ANNE DOUGHTY was born in Armagh but spent many years in England before returning to live in Belfast. Anne's writing is full of her great passion for the Ulster countryside and her fascination with the history of Ireland. Her first novel, *A Few Late Roses*, was longlisted for the *Irish Times* Literature Prize. *Stranger in the Place, Summer of the Hawthorn, On a Clear Day, Beyond the Green Hills, The Woman from Kerry* and *The Hamiltons of Ballydown* have all been bestsellers in Ireland.

PRAISE FOR ANNE DOUGHTY'S BESTSELLING NOVELS

'An ability to capture between the pages the tender beauty of the Armagh countryside ... Ms Doughty writes with insight and humour.'
Irish Times

'Anne Doughty brings the Armagh hills to life with her descriptive narrative which draws you deep into a fascinating world.'
News Letter

'Doughty writes charmingly and with genuine insight.'
Belfast Telegraph

RECENT TITLES BY ANNE DOUGHTY

A Few Late Roses
Stranger in the Place
Summer of the Hawthorn
On a Clear Day
Beyond the Green Hills
The Woman from Kerry
The Hamiltons of Ballydown

The Hawthorns Bloom *in* May

ANNE DOUGHTY

THE
BLACKSTAFF
PRESS

BELFAST

First world edition published in Great Britain in 2005 by
SEVERN HOUSE PUBLISHERS LTD of
9–15 High Street, Sutton, Surrey SM1 1DF.
First world edition published in the USA in 2005 by
SEVERN HOUSE PUBLISHERS INC of
595 Madison Avenue, New York, N.Y. 10022.
This edition first published in 2006
by Blackstaff Press
4c Heron Wharf, Sydenham Business Park
Belfast BT3 9LE, Northern Ireland

Typeset by Carole Lynch, County Sligo, Ireland
Printed in Great Britain by Cox & Wyman

A CIP catalogue record for this book
is available from the British Library

ISBN 085640-782-8

www.blackstaffpress.com

For Judith and Amanda,
without whom the story of the Hamilton
family would never have seen the light of day

Acknowledgements

The period from 1912 to 1916 was neither happy nor peaceful in Ireland, events both at home and in Europe casting dark shadows ahead of them. I am grateful to the librarians at the Linen Hall Library in Belfast for guiding me through the enormous number of books written about these events. I am also grateful to my friends at the Irish Studies Centre in Armagh who produced newspaper reports alerting me to errors in even the most highly thought of eye-witness accounts of the Easter Rising.

Kind neighbours have lent me unpublished material written during the First World War, shown me photographs and postcards from the front and alerted me to an important new book, published while I was still at work.

No doubt continuing new research will alter our perspective on some of the events referred to in the text, but, writing in July of 2005, my concern is not ultimately with the details of what happened, but with the courage and tenacity of individuals caught up in the events of their time, living in the shadow of anxiety, hardship, disease, rebellion and war.

My purpose is to remind the reader of the wisdom of Thomas Scott, a country blacksmith from Armagh, who said as often as need be that, '*Whatever way the world goes, the hawthorns bloom in May.*'

ANNE DOUGHTY
BELFAST, JULY 2005

One

The winter of 1912 was not a severe one in Ballydown. There had been very little snow and no long spells of bitter cold, though the regular hoar frosts iced the bare trees and left the straggling grass crisp and white in the morning sun. From the beginning of January, day followed day with cloud-covered skies and sudden sleety showers. The small windows of the south-facing dwelling that looked out across the Down countryside towards the rugged mass of the Mourne Mountains rattled under the onslaught, then trickled with streams of raindrops that turned the green prospect into a smudged watercolour landscape.

Rose had always felt the cold, even as a child. Now she gave thanks that February was over. The worst of the weather was certainly not past, no indeed, but with the evenings longer and the mornings less dark, there was at least a promise of spring. It would take time, months perhaps, before the edge went out of the wind, but the days would grow like the grey-green shoots of daffodils in the garden, and finally bloom into light and warmth.

Halfway through the first morning in March, she walked back into the kitchen from the chilly wash house where she'd been struggling with a pair of John's overalls. The clouds had dissolved, sun poured down from great patches of blue sky, the light was so brilliant it dazzled her. She was amazed at the sudden transformation.

She bent down, propped open the front door, then leaned against the doorpost. She closed her eyes and held up her face to the sun. To her surprise there was real warmth in its rays and the air was still and mild. Everywhere the birds were active and a robin was singing its heart out in a fuchsia bush on the eastern boundary of the garden.

'A pet day,' she said to herself, smiling.

It wouldn't last, not at this time of year, but it was lovely while it did. Something to be cherished, to be stored in the mind, to be taken out on the days when grey clouds again cut out the light and one's own spirits fell so low an effort had to be made just to keep going, doing the ordinary everyday things like keeping a welcome by the hearth for whoever might come, daughter or son, grandchild, neighbour, delivery man or stranger.

She stood quite still, a small, composed figure, her once dark hair now streaked with grey, her creamy skin marked with the lines of almost six decades of joys and sorrows, and the sudden laughter which so often came to her, a defence against solemnity and the dark thoughts that so often now came unbidden to occupy her mind.

'But not today,' she whispered to herself.

Today she would not think about the troubles and discontents filling the newspapers, the drilling and posturing that threatened the peace of the whole island, nor the grief in her own family, the death of her daughter Sarah's husband, Hugh, and the burden his going had placed on the shoulders of both Sarah and her own dear John.

Despite her resolution, she felt tears trickle down her cheeks. Still, after all these months, she could not bear to think of the magnitude of Sarah's loss. Hugh Sinton was older, of course, but he was a fine man and fit. He'd been their dear friend for years, John's employer, then partner, and for ten years Sarah's husband and her own son-in-law. Past his prime, one might say, but full of the joy his love for her had brought, and devoted to their two children. It seemed that every aspect of his life, even the heavy responsibility of running four mills when the times were so volatile, had become something he relished. And now he was gone. The typhoid fever that had taken its toll of both spinners and weavers at the height of last summer had taken Hugh as well.

'No, Rose, that's not the way,' she chided herself, as she wiped her tears on a corner of her apron. 'You mustn't dwell on what's past or you'll have no strength for the future.'

She gazed out over the familiar countryside and listened to the small familiar sounds that floated up to her on the still air, the muted pounding of the beetling hammers from Ballievy Mill, the bleat of sheep, the staccato bark of a sheepdog. From Rathdrum House further up the road at the top of the hill, where Hugh and John had worked together for so long and Sarah still lived, there was no sound at all.

As she stood listening, suddenly she detected a new sound, a rhythmic click that drew closer and then stopped. She opened her eyes promptly, just in time to see the postman prop his bicycle against the gate post and heave his sack of mail onto his shoulder.

'Great day, Missus Hamilton,' he greeted her easily, as he opened his sack. 'It's the quare while since I saw ye stanin' at yer door.'

'That must be one of the we'ans,' he went on cheerfully, as he handed her an envelope addressed in a large, childish hand which started well enough but then rapidly ran downhill.

She beamed at him. There were those who might think such a comment impertinent, but for Rose every word Dan Willis spoke was a pleasure. When he'd first got the job he was so shy and so uneasy he'd hardly been able to look at her.

Dan had lived on a remote farm with his mother for so long, seeing no one, visiting no one, that the world was a terrifying place for him. When she died, their neighbours at the foot of the hill had come up to ask John if he could find something for Dan in one of the mills. The poor man was dying of loneliness, they said. John had indeed found him a place, but after years of working on the farm, Dan couldn't bear being shut up indoors. It was Sarah who had found him a job he could manage. She'd gone to see an old friend of hers, Billy Auld, now postmaster at Banbridge Post Office, and found that he needed another postman.

'An' there's another forby,' Dan continued, delving in his bag as Rose stood smiling down at the envelope she already held. It was from young Hugh, Sarah's boy, writing from Friends School in Lisburn.

'It's from Donegal,' he added, as he passed over a bulging envelope. 'Full o' news by the luk of it.'

'It'll be from my brother Sam. Do you remember him? You met him in the autumn when he stayed with us.'

'Aye, I mind fine. Mister McGinley. The man with the red hair from New York. Nice man. He was goin' up to stay with yer sister in Donegal afore he went back to Amerikay. He'll likely be comin' to see ye again afore he goes,' he said reassuringly, as he humped his bag up on his back. 'Have ye any message for Missus Sinton?'

'Just the usual, Dan,' she said warmly. 'She'll be down this afternoon when she's finished her work.'

'Aye, well,' he said thoughtfully. 'I've a whole pile of stuff fer her. I hope it'll not houl' her back,' he said over his shoulder, as he picked up his bicycle and prepared to wheel it up the steepest part of the hill.

Rose hurried back indoors, fetched her spectacles from her workbox and tore open her brother's letter. It was not that she was anxious about him, for her older sister, Mary, with whom he was staying, would have let her know if he'd been ill, but it was some weeks since he'd written and Sam was normally such a regular correspondent. Over the long years he'd been in America, there'd been seldom a week he'd not penned a few lines. He always said writing to her helped clear his mind. Indeed, her letters to him had become such a part of her own life that she'd missed her own weekly effort when he'd arrived last autumn.

'Isn't it silly, Sam? I've got you here and I can talk to you till the cows come home, but I actually miss writing to you,' she said one afternoon as she sat sewing by the fire.

'Not a bit of it,' he replied promptly, looking up from the letters he was writing to his sons and daughters in New York and up-state Pennsylvania. 'The written word serves many purposes. For the writer as well as the recipient. Sometimes we don't know what we think till we write it down and look at it.'

She tore open the envelope and pulled out the thick wad of neatly written sheets.

My dearest Rose,
I hope you are sitting comfortably by your fireside as I propose to make up for my neglect of these past weeks. I really had not realised what an active life the Dohertys have here in Creeslough. I had, of course, committed myself to helping where I could with the shop and the farm, but I had reckoned without the social life. It seems all our nephews and nieces have some musical talent, which must come from their father's side, and consequently the house is never empty and certainly never quiet. I have had to excuse myself today from helping Michael with his drapery collection to find time and quiet to write.

Rose smiled to herself and breathed a sigh of relief. Whatever his news, at least she was sure he was well and in good spirits. She had quite forgotten to tell him how, one by one, Mary's children had taken up some instrument, except for Brendan, the youngest, who needed nothing but his own light tenor voice.

I have come to a momentous decision and, having come to it, I now feel somewhat sheepish about confessing. I have bought a farm of land. What a resonant phrase that is, *a farm of land*. Having done so, I have to face the fact that there is, after all, a peasant in me trying to get out. Despite all my education and my literary aspirations, I have purchased thirty acres of the most unprepossessing land I have ever surveyed. What madness can it be, Rose, that I, who have seen the richest land in North America and could have had a holding in Saskatchewan for the asking, return to visit my native shores and buy a slice of bog and mountain fit only for a few rigs of potatoes and a handful of intrepid sheep?

You know, of course, that Eva and I always planned to come on a long visit when the last of our six was settled, but when I lost her, I put the whole idea out of mind. I kept myself busy and travelled more than ever. That's why I took on the contracts for Western Canada. But I have to confess I found no rest from the loneliness that pursued me wherever I went until a few weeks ago when I stood in the rain on a hillside some six miles, as the raven flies, from our old home in Ardtur, a home which I have never even seen.

Rose blinked sharply. How long was it since the name Ardtur had entered her mind? Hardly surprising. It was more than fifty years since she'd held Sam in her arms, a red-headed baby wrapped in her mother's shawl, crushed into a wooden cart as the family made their way along a mountainside, their home in ruins behind them. Evicted. Sent out into the bitter wind of late April on a day of sleet and showers.

Despite the warmth of the stove and the golden light falling in patches on the well-swept stone floor, she shivered as her mind moved back to Donegal, to Ardtur where she'd been born, to Creeslough, where her older sister Mary had married a man who made a comfortable living from distributing and collecting the embroidery, the napkins and the hand-sewn shirts women worked in their own cottages.

Suddenly she remembered a visit to Mary when Sarah was still a little girl. She'd met a man one evening, newly returned from America, who'd come to join the music making. A man in his sixties who'd once lived in Kerry and was so happy to talk to her of the places she too had once known. She'd enjoyed his songs and his remembrances of Kerry, but one thing he said to her often returned when she thought of her dear brother and read his letters.

'It's a strange thing, Rose,' he'd said, 'but there's thousands go to America every year and we hear a lot about it. Sure the politicians are always talking about it. But you'd never hear of those that come back. They're the ones that hear *the calling*. I've met dozens of them. And I've met hundreds who've heard the same calling and either can't or won't come, but they die with that longing upon them. But what is even stranger,' he went on, leaning towards her, 'and you can believe me, or believe me not, as the saying is, that the calling is not to be denied. If it's not fulfilled in one generation, it passes to the next. We may not see it in our lives, Rose, but a time will come when the young will come back home, but they'll not be the same young that went away.'

Rose turned back to her brother's letter.

Of course, I should have begun by saying that I am not going back. I had decided to treat myself to a passage on this great new ship out of Belfast, but if I do go at all it won't be this April. In a couple of years, I'll go over and visit the family. Even if my piece of bog is a piece of fantasy that will not yield to the light of reality and is totally unable to support me, I am in the happy position of being able to stay regardless. The hard work of my lonely years has left me very well provided.

Do you remember, Rose, when I travelled steerage on the *Germanic* before the

Rail Disaster? You and John were thinking then of coming over and I advised you to try and afford second class as steerage would be so hard on the children. And now I can afford to travel First Class! Grand staircases and potted palms and à la carte restaurants in the French style. Can you believe it? I haven't been able to decide whether my reluctance to book my passage was my inability to square my conscience with my former poverty, or my feeling that there was something here still to be done. But now the die is cast. I've answered the calling. Uncle Sam America no longer exists. I'm here for good. To be called, no doubt, by whatever name your grandchildren dream up for me.

Rose burst into tears and wept unashamedly. Apart from John and her own children, there was no one she loved more than Sam, the little brother whom she'd always cared for and been so proud of. Now he'd come home. It wouldn't matter what he was doing, whether he was farming in Donegal or visiting Dublin, or their former home in Kerry, or renewing some of his old contacts in Belfast, or Limerick. What mattered was that he was here. In Ireland. No longer separated by the width of the Atlantic and the perils of ocean travel.

She sniffed and began to search for her handkerchief, finding one eventually in the pocket of her apron.

There is a farmhouse in keeping with the property. Small, rundown and neglected. The fuchsia bushes have grown so high they cut out all the light at the back of the house and getting round there is something of an obstacle race, the space full of rotting carts and rusting machinery. The roof, however, is slate and in remarkably good condition and despite the dirt and the debris the place is not actually damp.

So far, I have made no improvements except for removing a somewhat faded Virgin that dominated the downstairs room I propose to make my study. But I have beaten a path through the bushes to gain access to my stretch of mountain. You will notice the proprietorial tone has appeared even before the papers are signed!

Behind the house, outcropping some yards above roof level, is a slab of rock from which I can view my rush-filled fields and the track that runs along the mountainside from Swillybrinnan towards Derrykeel. It is a noble prospect, dominated by the full rise of Muckish Mountain to my right and the inlet of Sheephaven to my left.

If I am in danger of being overcome by the beauties of my new abode, I have only to remember the days not so very long gone when all this land belonged to one landlord and my job was to keep the evicted tenants from starving. There is no eviction now, but

the poverty of the small farmers and the
labourers is crushing. Perhaps there is still
something useful I might do.

She paused. Surely he'd said that before. She
leafed back through the neatly written sheets and
found the phrase that echoed in her mind.

'My feeling that there was something here still to
be done.'

She read the words aloud and let the letter lie in
her lap as she thought about them. Twenty years ago,
Sam had been politically active, so committed to the
rights of the tenant farmers and so involved with
Michael Davitt and the Land League that she and
John had feared for his safety. His visits to America
had been part of his work for the League. He'd carried letters, contacted sympathisers and collected
money. What she'd never really been sure about was
whether he returned to America solely because of
Eva, or because of his disillusion with Irish politics.

With a sense of growing unease she could not
identify she picked up the letter again and continued.

Naturally I shall want you to visit me as
soon as I have an establishment fit to be
seen, but that will certainly not be before
the summer. Even then, you may have to
stay with Mary, who will be only too
delighted to see you. She speaks of you so
often that I have come to wonder if it is a
feature of advancing age to cling to relation-
ships that were given rather than made. You

have often said that you and she were never close as children and yet she behaves as if you were. You certainly hold a place in her life that surprises me given the many years when you were not even in touch.

But that exploration is something for another time. I have written enough for one letter. I will let you digest this and write again quite soon for I should like to come and see you and John before the weather improves and I give my mind to the cultivation of my native soil, or rather, my rush-filled fields and mountain bog!

There was a further page to the letter, enquiries about herself and John, her elder daughter, Hannah, and his nephew and namesake, her younger son, Sam Hamilton, and his growing family in County Armagh. She read on quickly, pausing only when he mentioned Sarah.

I feel for Sarah in her grief. It is hard for any man or woman to lose a beloved partner, but she is still young. That may make the pain sharper at the time, but perhaps it also makes healing more likely. If I were a praying man, which you know well I am not, I'd be asking for a young man to remind her there is still joy in the world even if Hugh has gone.

Take care of yourself and write when you can to your little brother who, despite his own sorrow, is so happy to be home at last.

Rose sat quite still, the folded sheets held lightly in her hand, her mind moving backwards and forwards across her brother's life. She remembered how she had watched him, a toddler crawling round the housekeeper's room in Currane Lodge, when her mother took them to Kerry after their father died. They'd gone to school with the children of the other servants and she'd helped him learn his letters. Sam was bright, picking up things so quickly that even before he became a stable-boy on the estate, he'd been given permission to read the books in Sir Capel's library. She'd encouraged him to read in whatever time he had and, in the end, Sir Capel himself had sent him to train as a land agent. She had never entirely made up her mind whether to be glad or sorry that in Dublin, Sam had learnt more about land than its texture and quality, or its suitability for grazing, or cultivation.

Smiling, red-headed Sam, lightly built, good looking and friendly, had changed radically during his time in the city. She laughed to herself when she remembered the seventeen-year-old who'd been wildly in love with Lady Lily, the prettiest of the Molyneux daughters. After three years in Dublin, he'd turned his back on the job awaiting him on the estate and chosen instead to live on a pittance from the Land League. Now, at fifty-two, he was still a fit and good-looking man, even if his red hair had receded from his temples and was distinctly thinning on top. His passion for books remained with him and it looked as if his old passion for the land of Ireland had reasserted itself.

She shook her head slowly. It had never occurred to her that Sam might come back. But then, she said to herself as she looked around the comfortable kitchen, most of the important things that had happened in her own life she had never expected either. Neither the good nor the bad.

'Ah see ye've had a letter,' said John, peering up at the mantelpiece as they moved over to the fire when they'd finished their lunch.

'I have indeed, but you'd better read it this evening or you'll be late for your meeting,' she replied easily. 'It's my Sam, Uncle Sam America,' she said, laughing, 'and it's a big one. It took me half the morning to take it all in.'

'Is he all right?' John enquired anxiously.

'Yes, of course, he's fine,' she said reassuringly. 'He's just been very busy. What made you think he mightn't be all right?'

'Ach, no reason at all,' he said hastily, his eyes moving anxiously towards the clock.

'What's wrong, love?' she asked quietly as she handed him his mug of tea. She looked closely at him as he took it without meeting her gaze. 'Is there something amiss you haven't told me?'

'Shure I can't get Hugh out of my mind,' he said abruptly. 'I see him beside me. I hear him. I can nearly tell you what he's sayin' when someone asks me somethin'. One day he's there, happy and smilin', and a couple of weeks later he's dead and buried and our Sarah standing stiff as a post and the light gone from her eyes. I can't get it outa my mind.'

'Oh, John, love, I'm sorry,' she said, setting down her own mug on the edge of the stove. 'You were with Hugh more than anyone, even Sarah, so it's you misses him most.'

She stood up and was about to put her arms round him when she heard a step on the garden path and the scrape of boots on the doorstone.

'Anybody at home?'

A figure stood in the doorway, the sunlight blocked by his broad shoulders and tall frame. Their younger son, Sam, smiled at her as he flicked off his cap and hung it up by the door. For one moment, she was totally taken aback. Sam's bearing, his familiar gesture, his smile, was so like his father she couldn't think what to say.

'Hello, son, how are ye? What brings you here on a work day?' John asked, a bleak smile crossing his face as he collected himself.

'Handy delivery down in the town. It'll take them a while to unload,' he explained. 'Young Mickey has a sister married up in Seapatrick. He's away to see her. We agreed we'd take an hour and work later this evenin'.'

'It's lovely to see you, Sam. There's tea in the pot. Would you like a bite to eat?'

'Just tea, Ma. I've had my piece.'

'What about a bit of cake?'

'Aye, well . . .'

John laughed and looked easier as Rose crossed to the dresser. She took her time finding the tin, the carving knife and a plate, listening as John asked questions about the job. She was grateful Sam seemed happy enough, despite the changes there'd been in the management of the company he worked for, especially their work schedules.

'And how is Martha?' she asked, as she poured tea and passed him his plate.

'Oh, fine. Working away as always,' he said, dropping his eyes to the wedge of fruitcake on his plate.

'And the children?'

'Great. They're all well. Wee Rose looks more like you every day, Ma, and young Emily's walkin'. Inta everythin'. Oh, and one on the way,' he added, as he munched appreciatively.

Rose nodded and smiled, but her heart sank. Another child. There were six already. Surely enough to keep on one man's pay. She asked about each one in turn. Sam always answered her questions, told her about some childish illness safely past or some story to make them smile, but she always felt his answers left her none the wiser about how he felt.

'How do you like living on the farm, Sam?' John went on.

'Ach it's all right,' he said agreeably. 'The old uncle's a bit of a crosspatch at times. Sharp with the children. But sure they have space to play themselves in the fields and the orchard. There was nowhere for them but the street in that wee house in Richhill. I've one of the barns Uncle Joe doesn't use made inta a workshop and I do a bit of work for the neighbours in the evenings. It all helps.'

'What about the shoes, Sam?' Rose asked, as lightly as she could manage.

'Just the same, Ma. I tried,' he said steadily. 'I gave

her the money you sent me and she bought them all right, but she says they're only for Sunday. None of the neighbours' we'ans have shoes to go to school, she says, so why wou'd we make ours different? Her mind's made up an' I can see there's no use goin' on about it. That's the way with Martha, but I *did* try like you said.'

'I'm sure you did your best,' Rose said, nodding vigorously to cover her disappointment.

John got to his feet, clapped Sam on the shoulder and looked up at the clock again.

'I'm sorry to leave you, but there's a meeting at two. Maybe we'll take a run over one of these Sundays, Sam. Just for an hour or two,' he added hastily as he caught Rose's glance.

Martha had long ago made clear that she didn't welcome visitors on a Sunday when Sam was at home to look after the children.

'That wou'd be great, Da. I'd like fine to show you the workshop.'

'Well, see ye make a date with your mother. I must away,' he said quickly as he got up, kissed Rose, and headed off down the garden path.

'Where has he the motor?' asked Sam, puzzled.

'Oh, he leaves it down at Jackson's farm when he knows he's going back into Banbridge in the afternoon. It saves going up to Sarah's to turn. I think actually he enjoys the odd word with Michael Jackson. I'm afraid he's missing Hugh badly.'

Sam dropped his eyes to the remaining crumbs on his plate.

'How's Sarah?' he said abruptly.

'She's bereft,' Rose replied honestly. 'I've not seen her shed a tear yet. I don't know whether that's a good sign or a bad. But she's well enough in health, thank God, and she works hard.'

'Thank God indeed,' he said firmly. 'Sometimes it's a good thing to have your work to do every day. It stops you thinkin' long,' he added as he too got to his feet.

'Sunday or Sunday week, maybe?' she asked, as he picked up his cap and looked out into the sunshine.

'Ach, yes. Just come,' he said, turning back to face her.

He leaned down and kissed her.

'Sure I'm always there, even if Martha is away up to her father or visiting her friends. The we'ans 'ill be glad to see ye. Wee Sammy is lookin' for a ride in the motor. Ye may warn my father he'll give him no peace till he gets sittin' in the front seat.'

She laughed and touched his arm as he stepped over the threshold.

He took a few long strides along the garden path and turned down the hill. Even before she stepped back into the empty room, the echo of his footsteps had gone.

She looked at the lunch table and the mugs parked on the corners of the stove and began to clear them up, but as she moved back and forth to the dairy and returned items to the dresser, all she could see was the small, bright face of Martha Loney the first time her son had brought her home. She'd been pleasant enough in manner, and agreeable to whatever was suggested and pretty enough when she smiled. She'd been unsure then about the girl and about Sam's haste to get married.

Sarah had had no such doubts about Martha. From that very first visit she'd declared that Martha Loney was more in love with the idea of marriage and a family than she was with her brother.

'And she was right,' Rose whispered to herself, as she wiped the table with a damp cloth. 'Our Sam's made his bed and there's little anyone can do to help him.'

She wondered which was the greater loss, the loss of a dear husband who had brought joy for some ten years, or the loss of a hope, the image of a smiling girl dissolving into a young woman so entirely taken up with her children, her own life and her own affairs, there was little place for the man who had fathered her children and now worked so hard to give his family the very best he could afford.

Two

As Rose looked hopefully at her flowerbeds, seeking the first hint of colour in late March, she thought of all their neighbours anxiously watching the skies. Rainfall was always a problem at this time of year. A sudden dry spell would check the growth of the new grass. If that happened, animals would have to be fed hay, now both scarce and expensive. But if heavy rain came, sodden fields would delay ploughing and planting and wet conditions increase the risk of disease among the sheep and their young lambs.

As for the Sinton mills, seasonal storms could be bad enough to disrupt regular sailings across the Irish Sea, a serious matter when contracts were penalised for late delivery. Worse still, flooding was a danger on the low-lying mill sites and wet conditions meant more illness among the workers.

She sighed. Only one group of people seemed completely indifferent to the changes in the weather. Whether the day was bright and sunny, or teeming with rain, the early evening still light, or dipping towards dusk, the hundreds of local men who had recently joined the Ulster Volunteer Force were to be seen drilling. Outside Orange Halls, in open fields, or town squares, the sound of marching feet and shouted instructions was an everyday event.

Every weekend, she and John saw platoons tramping back to Banbridge along the local roads, or across the nearby fields, after some cross-country route march or exercise, heavy packs on their backs, a single billet of wood in their arms, the insignia of the Red Hand proudly displayed on their sleeves. When they met them on the hill outside the cottage or tramping across their back field, they could do little but step aside, nodding to those they knew, workers from the mills and lads from neighbouring farms, accompanied by their young officers, the sons of the manufacturers whose handsome houses dotted the Bann valley.

'Ah see they've got rifles now,' said John flatly one evening as he put down his newspaper and took off his spectacles.

'No, John, you don't mean it,' Rose said, horrified, as she looked up from the jersey she was knitting for young Hugh.

He raised his eyebrows, put his spectacles on again and read her a paragraph from the *Banbridge Chronicle*. A local carpentry firm had landed on its feet, it said. Seeing its opportunity, it was now supplying replica rifles to the volunteers, price one and eightpence each for pitch pine and one and sixpence for spruce.

She breathed a sigh of relief, but was not reassured by the look on John's face.

'Do you *really* think they'd turn against the government if Home Rule was granted?'

'I've no doubt about it,' he said promptly. 'They mean business all right. Sure there's tens of thousands of them now all over Ulster. The English papers can laugh all they like at them drillin' with bits of wood, but they're serious and there's those encouragin' them that'll find the money for rifles. It's only a matter of time. Even Hugh said that, an' you know how he felt about takin' up arms.'

'Hugh always faced facts,' she said quietly. 'Whether he liked it or not, if he saw something, he spoke. Sarah never had any time for making things smooth or comfortable either. I often thought that was one of the great bonds between them.'

To her great surprise, John laughed.

She smiled herself, delighted to hear a sound so unfamiliar. She waited hopefully to see what he might say.

'D'ye mind the first time she met Hugh?' he began. 'Sure she was only a wee thing, the night we arrived here with all our bits and pieces, an' he still had the bad leg from the accident, an' the scar. She looked up at him an' asks him did a horse kick him. An' then she wants to know did it hurt. Oh, she'd have gone on too till she'd found out the whole details . . .' He broke off, shaking his head.

'Aye, an' sure she does it still,' he continued easily. 'Nothin' gets past her. I sit at these board meetings an' I listen mostly, but it's Sarah asks the questions. Ach, ye'd be proud of her, Rose,' he added shyly.

'Yes, I am, John,' she replied, still smiling at the recollection of that first meeting. 'She has a sharp mind and great courage. I just don't know where she gets it from. It would be different if she was religious, but she's not. I know she went with Hugh to the Quaker Meeting, and helped with the charity work and the visiting, but she never became a Friend.'

John nodded and folded up his paper. Whatever he might think himself about being religious, his mind had moved on.

'Speaking of visitin',' he said abruptly. 'Are we for Liskeyborough on Sunday?'

She looked across at him and saw the sudden animation had vanished.

'Yes, I think we should,' she replied, her tone as neutral as his. 'It's a long time since we've been. Sam likes to see us there.'

'Why does Martha not like us, Rose? Tell me that an' tell me no more, as the sayin' is,' he asked directly, his brow furrowed with a familiar frown.

Rose sighed. It wasn't as if she hadn't given thought to the behaviour of their daughter-in-law, but she found it difficult to explain.

'I don't think she actually dislikes us, John, she's just indifferent. We don't matter to her,' she said steadily. 'All that matters to Martha is the children and she's good enough with them in her own way. After that, there's her father and old Uncle Joe, her two sisters and her girl friends.'

'An' what about our Sam? Where does he come in?'

'Well, they've six children and one on the way,' she replied, her tone sharper than she'd intended.

John just looked at her, his face grim. He shook his head.

'It's beyond me, Rose. Tell me what we ought to do an' we'll do it.'

The first Sunday in April was a lovely spring-like day, the air mild, the sky a cloud-scribbled blue, and although there was no sign of the trees bursting into leaf, the hawthorns were well sprayed with soft new leaves. As they drove along, Rose felt her spirits rise. In the cottage gardens they passed and along the roadside verges themselves, daffodils bloomed every-where. There were signs too that the birds were already nesting.

Rose could tell from the contented look on John's face that the engine was running sweetly and he was enjoying every moment of the drive. He enjoyed keeping his own and Sarah's motor in peak condition, but he seldom had time to do the job as well as he'd wish these days. She glanced sideways at him, delighted he was relaxed enough to point out new buildings that caught his eye and tell her a couple of amusing things that had happened at one mill or the other.

He was still in good spirits as he drove slowly down the steep and narrow lane leading to Richhill Station and turned off into the broad, well-swept yard of Joe Loney's farm at Liskeyborough. Two half-barrels full of daffodils bloomed cheerfully, a vivid splash of gold against the newly whitewashed walls of the long, low dwelling, its small windows reflect-ing the light, the upper part of the half door wide open to the sunlight.

'Place lookin' well, isn't it?' he said, as he

manoeuvred the motor and parked it with the bonnet facing outwards in the direction of the lane.

Rose nodded and looked around, surprised there was no sign of life, neither chicken nor child. Stranger still, no one appeared at the door.

'Hayfoot, strawfoot, hayfoot, strawfoot.'

They turned abruptly towards the barns behind them as Billy and Charley, the eldest of Martha and Sam's children, marched into view, commanded by an unknown boy somewhat older than Billy's ten summers. Both young Hamiltons carried billets of wood and both had tied a piece of old cloth round their waists as bandoliers.

'Hayfoot, strawfoot, hayfoot, strawfoot,' continued the sharp voice as he marched the two younger boys across the middle of the wide yard and into the nearby field.

Neither of their grandchildren so much as glanced at them, and one look at John's face told her his good spirits had evaporated like summer rain on a metalled road.

'What does he mean, "Hayfoot, strawfoot"?' she asked, unable to contain her curiosity.

'Ach, he's just repeatin' what he's heard,' replied John abruptly. 'Many o' these volunteers don't know their right foot from their left. When they started to teach them to march, they had to tie hay and straw round their ankles till they got the hang of it. It's not new to the UVF, though they'd tell you it is. Your brother Sam says the Americans invented it when they were trainin' up raw recruits for the Civil War.'

The children had disappeared and still no one had appeared to greet them.

'We may as well go on in,' said Rose, nudging him encouragingly as she pointed him towards the door and took his arm.

'Good day, Joe, are you well?' she asked, as she caught sight of a figure sitting close to the stove. She unlatched the lower part of the door and walked towards him.

'Well, there'd not be much point complainin' if I wasn't,' he replied ungraciously.

Unshaven and wearing his working clothes, Martha's Uncle Joe lowered his paper, but neither rose to his feet nor bade them welcome.

'Are you all alone?' she went on pleasantly, casting her eyes round the empty room.

'Aye. Martha's away up to see me brother. Your Sam's about the place somewhere. He's likely in the barn. Shure he's always in there fiddling with somethin' or other while Martha an' I are at our work,' he said in a tone it was hard to misread.

Rose raised an eyebrow to John, who said nothing, but pulled out two kitchen chairs for them to sit on.

'Ye've got a new coat of paint I see,' said John casually. 'Indoors as well,' he added, looking round the newly decorated kitchen.

'Aye. That was done a few weeks ago,' Joe replied, looking back at his newspaper meaningfully.

Rose followed his gaze. The fresh paint made the room seem larger as well as pleasanter. After the gloom of that tiny house in Richhill's main street, she could see why Martha had been so pleased when her uncle inherited the farm. He'd asked her to come with her family and help him run it and she'd jumped at the chance. Now Rose wondered if living with Uncle Joe still seemed as good an idea.

'An' the yard's well improved too,' continued John, who disliked Joe thoroughly, but did his best not to show it. 'Ye've got rid of a lot of old rubbish.'

'Aye. An' it wasn't before time.'

Silence fell and Rose wondered whether she should enquire about Martha or the children, or whether that would only make matters worse.

'Ach, hello, Ma. Hello, Da,' Sam said, crossing the room in a couple of strides. He kissed his mother and grasped his father's hand. 'Sure I didn't hear the motor. I was sandin' a bit o' metal an' it was only when I came out for a breath o' fresh air, I saw her stanin' there.'

'Sure the only time you iver hear anythin', Sam, is when you're called to your tea,' said Joe, without taking his eyes away from his paper.

Rose stood up and smiled at Sam.

'We were just admiring the new paint. It makes the room look so much bigger. Did you and Uncle Joe do it, or did you get help?'

'Help?' said Joe, staring up at her. 'Sure it's only gentry has "help". We've to do everythin' ourselves here. What way wou'd I get time for paintin' and doin' up the place wi' a farm of land and animals to run.'

'So Sam did it, then?' said John quietly, looking Joe full in the face.

'Sure he might as well. He's no han's for the farm,' he replied, as he turned away again.

John stood up and walked out into the sunshine.

'Well, we'd better go and see what Sam does have hands for, Joe,' said Rose, as she got up from the kitchen chair. 'There must be something Lamb Brothers think he's worth paying for,' she added quietly as she followed Sam and his father out of the house.

'Hayfoot, strawfoot, hayfoot, strawfoot.'

The three adults stopped outside the door as the three boys reappeared from their manoeuvre in the nearest field. Rose took a deep breath and watched anxiously to see what would happen.

Without a word, Sam walked out into the line of march, dropped on his hunkers in front of them and held out his hand for the billets of wood. Billy and Charley handed them over. He waited while they untied the bandoliers. Try as she would Rose could not hear what Sam said, so quiet was his tone, but she saw the two younger boys nod and make their way to the small orchard at the back of the house. The older boy looked uneasy, but made no reply to Sam's quiet questioning. Suddenly, he too turned away, and went running out of the gate and up the road.

'Who was the other wee boy?' she asked, as they followed Sam into the barn.

'Ach, that's Danny. He's one of the Hutchinsons,' he said, wiping a piece of cotton waste over a wooden bench so that she could sit down.

'He's a right wee lad, but the father's desperit strong against Home Rule. No matter what subject ye'd be talkin' about, whether it was motors, or factory work, or even the birds in the sky, he cou'd somehow bring it roun' to Dublin and the Fenians an' the Pope,' he went on matter-of-factly. 'Hasn't a good word to say for any of them. He's Master of the Lodge an' he has them out drillin' regular. That's where the wee fella picked it up.'

'What about your wee Sammy?' Rose asked. 'Did he not want to do what his older brothers do?'

''Deed I'm sure he did, but young Hutchinson must have said he was too young. He's away with Martha and Emily and the two wee ones up to Richhill.'

'Ye've yerself well set up, son,' said John, who'd been looking round him, inspecting the work-benches under the windows and the large space in the centre of the barn where a petrol-driven pump stood in pieces. 'Ah knew ye cou'd weld, but ah didn't know ye had weldin' equipment. That set ye back a bit.'

'Aye, it did, tho' I got it second hand,' Sam replied, sounding pleased. 'But sure it's near paid for isself already. The farmers roun' here can't afford new machinery, they just have to keep old stuff goin', harrows and reapers, an' suchlike. An' there's no smith near here since old Harry Pearson died over at Money. The nearest would be John Scott at Kildarton or our friends Thomas and Robert at Salter's Grange. An' that's a brave step if yer in the middle of a job.'

'So you're kept busy, Sam. Do you not get a day of rest at all?' Rose asked quietly.

'Well, I take Sunday mornin',' he confessed sheepishly. 'I've been goin' over to the Meetin' in

Richhill an' after that I go on an' meet a few friends down on the railway banks till dinnertime. We lie down there and talk about the news, aye, an' put the world to rights, as the sayin' is.'

'What do you do when it's wet?' asked Rose promptly.

Sam laughed, his face lighting up with the sweet smile Rose used to know so well and hadn't seen for a long time.

'Ach, then it has to be the goods shed. Tommy Buckley has the key to it if we're stuck.'

Rose settled herself to listen as John and Sam began to talk about the pump he'd been working on. She'd listened to so many of their conversations over the years, she could follow most of what they said, but before they'd decided the next step in the process, a small figure came flying into the barn.

'Granny, Granny, yer here,' cried Emily, scrambling up on Rose's knee with all the energy of a five-year-old.

'Hallo, Emily,' Rose said, hugging her warmly. 'Where's Sammy?'

'He's comin'. He can't run as fast as I can,' she added proudly, as six-year-old Sammy appeared breathless, with eyes only for his grandfather.

'Can I've a ride in the motor?' he gasped, fixing John with bright blue eyes.

John laughed and picked him up.

'Maybe if you said "Hello" to your granny, we could manage something.'

'Hello, Granny,' said Sammy, so promptly that all the adults laughed.

'And me,' insisted Emily. 'There's room for me too, Granda.'

'Come on then,' John said, smiling at Rose and Sam, as he took the two children by the hand.

Through the open doors of the barn, Rose watched him cross the yard, Emily swinging on his arm in her excitement, young Sammy talking nineteen to the dozen. She was about to comment on how much both children had grown since Christmas when she saw Martha come striding into the yard, the baby in the pram, young Rose perched across it.

'I'll away and say hello to Martha and the wee ones,' she said, as she stood up, and saw Sam now running a finger thoughtfully up and down a piece of metal.

'Hello, Martha, how are you?' she asked, as the younger woman lifted Rose from the pram.

Martha was heavily pregnant, but she swung the child to the ground with the greatest of ease.

'I wasn't expectin' ye,' Martha replied with a little laugh. 'I've the cows to milk before I can make tea for anyone,' she said sharply, looking down into the pram to make sure Bobby was asleep.

'Oh, we'll not stay for tea, Martha. You've enough to do,' said Rose, reading the familiar signal. 'We'll be off as soon as John gives the children their ride in the motor.'

Martha turned the pram to face away from the lowering sun and looked down at little Rose who was sucking her thumb.

'Here you are, Rose, here's your granny, come to see you,' she said quickly. 'She'll play with you while

Uncle Joe and I do our work,' she added as she picked up the weary child and handed her to Rose.

Behind them, Uncle Joe came to the door and strode silently past on his way to bring in the four cows from the low field.

'An' ye mean t' say that was all the conversation ye had wi' her, an' you hasn't seen her or the childer since Christmas?'

John took his eyes off the empty road and glanced at her as if he couldn't believe her words without seeing the look on her face.

'That's all, John,' she said firmly. 'I had a good deal more conversation with little Rose, for all she's not three yet and there wasn't so much as a doll or a wee toy for us to talk about. Sam hasn't much time for making toys from what I can see,' she added sharply.

'Aye, ye're right there,' he said sadly.

He pressed his lips together and looked up at the clear sky, now paling from blue to palest yellow.

'There's a quare stretch on the evenin's when ye get a good day to see it,' he said, looking round him carefully as they turned on to the Banbridge road. 'We did the right thing goin' on to Thomas and Selina's, diden we?' he said more cheerfully.

'Yes, you were right, and I was wrong,' she admitted, laughing. 'I know I said it was too near teatime to call, but they were so glad to see us, weren't they? I think it did us both good to be made that welcome. Even if Selina had nothing but baker's bread and shop jam, she'd have put it on the table. She's a great baker, isn't she?' she went on, her mind still moving on the warm welcome they'd had from John's old friend and his second wife.

'You don't think Martha and Sam are just very short of money?' Rose asked, as she thought of the scones and cake so generously provided.

'How would they be, Rose?' John replied, a note of irritation in his tone. 'Sam's a skilled man. He's earnin' far more than I iver earned before we moved to Ballydown. She's no money to find for her milk and eggs and as far as I know the farm has no mortgage on it, though it was in a bad way when Joe got it. An' forby that Sam is workin' all the hours there are, but for Sunday mornin'. He told me he earns a brave bit from the repairs and suchlike.'

Rose shivered and drew the car rug closer over her knees.

'Are ye cold, love?'

'No, I was just thinking of Selina's bright fire and her young Isabel running out to meet us. She's a pretty girl, isn't she? Though I can never look at her without thinking of wee Sophie.'

'Aye. That should niver have happened,' said John sharply, for he still felt angry over her death. A rabid dog had bitten the three-year-old and ended her short life, because the police hadn't taken the trouble to hunt it down when it was reported.

'I thought at the time Thomas wou'd niver get over it, but then Ned came along and then wee Isabel. Sure he's had a second family with Selina and it's healed many a hurt that Mary-Anne laid on him.'

John fell silent and the harsh and bitter words she'd once endured from Thomas's first wife came back into Rose's mind. A woman firm in her Christian views and active in her Bible reading but totally devoid of love or compassion. She'd shadowed many a good day when they'd lived in the house opposite Thomas's forge. Putting Mary-Anne firmly out of mind, Rose gazed round at the silent countryside as the evening shadows lengthened moment by moment. The air was cooling fast beneath a clear sky. Later, there would be a mass of stars and probably a touch of frost before dawn.

'Did ye notice when I asked Thomas if young Ned was thinkin' of goin' to America, that he diden mention *his* eldest boy? He's been in America for years now and I was waitin' for Thomas to say how he was doin' an' where he was. But Thomas niver said a word about him. D'ye think young James Scott might be like another James we know?' he asked, glancing across at her.

Rose took a deep breath. It wasn't often John mentioned their eldest son and it made her sad he still felt so hurt by the way James had rejected them, turning his back on the whole family, because he thought their Catholic relatives might somehow get in the way of his ambitions.

'Well, it's about the only reason I can think of why Thomas wouldn't talk about him,' she said slowly. 'We can't talk about our James either, even if we wanted to. What could we say? He's probably still with Harland & Wolff. I'm sure he's a manager or better, but he never let us know. We know he's married, but whether or not he has children we've never found out. It looks as if Thomas is in the same boat.'

'I suppose it happens in all families,' said John thoughtfully. 'Sure, look at my two brothers. When they went to America they wrote for a wee while and then that was that. My mother kept goin' for a bit longer and then she gave up. Maybe they just wanted to forget where they came from. Like our James. I've been told there's a brave few does that.'

Rose fell silent as he concentrated on the hill, drove to the top, turned in the wide space outside the gates of Rathdrum House and came slowly back down to park alongside their own wall. She was tired. Despite the pleasure of the visit to the forge house, she felt oppressed by what she'd seen at Liskeyborough.

While John lit the gas lamps, she stirred up the fire. It had almost burnt itself out, so she encouraged it with small sticks and fragments of turf. She thought back to the talk she'd had with Selina when Thomas and John stepped down to the forge to look at a new rotary drill and they'd laid the tea table together.

'What would you do, Selina?' she'd asked, as she spread the crisp, crocheted cloth. 'You'd be heart sore if you saw the wee ones barefoot in the cold weather. I'm sure you went barefoot as a child and so did I, but times have changed, thank God. I could help her out if she's short, but she bought shoes and boots with the money I sent and she has them in the cupboard. She told Sam they were for Sunday, but today was Sunday and all I saw was bare feet.'

'What about her mother, Rose? Is that the trouble?'

'Her mother died some years ago, but she has two sisters. They're both older, but neither are married.

She seems fond of them. Certainly she's always going up to see them when Sam's at home.'

Selina paused and put down the china cups she was holding.

'Poor Rose,' she said, smiling. 'Thomas has always said how kind you were to him and how good you were to your own wee ones. It'll be hard for you. But there's nothing you can do,' she said, shaking her head sadly. 'Sam's not chosen well, any more than I think our Robert has.'

'Oh, Selina, I wondered you didn't mention him. He's been married four or five years now, hasn't he?'

'Indeed he has. And I did my best to like the girl, but from the first day I met her she had something to complain about. Though in those days she made a joke of it,' she added wryly, as she filled the sugar bowl from a jar she took out of the corner cupboard. 'Well, it's no joke now. When Robert comes down from Church Hill to see us, I think it's the only peace and quiet he gets.'

'So what do we do to help them?'

'There's nothing we *can* do, Rose,' she replied steadily. 'They have to make their own lives and their own mistakes. Hard as it is, we have to stand out of the way until such time as something might change.'

Rose looked across the table at the older woman and knew she was thinking of her dear Thomas and the loneliness he'd suffered when he was married to Mary-Anne. She nodded and agreed. It was something her own mother had always said: interference only made things worse.

The fire burnt up and the kettle began to sing just

as John came back indoors after putting the tarpaulin cover over the motor.

'Cup of tea, John?'

'Aye, that would be great. I think we might have a frost.'

As she made the tea, Rose reflected that the prospect of either their Sam or young Robert Scott having a second chance to find happiness was remote indeed.

Three

Rose put down her pen, rubbed her neck, stretched her shoulders, and then read through her reply to her elder daughter's most recent letter.

12th April, 1912

My dearest Hannah,

Your long letter was much appreciated. Please don't apologise for the delay. If you've had workmen and decorators in your new London home, I'm amazed you can find a quiet moment at all, especially with both the boys on holiday from school and the two little ones becoming less little by the day.

Yes, we are well, though I must confess Hugh's loss still lies heavy. Your father misses him desperately, so I can't imagine how it must be for Sarah. She works very hard and does much of what Hugh used to do running the mills. She and Da are concerned just now that the work on the new machinery is going forward so slowly. Da complains a pair of dungarees lasts him a couple of weeks instead of a couple of days, because he's wearing a suit so much more of the time, attending meetings about the future of the mills.

I had a very long letter from Uncle Sam in America last week and it brought wonderful news. In fact, it's such good news I don't think I've quite grasped it yet. He means to stay here in Ireland permanently. He'd planned to go back this week, first class on 'the big ship', as everyone here calls her, and he sounded very excited about his plan, but a month ago he bought a farm in Donegal not far from Aunt Mary and her family and not far either from where he was born, though, of course, he was a tiny baby when he left Ardtur.

Do you remember, Hannah, when Sarah was little she kept asking for the story about the baby and the turf cart? I used to wonder then if she realised it was a memory of my childhood and not one of the stories I made up to keep you both amused on wet days!

Rose tried again to ease the crick in her neck. She enjoyed writing letters to family and friends, but however hard she tried to write slowly, she always ended up scribbling furiously and then her hand, her arm, her neck, or all three, started aching.

'Arthritis, I suppose,' she said wryly, as she cast her eye beyond the open door, pleased to see new growth in the flowerbed she and John had created last autumn.

A new ground-floor room with a large bedroom above had been added to the house last spring. It was ready just in time for Hannah arriving in the summer with all four children. When the fence was moved to accommodate the extension, the old flowerbed looked so strange. After twenty-two years, the precious cuttings brought from their home at Salter's Grange had grown into shrubs tall enough to take the light from the windows of the new sitting room.

She sighed as she remembered the struggle it had been to take them out. She wasn't having someone come to do a job that needed such care and thought, but afterwards her back ached for days.

When she visited her good friend Elizabeth and her doctor husband, she'd asked Richard about the pain and stiffness in her neck and the limp that sometimes slowed up her housework.

'Rose dear, we are all getting older. Even you. And you've worked hard all your life. You're bound to get bits and pieces of arthritis here and there. There's not much any of us can do about it,' he said matter-of-factly. 'Rest, if you can. Try aspirin. Elizabeth says a hot-water bottle is the best remedy, but I've pointed out the success of her method may be that in order to apply the said hot-water bottle she has to sit down. Neither you, nor my dear Elizabeth, have been much given to sitting down if there's work to be done.' He paused and grinned. 'Maybe you could write more letters.'

She laughed as she recalled the moment, always cheered by the thought of Elizabeth and the late marriage to Richard that had brought such joy to them both. Their only child, James, was but two months older than Hannah's eldest boy, Francis. She took up her pen and told her daughter about his recent successes at school. Then she added an account of the happy visit to Selina and Thomas Scott at Salter's Grange, making only a brief mention of Martha and Sam in passing.

You must be very proud indeed of Teddy taking his seat in the Lords while he is still so young. I'm sure he will do good work. I can imagine him and our old friend Lord Altrincham finding the means to reduce factory working hours even further. Sarah speaks of him often.

Does Lord Altrincham never consider retiring? I've no idea what age he is, but he must be older than your father-in-law. I know Lady Anne has pressed him to retire for years now, particularly since he's had trouble with the leg he hurt when he was shot at, back in the eighties. But with no success!

Richard says old injuries have a nasty way of playing up as you get older. I do hope Harrington and Lady Anne are still able to ride those lovely green paths at Ashleigh together. Which reminds me, are they planning to come up to town to see you while the boys are at home, or dare you leave your decorators to go and visit them?

She paused as she dipped her pen in the inkpot and listened carefully. She glanced at the clock. Only eleven, far too early for John, but it did sound like a motor on the hill. It would hardly be Sarah. She worked at her table all morning and called in the afternoon on her way to the Post Office, or to one of the mills.

Before she'd even put her pen down, a vehicle stopped outside, footsteps hurried along the garden path and Sarah stood in the doorway.

'Sarah dear,' she said, taking one glance at the pale, drawn face. 'Is anything wrong?'

Sarah nodded silently, crossed the room and threw herself down in her father's fireside chair.

'I've bad news, Ma,' she said quietly. 'I came to tell you before you'd hear it from someone else.'

Rose felt her stomach lurch. She thought of Sarah's children, Hugh and little Helen, just home for the Easter holidays. Something had happened to one of them. An accident. Or one of them was ill. Or perhaps Sarah herself was ill and hadn't told her.

She rose from the table with a steadiness that surprised her and sat down in the fireside chair opposite her. She shivered, suddenly chill despite the mild April morning and the warm glow of the stove.

'Da sent me a message up from Ballievy,' Sarah began. 'The big ship's sent out signals for help, but there's no other ship very near.'

'What! The *Titanic*?' Rose gasped. 'But how can she be in trouble? They say she's unsinkable. What's happened? What's gone wrong? And how did Da hear?'

Rose looked at her daughter steadily. She was sitting up straight in the easy chair, her hands stretched along its wooden arms, her fingers grasping the worn-smooth ends. She was wearing a high-necked blouse pinned at the neck with a favourite brooch and a plain dark-blue skirt, her favourite colour. Apart from the look on her face, she seemed the calm, controlled Sarah who'd taken up her life and Hugh's work with so little hesitation and such steadiness immediately after his death.

'Someone got the news from the White Star office in Belfast this morning and it went round the mills like wildfire,' she explained. 'Some of the men have brothers in the crew or know someone in the handover group and several women have relatives who are passengers. There's two families in second class emigrating from Belfast. My Mrs Beatty has a niece who's a stewardess,' she went on, taking a deep breath. 'You've met her, Ma. She used to be on the cross-channel ferry, before she was moved to the *Olympic*. They were short-staffed for *Titanic*, so they moved her again. Mary Sloan?'

Rose nodded silently. She'd had more than one conversation with her over the last years when she'd crossed the Irish Sea to visit Hannah and her mother-in-law, her own oldest friend, Lady Anne.

'Oh Sarah,' she began, waving her hands helplessly. 'Whatever *has* gone wrong? Was it a storm?'

Sarah shook her head again, but did not look away. Her blue eyes lacked the old animation, gone with Hugh's death, but they never wavered. However painful the news, she'd tell her straight.

'Da telegraphed our agents in New York first thing this morning. They said nearby ships had taken off all the passengers and she's being towed to Halifax. But a little while ago, they heard from the London office. Montreal had telegraphed that she'd gone down. Apparently, she sent out CQD for a couple of hours and then this new signal, SOS. But then all went silent.'

Rose was so shocked she could hardly get her words out.

'Sarah, Sarah, dear. All those poor people. She'll be so anxious about Mary. Is there nothing we can do to find out what's really happened?'

'I'm on my way to the Post Office. I'll talk to Billy Auld. If anyone can find out, he can. He's in charge of telegraphs now,' she said abruptly, as she stood up.

Rose sat where she was, still staring at her daughter, who walked across the kitchen but made no move to leave.

'Who were you writing to, Ma?' Sarah asked, as she caught sight of the unfinished letter on the table.

'Hannah. I was telling her the good news about Uncle Sam in America . . .' Rose broke off, aware that Sarah was watching her closely. For one more moment she sat, confused and bewildered, and then it dawned on her why Sarah had come. She put a hand to her mouth and gasped.

'Sam,' she said, in a whisper. 'Your Uncle Sam,' she said, looking up, her eyes wide. 'He should've been on her.'

Sarah smiled bleakly, came and put an arm round her, kissed her cheek.

'Yes, I know. He showed me the newspaper advertisements when he was last here. He said a touch of Louis Quinze and potted palms would be quite an experience after years of travelling steerage. It would be something to remember.'

Tears sprang to Rose's eyes and trickled unheeded down her cheeks. First Hugh and then Sam. The very thought of losing her own brother after the loss of their dear friend and son-in-law. It was just too much for her. She sobbed and Sarah comforted her.

By the end of the day, everyone knew that the big ship, such a part of life since her launch the previous year, had indeed gone down, but it was an enormous relief that all the passengers were safe. A list of ships in the area, many of them with familiar names, were said to have come to her aid. Some of them were White Star liners, like the *Titanic* herself. Others had been built in Harland & Wolff's yards in Belfast where she too had been built. But *Titanic* was lost. The ship launched with such pride and celebration less than a year ago now lay some two miles below the Atlantic waves.

Rose and John sat silent by the stove after their evening meal. The daily paper had no knowledge of what had happened in the early hours of the morning on the other side of the Atlantic. They were both fully aware that, whatever messages were being tapped out back and forth across the ocean, no further news would reach them till the *Belfast News Letter* arrived in Banbridge on the earliest of the morning trains.

'D'you remember Sarah and Hugh taking the children to see her?' Rose asked suddenly, breaking the heavy silence.

'Aye. An' wee Hugh was that excited he couldn't eat his breakfast,' replied John, looking up at the clock, as if it would tell him something he needed to know.

'When they got back he tried to tell me how big she was and he just ran out of words,' she said, smiling sadly. 'Then he said it would hold everybody in Banbridge and they could go for walks along her decks just like we do on Sundays.' She paused. 'How many would there be on board, John?'

'Some say two thousand, some say three. Wee Hugh isn't far wrong, though, she's the biggest ship that's ever been built. It's an awful blow for all those that wrought on her, never mind the White Star Line and the owners.'

'But how would you get them all off and onto other ships?' Rose demanded, thinking of the huge cliff that towered above them when they'd gone with Richard and Elizabeth to the launch.

John rubbed his chin and studied the toes of his shoes.

'Ye might be able to get another ship alongside if the big ship's engines weren't runnin', but more likely ye'd have to lower the lifeboats and move people that way. It wou'd depend on the sea, too, if it was rough. It wou'd be a hard job with childer and older folk.'

'And it would be cold, wouldn't it?'

'Ach yes, sure it's only April. There's talk about icebergs, so it must be,' he said, standing up and putting out the gas lamp on his side of the fireplace.

'And we'll go to our nice, warm bed and pray those poor people are safe,' she said, her voice wavering.

'That's all we can do, love,' he said kindly, as he lit a candle to see them upstairs to the large, new bedroom where they now slept.

But Rose's mind was still racing. For a long time she lay motionless, reluctant to disturb John, who'd fallen asleep within moments of getting into bed. Then, she slid out gently, drew on her dressing gown and tiptoed barefoot to the window. She drew back an edge of curtain and saw the moon appear through a mass of racing storm cloud. For a moment, it beamed a cold, silvery light over the familiar fields, then, as the clouds closed over again, the details of the landscape were blotted out, only the shape of the little hills, dark upon even darker, rolled away to the horizon. She looked in vain for a light, a friendly signal in the empty space. But it was late and all their neighbours were in bed. There was no light to comfort a passing stranger, or someone adrift in the darkness in the cold night hours.

She shivered and felt her teeth begin to chatter, told herself firmly to get back into bed and put away such desolate thoughts. 'Think of something pleasant,' she said to herself as she slipped cautiously beneath the blankets. 'Flowers and trees and the song of birds.'

She tried, but it was no good. She lay on her side, her feet two blocks of ice, her arms folded across her breasts as she felt her body shake and a cold sweat break on her face.

'We'll divide the ship here,' the man said, looking up at her, his hands full of stones. 'An' we'll take the first piece down to the bottom an' come back for th'other. The doors is locked so you'll be safe.'

She looked around in the darkness and saw she was in a boat. It was full of children. At first, she thought she had never seen any of them before. Then she looked more closely. In the dim light she caught sight of Hugh and Helen holding each other's hands, then Charley and Billy and little Sammy. Emily and Rose were hunched together with the baby, Bobby, all wrapped up in a white sheet. They were all frightened and so was she. She was sure the water was deep and she knew none of them could swim. What would she do when the men came back for the other piece of the ship to take it down to the bottom?

'Don't worry yourself, Rose. Sure, haven't we got through worse than this?'

She heard a familiar voice, felt a touch on her hand and a soft arm slide round her waist. Even without seeing her face, she knew it was Mary Wylie.

'Sure this boat's unsinkable,' said Mary, laughing. 'It's like you an' me. We'll always come back up again. If Mary-Anne didn't do for us, who could? Will we get out the griddle and make pancakes for the we'ans?'

There was a sudden threatening rush of sound. Rose woke with a start and heard a shower of sleet rattle fiercely against the bedroom window. In a few moments, it died away and left the room in silence.

'Mary Wylie,' she said to herself. 'Oh, my dear Mary, how I wish you'd not died in the Rail Disaster. You always understood without having to be told. You knew what I was feeling when I didn't even know myself.'

She lay still, warm and comfortable now, soothed by the steady rhythm of John's even breathing. Here and now, at this moment, she was safe. And so was John. And so was her brother Sam. And so were all the children, her own children, Hannah and Sam and Sarah, and Sarah's children, Hugh and Helen. There was nothing to be done about the disasters and disappointments that life brought to everyone. She must give thanks for this moment of warmth and security and the memory of her dear friend, and store it up to give her courage in the future, whenever she should need it.

The morning brought more squally showers and intermissions of brilliant light. John left early and promised he'd send a messenger with the Belfast paper. There was nothing to do but get on with her morning's work until he arrived.

'Missus Hamilton?'

Rose closed the oven door and straightened up cautiously, her back protesting after the effort of sliding a heavy casserole into position.

'Yes. Yes indeed,' she said, hurrying towards the young man who stood awkwardly against the door-post, his waterproof cape dripping from the last heavy shower.

'It's all bad news, Missus,' he said, drawing out a

folded newspaper from under the cape. 'She hit an iceberg and sunk a couple of hours later. There's fifteen hundred lost and no news yet of who's saved and who's drowned,' he said, handing it to her. 'Desperit business,' he went on as she unfolded the paper and stood staring at the banner headline.

'Had you anyone on her?' Rose asked cautiously.

There was something in the tone of his voice that made her wonder if all the drops of moisture on his face were actually raindrops.

'Aye, surely. Ma cousin Hugh's a boilermaker. Me mother's people all work in the yard, but they're platers and riveters, except Hugh. He was that excited he was goin' and they cou'd only stan' an watch. But they're safe enough now, an' likely he's gone,' he said matter-of-factly.

'But there's still some hope, isn't there?' Rose began tentatively. 'He might be among the saved. There are no names yet, are there?'

The young man smiled at her and shook his head.

'Not much chance wi' all them millionaires on board forby weemen and childer,' he said, pressing his lips together. 'He wou'd have deeved ye when he talked about them boilers, the size o' them and how they worked together like,' he said suddenly. 'I diden understan the half o' what he said. I wisht I'd lissened to him rightly the last time I saw him.'

He turned away quickly without another word.

Rose sat down by the stove and read everything she could find about the *Titanic*. Some of the reports contradicted each other. One said there were 3,359 souls on board and 1,500 had been lost, but elsewhere it said

600 passengers were transferred without mishap. The figures simply didn't add up. One report said the survivors were going to Halifax, another to New York.

No, there was nothing to give so much as a grain of comfort. Sir Bruce Ismay, the Chairman of the White Star Line, was among the victims, it said, but no names of survivors were given. There was a great deal about 'the space-annihilating speed of wireless telegraphy', the number of American millionaires on board, the likelihood and possibility of icebergs at this time of year, and 'the need for incessant watchfulness on the part of mariners traversing the North Atlantic'.

Life was full of danger, she told herself, as she dropped the paper by her chair and leaned forward to stir the fire. There was nothing new in that. It was just that sometimes it came so close, as it had on her thirtieth birthday, the day of the excursion to Warrenpoint, the day dear Mary Wylie threw her youngest son out of the window of a train with locked doors, as it ran backwards down a steep gradient into an oncoming passenger train. Ned had survived unscathed. He'd married a local girl only last summer.

For years she had been haunted by dreams of that awful morning, the sun beating down remorselessly as she tried to get the children home across the fields without them seeing the devastation, but the dreams had passed. She thought of Mary often enough, but until last night she had never dreamed of her.

They'd bought all the newspapers then, too, looking for news of the injured, and details of the Board of Trade inquiry, but their own information had been more accurate than anything in the papers, for they heard immediately who had died overnight from injuries and who still lay critically ill in the infirmary in Armagh.

All the people involved had been friends or neighbours, or the friends and neighbours of someone they knew. This was different. So many, many people. People of all sorts and conditions. Millionaires and film stars. Owners of big American companies. Poor people emigrating with only a suitcase. Only some of these people were known, even indirectly, but it seemed the fate of each one became a personal matter because the ship they'd sailed in, confident they were safe, had been built by thousands of work people in Belfast.

She sat silent for a long time, just gazing into the warm glow of the stove and asking herself, over and over again, what could anyone do.

For the rest of the week no one talked about anything else but the loss of the *Titanic*. Each day brought new information to set against the rumours and speculations which had circulated as freely as the newspapers themselves. There was now no doubt about the cause of the disaster. The *Titanic* had hit an iceberg which had opened one side of the ship, allowing the sea to flood to the so-called watertight compartments. Only some 680 people had been accommodated on the lifeboats, mostly women and children. They were rescued by the *Carpathia* some hours after the big ship went down. One hundred and ninety bodies had been found and taken to Halifax for burial. The Americans had opened an inquiry and the surviving crew members and passengers were giving evidence.

Despite the claims of the White Star Line, there were already questions being asked about the speed of the ship and the route it had taken. It was now known that *Titanic* had received many warning messages about ice and icebergs and at least one passenger had 'smelt ice', a distinctive smell familiar to those who sailed regularly in these waters. Why had the ship not altered course or reduced speed? Why was the captain not on the bridge? Why the delay in responding to the iceberg warning?

Every new detail to emerge from the American inquiry and the interviews with survivors was read and considered. For the people who built the ship and the families of those who had sailed on her, it seemed as if understanding precisely what had happened would ease the pain. But it didn't. It only provided a way of expressing some of the hurt and grief.

On Sunday morning, Rose and John attended a memorial service for the 1,500 victims in Holy Trinity, Banbridge. That afternoon, Sarah joined them and they went up to Belfast to the cathedral service, so that John could add to the collection for the widows and orphans of the Belfast crew members the contribution from the four mills.

To Rose's great surprise, Sarah wore black. Quakers did not hold with this sign of mourning and when Hugh died, she'd not given a thought to mourning dress. Now, standing in the packed cathedral, a small dark figure, she looked pale, ravaged and heartbroken, though she held herself erect and composed and managed to sing 'Nearer my God to Thee' without crying, which was more than Rose was able to do.

'Hello, Ma. How's your back?'

Rose looked up from her book some days later, surprised there'd been no sound of a motor.

'I can't complain. It was entirely my own fault. I should know better than to garden for more than an hour or two, but the day was so lovely,' she replied ruefully, getting awkwardly to her feet and kissing her daughter.

'Have you time for a cup of tea?' she asked automatically, for Sarah had seldom time for more than a short visit these days.

'Yes, I think so,' she replied, dropping her document case by the door and slipping off her jacket.

Surprised, but pleased, Rose drew the kettle forward on the stove.

'Did you get Helen and Hugh safely back yesterday? I'm sure they didn't want to go,' Rose said, looking over her shoulder as she crossed to the dresser.

'Actually, they were quite keen when it came to it,' Sarah replied thoughtfully. 'I think all this *Titanic* business upset them, and Mrs Beatty wasn't herself at all till we got the good news about her niece.'

'Has there been anything further from her?'

'No, just that one word, "safe". I expect she'll have to stay for the American inquiry, but the Americans have been very kind. I read that complete strangers were waiting at the docks with clothes for the survivors when the *Carpathia* arrived.'

'Yes, I read about that too. And they paid the fares of the steerage passengers to wherever they'd been going. It's some comfort to see such kindness,' said Rose, as she collected china mugs and a jug of milk and came back to the stove.

'It is, indeed,' Sarah agreed. 'It makes up for the likes of Sir Bruce Ismay getting off in the first lifeboat with his wife and secretary and enough empty places to have saved three or four whole families,' she said bitterly.

Rose looked round quickly from spooning tea. She thought she saw Sarah flick something out of one eye as she sat staring fixedly into the orange glow of the fire.

'Did you read about Isador and Ida Straus, Ma? They own Macy's, the big store in New York.'

'No, love, I don't think so. Was it in the papers you brought yesterday?'

'Perhaps it was today's,' Sarah replied uneasily. 'I've brought them for you,' she added flatly, as Rose handed her a favourite mug decorated with delicate sprays of forget-me-not.

There was a look on her face that Rose could not read. She seemed quite in command of herself, but then she always did. The last time Rose had seen Sarah upset was more than a year ago, after a particularly bad accident at Ballievy. A machine guard had not been replaced after cleaning and a girl had been caught by her hair and died from her injuries.

They drank their tea in silence.

'What happened to the Strauses, Sarah?'

'They went to the lifeboats and said goodbye, and Mrs Straus got in and sat down,' began Sarah coolly. 'And then she got up again and climbed out of the lifeboat and went back to her husband. She said they'd been together all these years and they weren't going to be parted now. Then they went away along the deck together.'

Her tone remained steady almost to the last word, but when she said 'together' her voice broke into a choking sob and tears streamed down her cheeks. She covered her face with her hands, her narrow shoulders shaking as she rocked back and forth in her father's fireside chair.

'Sarah, Sarah, love, what is it? Tell me what it is,' Rose whispered, jumping to her feet and putting her arms round her. She stroked her hair and kissed her neck and the small piece of forehead that emerged as Sarah wiped her face ineffectually.

'Sarah, love. Tell me. Is it Hugh?

'No, it's me,' she gasped, as she pulled out a handkerchief from her skirt pocket. 'I wish I could have gone with Hugh. That's wicked, isn't it? The Strauses were old and their children grown up. If Hugh and I had been on the *Titanic,* he'd have made me go because of Helen and young Hugh. But I wouldn't have wanted to go. Not even for them. And that's all wrong, isn't it? I ought to love my children and I don't.'

'Oh Sarah, Sarah, you're not *wicked*, you're bereft. You've lost the man you loved. You've loved him all your life.'

'I still love him. I'll never love anyone else,' she sobbed. 'Whatever he says, I'll never love anyone like I loved him.'

'Of course you won't. You can't love any two people in the same way. You can't love the children like you loved Hugh, but that doesn't mean you don't love them.'

'Doesn't it? Sometimes I can hardly bear to look at them because they're so like him. Hugh even *sounds* like him when he's trying to be grown up,' she went on, her voice stronger, though the tears still flowed. 'I simply *cannot* imagine how I can go on living without him. Without joy. Without comfort. Just work and the children. No motor coming into the yard. No footstep in the hallway. No warm arms at night or in the morning. Never, ever again.'

'Sarah, you're too hard on yourself. It's not a year yet,' Rose said firmly, wiping her tears with her own hanky. 'You've done nothing but work. You're tired out and everything's worse when you're tired. Do you remember when you were a little girl, how irritable you got? You were so cross the others used to be afraid of you.'

Rose paused, grateful for the sniff that might have been the ghost of a laugh.

'But now you're so good, so grown up, so sensible, you've forgotten how to be sad or upset.'

'But isn't that what one's supposed to do? When one has children and responsibilities?' Sarah countered, as she blew her nose loudly.

'Oh yes, we have to try,' said Rose, whose back was aching furiously with bending over. 'But how can we be comforted if we don't admit our pain and hurt?'

'I thought comfort was only for children,' Sarah came back at her again as she wiped her face with Rose's drier hanky.

'But we're all children when we're hurt, Sarah,' Rose said firmly, taking up her stone-cold hands in her own warm ones.

'Did you never see Hugh cry?' she went on softly.

Sarah nodded silently, swallowed and blew her nose. 'He was always ashamed when he cried,' she said awkwardly.

'That's a great pity, Sarah,' Rose nodded. 'But it's common enough. It was years before I persuaded your father that tears are nothing to be ashamed of.'

'Da?'

'Da, and my brother Sam, and Thomas Scott,' she said firmly, 'and the messenger who came whose cousin the boilermaker was lost.'

Sarah stared at her, her eyes red and swollen, her cheeks still damp. 'Ma, what *am* I going to do? Some days I think I'm going mad.'

Four

Sarah walked slowly back up the hill to Rathdrum, her gaze moving along the hedgerows and over the sloping fields as if she hadn't laid eyes on them for a long time. The afternoon was sunny. Great patches of blue sky were scribbled with light cloud and the breeze was fresh but not chill. With the air clear, the mountains seemed so close, their familiar craggy shapes sharply outlined. She stopped on the steepest part of the hill and stared at them till her eyes blurred in the strong reflected light. Yes, that was it. It was as if a photographer had enhanced the outline with the slightest touch of Indian ink on a very fine brush.

To her surprise, she found herself thinking about the photographic studio in Belfast where she'd worked before she and Hugh were married. She could almost smell the sharp odour of fixer that greeted you at the top of the steep, narrow stairs and hear the voice of her boss, that awful man, Abernethy. Photographing the great and the good was the mainstay of his business. She hadn't had much time for most of them, but she'd learnt a lot about portraiture. She had pictures of Hugh and the children that she was pleased with, though she hadn't looked at them since he died.

The big chestnut that stretched its lower branches over the road at the entrance to the driveway was beginning to leaf. The sticky buds had burst. Still a pale, downy grey-green, the delicate leaves were beginning to unfold. The driveway was adrift with outer coverings, sepals of pale brown and pink mixed up with the fading white blossoms from the flowering cherries they'd planted five years ago to replace two elderly limes lost in a winter gale.

Snow in springtime, she thought, as she walked slowly towards the handsome front door that no one ever used.

'Elizabeth, Elizabeth, come quick! Ma's ill.'

Suddenly, she saw herself, a schoolgirl, running along this same drive, ploughing through deep snow, her heart pounding, gasping for breath, intent only on reaching that same front door where a gleam of light spilled out through the fanlight into the darkness of a winter day.

'So very long ago,' she thought. 'And in another life.'

She and Hannah had tramped up the hill after school and found their mother lying icy cold on the bedroom floor. Hugh had gone for the doctor, but she'd met the doctor herself the previous day. She knew he'd be no good. The only hope was Elizabeth. Dear, sensible Elizabeth, Hugh's sister, who'd collected brandy and herbs and friar's balsam in her basket and saved her mother's life.

But Elizabeth couldn't save Hugh. Neither she nor Richard had been able to do anything but watch and hope. They had been so loving and so good to her, knowing her distress, but as the days passed they had warned her Hugh was weakening, his body no longer strong enough to fight the fever, and their honesty had given them one last night together.

She walked round to the kitchen door, pushed it open and called out a greeting to her housekeeper. Then she remembered she'd sent Mrs Beatty to Belfast to spend a night or two with her sister, to comfort her if her only daughter should have been lost with the *Titanic*. The house was silent. Even more silent than usual.

She put down her document case in the dining room where the big table was covered with neat piles of papers. Across the hallway, the door to the sitting room stood open, a pleasant room with its well-polished furniture and marble fireplace, now filled with sunlight, the grate laid ready with sticks and fir cones. She moved back into the hallway and stood for a moment, looking at the spill of brightness from the fanlight and the pattern it made on the carpet, unsure of what to do.

In all these months, she could not recall being completely alone in the house before. Elizabeth had stayed with her for a few days after the funeral. She herself had honoured the entertainment of Friends from various parts of England to whom Hugh had already offered hospitality. The children had come for holidays. Mrs Beatty had remained, steady and reliable, saying little, ensuring that Sarah ate what she put in front of her.

Sarah made up her mind and walked quickly upstairs. She crossed the landing to the bedroom she and Hugh had shared, kicked off her shoes and lay down on her own side of the large, high bed. She closed her eyes, felt tears press through the lids and trickle past her ears.

The August night had been dark and airless, the windows open wide to catch any breath of air. Hugh lay motionless, beads of moisture on his forehead, his breathing shallow.

'Now, Mrs Sinton, you must go and get some rest. I'll come for you immediately if there's the slightest change.'

The night nurse Richard had found for Hugh was both efficient and kind. Neither she nor Elizabeth ever tried to send her away when she sat through the long hours of the day with Hugh. They just encouraged her to walk in the garden when he was deeply asleep and to eat her meals downstairs while they washed his fevering body and changed the sheets.

But that warm August night, despite her weariness, she could not sleep at all. Hugh was slipping away. Even without Richard and Elizabeth's cautious words, she could see that for herself. His body was weary, flagging, bathed in sweat. There was nothing anyone could do. Nothing. No magic potion. No miracle.

She'd got up and dressed, gone to their bedroom, pushed open the door and seen the white-clad figure sitting by the bed, reading in a tiny pool of light. To her surprise, the nurse said nothing when she appeared, merely got up from her chair, nodded to her and left the room, closing the door quietly behind her.

Very carefully, so as not to disturb him, Sarah had climbed onto the bed and moved herself slowly across till she was close enough to put her ice-cold hand on his hot, damp forehead.

'Sarah, my love . . .'

'Hush. I didn't mean to wake you. Go back to sleep,' she said softly.

'I don't think I was asleep. Or perhaps I was dreaming of you. I was thinking of you. I'm so glad you've come.'

His voice was weak but perfectly clear. She sensed that each word was an effort, but an effort he chose to make.

'Sarah, I have been so happy since we married,' he said, turning his head slowly to look at her, as she took his hand. 'I can hardly believe how happy. There is only one darkness on my spirit. Were it gone, I could go in peace, though it is not my will but God's.'

'What's that, Hugh? What darkness?' she asked quietly, as she gazed at his worn and ravaged face.

'Your grief, Sarah,' he said steadily. 'I cannot bear the thought of your grief, but I cannot ask you not to grieve for what we have lost.'

He paused, as if to gather the little strength he had. 'I would be so happy if you could promise me to live in hope,' he continued, his voice now a whisper. 'To love again wherever love is to be found.'

He stopped, totally exhausted by this longer effort. Sarah leaned across his body to the bedside table, dipped her fingers in a glass of water, moistened his lips and then wiped the sweat from his brow.

'I can never love anyone as I have loved you,' she said honestly.

He pressed her hand weakly.

'I know that,' he said steadily. 'But you are young and may have a long life ahead of you. Think of Elizabeth. Think of me. We neither of us expected to find joy in a loved one. Please, my darling, promise me you will not turn away from what could bring you joy.'

Sarah could think of nothing in the whole world that could bring her joy without Hugh to share it, but his eyes were upon her, moist, red-rimmed, yet full of love. What could she possibly say? They had always been honest with each other. Even when she was very young she'd told him what she thought and he'd listened and pointed out other possibilities she might not have been aware of. But now there was neither time nor energy for argument or discussion. She could not be dishonest, but neither could she deny him anything that might comfort him.

'I promise you I'll not turn my back on the world – the good and the bad. If I could ever love anyone it would be because I've loved you for so long. You taught me what love was.'

'You will love again, my dear. I know you will. And I bless the man you give your love to. Only I know how fortunate he will be.'

He closed his eyes and lay so very still she thought he'd fallen asleep, but a few moments later he opened them again and smiled.

'Don't go away, Sarah. Close your eyes and we'll both have a little sleep. You're tired too.'

And she had slept. With his hand in hers, she had dozed off and not wakened till she heard the song of a blackbird through the open window. She had shivered slightly in the cool air of the early dawn and looked carefully at the sleeping figure beside her. He seemed paler and more deeply asleep.

She'd gone to the window and stretched, drawn in the freshness of the very early morning and returned to the nurse's chair to take the cold hand that lay inert on the unruffled bedclothes. How long she sat watching him she could not measure, but she did know he died peacefully before the first sunlight had dispersed the shadows of the night.

She wiped her tears with the back of her wrist and lay looking out at the garden. Despite the cold, frosty nights, growth had begun. The same weeds that tempted her mother to start work would be springing up in the flowerbeds she and Hugh had tended together. It was one of the pleasures she'd encouraged him to enjoy. Something to set against the hard work, the endless pieces of paper, the decisions about what raw materials to buy, or what to charge for finished goods and how best to transport them to their far-flung customers.

She hadn't set foot in the garden since Hugh died, as her mother had reminded her that very afternoon, as near to chiding her as she would ever come.

'Sarah dear,' Rose had said, 'we all have our work to do and sometimes it seems to take all the time and energy there is, but you have to have other things too. Small pleasures. Little enjoyments, like flowers on the table. We need encouragements, even when we're happy and things are going well for us. We need them even more when we're unhappy.'

'But what difference can it make, Ma?' she'd thrown back at her. 'Hugh was all the encouragement I ever needed and now he's gone. What point is there in life at all, except his work, which I do for him?'

'Sarah, what would Hugh say to you if you said there was no point in life, except work?'

Rose had got up to make a fresh pot of tea, for their two china mugs sat cold and untouched on the corners of the stove. She looked over her shoulder and saw Sarah glance down at her hands, her tears past now, her cheeks no longer streaked and puffy.

'Hugh would say we're given life to live to the best of our ability.'

'And what about using one's talents?'

To Rose's great delight, her daughter laughed, recalling an old contention the two of them had argued about for years.

'He said one had to use all one's gifts, not just the useful and everyday,' Sarah began, her voice now quite steady. 'Being able to love was a talent some women had in great measure. He'd been lucky. Before me, he'd had Elizabeth and you. He said you'd saved him from being a crotchety old bachelor, just as Da had saved him from loneliness for want of a friend.'

'Hugh was always so generous in his appreciation,' Rose had said as she poured fresh mugs of tea. 'I know Quakers speak out as their conscience dictates on important matters, but Hugh would speak out about quite ordinary things as well. If there was something good to say, he always said it.'

'Ma, do you think the pain will ever heal?' Sarah asked abruptly.

'Sweetheart, I've never suffered such a loss as you have,' Rose had said quickly as she put Sarah's tea into her hand. 'But I can tell you what my own mother said when I was old enough to ask her how she coped when your grandfather died. She said there was no point at all in trying to forget what had been, or to run away from the sadness. If you did that, you lost all the good things that would otherwise come to you and give you strength. Every time she put food on the table she thought how delighted our father would have been that we had enough to eat. It was the thought of his pleasure in all she now did that finally comforted her.'

Sarah woke with a start, surprised she should have fallen asleep in the middle of the afternoon. She swung her legs out of bed, walked in her stockinged feet to the window and leaned out, looking down at the garden. She was almost sure she could see the bright faces of polyanthus at the edge of one of the flowerbeds.

Despite the fact that she hadn't worked in the garden since Hugh died, the little flowers had bloomed without any help or attention from her.

Suddenly and unexpectedly, she remembered a saying of their old friend Thomas Scott; one which her mother often quoted: '*Whatever way the world goes, the hawthorns bloom in May*.'

Strangely comforted, she went on staring down at the small patches of colour that were pushing up between the weeds.

'Later,' she said to herself, Thomas's words still repeating in her mind as she closed the window and put her shoes on. 'There'll be time to do a little bit before dark.'

She crossed the landing to the guest room where she had slept since Hugh had become ill, gathered up the comb and brush, the hand mirror and the bottles on her dressing table and carried them across the landing in her arms. Back and forth she went, carrying her underwear, her clothes and shoes, her hats and handbags, until the room was empty and the large double bed was covered with things to be put away.

When she had found a place for everything in the empty cupboards and drawers, she went to the linen cupboard and took down a carefully folded bed-spread wrapped in spoilt linen. She removed the crumpled bedspread on which she had fallen asleep, shook out the folds from the new one and spread it carefully over the bed. When it was straight and smooth, she looked at it and smiled. Made by her mother and Elizabeth with treasured fragments from dresses and blouses she could still remember, it had at its centre a beautifully embroidered diamond panel.

'Sarah and Hugh', it said, within a circle of flowers.

Five

As April turned to May, springtime came with a sudden rush, the trees bursting into full leaf, the road verges swaying with tall, delicate stems of cow parsley. By the middle of the month, creamy-white hawthorn blossom lay thick on the branches, its heavy perfume drawn out by the warm afternoon sun. The days grew long and the evenings light, the smell of the first cut grass mixing with scents from cottage gardens.

Since the end of February, Rose had been longing for the warmth of summer and the first blooms in her garden. Now she had the sun on her back, her hands were full of prunings and the scent of flowers was all around her, yet her thoughts kept moving away and her mind filled with dark shadows and anxious fears.

Morning after morning she would rise cheerfully, see John off to work and then find her plans for the day falter and fade. Baking and sewing seemed a labour. She was even reluctant to write letters, something that had never happened before.

'This won't do, Rose. This really won't do,' she said to herself as she studied the soft foliage she'd cut from shrubs overspreading the path.

She chose some sprigs of red weigelia to add colour to the prunings she couldn't bear to throw away, turned back into the house, arranged the assorted fragments in a vase and set the result of her efforts in the middle of the kitchen table. She dropped down into her chair and sat staring at the fresh foliage and bright blooms, trying to work out what made her feel so sad on such a lovely morning.

From long ago, she heard the familiar voice of her mother-in-law, Sarah, with whom she and John had lived happily for the first ten years of their married life.

'We all get depressed, Rose. Sometimes it's just our bodies telling us we're tired. Or maybe there's something we should be paying attention to that we're not.'

Well, she wasn't tired. She had plenty to do, sure enough, but never so much that she couldn't sit down and sew or read her book if she felt weary. She hadn't been sleeping well, her nights broken with sudden fevers and bizarre dreams, but she often closed her eyes in her chair. Surely that would make up for any sleep she'd lost.

'*Don't lose any sleep over it, Rose dear.*'

That was her mother's voice. Strange she could still hear it so clearly after all these years. When she'd had problems with her young mistress, Lady Anne, or been scolded by Mr Smithers, the butler of Currane Lodge, she'd ask her mother what to do and Hannah would reassure her that it wasn't as bad as it seemed. It never helped to worry. She'd be all right if she just did her best.

Time and time again, events had proved her mother right, but on this lovely May morning the problem was she could put no name to what was troubling her.

She sat still, listening to the tick of the American clock. The sun climbed higher and the bright patch it cast on the floor moved slowly towards the hearth rug. Soon the brightness would fall on her boots like a rising tide.

She shuddered and pushed out of mind the now familiar thought of a rising tide. It had been with her for weeks now, ever since the first news of the *Titanic* disaster. No matter how she had argued with herself, she could not be free of the image of the water slowly rising. The thought of standing on the deck, knowing there was nothing you could do. That there was no seat in a lifeboat for you, no way back to the loved ones who had already left the sinking ship.

'Waiting. Just waiting for what you know is going to happen. And having no power at all to stop it,' she said, looking round as if she hoped there would be some reply from the empty room.

She leaned her head back and closed her eyes as the bright beams of light moved closer.

'*What are we gonta do, Hannah?*'

That voice was her father's. He was standing by the door of their house in Ardtur. She could hear the sound of walls falling and smell the dust that was swirling round him as Adair's men demolished their neighbours' houses. But when she looked at him again, it wasn't her father, it was John. He had a white envelope in his hand.

'They can't put us out, can they? And us with children?'

'Oh, yes they can,' she said to herself. 'Anything can happen. All those poor people on the *Titanic*. They thought she was unsinkable, but no one is safe from disaster. You can lose your home, your livelihood, your health, your loved ones. Whether you're the richest mill-owner in Belfast or the poorest widow in Banbridge, you can still lose what is precious to you.'

She opened her eyes with a jerk, blinked in the sunlight and saw her daughter appear in the doorway.

'Sarah, I wasn't expecting you. How lovely to see you.'

Sarah looked at her closely.

'Were you asleep, Ma?'

'Yes, I must have been,' Rose agreed, stretching. 'I sat down to have a think and I found myself back in Ardtur and then in Annacramp.'

'Was it a nice dream?'

Rose smiled. There was something in the way Sarah had asked her question that reminded her of the dark-haired child who would ask and ask and ask again till she was satisfied. It had been wearing at times, but she'd never resented it, for Sarah made such an effort to understand what was happening around her, even as a little girl.

'No, it wasn't,' she admitted, shaking her head. 'It was about the bad times. And it made me think of the *Titanic* all over again.'

Sarah nodded as she sat down opposite.

'I was talking to Richard the other day,' she began easily. 'He says he has patients coming to him with a whole variety of complaints and when he sits down to talk to them, they end up asking him what he thinks about the *Titanic*. He says there've been so many, he's watching out for it now.'

'Why does Richard think it's upset them?'

'He says it's made them feel insecure, but Elizabeth says it's just *reminded* them how insecure we all are.'

Rose smiled.

'Dear Elizabeth, she can always go one step further. What do *you* think, Sarah?'

Rose watched as a familiar frown appeared on Sarah's face. There was something about her today that kept reminding her of the lively child and passionate young woman she'd once been. Just seeing her had made Rose feel better already.

'I think the only security we have is knowing there are a few people who care about us,' she began. 'We can't do anything about being killed in a rail crash, or drowning on a voyage, or catching typhoid in the summer, but if we have a few people who love us, we can do something about being sad, or hurt, or in despair. As I was a few weeks ago when I sat in this chair and bawled,' she finished with a sudden beaming smile.

Rose got up and gave her a kiss.

'I'm so glad you came, love. I wasn't crying, but I was very low. And I couldn't see my way. I think I can now.'

'What was upsetting you, Ma?'

'I'm not sure, but it was certainly about not being able to stop things happening. I worry about your father. He gets so tired these days and the board meetings are a great burden to him. And then there's Sam and Martha and the wee ones. I can't see what life Sam has apart from his work. And I doubt if Martha will ever change.'

'No, *she* won't change,' Sarah agreed, nodding vigorously. 'She's too committed to her own invincible ignorance. She'd see any change as giving in. She'll never give in. And there's plenty like her.'

'Sarah!' Rose expostulated, amazed she should be quite so ferocious.

'Not much point mincing words, Ma – she's irredeemable,' Sarah added cheerfully. 'She's absolutely convinced that what she thinks is right and whatever she does is the only possible way of doing things. Don't you think?'

'Yes, to be honest, I do, but I was trying to keep an open mind or give her the benefit of the doubt,' she replied, nodding. 'Perhaps I just couldn't face the thought of what Sam has to live with.'

'Sam'll find a way. But he won't find it till he stands up to her. He hasn't done that yet, but he will. He's not as soft as he looks, Ma.'

Rose nodded, sure that Sarah was right, as she'd been right about so many people, even as a child. Suddenly and unexpectedly, she realised that she and Sarah hadn't talked like this for a very long time. Before Hugh died and the children had gone away to school, Sarah had worked as long hours at the mills as Hugh himself. What little leisure time they had, they'd devoted to the children. Since his death she'd seen her almost every day, but it wasn't the same Sarah who now sat opposite her, talking about her older brother.

Rose got to her feet, feeling a lightness she'd not known for weeks.

'I hope you've got time for a cup of tea, love. I've just remembered a story I want to tell you, even if I have told you it a dozen times before. It's the story of the night *after* we left Ardtur.'

'You know, Ma, you *haven't* told me that story before,' Sarah said thoughtfully as Rose took up her neglected mug of tea and drank thirstily.

'Oh, I must have done, Sarah. You and Hannah were always asking me for stories when you were little. I had to make use of anything I could lay hands on,' she said, laughing. 'I'm sure I've told you about Daniel McGee's house and the last story that was ever told there.'

'Yes, I know we kept asking,' Sarah said quickly. 'But I'm sure I can remember everything you told us. I could describe your house and the new school and the path you took the day you decided to go off up the mountain all by yourself to see the landlord's castle. I can remember Owen Friel and Danny Lawn, and old Aunt Mary . . .'

Rose listened, amazed as Sarah reeled off the names of friends and neighbours from that far-off life, names that hadn't been mentioned for years.

'But you've never told me about Daniel McGee, Ma. And I've never heard you even mention

Casheltown,' she said quite firmly.

'That is strange, Sarah. It really is,' said Rose, shaking her head. 'We all tell the stories that are important to us, and we all forget we've probably told them dozens of times before, but this time it's the other way round, isn't it? I could have sworn I'd been telling that story for years, it's so clear in my mind.'

'Maybe you've been telling it to yourself in your dreams. Or maybe you've just been practising what it preached . . .'

'What do you mean, love?'

'Well, it was a very sad occasion, Ma. All the people gathered in Daniel's house knew that it would be their turn tomorrow. Adair's men were working along the valley. By the end of the day, their homes would have gone. This was the last night. Tomorrow, they'd be adrift. No work, no shelter, no food . . .' Sarah broke off as a sudden thought struck her. 'Ma, do you think maybe it was the *Titanic* made you remember?' she asked quickly. 'When I said "adrift", I thought about the lifeboats again. And then I thought about the people left on board, listening to the band, knowing there was only a little while left.'

'Certainly it's strange, Sarah,' Rose said, nodding. 'Strange I thought I'd told you. Strange I wanted to tell you again. I wonder why?'

'Well, I could make a guess.'

'Please do,' said Rose quickly.

'Well, it seems to me that Daniel was looking for something to give hope to those in despair and he'd a feeling that Granny Hannah had what he needed.

And he was right. She told her story about how her father and uncle had survived after *their* eviction, walking the length of Scotland on burn water and berries from the hedgerows. Then Daniel asked her about what her father said to her when she was about to marry a man of a different religion, from a different country. That's the story that really mattered that evening.'

Sarah paused and collected her thoughts.

'I can't remember the exact words, but the core of what he said was that none of us pass through life without sadness and sorrow. "We must shed tears for our grief but not be bitter",' she went on slowly and carefully as she watched her mother's face. '"Bitterness stuns the spirit and weakens the heart. Accept what you cannot change and ask God and your fellow men for comfort. In that way you will live well however short your span."'

Rose nodded, amazed that she herself could have remembered these words from so very long ago.

'And then he warned her that if you give in to bitterness you will never fully live, "though you go beyond three score years and ten",' Sarah ended with a sigh. 'You've never been bitter, Ma,' Sarah said abruptly. 'No matter what's happened, you've tried to do your best. I hope I can do half as well.'

'Oh, Sarah, you're not bitter about losing Hugh, are you?

'No,' she said, shaking her head vigorously. 'But I do feel bitter when I see poor people exploited. When I see the conditions that some of them live in. I can't accept that, it makes me too angry. Hugh tried to help me, but even he couldn't manage it,' she admitted ruefully.

Rose said nothing, her mind moving backwards and forwards over events in Sarah's life. Time and time again she had indeed seen her beside herself with anger. Often she'd feared for her, feared for the passion that exhausted her, helping anyone she found in distress, but she'd hoped the years with Hugh, his steadying presence, his willingness to listen, had eased the burden.

'Is it still as bad as before you married?' she asked quietly.

'If anything it's got worse,' she admitted easily. 'I knew it troubled Hugh, so I tried very hard to be steady and calm, but I read an article about byssinosis the other day and I was so furious I couldn't sleep that night . . .'

'Byssinosis?' Rose repeated quietly.

'*Byssos*. Greek word for flax or linen, Ma. Byssinosis is the result of breathing in dust and fibre. It's better known as Monday wheeze, because wheezing after the weekend is the first symptom. Spinners and weavers and bakers all get it. That's why we put in extractor fans years ago and bought the holiday houses at the seaside. Now a group has produced figures for byssinosis in the cotton industry in Britain. They're appalling, but the government won't act. They say the disease isn't fatal. Do you know why it's not fatal, Ma?' she said, her voice dropping to a whisper.

Rose shook her head and noted how pale Sarah had grown.

'It's because, Ma, as it gets worse, the workers don't have enough breath to do their job. They have to give it up. When they die, they aren't working, so the report is able to state that "there is no morbidity with byssinosis; there is therefore no need to legislate".'

'Oh, Sarah dear, no wonder you're angry,' said Rose sadly. 'But is the anger going to help?'

'That's what Hugh always said, but he's not here to say it now,' she said flatly.

'Then perhaps I could say it.'

Sarah smiled weakly.

'You might get fed up.'

'Well, I'd be willing to try. But there's one condition,' replied Rose, pausing when she saw Sarah look surprised.

'Yes . . .'

'If your weakness is anger, Sarah, then mine is despair. I often fear I just haven't the courage to keep going and cope with the next disaster, whether it's public or private,' she said quietly. 'How would it be if we agreed to watch each other?'

'And remind each other of the last story ever told under Daniel McGee's roof?'

'Yes,' said Rose, warmly. 'Maybe that's why it came back to me today, after all these years. Maybe we *both* needed it.'

Six

'You *will* remember to water our gardens, won't you, Mama?' young Hugh had insisted on the pleasant April day Sarah had taken them back to school. 'Even if it rains,' he went on solemnly, 'it may not provide enough moisture when plants begin to grow vigorously.'

Sarah smiled to herself as she visualised the look of concentration on his face as he instructed her. She'd never thought of herself as much of a gardener, and clearly her son shared her view, but she had to admit she'd thoroughly enjoyed keeping her promise to the children during these last few weeks.

Some three years earlier both Helen and Hugh had asked to have their own piece of garden. Encouraged by their Aunt Elizabeth and Grandma Rose, to whom they had applied for things to grow, they had dug and planted with great enthusiasm, even if she'd had to tidy up a bit after them.

'The early morning is probably the best time to water,' her son had explained, fixing her firmly with his gaze, 'but if you forget, then you must wait till the sun has gone round to the south-west and our part of the garden is in shade.'

'You need to poke your finger in the soil like

Grandma does,' added Helen helpfully.'If your finger's still clean afterwards, then you do *need* to water.'

Determined not to disappoint them, she'd made a large notice and propped it up on her desk at the beginning of June when the weather turned warm rather earlier than usual. Now, when she came into the dining room each morning, instead of making a start on the papers she'd left ready, she'd look up at the sky and fill her watering can instead.

Helen's garden was a mass of bloom. Foxgloves, Canterbury bells and lavender were her favourites. Already, the worker bees were harvesting nectar, so involved with their own affairs that Sarah's only concern was to avoid sprinkling them as she pushed the spout of her can below the flourishing plants. She watched the fine rain of moisture pit the dusty soil and trickle off the white stones and seashells which marked its boundaries.

Hugh's garden was easier to water. In a rectangular space the same size as Helen's, but on the opposite side of the path, he had planted seven chestnuts and seven acorns. Every single one had sprouted and several of them had grown so vigorously, they would soon have to be found new homes. Between the young trees, small annual weeds were springing up in the bare earth, just as he'd told her they would.

The ground was *very* dry. Even without her mother's finger technique, she could see the water running across the dusty surface and forming tiny pools. She went back into the kitchen, refilled her can and worked her way slowly round the trees a second time.

'*Great oaks from little acorns grow.*'

She couldn't remember who'd said it, when they'd said it, or where they'd said it, but she could certainly see now *why* they'd said it. From those acorns, brought home in a trouser pocket, here were these seven vigorous specimens. If they grew this fast, where might they be in ten years, or twenty?

Tempted by the freshness of the morning and the quiet of her own thoughts, Sarah fetched a hoe and started dislodging the weeds in the soft, damp soil of her son's plot. Later it would be warmer, much warmer. No papers were needed at the mills today so they could wait a little longer in the cool, shady dining room.

'Mmm, perhaps I have picked up a thing or two,' she said to herself some time later, when she straightened up and looked down at the trim edges of the grass path where she had been weeding the borders. As she went along, she'd found self-sown seedlings of borage and thyme and used them to fill in the odd empty space, stirring up the compacted soil to let it breathe. Now, looking down at what she'd done, she felt pleased, just as she did when she tidied up the sitting room or put fresh flowers in vases in all the windowsills.

Perhaps there were times when you learnt just by doing what needed to be done. Only when you began to take pleasure in what you'd achieved did you register the fact. She smiled to herself, wondering if either Helen or Hugh would observe her new-found skills, or whether they would both go on telling her how to look after their gardens with that slightly superior tone children sometimes adopt when they're sure they know better than their parents.

She paused under an archway covered with a flourishing rose. There were no blooms yet, but the long, soft branches of new growth were shooting out in all directions, well covered with fat buds.

'*A little guidance needed here, as usual.*'

The words echoed in her mind and brought a smile to her face. She could see Hugh threading the long stems back through the trellising, his tone slightly amused, as it always was when patience was required. He insisted he wasn't a patient man, but he'd been practising for so long that no one believed him any more, even her.

'Mrs Sinton, Mrs Sinton, where are ye?'

Sarah released the soft stem immediately and hurried back to the central path. Mrs Beatty, her housekeeper, was standing on the back steps peering anxiously into the garden, her eyes shaded against the strong light.

'Here I am,' Sarah said, hurrying up to her.

'Ma'am, there's a lad here from Ballievy,' she began hastily. 'He has a message from yer father, but he wouldn't tell me what it was.'

'Where is he?'

'I put him in the dining room. Was that right?'

'Yes, it was,' she said reassuringly. 'I'll just wash my hands and see what's up,' she said with a lightness she most certainly did not feel.

'Jimmy, you have a message for me,' she said quietly, as she slipped into the cool dining room, where Mrs Beatty liked to keep the curtains drawn for the sake of the furniture.

'Yes, ma'am,' he replied, jumping to his feet and twisting his cap awkwardly in his hands.

'Yer Da . . . Yer father,' he began, correcting himself hastily, 'phoned our Mr Quayle from over at Millbrook. He said he'd like ye to go over t'him there right away. He said there wus a meetin' in the dinner hour in the recreation hall.'

'What kind of a meeting, Jimmy? Did Mr Quayle not tell you?'

'No, ma'am,' he replied, shaking his head vigorously. 'He jus said t'get on me bike an' come up an' tell ye an' there wus no time to waste. He seemed awfall put out.'

'Well, I'm sure you've been very quick,' she said briskly. 'Now, go back to Mr Quayle. Tell him to phone my father and say I'll be over very shortly. I'd give you a ride in the motor, but you'll be faster on your bike by the time I get it out of the motor house.'

'Aye, ma'am,' he said, venturing a smile at last. 'It's a good steep hill and ye can get up a grate speed if you mine th'holes.'

'Well, see you mind them. There's a few need filling that haven't been seen to recently,' she said, as she let him out through the front door.

'A meeting,' she said aloud, as she walked back down the hall and peered at her reflection in the tall mirror of the hallstand.

'Not a board meeting on a Thursday, surely,' she thought, as she decided she'd have to change her clothes.

Robert Sprott and Gerald McHammond she couldn't speak for, but Elizabeth and Richard were never available on Thursdays, and Harry Cunningham, their legal adviser, always worked from his Belfast office during the second half of the week.

It was as she straightened her blouse and skirt and reached for a brush to run through her dark hair that she remembered Jimmy had said the recreation hall. She stared at her reflection in the mirror. She looked solemn and unblinking, like her own son had when he'd instructed her how to water the garden. She smiled at the thought of young Hugh. But the relief was only momentary.

Whatever had caused her father to send for her was no smiling matter. Built some five years earlier at the west end of the solid brick mill building, overlooking the new lake, the recreation hall could seat five hundred people. It could more than accommodate the entire workforce of Millbrook.

It was market day in Banbridge, the centre of the town full of stalls, carts, animals and crowds of people who spilled out over the road with complete indifference to passing traffic of any kind. Although there were few motor vehicles other than her own, Sarah's progress was slow. She had to stop for straying cows and groups of curious onlookers. As she finally cleared the town, she reflected that she'd made better speed eleven years earlier when she'd heard there was a fire at Millbrook and had borrowed a bicycle from a neighbour to get there as quickly as she could.

Two miles north of the town she turned off the public road and made her way cautiously down the steep slope towards the main entrance. To the right of the centrally placed double doors her father's motor was parked beside Tom, the mill manager's. No sign of any of the other directors. She drew up beside them, her sense of unease growing all the time, for the air itself felt full of tension.

As she climbed down from the motor, suddenly it dawned on her why she felt so uneasy.

'There's no noise,' she said to herself.

The entire length of the four-storey mill sat bathed in sunlight and silence. Not a thread of steam hissed through the vents. Not a single spindle was turning. As she made her way through the entrance hall and turned towards the mill manager's office, a straggle of women passed her going in the direction of the recreation hall. She smiled and greeted them. Some of them she knew, some she didn't, but all of them dropped their eyes and avoided her gaze as they hurried away.

'Da, Tom, what on earth is going on?' she gasped as she closed the office door behind her and looked from one to the other.

Her father, grey-faced and anxious, nodded towards Tom who shook his head in despair.

'I niver thought I'd live to see the day, Miss Sarah. There's been bad times afore, but nothing like this,' he said despairingly. 'The men's turned off the power, so that everyone can go to this meetin' at twelve. They're goin' to call a strike here, so's they can bring out the other three mills. They'll close down the whole show.'

'But who, Tom? Who's behind this?'

'We don't rightly know,' he said with a great heaving sigh. 'Some o' the men's been goin' up to Belfast to these Trade Union meetings and readin' this man Connolly about a minimum wage of thrippence an hour. One o' the greasers told me about it las' week, but I diden take it serious. I'm sorry, Miss Sarah, I feel I've let ye's down.'

Sarah dropped into the nearest chair and looked up at the huge clock that ticked out the individual minutes of the day and gave the signals for the change of shifts and the beginning and end of the working day.

'Five to twelve,' she said ruefully. 'What are we going to do?'

'If Hugh were here, he'd speak to them,' said her father flatly. 'But shure I coulden face them,' he added honestly. 'I coulden put two words together against them clever talkers.'

'If I thought it wou'd be any use, I'd try, Sarah,' said Tom, nodding his agreement with John. 'I'd do anythin' I could for the Sintons after all they've done for me an' mine, but I have no gift that way.'

'Well, we'll just have to see what happens,' Sarah said, glancing up again as the huge minute hand of the clock moved with an audible click.

'If it comes to the bit, I may have to say something, Da,' she went on, an awful sense of dread coming upon her. 'And it's time I was going. Would one of you like to come with me?'

'Aye, certainly I'll come,' said Tom promptly.

'I'll not come, Sarah. Ye might do better without

me,' said John, dropping his eyes to the pile of paper in front of him.

'Right, Da,' said Sarah, managing to smile at him. 'Say one for us. It'll all be the same in a hundred years, as the saying is,' she added lightly.

There wasn't a soul in sight as they turned out of the building and made their way along the front, the heat reflecting from the warm bricks, the windows flashing in the bright sunlight. As she strode out, all Sarah could think of was the day of the fire, when she'd tramped the length of the mill to climb on the engine-house roof to take her pictures. That was the day she'd found out for sure that Hugh loved her. The engine houses were at the east end of the mill now, but the change in colour in the brickwork where the west end of the mill had been rebuilt was still quite obvious. She cast her eye up the line of the new brickwork as they hurried past, turned the corner and saw a small cluster of people disappear into the large one-storey building in front of them.

The hall was packed. One glance told Sarah that groups of weavers from Lenaderg, hemstitchers from Seapatrick and bleachers from Ballievy had also come to the meeting. They were being greeted at the back of the hall by some men she'd never seen before.

'Front or back?'

Even in such a large, crowded gathering, Tom knew there would be empty seats at the front. It was always the same, whether it was the local church or a public concert. The first arrivals were always too shy to sit in the front row. They would choose the second or the third. The front row was usually filled by latecomers.

'Front,' she said quietly, as they slipped through the groups of men still congregated by the entrance and made their way down the central aisle between solid rows of women who sat silent, nudging each other as they passed.

The hall was thick with heat and the smell of sweating bodies. Only now was a man with a window pole opening the top sections of the tall windows that ran down both sides of the high-roofed building. Sarah watched him quietly as if she had no other concern than the discomfort everyone must be feeling.

For a moment, before the first speaker climbed the steps to the platform, she had a clear view through the window he was opening on the north side. Dug after the fire to provide work and a new water supply, the waters of the new lake lay gleaming in the sunshine, willows dipping their lowest branches into the shallow margins.

'Comrades, I have come here today . . .'

Sarah took a deep breath. The blow had fallen as Hugh had told her it would. As she drew her eyes away from the cool vision of peacefulness and prepared for what was to come, she caught a movement in the corner of her eye, glanced back again at the dazzling water and saw two swans move slowly, side by side, across the whole width of the lake she and Hugh had planned together and watched grow in the year of their marriage.

There were three speakers, one with a Lancashire accent from a Trade Union group she was quite familiar with, a second from Belfast whose articles she had read in *The Worker* and the third, a pale young man from the works at Lenaderg, whom she knew only by sight. They all said the same thing in different ways, put their case clearly and persuasively, and drew murmurs of agreement and sometimes cheers from their audience.

Sarah could feel Tom fidgeting in distress at her side. Having worked all his life at Millbrook and been devoted to Hugh, she could imagine what he must feel at the hostile references to slave drivers and parasites, but she knew that if anything were to be done, she must not react to this familiar rhetoric. Only if she kept calm was there a remote possibility that they might listen to a different view.

She and Hugh had often discussed the threat of strike action, genuinely aimed at improving the lot of all workers, but failing through lack of funds. He had seen clearly enough what success might achieve if every textile factory in the north were to close, but the most likely outcome in the present state of the labour movement was the kind of disruption that would leave families penniless.

'So, comrades, the case is clear. . .'

The original speaker, the one from Lancashire who'd said his name was Michael Donaghy, stood up again and began a vigorous summing-up.

'Unless we take action and bring the employers to their knees, you good people will be sweating your guts out to feed your families while others enjoy the fruits of your labour,' he said, his arms embracing his silent audience. 'Only by joint action can we achieve any progress. And I would speak particularly to you women,' he went on, adopting a more confidential tone. 'Women have not been active in the labour movement in this country and yet it was women who backed up the men that fought in the Land League to get a decent life for those who worked the land as tenants and labourers. Surely *you* are not going to let those women down, women that fought for their families, for a decent living, for a future for their children. Are *you* just going to pass by on the other side, or are you going to stand shoulder to shoulder with your menfolk and win this battle against those who would exploit and oppress us?'

Michael threw out his arms in another all-embracing gesture. There was a spatter of applause from the ranks of seated women and cheers from some groups of men who had chosen to stand in the side aisles and at the back of the large hall.

Before the applause had died down, Sarah left her seat, slipped quietly across the front of the platform and ran lightly up the steps to stand beside him.

'How do you do, Michael,' she said, holding out her hand. 'I'm Sarah Sinton. I work at all four mills,' she said in a normal voice, just loud enough to carry to the front rows. 'I'd like to add a word or two, if I may,' she said, smiling, as he took her hand.

The look of amazement on his face as he shook her hand was almost enough to encourage her, but not quite. She knew perfectly well she was taking a desperate risk, but as there was no one else to speak, she would simply have to do her best.

'Ladies and gentlemen,' she began, before anyone could object. 'I've listened very carefully to what our friends have had to say and most of what they've said I agree with. The rates of pay in the textile trade are far too low. I would also add they are *grossly* unfair to women. We are entirely in agreement about that,' she added, glancing behind her at the three men, now seated and watching her carefully.

'In many cases also, the working conditions in mills are both dangerous and damaging to health, as two of our speakers have pointed out. I hope you would agree with me that this isn't the case here,' she went on, as she looked around the audience for the first time.

There was a murmur of assent, particularly from the women. The men sat or stood in silence. Some of them had begun to look a little uncomfortable.

'What Michael and I might disagree about,' she went on, raising her voice to reach the back of the hall, 'is how best to put this situation right without causing unnecessary hardship. Sometimes it's very hard to see a problem from a different side. I learnt that when I was still a schoolgirl and I had my first disagreement with the man who became my husband.'

She knew there was a slight catch in her voice when she referred to Hugh, but she also knew that the silence in the hall had grown deeper and that everyone was listening to her. She felt sure the audience wondered what was coming next, even if it was only from curiosity.

'One bitter winter's day, with snow falling, a woman came to the door of my home at Ballydown. She was carrying a baby and she was exhausted. She was on her way to the top of the hill to Hugh Sinton's house, Rathdrum, to get a ticket for the dispensary. Some of you will remember the old ticket system before there was a dispensary in each village,' she added, as an aside.

'While my mother gave her tea, I ran up the hill, asked Hugh Sinton to get the brougham out and we took her to the doctor.'

She paused and took a deep breath. The heat of the hall and the tension she felt were making her chest painfully tight.

'By the time we got there, the child was dead,' she went on steadily. 'I was so angry, I blamed Hugh personally and wouldn't speak to him for months. When finally I did, I demanded to know why he didn't pay his workers properly, so they could afford doctors when they needed them without a silly ticket. The answer was quite different from what I might have imagined. He agreed with me about rates of pay. Then he asked me if I knew what would happen were he to pay workers more, so that he would have to charge more for his cloth.'

Sarah paused and shook her head.

'It never occurred to me the mills would close if Sinton's put up their prices and lost their orders. There would be *nothing* then for the people who had worked there. There would be no money *at all* to buy food. And very little prospect of finding any other work. If the mills had closed, back in the nineties, there wouldn't even have been a handful of public works to help out, as there had been during the time of the famine. There would be *nothing*.'

She paused and looked around her. Many of the women were nodding.

'I don't disagree with your analysis of the situation in the textile industry,' she went on, turning to the three men who sat behind her. 'I only disagree about how we go about changing it without putting hundreds of families at risk.'

'And what would you suggest?' Michael asked, courteously enough, as he stood up and came to stand opposite her.

'I suggest that we continue to press for government legislation to shorten hours and increase earnings. Progress *has* been slow. It doesn't please me, or you, but it's better than risking the well-being of whole communities.'

There was applause from the crowded hall, but Sarah felt no easement in the tension that surrounded her. The two other Trade Unionists were whispering together behind where she and Michael Donaghy stood facing each other.

'Comrades,' shouted the man from Belfast, jumping to his feet, 'you have heard what Missus Sinton has to say. And she puts it very nicely too,' he said, nodding his head in her direction. 'Do nothing. Go back to work. Continue to make money for me and my family. That's what she's saying.' He paused and drew himself to his full height, ignoring some hostile murmurs from the body of the hall. 'Then let me tell you good people just how much money is stacked up in the Sinton Mills account in Banbridge and let you judge for yourselves whether this family could meet your legitimate demands for a minimum rate of thrippence an hour.'

To Sarah's amazement and horror, he named an extraordinarily high figure, which made his audience gasp. She saw Tom shake his head and drop his face into his hands.

'Maybe Missus Sinton would like to tell us what *her* plans are for *your* money,' he said, with an unpleasant sneer as he sat down again.

As there were only three chairs on the platform, Sarah had remained standing. She was beginning to feel quite faint, what with the heat and tension, and the need to look calm when her chest felt tight and her stomach grumbled uncomfortably. She nodded to him as he sat back in his seat with a show of preparing himself to listen. Michael glanced at her with a look she could not read, turned his back on her and went and sat beside him.

'I am not sure the sum you mention is quite accurate,' she began coolly, 'but for the sake of argument we will assume it is. I should be delighted to find that it is the case,' she said, turning back to her audience. 'There are three reasons why this sum is so high. Firstly, we have had two very good years of trading. Secondly, unlike other companies, the directors do not share out the profits among themselves, build grand houses, take themselves off to live in London or Bath, or give substantial gifts to the right people so as to end up with titles,' she said firmly. 'The directors are paid a salary which you can look at in the annual report. Until recently, *all* profits have been redeployed within the company.' She went on, 'They've been used for new machinery and equipment, so that our technology doesn't fall behind. They've also been used for housing, for the co-operative shops, the dispensaries and the holiday homes at the seaside. And this recreation hall,' she added easily, as she looked around the sea of faces. 'Two years ago a decision was made to accumulate profits where possible and to launch a public company . . .'

There were jeers from the back and sides of the hall and remarks from the three men seated behind her.

'Ohhh, that's great news for the workers.'

'Going public, are we?'

'Give the money to the shareholders.'

'I haven't finished,' said Sarah, more sharply than she intended, as she turned to look at them. 'The plans to go public have been delayed by the loss of a director,' she explained. 'But what *is* under way is a scheme whereby all the workers with more than two years' service in any of the mills will become shareholders. If we cannot pay threepence an hour without putting the company at risk, we intend to compensate the workforce by returning to them the profits they have helped to accumulate. Perhaps the person who investigated the company's bank account could also consult our legal advisers to ensure that what I am saying is true.'

Sarah stopped speaking, knowing that she could do little more. Her mouth was dry, her back ached and she was longing to sit down. What happened next took her completely by surprise.

A small figure wearing the white apron of a doffer erupted from the steps at the side of the platform and advanced furiously on the three men who were once again whispering together.

'Get up,' she said, her hands on her hips as she stood over them. 'Have ye no manners atall? Give Missus Sinton a chair.'

Michael Donaghy got up sheepishly and, amid laughter, walked across to Sarah and placed his chair behind her. She sank down gratefully amidst a round of applause.

But the newcomer on the platform had only just begun. She came forward to the edge of the platform and addressed herself to the great block of seats occupied by the spinners of Millbrook.

'Have you people all lost leave o' your senses?' she demanded. 'Can ye not mind who helped you out in the bad times? Have any of you iver been in such trouble that ye diden find help here at work? You'd only to go to Doctor Stewart or Missus Sinton or Mister Hugh, God rest him. They've done their best for us, and most of us wou'd do our best for them. I'd be up there workin' my frames if it weren't for a handful o' men who turned the power off. They ought to be ashamed of themselves. Did they ask us for our opinion? No, they didn't,' she said, her eyes blazing. 'Well, I'm goin' to ask ye now, in a minit,' she said, pausing to catch her breath. 'That wuman,' she said, pointing unexpectedly to Sarah, 'carried me on her back out of this mill when it was on fire eleven year ago. I had a bad leg an' coulden run when the fire took hold and I took fright. An' what none of ye's knows was who it was that started that fire, the lad that told me to go up an' watch the fun when I was a wee girl wi' no wit at all.'

She glared round the groups of men and boys now being scrutinised by the women sitting nearest them.

'No, I'm not goin' to shame him, for Mr Hugh told me I was niver to say. I'll not break my word,' she went on more quietly. 'But what about youse'ns?' she demanded in her former tone. 'He forgave one of you for a fire that cost him dear an' might have cost me my life. D'ye not think you'd be better to trust the likes of him and Missus Sinton here, than these men that wou'd have us out on the street? Has any of them said one word about strike pay? Do they think because we're not up in Belfast we're stupid? Do they not know that we can go to classes in the evenin' an' read the same books as them and make up our own minds?'

There were cheers and cries and loud applause.

For the first time since she'd burst onto the platform, Sarah saw the young woman take breath. Momentarily, it seemed she was taken aback by the storm she had called up, but it was only for a moment.

'C'mon then,' she called, shooting one arm vigorously in the air and staring at the assembled company. 'I'm goin' back to work. Whose comin' with me?'

A forest of arms shot into the air as every single woman registered her vote. Only among a cluster of men by the door was there no show of hands. They simply moved silently out into the bright light. A round of applause marked their going. Everyone in the hall knew they were the engine men going to switch on the power.

Seven

It was only as Sarah settled herself by Rose's fireside and began to tell her why she'd gone over to Millbrook that the full magnitude of what had really happened slowly dawned upon her.

'And the men simply turned off the power?' Rose asked, her eyes wide with amazement, the tone of her voice giving away her growing anxiety. 'What about your father?'

'He was badly upset,' Sarah said flatly. 'He made no bones about it. He didn't know what to do. To be honest, Ma, I'd no more idea than he had. Da's never been one for public speaking, but I think he felt it so badly because he's so sure Hugh would have known what to say and he never wants to let Hugh down.'

Sarah shook her head sadly.

'To be honest, Ma, I'm not so sure he could have done any better than Da. It was the men who were so hostile and if it hadn't been for the women and wee Daisy, I mightn't have got far either. The two men from Belfast and Lancashire were trying to make out the spinners were cowards for not supporting their menfolk like the women did in the Land League. The spinners didn't like that, but most of them didn't know what to do until Daisy said her piece. Another time it might not go the same way,' she ended sharply.

Rose looked at her daughter. No, she was taking no joy in her success. Before she could think of anything to say, however, Sarah went on: 'Here am I, Ma, working as best I can for women's rights, for better conditions in the mills, shorter hours and better pay, and along come these men with their great ideas. "Bring the employers to their knees." "Strike for better pay",' she said angrily. 'Have they no sense at all? It's not as simple as that. Don't they ever look and see where that road leads?

She stood up abruptly and paced back and forth across the room.

'Sometimes I think Hugh was right,' she said, pausing and looking down at Rose. 'He used to say the worst thing that ever happened to him was inheriting four mills.'

Rose remembered an autumn morning long ago when Elizabeth told her how hard Hugh had struggled with the work in the mill office when his father had sent him to learn the business. Before he'd discovered his talent for repairing and inventing machinery, the mills and everything about them had been nothing to him but a constant source of anxiety and misery. That Hugh had gone on feeling the burden even after he and Sarah were married had never entered her head.

'You worked so well together, Sarah, I don't think I realised how hard it was for you both.'

'No, I don't think I did either.'

Sarah came and dropped down wearily in her father's chair.

'And now the burden is falling on Da,' she said, looking her mother straight in the face. 'I think he feels just like I do, that he has to keep things going for Hugh's sake. But I'm not so sure that's what Hugh would want. So many things have changed, Ma. And they'll go on changing and not for the better. Today is only the beginning.'

'Oh Sarah, do you really think it's as bad as that?' Rose asked gently. 'You're very tired and it must have been quite dreadful standing up there in front of all those people. I think *you* were very brave.'

'Thanks, Ma,' she said, smiling suddenly. 'Who was it said that the only really brave people are those who are scared but still do it?'

'I don't know, love, but I'm sure it's true. Do you think Daisy was scared?'

To Rose's surprise, Sarah laughed.

'No, I think she was so furious with those men behaving as if the women needed jollying along that she just flew in and said her bit,' she said cheerfully. 'Do you know, she doesn't even limp now? That was Richard's doing.'

'And Hugh's,' Rose added gently.

'Yes, I didn't know about Hugh's part till today,' said Sarah, leaning back in her chair and glancing away towards the open door. 'He must have taken her to see Richard himself. That's probably when she told him who started the fire,' she added, as she picked up her cup and drained it.

'And she's known all this time who started the

fire back in 1901?' asked Rose, shaking her head in amazement.

'What's funny, Ma?' Sarah demanded, as Rose suddenly began to smile.

'Oh dear, the things that come into one's mind. I had a sudden memory of you standing at that door, looking like a well-dressed tramp, great dark circles under your eyes, your hair grey with ash. Do you remember you were so exhausted I had to wash your face for you?'

Sarah smiled herself and then laughed wryly.

'And wasn't Martha Loney sitting by the fire and Sam not able to take his eyes off her?'

They were both silent for a few moments.

'An awful lot has happened in eleven years, Sarah dear,' said Rose slowly. 'I often wonder where another decade will take us. *If* we're here to see it, that is.'

'Of course you will be, Ma,' Sarah protested. 'In 1922, you'll only be sixty-nine.'

Rose smiled and shook her head.

'There's no decade of my life, Sarah, where I could have guessed what was going to happen, good or bad. When we were put out of Ardtur, did we ever think of Kerry, or Annacramp, or Salter's Grange, or Ballydown? Did I ever think I'd marry a man from the north and have two fine sons and two beautiful daughters?'

'And lose one son to pride and the other to a self-centred woman?' Sarah retorted.

'No, I never imagined that,' Rose said steadily. 'Perhaps it's as well we don't know what lies ahead of us. Often we can find courage when things jump up and hit us, like you did this morning, but sometimes if we *think* too much about what *might* happen, it undermines our good spirits and disables us. I think it's better to travel hopefully, even if one is upset or disappointed, rather than always looking over your shoulder.'

'Yes. In principle, I agree, but there are times I just can't manage it,' Sarah admitted. 'I worry about the children, about the world we live in, about the poor, the hungry and the exploited,' she went on sadly, a look of real dejection taking the light from her eyes and the animation from her face.

Rose stood up, came over and kissed her.

'So do I, love,' she said reassuringly. 'We wouldn't be much good to each other if we didn't, now would we?'

Beyond asking if Sarah had called, John said little that evening when he came in, late and tired, and Rose did not press him. In the days that followed, however, she became increasingly anxious about him. He seemed distracted, almost unaware of her gentle enquiries and certainly more tired than usual, whether the day had been spent in the workshop or the boardroom.

'What about the big order, love? Did it go out on time all right?' she asked one humid July evening some three weeks after the stoppage.

'Aye, it did,' he said, nodding.

She watched as he took off his suit jacket, hung it over the back of a chair and came to the table for his supper. She served up their meal and waited, hoping he might volunteer some comment about the day, but he didn't. He just began to eat slowly and automatically.

Her mother-in-law, Sarah, had once said that all the Hamiltons had good appetites and indeed there was a time when both Sam and John had never failed to look hopefully for a second helping. But not tonight. She knew even before she offered that John would just shake his head and say, 'That was very nice.'

She tried changing the subject, passing on scraps of local news brought by Emily Jackson, the lively young niece of their closest neighbours who worked the farm at the foot of the hill, but there was no response beyond a nod or a raise of the eyebrows.

'Are you *very* tired, love?' she asked, as they sat down by the fireside after their meal.

'Ach no, no.'

He seemed about to say something, but no words emerged. Preoccupied with the way he looked, his face grey and immobile, she handed him a mug of tea instead of setting it on the edge of the stove as she usually did. He put out a hand to grasp it, but it slipped from his fingers and smashed on the stone floor. As he bent towards the broken pieces, she saw a look of pain cross his face.

'Dear, dear,' he said breathlessly, as he bent to pick up the fragments, but the pain caught him again and he had to lean back in his chair.

'John, love, what's wrong?' she asked, as calmly as she could manage.

'Ach, it's nothing. Ah must have done something awkward in the workshop. It gives me this pain across m'chest.'

'And when did it start?'

'A while back.'

'And you didn't tell me?' she said softly.

'Sure we all get pains and aches, Rose, at our age. It goes away in a while,' he said, sitting back awkwardly in his chair.

'Are you telling me the half of it, John Hamilton?' she said, managing a smile.

'Ach, maybe I'm not, but sure I didn't mean to keep anythin' from ye,' he said sheepishly. 'You have your worries too. I know yer not happy about Sam and Martha and those wee childer, and sure Sarah's not her old self at all.'

'And are you going to add to my worries or will you go over and see Richard tomorrow?'

'D'you think I should?'

'I do.'

'Well . . .'

'Good, then that's settled,' said Rose briskly. 'Now take off that shirt and I'll rub your shoulders with Elizabeth's oil. Then I'll make another pot of tea and you can tell me what's been happening that has you holding one shoulder higher than the other.'

Rose knew she could rely on Richard to be honest with them, and he was. He took them into his surgery, settled Rose in a comfortable armchair and then spent a long time examining John's chest, making him move in various directions and breathe to a particular rhythm.

'There's a great deal of tension in the muscles, John. What I can't tell for sure is what's causing it. It could be anxiety in itself, but it could be something more serious,' he said coolly.

'*Angina pectoris* is only the Latin name for a pain in the chest,' he said, as John put his shirt back on. 'But it can be a symptom of heart trouble. What is somewhat comforting about angina is that the pain is a warning and, if properly heeded, it is not a threat in itself. I've known patients with angina live to a ripe old age, but they do have to take care and rest when the pain tells them they've done enough. They also have to avoid anxiety,' he ended more firmly.

'Aye, well,' said John wryly.

'Yes, John, I know you well enough by now,' said Richard, eyeing him as he reached for his jacket. 'There's no patent medicine for your problem, or if there is, I wouldn't prescribe it anyway, but there *is* something we can do. We'll summon Elizabeth and Sarah to join you and Rose and we'll have a *family* board meeting. Whatever's causing this pain, John, part of it is the weight of Sinton's Mills. I've never operated on a mill before, but there's always a first time,' he said grinning. 'And I'll have three great nurses to help me.'

The family board meeting did a great deal to comfort John. Both Elizabeth and Sarah, the other major owners of Sinton's, were quite clear that the changes they'd planned before Hugh's death would have to be advanced more quickly. At least two more working directors were needed to help, or replace, the directors who were simply consultants. The plan to go public had to be speeded up. With two more directors to handle the day-to-day overseeing of the mills, John could return to his major role, the responsibility of keeping the current machinery working and buying the new machinery that would keep all four mills properly up to date.

The decisions made in Elizabeth and Richard's comfortable sitting room did bring some relief, both to John, who now admitted how anxious he'd been feeling, and to Rose, who noticed within days that John was looking better and had started talking to her again. But it was not until the beginning of September, on a warm, sunlit afternoon, that something happened which changed the whole situation in a way the family board meeting could never have imagined.

Rose had been gardening and had just washed her hands in the dairy when she caught the vibration of a vehicle on the hill. Assuming it was Sarah, she went to the door to wave to her as she passed or greet her if she slowed down and stopped. To her surprise, the motor which appeared, its bodywork gleaming, its lamps polished till they flashed in the sun, was much larger and far grander than Sarah's. She reached the front door just as it drew up beside the garden wall and first one young man, then another, stepped down and made their way round the vehicle towards the garden gate.

'Good day,' she greeted them, as they strode up the narrow path one behind the other.

'Missus Hamilton?' said the first, a small, robust young fellow with clear blue eyes that looked straight at her.

'Yes, the very person,' she said easily.

There was something familiar about his face. She felt sure she ought to know him, but she couldn't place him. For a moment, she wondered if he might be a friend of Sam's from the days when he worked down at Tullyconnaught, before his move to Richhill, but she doubted if a friend of Sam's was likely to arrive in such state.

'Ned Wylie,' the young man said cheerfully. 'You'll not remember me.'

Rose laughed. 'I *would* have known you, Ned, if I'd thought a bit longer. You've got your mother's eyes. Come in, come in,' she said warmly, her smile including the stranger who stood patiently watching them.

Ned followed her into the house, then turned to his companion, a tall, sombre-faced man of about his own age with dark hair and eyes and noticeably broad shoulders.

'This here is Alexander Hamilton,' he said, introducing him to Rose with a brief nod. 'He wanted to meet you, so I said I'd bring him over on my day off. He's got somethin' to ask you,' he went on cheerfully. 'Aye, an' indeed, so have I.'

'Hamilton?' said Rose, turning to the young man whose dark eyes were fixed firmly upon her. She shook his hand, beaming at him. 'Are you one of our long-lost relatives?'

'Well,' he began awkwardly, his eyes flickering away from her face for the first time. 'I think it's just possible, ma'am, but I've such a bad memory I'm not sure myself,' he said, his soft Canadian accent in marked contrast to the strong lines of his face and the obvious strength of his body.

Rose insisted on making tea and was pleased to see both her visitors settle comfortably by the fire. Alexander Hamilton, she noted, was looking round the room, taking in its every detail, while Ned Wylie was extracting a well-wrapped parcel from the bag he'd been carrying. He set it down carefully on the corner of the kitchen table.

So amazed and intrigued was she by her un-expected callers, Rose discovered she had the greatest difficulty keeping her mind on the simple business of making tea.

'Ned, it's a beautiful motor,' she said, glancing through the open door as she lifted a fruitcake from its tin, cut generous slices and arranged them on a cake plate.

'She is indeed, Missus Hamilton. I wish she were mine,' he said, laughing. 'I work for Loudan's in Armagh. Weddings, funerals and visitors wi' plenty o' money. He lets me have the motor for the odd day when I've had a lot of extra work an' we go a bit slack. I keep her runnin', ye see, an' I tell him she sometimes needs a real old run to keep her in good heart. It's true all right, but Peggy says I'm the crafty one tellin' him that an' gettin' the car for the day,' he went on happily, his blue eyes moving between Rose and the plate of fruitcake.

'*This one has them all beaten for guile.*'

Rose smiled to herself. She was back in the

kitchen of the house opposite the forge, making tea for his mother, her dear friend, Mary. She'd been feeding him and had put him down on the bed to sleep, but she wasn't hopeful. Waving her arms with fingers crossed on both hands she'd come back out of the bedroom, waiting for his usual outburst, but on that day young Ned *had* slept.

'Yes, I know about motors, Ned. You have to in this house,' she explained, turning towards the stranger. 'My husband's been mad about motors since ever I've known him,' she went on. 'Sam, my son, is just as bad. Even Sarah, my daughter, can fix her own if it gives her trouble and her father's not about,' she went on, coming between them to the stove to make the tea.

'How is Aunt Peggy? I owe her a letter,' said Rose, glancing down at Ned as she put the lid back on the teapot.

Every time she looked at him now, she could see his mother. It was quite disconcerting. This was the child Mary had thrown through the window of the runaway excursion train a few minutes before she herself was killed in the crash that followed. Ned had been found, unmarked, in the middle of a bush. His two older brothers lay with Mary in the shadow of the church at Salter's Grange.

'She's well. An' Da too. An' my wee sister's gettin' married next month,' Ned went on with a grin. 'That's us all married now.'

Rose asked one or two more questions and Ned chatted on happily, filling her in on the latest news from the Wylie family while the tea brewed, but then, concerned he might feel neglected, she turned to speak to Alexander Hamilton.

To her surprise, before she had opened her mouth, he immediately got to his feet.

'You come here, ma'am, to your own chair, opposite Ned. I'll sit over here.'

Without the slightest fuss, he drew a kitchen chair from under the table and settled himself between them as if the only thing he wanted to do was share their enjoyment in their talk.

Apart from pausing briefly to demolish his cake in generous mouthfuls, Ned moved on from the Wylie family to tell Rose the news from Annacramp and Salter's Grange. He passed on good wishes from old neighbours and particularly from Selina and Thomas Scott, who were hoping to see them again soon. It was some time before he paused and remembered the parcel sitting on the table.

'Peggy gave me this last year when Jeannie and I got married,' he said with a sideways look. 'She said it might come in handy. An' indeed it won't be long now. Jeannie's expecting next month,' he said, colouring slightly, as he handed her the parcel and waited while she opened it.

'She said she wasn't sure, but she had a good idea that it was you made that. I'd made up me mind to come an' ask you, even before yer man here turned up,' he said slowly, casting a quick glance at Alexander before turning back to watch Rose closely as she unfolded the christening robe she'd once made to thank Mary for all the help she'd given her with the children after Granny Sarah had died.

'*Shure he'll look like a wee prince.*'

Rose spread out the delicate fabric on her knee. Her eyes misted as she recognised the pattern of flowers she had scattered across it. She nodded at Ned, an uncomfortable lump in her throat.

'That's a beautiful thing, ma'am.'

Rose was almost startled at the softness and unexpectedness of Alexander Hamilton's comment. She turned to him and saw he was holding out his hands towards her.

'May I?'

'Yes, of course,' she said, touched by the gentleness of the request and the way he handled the fabric, as if it were infinitely more delicate than it actually was.

There were several moments of absolute silence, when even the irrepressible Ned said nothing. Then Alexander, who had studied each tiny flower individually, handed her back the robe.

'You're a lucky man, Ned,' he said soberly, looking Ned full in the face. 'That's a beautiful thing, ma'am,' he repeated, as if it was a matter of great importance to him.

'Well then, Alexander, I'm dying to know what's brought you all the way from Canada to Annacramp. What part of Canada do you come from?'

Rose saw a sudden flicker of anxiety in Alexander's dark eyes, but it was so fleeting she wondered if perhaps she was mistaken.

'I've moved about a bit,' he said, easily enough. 'I was in Canada a long time, but my last place was in

Pennsylvania, a place called German Township, in Lafayette County. That's where I met your brother, ma'am, Mister Sam McGinley. About two years ago.'

'You met Sam?' Rose cried, delighted and amazed they should have met in this unknown place, so far away. 'How extraordinary. But how did you meet him?'

'Well, it was a meeting of farm labourers he was addressing. You probably know, ma'am, farm workers don't get very well paid. Some get nothing much beyond their keep. And poor food and a bed in the straw at that.'

'Yes, Sam's told me all about it. Did you know he's come back to Ireland?'

'No, ma'am, I didn't. I just met him the once after the meeting,' he said, looking slightly startled. 'That's when he mentioned Annacramp.'

Rose looked puzzled, but said nothing.

'When I went to ask him some questions, I told him my name and he said, "That's a good Ulster name. My sister Rose is married to a Hamilton from Annacramp." And I asked him where that was and he told me it was about three miles outside of Armagh on the Loughgall Road. So I knew where to go.'

'But what made you come?'

Rose watched his face, trying to grasp the difficulty he was having in finding words.

'My mother once said that my grandfather had come from Ireland. I'm nearly sure she said Annacramp, for I kinda knew the name when your brother said it, but I was only a wee thing when she died.'

'And your father?' Rose prompted gently.

'My mother was a widow. I don't know what happened him at all,' he said matter-of-factly. 'I can hardly remember my mother.'

'And what happened you when your mother died?'

'I was put in an orphanage till I was old enough to go to work.'

'And what age was that?' asked Rose, who couldn't bear not to know the rest of Alexander's story.

'I was big for my age, so they let me go at nine. Though ten's the age, I'm told,' he said, in the same matter-of-fact tone in which he'd answered almost all of her questions.

Rose put her hands to her face and thought of her own children. Even Sam, who was taller now than Alexander and had shoulders just as broad, was only a wee thing when he was nine, still liable to shed tears when he was upset and to climb on her lap to be comforted.

'So you decided to come and find your family?'

'Yes, ma'am,' he said awkwardly. 'And I'm not sorry,' he went on more firmly. 'I've had more kindness since I stepped off the boat in Belfast than I've ever had before. I'll not forget that, whatever happens me now,' he said, smiling unexpectedly.

Rose was completely taken aback. She had never before seen a face so utterly transformed by a smile. At this moment he seemed so full of warmth and liveliness that she found it almost impossible to imagine his former sombre appearance.

'Are you going to stay?' she asked tentatively.

'I'd like to stay, ma'am, but I need to find a job. Ned here took me to Thomas Scott and he said he'd be happy to have me if there was more work, but he and young Robert have only enough to keep them both going. It was he suggested I come and speak to your good man,' he said, looking at her quite directly. 'I don't want to impose on your kindness, but I'm a good worker and I'll not let him down if he can find me a place in one of his mills.'

'Aye, he's as strong as an ox,' said Ned, his sudden intervention and easy manner lightening the tension Rose was feeling.

'Sure when Peggy said he could stay with her a day or two and look round him, there was no stoppin' him. The place doesn't know what's hit it. Forby mending the reaper and the harrow.'

Rose felt her heart lift and a great wave of relief envelope her. Even before she asked the question shaping in her mind, she had a marvellous sense that she knew what the answer would be.

'What is your line of work, Alexander?'

'I was trained up to do farm work, but down in Lafayette I worked with a blacksmith and he let me mend machines. I like machines,' he said simply, with a glimmer of a smile.

Eight

Rose was surprised at how easy John appeared to be when he walked into the kitchen and found a totally unknown young man sitting by the fire absorbed in the pages of one of Sarah's picture albums.

'John dear, this is Alexander Hamilton,' she began, hurrying in from the dairy. 'Ned Wylie brought him over from Annacramp and our friend Thomas sent you a message with him,' she went on. 'He says he'd like fine to have him but his loss might be your gain.'

Alexander stood up and the two men shook hands warmly.

'And how would that be?' John asked, nodding with pleasure at the mention of Thomas.

'I need a job, sir,' said Alexander quietly, 'and Thomas said you might be able to find me something in one of your mills.'

'Now sit down to your supper, both of you,' Rose interrupted before either of them could say another word. 'There's the whole evening to talk about jobs and I'm sure you're hungry.'

Rose had had to think quickly as to what she had in the house that would make a supper when there was an unexpected guest. As she served champ with a well for butter and crisp slices of bacon to garnish it, she was delighted to see John's eyes brighten and the young man's face break into a broad grin.

'My goodness, ma'am, this smells good,' Alexander said, as he picked up his fork.

'Aye, she's a great cook,' said John, making vigorous inroads into his own meal.

It was when John paused to take a long drink of water from his glass that he suddenly looked at Alexander.

'Did I hear right that yer name's Hamilton?'

'Yes, sir,' Alexander replied, nodding, his mouth full.

John looked across at Rose to see what he was to make of this.

'It looks as if Alexander might be the grandson of one of your brothers, John,' she began, smiling at him reassuringly. 'He was born in Canada and his mother mentioned Annacramp to him when he was a wee boy, but sadly both his grandfather and his parents are dead.'

'Ach dear, that's a hard thing,' said John kindly. 'What age were ye when ye lost them, Alexander?'

'I think I was about seven when my mother died, but I've no great memory,' he began awkwardly. 'I never knew my father at all.'

Rose noticed his faltering tone and the anxious look that returned when John asked his question, but he just nodded sympathetically at the thought of the young man's loss. What he said next took Rose completely by surprise.

'Well, there's one thing for sure, you have the Hamilton shoulders. Both m' brothers had shoulders broader than mine. An' yer dark forby, ye look just like m' father in his prime,' he said matter-of-factly, as he handed his plate to Rose, the first time he'd asked for a second helping in months.

Next morning, Rose watched the two of them walk down the garden path together, Alexander wearing a pair of John's dungarees, the legs turned up at the hem until she had time to shorten them, the shoulders showing signs of strain.

When they arrived back for lunch, it was hard to tell which of them was the more pleased.

'I've got m'self a new helper,' John said, beaming at her, as he bent to give her a kiss.

Alexander's eyes were bright and his smile had become an almost permanent feature as they settled to eat bread and cheese with small pieces of cold bacon.

'Is it a big change from farm equipment, Alexander?' Rose asked, as she cut slices of new-baked wheaten for them all.

'It is in one way, ma'am,' he said, looking up at her. 'The textile machines are more complicated, but they run on the same principles. They're more interesting to work with,' he said, pausing as he spread butter very thinly on his bread.

'Aye, he has the measure of it, Rose,' said John warmly. 'Far better than I had when I first worked with Hugh.'

'Did you meet Sarah, Alexander?'

'Yes, ma'am.'

'Ach, it was a quick word, Rose, for Sarah had the motor out,' John explained. 'She was goin' over to

Elizabeth and Richard's to see about this new scheme for medical examinations. There'll be plenty of time for them to get t' know other now all's settled,' he added reassuringly.

September, which began with anxiety over John's health, now moved on in a glow of sunlit autumn weather that would have brought delight to the whole family had the political situation in Ulster not stirred up a whole set of new anxieties.

Encouraged by the activists in the Orange Order and by Sir Edward Carson in particular, the 28th of September had been designated Ulster Day. On that day, after church services to appeal for the help of the Almighty, all true born Ulstermen were expected to sign the Solemn League and Covenant, committing themselves to use 'all means which may be found necessary to defeat the present conspiracy to set up a Home Rule Parliament in Ireland'.

After the recent changes to the power of the House of Lords, everyone knew they could no longer veto bills passed by the House of Commons and there was every likelihood that the Home Rule Bill would pass. With two opposing volunteer forces recruiting and training vigorously, what would happen next lay like a dark shadow on many a household beyond that of the Hamiltons and their friends.

Along with every other place of work, the mills were forced to close on the day. In city, town and village, locations were set up where men could sign the covenant and their women folk could add their support by adding their names to the accompanying declaration. All over the province, there were queues outside Orange halls and Temperance halls, church halls and school halls. Beyond Ulster, covenant sheets had been distributed abroad as far away as China so that no mark, or signature, would be lost in the effort to register the unity and magnitude of Ulster's hostility.

Neither Sarah nor Rose nor John signed the relevant document, but they did go to the church service in Holy Trinity. While they could not be forced to sign the documents, their neighbours would have found it very strange indeed if they had not appeared at a church service which purported to ask for God's blessing on Ulster. In the event, not unexpectedly, they were dismayed by the tone of the minister's address, his references to the idolatry of the Church of Rome, or his harping upon the threats to religious freedom should an Irish parliament ever sit in Dublin.

Sarah found the whole business utterly depressing. The newspapers fulminated against the wicked English government, who could even consider allowing a situation to come about in which Catholic farmers would have the power to dictate to the loyal Protestant industrialists of the North, who by their wisdom and hard work had made the province so prosperous. She had heard it all before and wished she might never hear it again.

A few days after the great signing itself, Sarah arrived at Millbrook to be greeted once again by silence. She felt such a reluctance to cope with yet one more problem that she had the greatest desire to turn the motor in front of the main doors, accelerate up the slope and never come back. But she knew her father was working at Ballievy. Even if Tom had telephoned to ask him to come, he probably couldn't just leave what he and Alex were dismantling or repairing. She pushed aside the thought, took a deep breath, parked the motor alongside Tom's and made her way into the office.

Tom looked up from a document he'd been trying to read, his face moving from anxiety to relief.

'What is it this time, Tom?'

He shook his head and let out a great sigh.

'Some Catholic women were saying that the blood for signing the covenant wasn't the only blood there'd be after Home Rule.'

Sarah looked puzzled.

'A lot o' the men that signed, in Belfast particularly, cut their fingers and signed in their own blood,' he explained flatly. 'There's no use at all me goin' to talk to Catholic women, for they'll just say I'm a Protestant and as bad as the rest of them,' he said, shaking his head angrily. 'I sent yer man the Trade Unionist. He's always goin' on about the bosses usin' sectarianism to divide the workforce. We'll just have to see what *he* can do to get them together.'

Sarah dropped down in the nearest chair.

'In this country even the atheists are Catholic or Protestant,' she said bitterly. 'How long's he been gone?'

'About half an hour. I told him to come back here as soon as he had any word.'

Before he had finished speaking there was a perfunctory knock on the door and the man Sarah had last seen recommending strike action on the platform of the recreation hall stood in front of them.

'I'm sorry,' said Sarah, standing up. 'You know my name but I don't know yours.'

'I'm John Joseph Shiels, Missus Sinton, and I don't approve of this stoppage, whatever you might think,' he said irritably.

'I don't think anything, John Joseph, till I know what's going on. I hope you're going to tell me what's the issue,' she said calmly.

'Flags and party tokens,' he said sharply. 'There's portraits of Carson and Orange symbols on some of the looms and Emmett and Tone and O'Donovan Rossa on the others.'

'Is there any reason why we shouldn't remove them?' Sarah asked, looking him straight in the eye.

'It would cause bad feeling,' he said cautiously.

'Haven't we got bad feeling already? Would it make it any worse?'

'I don't know, Missus Sinton. I wouldn't want to be the one to do it.'

'All right then, I'll do it,' she said wearily. 'But you can both come and help me,' she went on, swinging round to include Tom. 'We remove *everything*, put all the bits in a basket and leave them to be collected with the wages on Friday. All right? I'll speak to the other directors tomorrow. I think what we need is an agreement that we employ neither Catholics nor Protestants in this firm, only men and women,' she said severely. 'I hope you think that's acceptable, John Joseph.'

'Yes, I do,' he said, more enthusiastically than she'd expected. 'But I shou'd warn you, Missus Sinton, there's those few on both sides that won't lissen to a word I say. I can only promise you I'll do m' best. You're tryin' to be fair, but there's some that won't have it no matter what ye'd say.'

'Thank you, John Joseph, I appreciate that,' she replied with a bleak smile. 'Let's go and get it over with. Is the power off, or is it only the individual frames?' she asked as Tom opened the door and she walked ahead of them out into the silent mill.

There were no signs of life at Ballydown as Sarah drove home. The front door was shut, which meant her mother had gone into Banbridge. When she closed the door of the motor house and came into the kitchen, Rathdrum was silent too. No sign of Mrs Beatty and no sound from the workshop. Her father and Alex must still be down at Ballievy.

She looked disconsolately out of the kitchen window as she waited for the kettle to boil. She wasn't sure about this Alex, as everyone now called him. He was courteous enough and clearly a good worker. Both her parents seemed delighted by his advent and there was no doubt whatever that her father was a different person now he had someone to help with the repairs and to assess the new technology that kept appearing.

'If they're happy, shouldn't I be happy for them?' she asked herself.

She wondered if perhaps she was envious. Her father had found a friend to help him and Rose clearly enjoyed the young man's company and the stories he told her about working on farms in New Brunswick and Pennsylvania. Her mother had suggested to John that they have Alex to stay at Ballydown as they had three empty rooms. Her father had said no, but only because he thought a young man should get away from his work. He needed to get out and meet other young people, not spend his time with them. Everyone seemed delighted when Mrs Jackson at the foot of the hill offered to have him as a lodger, now all their sons were gone and only their young niece, who had lost both her parents, lived with them.

The kettle was rattling its lid before Sarah turned from the window and her thoughts. She made a pot of tea and looked out again over the broad cobbled space in front of the workshop while she waited for it to draw.

Often, in the morning, while she was still tidying the bedroom, she'd see the two of them arrive for work, walking companionably side by side across the yard. Suddenly, Sarah found tears trickling down her face. Side by side. That was it. Alex walking with John. Keeping John company. No wonder her father looked better. No wonder the pains in his chest had vanished. Something, *someone*, had come to fill the aching space of Hugh's loss, but nothing had come to help her, only the hurt and vexations of the work she tried to keep up for his sake.

'Stop it, Sarah. There's no way forward through self pity,' she reminded herself angrily, but the tears would not stop. She went upstairs and lay on the bed and cried till they were spent.

When Mrs Beatty arrived back from Jackson's with the week's supply of eggs and butter, she wondered why there was a full pot of tea, still slightly warm, but untouched, on the draining board. She drained the tealeaves, rinsed the pot and put it away. Kind woman that she was, she had long since learnt when not to notice things that seemed awry.

It was some weeks later, a day or two before her brother Sam's birthday, that Sarah decided she must make up her mind about Alex Hamilton. She knew she'd been rather cool with him. Not unfriendly, but certainly not as welcoming as her parents and the Jacksons and all their neighbours.

As she looked down from her bedroom window that morning, she saw him once again striding along beside her father, the two of them deep in conversation, but while Alex wore his new dungarees, still almost unmarked by oil or grease, her father wore a suit. She smiled to herself. Poor Da. He'd have to leave shortly to see the bank manager or the accountant. He was no longer anxious about such matters, but she knew where he'd prefer to be.

'Cup of tea, ma'am?'

When Mrs Beatty put her head round the dining room door at half past ten, Sarah nodded.

'Could you put Alex's mug on the tray, Mrs Beatty, and tell him I'm in the conservatory? We don't seem to have exchanged two words all week, we've both been so busy.'

She looked out on the October morning. It was

soft and grey, the sky overcast, but not sombre. The first drifts of leaves had accumulated against the garden wall, pale gold from the limes in the avenue mixed with a scattering of bronze and copper from the large beech tree in the garden itself.

As she waited his coming, she realised she had no idea at all what she was going to say to the young man whose arrival seemed to have brightened life for everyone but herself.

'Good mornin', ma'am,' he said, shutting the glass door carefully behind him. 'This is a pretty place,' he added, his eyes moving round the broad windowsills where geraniums still bloomed prolifically.

'I'm not much of a gardener really,' Sarah said easily, 'but my sister-in-law always had it so nice, I've tried not to let her down. My mother's the gardener in the family, as you know. She keeps me right,' she went on, as she filled his mug and handed him a plate of Mrs Beatty's biscuits. 'Most of these are cuttings from her. Do you like flowers?'

'Yes,' he said, looking round him again. 'I worked for a couple once where the wife had a little summerhouse. The man was a hard man and a lot older and she was young and loved pretty things. Sometimes I'd bring her wildflowers from the field where we were working, but I had to creep in so your man didn't see me. He'd have beaten me black and blue if he'd caught me,' he said matter-of-factly, as he crunched a biscuit between his teeth.

'What age were you then?'

'Nine,' he said, without any hesitation. 'It was my first job. That's when I learnt to speak English.'

'To speak English?' Sarah repeated in amazement. 'So what had you spoken before?'

'French. It's all French on the farms in Québec.'

'And was your mother French?'

'No . . . she was English . . . or rather she spoke English,' he went on, flustered. 'But after she died, I had to speak French. I forgot my English. I was only four or five,' he added hastily, a slight flush appearing on his cheekbones.

Sarah turned this over as she offered him more tea. She was quite sure her mother had told her he was seven when his mother died.

'What I like best is trees,' he said suddenly, looking out towards the garden. 'Up in the Laurel Highlands, the colour is wonderful in the fall. Here the colours aren't as bright, but the fields are greener. It sets the trees off better. It's just as beautiful, but different.'

'You must find a lot of things different,' she said, filling in the space, wondering what she could say next.

He was so open, so direct in his way of speaking. Only when his mother or his family were mentioned did his candid gaze flicker and fail. Despite herself, she found she liked the man.

'Yes, and everything better than I could have hoped,' he said, smiling, the warm smile that even Mrs Beatty had commented on. 'It's been like a homecoming.'

'But surely it *is* a homecoming,' replied Sarah quickly. 'You've found your family. Isn't home where one's family is? Or is home where one feels "at home"? What do you think?'

He paused, looked out across the cobbles and moved awkwardly in his chair. 'I think, ma'am, home is where you feel right in yourself. A place where you can do your best and not always have other people telling you what to do all the time and never a kind word when you do it.'

It was Sarah's turn to look away. While Hugh was alive, the work they did was hard, but rewarding. They supported each other. Now he was gone, she could no longer do her best. Her heart had gone out of it. She could not bear the anger, the hostility she saw all around her, in the mills, in the town, out in the countryside of marching feet. She could put up with the boredom of papers and orders and countersigning documents, but more and more she felt alone, looking out at a world that no longer had a place for her. The feeling seemed to be getting worse, not better.

'I ought to be getting back to my work, ma'am. That was very nice indeed, thank you,' Alex said, getting to his feet.

'No, don't go yet,' Sarah said hastily, aware that she had fallen silent. 'There's something I want to ask you.'

He sat down again awkwardly, his large frame filling the woven conservatory chair.

'Is Alexander Hamilton your real name?' she asked softly.

'Yes, ma'am. It is,' he said firmly, looking her full in the face.

She met his gaze and said nothing. She waited, a tension growing that she could not explain.

'But you're right,' he said at last, his shoulders drooping. 'You're the only one who's seen the lie I told,' he said sadly, his face the picture of misery. 'My name's the only thing I *do* possess. I have neither mother nor father. I was an orphan on a ship out of Liverpool to Québec. I remember the grey of the sea and being sick. I remember the label tied to the collar of my coat scratching my neck. And I remember working for the orphanage for all those years till I was sent out to work on a farm. I've tried to forget it. Pretend it happened to someone else. And maybe I could if I could stay here and be Alex Hamilton. But that's not to be, is it?'

'Why shouldn't it be?' said Sarah, close to tears, the bare details of his story unrolling in her mind.

'Because you know I'm a liar, and you'll tell your parents and they'll throw me out, just like I've always been thrown out from anywhere I found a place that was kind,' he said, two bright tears shining in the corners of his eyes.

'You are *not* a liar, Alex,' she said firmly. 'That's the trouble. If you *were* a liar, you wouldn't have made mistakes. You'd have your story off pat. And you *do* have a mother and father. We just don't know who they were. Who knows but you're one of the Scottish Hamiltons. It doesn't matter to me.'

'It doesn't?' he said, his voice breaking slightly.

'No, it doesn't matter who your family are, or were. I just needed to know the truth.'

'And you'll not say anything to anyone?' he asked slowly, after a long silence.

'Not a word,' she said, smiling. 'Our secret,' she added, holding out her hand. 'Like children when they promise eternal friendship.'

He looked puzzled but took her offered hand and shook it firmly.

'I'm sorry, Alex,' she said, guessing what the problem was. 'You probably didn't have much of children's promises and that kind of thing in your childhood,' she said quickly. 'I was lucky. I had good parents and Hannah, and Sam, and friends at school. And there was always Elizabeth and there was Hugh, long, long before I married him. I had no idea how much love there was in my life until I heard your story. Now it's my turn to feel I'm on my own,' she said, her voice faltering unexpectedly.

Alex stared at her uncomprehendingly, his good spirits vanished in a flash.

'But how is that, ma'am?'

Sarah hoped that the tears which had sprung to her eyes would disappear if she blinked a few times, but they didn't and the look of concern on Alex's sombre face made it even worse.

As they trickled down her face she wiped them with the back of her wrist.

'You've been honest with me, Alex, but I've not been honest with you,' she began, taking a great deep breath.

'I love my parents dearly, and my children, and this house and even this garden, but the light went out of my life when Hugh died,' she began steadily enough. 'I tried to keep up his work – our work it had been – but now I dread going to the mills, I can't bear the squabbles and the bitterness, the marching men and the shouting women. I thought I would spend my life here, working to improve social conditions and particularly the lot of women, but everywhere I look I see exploitation by the privileged and disagreement and discontent among those who ought to stand together and help each other and I have no heart to fight it any more. I just wish I could go away, far away, like you've done, to somewhere I could be myself again.'

She paused, overcome by the enormity of what she had admitted.

'I think perhaps I envy you, Alex,' she said, collecting herself. 'You've had a hard time, but you've been brave. It was a very brave thing to come to Ireland with nothing but a slender hope,' she continued firmly when she saw him look doubtful.

'You've had your homecoming. I wonder if I will ever have mine,' she ended, as she wiped her eyes again with her wrist and began to search for her handkerchief in the pockets of her skirt.

'If it's a matter of courage, you'll make it,' he said, so promptly that she stopped her search and stared at him.

'You don't lack courage, from all I hear,' he went on. 'I know you've a good mother, but sometimes what we need most is a friend we can tell our secrets to,' he added softly, as she wiped her eyes and blew her nose. 'I used to pretend I had a big brother, a really *big* one,' he said, smiling at her. 'He'd beat up all the boys that ganged up on me and never split on me when I got into trouble. He'd be on my side whatever I did.'

She nodded sadly.

'I even had a big brother,' she admitted, with a shake of her head. 'Two of them, in fact. But I've lost them too.'

'Yes, I know about James. And I know about Sam and Martha and about Hannah too. Rose talks to me a lot about them. She talks about you, too, but she doesn't know what's making you so unhappy.'

'No, and I can't tell her. Not yet. Not until I can see some way ahead. Not until someone says "Annacramp" and I decide to go, like you did when you met Uncle Sam in German Township. Then I'll have to tell her. And that will be hard, because we've been so close.'

'It might be easier when the time comes,' he said kindly. 'We always think the future will be like the past, but it can be utterly different from what we imagined. I couldn't ever have imagined what's happened since I got off that boat in Belfast.'

She thought of the cross-channel ferry tied up at the quay. Of the many times she'd crossed to England to visit Hannah or Lady Anne, taking the children to see their cousins, or travelling with Hugh to meet Lord Altrincham.

'I'll have to go too, Alex,' she said sadly. 'You promise you won't tell anyone, will you?'

'I'll promise all right,' he said, nodding vigorously. 'We've both got a secret. Perhaps,' he went on, very tentatively, 'we might be able to help each other.'

She nodded encouragingly and waited to see what he might say.

'I'm not an educated man. I wish I was,' he began, speaking quickly. 'You'd have to explain all these different parties and factions to me and all these problems at the mills, but if you did, I could maybe encourage you a bit with the work you have to do. The way your brother Sam might do if he were still at home,' he suggested gently.

Sarah smiled, thinking of how little Sam would actually be able to help her these days, except by his gentle presence, but Alex was a different matter. He had a quick mind and he listened to everything anyone said, absorbing it instantly, avid for the knowledge and experience his hard working life had denied him. She would never have to explain anything to him a second time.

'It might be very boring,' she said promptly.

'I'll take a chance on that,' he said cheerfully, looking her straight in the face again.

She returned his gaze. He looked so enormously pleased with himself she couldn't help laughing.

'Why are you so pleased?' she asked.

'Well, Sarah,' he began cautiously, as if she might suddenly bridle at the use of her name, 'I always imagined a big brother. I never in all my dreams thought I might have a big sister.'

'Life is full of surprises, Alex. And some of them are nice. That's what Da always says. He had it once in a copybook, but he never paid any heed to what it meant until Ma reminded him. She'd had the same copybook at the other end of Ireland.'

They rose together, knowing there was work to be done and the morning was moving on.

'Alex,' she said, as he put his hand on the door. 'Would you come with me to see Sam on Saturday afternoon? He's your cousin after all,' she added, smiling. 'It's time you met him. And besides, I can't stand Martha, and I never know what to say to her. Will you come?'

'Yes, I'll come. Any time you want me, I'll come. Just say the word,' he said easily, as he shut the door behind him and strode across the cobbles.

Nine

As she drove through the quiet autumn country-side on a sunlit October afternoon, Sarah felt her spirits rise and she breathed a sigh of relief. It was just so good to be away from both house and work and to have someone she could talk to about matters other than the everyday business of the mills. What amused and delighted her and fed into the lightness of her mood were Alex's honest and often unexpected responses to her questions.

'But why was it, Alex, that you hit upon Annacramp?' she asked, as they passed through Richhill village, where a dog lay asleep in the sunshine, the only other vehicle in the broad main street a horse-drawn baker's cart.

'I think Annacramp hit *me*,' he said, laughing. 'When your Uncle Sam made that remark about Hamilton being a good Ulster name, I had this sudden, strange feeling he was about to say something of enormous importance to me. It was almost as if I'd heard it all before, but hadn't been paying attention. Have you ever had a feeling like that?' he asked, looking at her directly.

'Don't think so,' she said shortly, as she manoeuvred the motor across the deeply rutted surface where the heavily-laden road engines had swung round on their way down to the railway station.

'Well, it was like getting a telegram,' he went on cheerfully. 'I know it sounds peculiar, but the minute he said "Annacramp", I thought that's it, that's where I have to go.'

'So you just went?'

'Not quite,' he said, shaking his head ruefully. 'There was the small matter of the fare and I had nothing but working clothes. I couldn't turn up looking like a tramp, could I?' he said, smiling suddenly.

She glanced at him briefly as they moved between high hedgerows, the almost leafless hawthorns glowing red with a mass of berries.

'So how did you manage the money?'

'Got a second job,' he replied promptly. 'Worked on a farm by day and wrote letters at night. Writing letters actually paid better than the farm work.'

'But what sort of letters did you write that you got paid for?' she asked, turning to look at him, for the lane was quite empty.

'Emigrant letters,' he replied with a sigh. 'Telling the folks back in Ireland, or Scotland, or France, or Germany, how well they were doing, what a great place Pennsylvania is, how good the weather, the food, the profits from the shop, or the farm. Asking for all the family and the neighbours by name and for the news from home.'

'But why didn't they write themselves?'

'Some couldn't. Illiteracy is high outside the towns,' he said matter-of-factly. 'Some could manage a pen perfectly well but didn't know what to say.

Once I'd thought about it, it was easy. They all wanted to say the same thing, whichever country they'd come from. "We're doing great, why don't you come over too? But in the meantime we need to feel part of the life we left behind. So tell us how everybody is and how life goes on with you." '

'And were they doing great?' she asked, picking up a sadness in his tone that surprised her.

'No, not always, but the less successful they were the less they admitted it. No one ever said in a letter that they were homesick or wished they'd made a different choice, but you should have seen the relief on their faces when I suggested a few phrases that sounded good without actually telling a lie.'

'So you were a professional letter writer?' she said, shaking her head and smiling to herself. 'In English *and* French?' she asked, looking at him again briefly.

'And German,' he added, looking away as she changed gear and manoeuvred carefully through the entrance to the yard.

The whole area in front of the low-set farmhouse was full of children who made her anxious by dashing towards her as she drew to a halt. Before she had even pulled on the handbrake, the back doors of the motor had been thrown open and two boys had hopped up into the back seat, followed more slowly by a small boy whose legs weren't long enough to step up on the running board and a little girl who pushed him from behind in her haste to follow him.

Before Sarah had time to protest, Sam emerged from the barn. He looked once at the back seat, then waited silently while the boys climbed down and the two smaller children tried to look as if they'd just been standing there quietly all the time.

'Hello, Sarah. Alex. You're very welcome,' he said, giving his sister a kiss and holding out his hand to Alex. 'Ma dropped me a line to say ye were comin', so I made sure I was here. I'm afraid all the boys are motor mad. It must run in the family,' he said agreeably, turning to Alex. 'I hear Da has you working on the new stenters.'

Alex smiled warmly. There was something about the way the two men greeted each other, something about the set of the shoulders, the ease with which they acknowledged each other, that made Sarah ask herself yet again if Alex might not be their cousin after all.

A figure appeared in the doorway. Martha was holding a small baby awkwardly against her already swollen stomach.

'Martha, this is our cousin Alexander Hamilton,' Sam said as Alex stepped forward and held out his hand.

'Pleased t' meet ye,' she said without enthusiasm, her glance taking in both Alex and Sarah in one calculating sweep. 'D'ye want a cup of tea now or before they go?' she asked, addressing herself to Sam. 'I have the calves to feed.'

'Well then, we'll have a look at the workshop till it suits you,' he said steadily. 'Send one of the children to tell us when it's ready,' he added, as she turned on her heel with the sleeping child.

Sarah did her best to show an interest in the workshop but the sight of Martha's sharp little face and the screams of the children running around on the tramped earth of the yard had totally dispersed her good spirits. Sam seemed unperturbed, however, enjoying his conversation with Alex, demonstrating some of his newly acquired equipment and listening attentively when Alex described the kinds of machinery he was familiar with in Pennsylvania.

They were in the midst of an extended exploration of the merits of tractors as opposed to ploughing engines when a small child appeared. Barefoot, with dark hair and dark, sparkling eyes, Sarah watched her as she went straight to Sam, who picked her up and held her close without interrupting for a moment what he was saying.

Sarah saw a small arm encircle his neck as the child whispered a word in his ear. She leaned her head against her father's cheek, kept silent and observed the visitors with interest from her vantage point.

'Time to go and have a cup of tea, Rose,' Sam said, lowering her gently to the ground some minutes later.

He reached out for a piece of cotton waste to wipe some traces of oil from his fingers and had almost finished when Rose, who'd been looking up at Alex, questioned him in her small, clear voice.

'Are you Aunt Sarah's new man then?'

Sarah had been watching Sam as he wiped his fingers slowly and methodically. It was such a Sam-like gesture, slow, steady and effective, but when Rose spoke, she saw a look on his face quite unlike anything she'd ever seen before. Sam was angry, furiously angry, but with an enormous effort of control, he was holding on to his temper.

'No, Rose dear, I'm nobody's man,' Alex replied, dropping down on his hunkers to look her straight in the eye. 'I haven't even got a Ma and Da like you have,' he added quietly.

'What happened them?'

'I'm afraid they both died when I was small.'

'As small as me?' Rose continued, her eyes fixed firmly on Alex's face.

'Yes, as small as you, Rose,' Alex said, with a confidence Sarah had not heard before.

'Run on over to the house, Rose,' said Sam quietly. 'Tell Ma we're comin' right now.'

The child turned on her heel and shot off immediately. As the three adults came out of the workshop Sarah saw her skipping across the yard and disappearing into the house. In silence, they followed her.

To Sarah's great amazement, Martha had laid the table with a clean cloth and set out four places. There was bread and butter, two small dishes of jam, a plate of scones and a fruitcake. A lavish spread for so early in the afternoon and an unheard-of effort on Martha's part.

'There y'are. Sit down now, it's ready,' she said, without looking at them, her whole attention focused on a large teapot which she lifted from the corner of the stove.

She waved the visitors to their places, began pouring tea, but made no effort to engage them in conversation or sit down with them. A few moments later, they heard the scrape of boots at the door.

'I've poured your tea, Uncle Joe. Come and sit down,' she said briskly.

Joe glared at the assembled company, dragged out the empty chair and threw his cap on the floor at his feet as he sat down. He produced his hand reluctantly when Sam introduced 'our cousin, Alex', who was sitting on his right. Sarah, on his left, he dismissed with a glance as he addressed himself to the plate of wheaten bread. Having poured tea for herself, Martha now retreated to an armchair by the stove where she could watch her guests without having to be any part of the company.

In the uneasy silence that followed, Joe made short work of a couple of slices of bread and jam while Sarah was still doing her best to eat a scone. There was nothing wrong with the scone, but the atmosphere in the room made her wish she could run out to the motor and drive straight home.

'Ye must find things here a bit differen' to yer way of goin',' Joe threw out sharply, addressing himself to Alex.

'Yes, very different in one way,' said Alex nodding agreeably, 'but the work's not so different and I've been made very welcome.'

'Aye, so Ah see,' said Joe unpleasantly as he looked from Alex to Sarah and back again. 'Did yer *cousin* drive you into Banbridge in her motor to sign the covenant?'

'No, sir. I didn't think the covenant was any of my business.'

'Ah, ye'll do well then with the Hamiltons,' he said, nodding across the room to where Martha sat watching them. 'Shure there's not one of them has any time for anyone but themselves and making money. Either that or they don't know how to write their names,' he added, laughing at his own joke. 'Yer sittin' beside two of them, Alexander. Brother and sister, an' neither of them one bit loyal. An' the father an' mother the same.'

'Loyalty, as you call it, is a personal matter, Joe,' said Sam quietly.

Sarah was startled, for there was a firmness and a coldness in his tone she'd never heard before and what he said next surprised her even more.

'There are higher loyalties than membership of any political party.'

'Aye, well, joining the Quakers is yer excuse, Sam, an' Martha an' I are well sick of it,' said Joe, reaching for another scone. 'What about yer sister then, what's her excuse?' he asked, without so much as a glance at Sarah.

Sarah had abandoned her scone and was silently watching the grimaces of Joe's dirty, lined face, as he scrunched it up into yet further unpleasant gestures. Were it not for Sam she most certainly wouldn't sit at this table for another moment. But this was Sam's home, and Martha, who was watching Joe's perform-ance with barely concealed pleasure, was Sam's wife.

'I don't need an *excuse*, Joe, for anything I do, or don't do,' she said, as coolly as she could manage. 'I need a *reason*, and I have one, just as Sam has.'

'Oh aye, Sam's a great man for reason,' he agreed, nodding his head at Sam, as he swallowed a large mouthful of tea and rattled his cup for Martha to come and refill it. 'He gives Martha an' me plenty of benefit of his reason,' he went on in the same sour, querulous tone, glancing up at her as she came to pour it for him. 'What he'll do and what he'll not do. It's a great life when ye can get others to work for ye an' put a roof over yer head and spread up a table for yer comp'ny like they was gentry.'

He reached across the table for a slice of cake and turned towards Alex.

'Maybe they'd like ye t'think they were someone, but let me tell you somethin',' he continued, adopting a confidential tone. 'Yer man Sam's mother was a servin' girl down in the south an' her brother had t' get away overseas outa trouble with the pollis. An' now he's back lukin' for more trouble, up an' down to Dublin from Donegal. That's where all their Papish connection live.'

He paused, drained his cup in one go, snatched up his cap from the floor and stood up abruptly.

'Irish Volunteers, they call themselves. Nothing but a lot of Shinners. An' now Sam McGinley's in the thick of them. God knows what he's up to. Just watch yourself, Alexander,' Joe said, his voice lingering sarcastically on the full name he insisted on using, as he paused in the doorway. 'That's my advice to ye. Ye don't know these people and the shifts of them. Ye cou'den be up to them with all their fancy ways. They'll have ye as bad as they are if ye don't watch out,' he threw back over his shoulder, as he pulled open the lower portion of the half door and banged it closed behind him.

For what seemed to Sarah like a very long time, no one spoke. Then Sam got to his feet, picked up her teacup, walked to the door and threw the cold, unpleasant-looking contents into the drain that took the rainwater away from the front of the house.

'Is there still a drop of tea in the pot, Martha?' he asked, as he came back into the room and held out the empty cup in front of her.

'Shure there's half a potful. Didn't ye say to use the big teapot?' she said shortly as she filled the empty cup.

'Here ye are, Sarah,' he said quietly as he put the cup back in her saucer. 'What about you, Alex?'

'I'm fine, thanks,' Alex said. 'That was a very nice tea,' he said, looking over at Martha. 'Lovely fruit-cake.'

'Does Rose not give you fruitcake for your tea?' Martha asked, a sarcastic note in her voice.

'I'm sure she would if I ever went for tea,' said Alex cheerfully, 'but I'm at work all week and I give Michael Jackson a hand on Sundays. I find I miss farm work, now I spend all my days with machinery.'

'Ye wou'dn't miss it if ye were here, that's for sure,' Martha replied sharply. 'I've the milkin' to do,' she went on, getting to her feet. 'The two wee ones are asleep in the room, Sam. Ye may give them a bottle if they wake up,' she added quickly, as she left the kitchen without a word of farewell.

'That reminds me,' said Sarah, standing up and smiling at Sam. 'Ma's sent a wee dress for the new baby and a jersey for Sammy. They're out in the motor.'

'I'll fetch them, Sarah,' said Alex promptly, disappearing outside before she could object.

'Take no notice of Joe,' said Sam, turning towards her and putting his hand on her shoulder. 'He an' his brothers are all the same. Ye wou'dn't get a civil word outa one o' them. Don't pay a bit of attention,' he finished quickly, as Alex reappeared with two paper bags.

Sam opened the first bag and held up the tiny dress in his large square-fingered hands. 'Ach, that's lovely,' he said softly. 'An' so's that,' he added, as Sarah drew out a brightly coloured Fair Isle jersey. 'Wee Sammy'll be as pleased as Punch,' he continued, turning to Alex. 'Ma has great hans. She takes it in turn up and down the family for sweaters and Sammy's been askin' every week since Charlie got his.'

'Well, tell Emily it's her turn next,' said Sarah, making an effort to show Sam she was herself again. 'And then it's Rose.'

She looked around her and out through the door, suddenly aware of the complete absence of children. 'Where's she got to? And where have the boys gone?'

'Martha sent her down after Sammy and Emily to play at Loneys,' he said, pulling a kettle back onto the hottest part of the stove. 'Billy and Charley are up the road helping the Hutchinsons lift their potatoes, and Bobby and Johnny are asleep. An' I hope they'll sleep till I have their bottles made,' he said, breaking into a broad grin.

'Now I could give you a hand with a bit of welding, Sam, but I'd be no good at all at making bottles,' said Alex lightly.

Sam laughed and looked pleased and Sarah decided it would be best to go before Martha reappeared again.

'And we'd better be going, Sam,' she said quickly. 'I still don't like driving in the dark even with the more powerful lamps.'

'Aye, ye need to be doin' it regular to get the hang of it,' he said sympathetically. 'The days is gettin' very short already, but ye shou'd be home before dark.'

It was not until they'd passed through Richhill and turned south towards Banbridge that either Sarah or Alex said anything. Finally, it was the young man who broke the silence.

'I don't think Uncle Joe would be quite my favourite relative,' he said, with great deliberation.

Sarah looked at him, caught the sparkle in his eyes and burst out laughing.

'Thank goodness for that,' she replied, relaxing her fierce grip on the steering wheel. 'It might have been the end of a beautiful friendship.'

They drove on, talking easily now, the afternoon sun declining into a glow of gold on the horizon, the sky paling above, the temperature dropping rapidly. By the time they reached Seapatrick, they could see their breath streaming on the crisp air as they glanced across at each other on the empty road.

'Sarah, what's a Shinner? I don't think I've heard of them before.'

'Sinn Fein. Political party. Very active in America in the last century. Not much talked of these days, but then Joe has a long memory.'

'Of course, I've heard of them,' he said, shaking his head, 'But your Uncle Sam's a socialist, isn't he?'

'All the same to Joe,' she replied, now laughing

easily. 'If you don't agree with Joe, it wouldn't matter what you were, he'd find a way to disparage you. Uncle Sam worked for the Land League back in the eighties, but he was opposed to violence. He always has been. He did go to America to take letters and raise funds for the League, but it was because of Eva he stayed,' she explained. 'He was probably on some of the police lists, but anyone who worked for the League was then. He's told me often how any organisation can be infiltrated by people who want to use it for their own purposes. There were people in the Land League who moved to the IRB when it was founded.'

'Irish Republican Brotherhood?'

'Yes. I'm afraid I don't know anything about them. Hugh always tried to keep up with politics, but I'm afraid I feel defeated by great causes and marching men,' she went on, as they drew to a halt and let a column of Ulster Volunteers cross the road in front of them.

Weighed down with heavy packs, some carrying rifles, they tramped solidly along behind their officer, scaling the wall alongside the road with practised ease.

'All I can do is try to see that no one in the four mills goes hungry or dies for lack of care,' she said sadly. 'But even that seems a struggle at times,' she added, as the last of the long column disappeared into the nearby fields.

'Wouldn't anything be a struggle when you lose the man you love?'

Tears sprang to Sarah's eyes and she had to blink furiously as she revved up the engine and moved off again.

'Maybe one of the lives you save will do more for mankind than all the political groups and volunteers put together,' Alex went on without looking at her.

'I'd never thought of that,' she replied honestly. 'I'll try and remember next time there's a threatened strike or a punch-up over a bit of coloured ribbon.'

'Well then, Alex,' said Rose, laughing, 'you've met Uncle Joe and lived to tell the tale. Are you sure you shouldn't take his advice about the Hamiltons before it's too late?' she went on as she and Sarah led the way into the new sitting room where a log fire blazed invitingly.

'I think I'll take a chance on my own judgement,' Alex answered her with a broad smile.

The roast dinner Rose had ready for them had gone down well. In the warmth of the kitchen, the events of the afternoon were recalled, softened somewhat by distance and touched with humour by both Sarah and Alex in the telling.

'I don't know how our Sam puts up with it,' said John slowly, straightening up from putting another log on the fire.

'I forgot to tell you, Ma, Martha's expecting again,' said Sarah, as she looked across at her mother.

Rose sighed, took one look at John's face and wished Sarah hadn't mentioned it just then.

'Well, she certainly keeps my hand in with babies' dresses,' she said, as she bent down to leave the teapot on the hearth.

'I think Sam is very fond of children,' said Alex unexpectedly. 'Maybe that makes up to him for something in Martha. He has only to say a word and they do what he tells them. Little Rose seems to adore him.'

'Yes, Alex's right,' added Sarah. 'He's stronger in himself than ever I remember. I used to think Martha walked all over him, but it's different now. I just wish he didn't have to work so hard, evenings and weekends as well as a long day.'

'Aye,' said John, 'I know what ye mean, but he once said to me that work keeps you from thinking long. When he's working he has a whole world inside his head, figuring out things, planning things . . .'

'Like you used to do yourself, John, on the forti-eth horseshoe,' said Rose, smiling at him across the fireplace. 'Maybe we can only see one side of things. I must say Sam never seems unhappy when he comes here.'

'Ach, how would he, love, an' this his home an' him so welcome?' said John hastily.

'Yes, but sadness hangs round a man like a cloak,' said Alex promptly.

Rose and Sarah exchanged glances and they both smiled. They'd got used to it now, but to begin with some of Alex's sudden offerings had taken them by surprise. He had a way of summing up a situation or observing a characteristic in a person that was perceptive and shrewd.

'Ye said, Sarah, that yer man mentioned Uncle Sam,' began John, as he settled himself more comfortably in his high-backed armchair. 'What was this about goin' up and down to Dublin? Where did he get that?' he asked, looking at Rose. 'Has your Sam been to Dublin?'

'Yes, he has,' Rose said, 'but I don't know how Joe found out. Maybe I told our Sam that Uncle Sam had been down to see Lily.'

'Lily?' Sarah gasped. 'Ma, you never told me he'd seen Lily.'

'Did I not? I must have forgotten,' she said, laughing. 'It seems to be a feature of getting older,' she went on cheerfully.

'Lily is the younger sister of my friend Lady Anne,' Rose explained, turning to Alex. 'When Sam was seventeen or thereabouts he thought he was going to die of love for the beautiful Lily,' she went on, as both Sarah and John began to smile. 'She was very pretty, I admit,' added Rose, 'but Sam might as well have been a sparrow in a tree for all Lily noticed him.

'Lily took care of her father when he moved from Currane Lodge to their Dublin house. She still lives in Dublin but when he died she found a smaller house in Dawson Street. We met her again at Hannah and Teddy's wedding and she insisted John and I would go and visit her. Teddy is her nephew, of course. She was very welcoming I must say. I think she's rather lonely with all her sisters in England or America. She never married herself,' added Rose, with a sigh, 'despite all the admirers she had. When I wrote and told her Sam was home on a visit, she wanted to see him too. I think he went out of curiosity, but they seem to have got on very well.'

'But Joe said "up and down to Dublin". Was he just exaggerating? He'd be capable of it,' said Sarah sharply.

'Well, I think Sam *has* been several times,' she began thoughtfully. 'Now that I think of it, he has mentioned in a couple of letters what an easy journey it is on the train from Creeslough and how much he always did love Dublin. Last time he was here he said Lily has no one to talk to about the old days in Kerry. The cook and butler from Currane Lodge are long gone. Her only friends seem to be in the artistic world, mostly young men trying to make a living. She's a very good watercolourist, Alex,' she added, nodding to a landscape of sky and water in the alcove by the fireplace. 'She's promised me a painting of Currane Lodge the next time we go down.'

'It's a pity she didn't take your Sam when he was so keen on her,' said John thoughtfully. 'But then I suppose he wouldn't have met Eva and had a grand family and done so well for himself. It would always have been Lily's house and Lily's wee bit of money, once Currane Lodge went. And who knows how Sam would have made out.'

'And I wouldn't be sitting here,' said Alex, looking him straight in the eye. 'I must be very grateful to Lily Molyneux. If it weren't for her I'd never have met Sam McGinley. And maybe I'd never have got back to where I belong.'

'Ye have a point, Alex, indeed ye have,' said John vigorously. 'Sure if a groom at Castledillon hadn't had his old mother ill, I'd never have laid eyes on Kerry m'self.'

'And *I* wouldn't be sitting here either,' said Sarah, so promptly that they all laughed.

Ten

Sam McGinley smiled to himself as he took his sister's letter out of its envelope once more. He had read it the previous day, but now he laid it on his breakfast table where he could see her generous signature and the scrawl of kisses with which they'd always decorated their letters. Whether Rose wrote about the ordinary everyday things of her life, or asked for his opinion on matters political, literary, or personal, he always found her letters soothing. Not because they were pleasant or without distress or anxiety, but because he could always see her small figure sitting at the table, totally focused on what she wanted to share with him. It was an image that had comforted him for most of his life.

Sometimes it seemed her very existence helped him to keep at bay the sadness – the despair, even – which came upon him as he considered the world around him, a world which he'd struggled to change since his mid-teens. Now, at fifty-four, his sons and daughters married with growing families of their own, he wondered just what, if anything, had been achieved for Ireland, or for the millions of Irish who laboured on the other side of the Atlantic, in the three decades he himself had spent as an exile working for their betterment.

Long ago, in a cottage opposite the forge at Salter's Grange, he'd broken it to Rose that he was going to America carrying letters for the Land League. A year later, after he and Eva had fallen in love, he had told Rose and John he was going back to America. He'd spoken with such sadness of the Ireland he was leaving that John, usually so silent on matters of feeling, encouraged him by suggesting he might achieve more for Ireland in America than he'd ever achieved in Ireland itself.

Sam poured himself more tea, smoothed out the letter, ready to read it again, and then sat looking up at the sky. In the world's terms, he *had* been successful. He'd worked hard and bought small pieces of land on the outskirts of New York with his savings. When he'd begun to sell them, to help his sons and daughters set up their own homes or businesses, twenty years later, he'd been truly amazed at the extraordinary sums of money he'd been offered.

But making money was not what he'd set out to do. Sometimes he wondered whether he would have been able to achieve some satisfaction through philanthropy had he put his mind to making money, but the question was academic. He hadn't made the huge sums that would have made a real difference, like Rockefeller or Carnegie, nor had his work for the labour movement produced the growth in numbers and activity needed to lift thousands of workers out of abject poverty in a flourishing land.

He pushed away his sad thoughts and took up the letter.

Ballydown
10th May, 1913

My dear Sam,

I was so delighted to get your long letter and know that you and all Mary's family are finally well again. John and I have both recovered, though his cough went on for weeks. Little Hugh caught a chest infection when he went back to school and was too ill to come home again. Sarah went and stayed with friends in Lisburn until he was over the worst, but it upset her badly. She's not like her old self at all at the moment.

I must tell you that you've become a great-uncle, yet again, up in County Armagh. Martha had a little girl last week. That makes eight. I sometimes wonder if losing her first two children so soon after birth made her determined to show everyone how good she really is at rearing children. I have to say they are all remarkably healthy, though it still breaks my heart to see them running barefoot in winter when it is not necessary.

What news from Pennsylvania, Sam? Is Patrick still planning to visit Eva's family in Germany? Are you still concerned that his visit is political and that he's not telling you the half of it, as John and I would say? What *do* you think of the situation in Germany at the moment?

As for our own country, I sometimes despair. Given the way all the young men *here* are flocking to the Ulster Volunteers, it is hardly surprising that Brendan and young Sean have joined the Irish Volunteers, especially since, as you say, the Gaelic League is so active in Donegal. It seems as if our poor island is turning itself into two opposing camps, while all the time the news from Germany becomes more and more alarming. Sometimes I just try to give thanks that all is well for the moment, though often it's difficult when John comes in with a long face and not a word out of him till he's put the day behind him.

I've been meaning to ask you about Lily since your last visit to Dublin. Did she have her pictures hung at the Academy? I think they are very good, but then I am totally captivated by her way of representing sea and sky. I was so delighted when she sent me the watercolour of Currane Lodge she'd promised me. Can one really be objective about pictures of places one has once loved? Do you think it is our advancing age that makes us so willing to collect up fragments from our past?

You asked me how Helen and Hugh had resolved the problem of your name, following your relocation. Sarah tells me she overheard a most serious conversation in which Helen insisted that you were still

Uncle Sam America because *you* hadn't changed, only where you lived. Hugh, ever logical, disagreed. Uncle Sam Richhill had become Uncle Sam Liskeyborough, when he moved, he said, so therefore you had to be Uncle Sam Donegal. As always, in such matters, Hugh carried the day.

Now, my dear, I must stop. I have been turning my back on a number of jobs and if I leave them much longer I can be sure my sins will find me out, the weeds in my flowerbed will be even further entrenched, there will be no clean shirts and only crumbs left in the cake tin . . .

A shaft of sunlight struck the surface of the table. The clouds were now dispersing in all directions. It was going to be a good day after all. He cleared away his breakfast dishes, made neat piles of his papers, tidied his books, walked out the back door and climbed the dozen steep steps he and Brendan had cut and laid with stone one windy day the previous autumn.

From the top, he could look out over his own slate roof, but he strode on up the narrow path he had trodden day by day to the fence which bounded the mountain land where he kept the sheep in summer. He leaned on a stout corner post and surveyed the whole of the countryside spread out before him. To his right, the great hump of Muckish Mountain was still wisped with cloud, but the valley below was bathed in sunlight, his own small fields and those of his neighbours green with new growth, dotted with sheep and the sturdy crop of lambs the mild winter had brought. To his left, the rough track-way that passed his own front door led down to the coast. He shaded his eyes from the dazzling light and saw the dark blue waters of Sheephaven still ribbed with white horses from the strong wind that had wakened him in the night, whistling and roaring round the eaves.

He climbed over the fence, scrambled up a slab of rock and found himself in the eye of the breeze. On this exposed point, it threw locks of red hair across his forehead and made his eyes water, but long ago he'd accustomed himself to wind and cold. He looked around him once more and listened carefully.

From somewhere up near Muckish, he heard the harsh cry of ravens soaring in the uprush of air that rose all along the flanks of the great, bare mass of rock, its sides scarred and seamed like an ancient creature, the survivor of many battles. He smiled, satisfied.

The fuchsia bushes surrounding the house were recovering from the fierce pruning they'd needed when he first began work. Soft new growth con-cealed the saw-cuts that had opened up the path and let the wind dry out the sodden earth. Soon there would be a mass of blood-red tassels swinging in the breeze. Already on the mountainside below him, orchids bloomed in the grassy spaces between the heather-covered peat hags. Where the rock broke through the thin soil, milkwort, thyme and silver-weed had found a place, plants he had never even heard of till he saw them at his feet and bent to look at their delicate colours and bright faces.

'Uncle Sam Donegal,' he said, smiling to himself, as he looked around him.

Whether it was the soughing of the breeze or his preoccupation with his own thoughts, he wasn't sure, for he had heard no sound, but suddenly, there at the fence was Brendan, the youngest of his sister's children. Now in his mid-twenties, short and robust with a shock of straight, black hair, Mary always said Brendan was the image of their father. Sam took her word for it, for he had no memory at all of Patrick McGinley, only of Rose and Hannah, his mother.

'Well, have ye still a mind to go?' Brendan asked, as Sam climbed down from his perch, tramped through the rough grass and climbed back over the fence to greet him.

'Yes,' he said, nodding vigorously. 'Isn't it going to be a great day? Did your father lend you the trap all right?'

'He did. He said if we went, it wou'd make him sit in the back room and do up his books. Shure he'd far rather be out.'

Sam laughed as they made their way down to the road where the tethered pony stood nuzzling the new grass by the gatepost.

'Ma made us sandwiches and cold tea,' Brendan announced, as Sam pulled shut the front door and pocketed the key.

'That was good of her,' Sam replied warmly. 'Did you ask her to come herself?'

'Oh I did, aye,' he replied, nodding vigorously. 'Shure ye told me to be sure an' ask, but she said no, that maybe Aunt Rose wou'd come if she were here, but no, she diden want t' go.'

The journey took much longer than Sam had expected. What the map he had studied could not tell him was how broken and potholed the tracks were after the frost and rain of winter. Where they served a scatter of farms, they'd been roughly mended, but where houses stood empty, the thatch grass-grown, the bushes run wild, then their progress was slow, the holes neglected for many a year, filled now with rainwater from the previous night's storm.

It was a rough and bumpy ride, but the freshness of the day, the warmth of the sun and the brilliance of the morning sky made up for their discomforts.

'Will we give her a bit of a rest?' asked Brendan, as they crossed the Calaber Bridge and joined the road that turned east.

Above them the curved slopes of the Derryveagh Mountains were crossed with the straight lines of the deer fences which surrounded the Glenveagh estate. The road eastwards was well mended for the benefit of the coaches and the motors of those who were invited to visit Adair's castle down by the lake.

They sat on the parapet of the bridge, the countryside brilliant in the morning light, silent but for the noisy babble of the river below and the cheeping of finches flying from bush to bush in small oscillating flights. Even through his tweed jacket, Sam could feel the sun's warmth on his shoulders. He watched Brendan scanning the mountainsides, his eyes half closed against the light.

'There was a golden eagle here last year,' the young man said suddenly. 'One of the gamekeepers told Da. But sure it stayed by the lake where the feedin's good an' the likes of us aren't welcome,' he added bitterly.

Sam smiled wryly as he got to his feet. For all the struggles of the Land League and the Land Acts that had given opportunities for tenant farmers to buy their land, there were still these vast estates, owned by people so rich they could afford to run a castle and dozens of square miles of mountain and lough simply for the hunting or the entertainment of guests in summer.

Adair himself was dead but it was said his wife loved the place. With her income from the Adair estates in Texas, she could afford to keep up a holiday castle.

'She does provide some employment,' Sam said steadily, 'and I hear she's not as indifferent to starvation as her husband was,' he added wryly, as the two of them climbed back up into the trap.

'I've been this far with m'Da,' said Brendan, some time later, as they rounded a corner and found themselves looking along the length of Lough Gartan, calm and shimmering in the noonday sun. 'But I don't know m'way from here.'

'We go right here towards Glaskeelan Bridge,' said Sam, consulting a small notebook. 'Provided we find the bridge, we're on our way. The track runs the whole length of the lough, but Ardtur is only just over halfway.'

They heard the river before they saw it. Swollen by heavy rain in the previous week, it poured down the hillside, collecting small streams from the sodden vegetation as it went. The brown, peat-stained waters had spread wide on each side of the single-arched bridge, but the roadway itself was dry.

Apart from signs of repairs to the deer fence, there was no mark of human hand on the lower slopes of the mountains or on the damp margins of the lough. Everywhere, bushes and moisture-loving trees, newly leafed, gleamed in the sunlight. On bare mossy banks, primroses bloomed prolifically, ivy and bramble scrambled over low stone walls and the golden flare of gorse blazed out against the dark residues of last autumn's heather. Already tall, the vivid green branches of young bracken were beginning to unfurl.

'Have ye any idea where yer goin?' Brendan asked, as he slackened the reins and let the pony pick its own way on the grass-grown track.

'Well, there *was* a school,' said Sam doubtfully, as he ran his eye over the rush-filled land to their right where no trace of habitation could be seen. 'It *would* have been on the left,' he added, waving his arm towards a cluster of hawthorns whose creamy blossom was just beginning to show white on the green branches.

The track steepened. They got down from the trap and Brendan led the mare, his eyes still seeking any sign of human life in the prolific but unpeopled landscape.

'There it is,' said Sam suddenly, his voice high with excitement.

'Where?' demanded Brendan, who could see no trace of a building of any kind.

Sam beamed at him as he strode ahead and hurried up the slope.

'The apple tree,' he said, waving his arm in triumph. 'Rose told me a man who only spoke English came and planted it at the gable end. There it is. Would you look at the size of it!'

Brendan caught up with him. High above their heads, its crown rising above the birches and elderberries, the pale grey twigs were newly leafed. Here and there, where the morning sun shone most directly on the low, sheltered branches, tight pink buds were already beginning to open.

'It was here all right,' said Sam, kicking his way through the undergrowth. 'Look, here's one corner. They must have missed this bit. You can see where even the foundations have been dug out for the stone.'

'And this was where Ma and Aunt Rose went to school?'

'Yes, it was a brand new National School. They came in different sizes. This one was the smallest. I've seen the specifications in the Public Records Office in Dublin,' Sam explained. 'But it only lasted two years,' he added, as he turned his back on the apple tree, ran a practised eye back and forth across the track and the low stone wall bounding it.

'Why? Why was that?'

'Adair,' he said abruptly, as he considered the overgrown fields beyond. 'If you evict all the families, there'll be no children left. No need for the school. I wonder who it was carted away the stone and what they built with it.'

'May he rot in Hell,' said Brendan softly, as he followed Sam across the roadway and along the side of an overgrown stone wall that joined it at right angles.

After a short distance, Sam struck to his right, heading for a small bracken-covered eminence.

'Where are ye goin'?' Brendan protested, as he struggled to follow him through the undulating ground. ''Tis desperate rough goin'.'

'Spade rigs,' said Sam without stopping, as he pushed through the thigh-high bracken and made a beeline for the highest point of the low rise.

Brendan watched patiently as Sam kicked his way through patches of nettles and brambles and walked up and down, casting an eye first towards the school, then towards the piled-up stone boundary wall which ran along the foot of the mountain itself. He stopped eventually on a slight rise covered with shorter grass.

'Here, Brendan, here,' he said at last, dropping to his knees and studying the ground in front of him. He took out his penknife and made three long shallow cuts. Then he peeled back the sod like rolling up a mat and revealed a broad, smooth-worn stone. On either side of it, half hidden in brambles, were the fragments of two rotten posts.

'That's the doorstep of your grandfather's house,' he said firmly, as he rubbed soil from his hands and stood up. 'Part of what we walked across would have been *his* potato garden. And over there,' he went on, pointing to where bleached, straw-pale heads of last year's corn stood swaying in the breeze, 'is where he kept a horse or pony.'

He looked back again the way they had come, his eyes half closed in the bright light, his arm waving in a leisurely way.

'Where the grass is shortest is where the street was. The houses weren't lined up, they were set at angles to each other,' he began. 'Nettles thrive on human waste, so where the nettles are thickest is where the barns were. You can see a patch at the back of each house and this one here, McGinley's, is just a wee bit higher than its neighbours. Rose remembered that from the day she set off to climb the mountain to see what was on the other side. She stood and looked back and she still remembers everything she saw, even the apple tree at the school gable.'

'So what happened all these people?' Brendan asked sharply.

'Did your mother never tell you?'

'No, she always said it was better forgotten. She told me Granny took you and Auntie Rose to Kerry and my two uncles went back to Scotland after Granda died. I know one of them went on to Nova Scotia. But she didn't know where any of the neighbours went.'

'Those that survived,' Sam added automatically.

Brendan looked startled.

'Do you really want to know?' he went on, raising an eyebrow.

Brendan nodded and sat down on one side of the newly excavated doorstone. As he waited for his uncle to seat himself on the other, it occurred to him that this must be a very strange homecoming for the older man. Of it being also a homecoming of his own, he was completely unaware.

'I was a babe in arms when it happened, so I've no memory at all of my own,' said Sam, twisting a stem of grass between his fingers. 'But your Aunt Rose has never forgotten that day. She remembers how cold it was and how she knew something was wrong, but nobody would tell her. She saw Ma and Da out talking to a neighbour and watched a lad they knew bringing news from further up the valley where the evictions started.'

He shook his head and smiled.

'She was only eight and so small for her age, they put her in the wee turf cart with me and a few odds and ends of food and kindling. She says they just walked away when Adair's man told them to get out. Your Granny told them all they were not to look back.'

'And they destroyed the house?'

'Oh yes. In other parts of the country, where they pulled the roof off or knocked down the walls, the people came back and lived in the ruins. A bit of a wall's better shelter than nothing. Adair's men had orders to do a good job. He didn't want anyone sneaking back when they'd gone.'

Sam looked at his nephew and saw that his hand was moving back and forwards across the surface of the wide doorstone on which they both sat. Worn by the passage of feet and the fall of rain for over a hundred years or more, and untouched by either for the last half century, it was now exposed to the hot sun, the soft mould of its covering drying to dust which Brendan was gently sweeping away.

'How many?' Brendan asked sharply.

'According to the *Londonderry Standard*, forty-seven families, some two hundred and forty-four men, women and children,' Sam replied. 'Only forty-two of the houses were destroyed. I think he saved the others for the shepherds he brought in from Scotland,' he continued. 'I went and looked up the newspaper reports last year. There *was* a great deal of anger about what he was planning to do and questions were asked in Parliament, but no one lifted a hand to stop him. There were even two hundred police standing by to make sure there was no disturbance of the peace.'

'Why d'ye think Ma diden tell me when I asked her?' Brendan demanded, his eyes wide with amazement.

'Well, it might have been because of *her* Aunt Mary,' said Sam thoughtfully. 'I think Aunt Mary was actually your grandfather's aunt, but she was certainly an old lady. Lived further up the valley. I've forgotten the name of the townland just for the moment. She had bad legs and could barely walk. Your mother used to go over every day and do the jobs, fetch the water and turf and boil the spuds for her meal. The morning of the eviction your grandmother sent your mother over with a can of milk, but she told her she was to hurry back. I think your mother was fond of the old woman,' he said quietly. 'Rose said she was worried about what would happen to her and she cried her eyes out when she heard she was dead.'

'What happened her?'

'It seems she wouldn't go to the Workhouse, but in the confusion no one actually saw *where* she went. About a week later, your grandfather and one of my brothers found her curled up behind a stone on the mountainside with her Rosary in her hand. Goodness knows how she'd got there. She'd been dead for some time. It was very cold and there was frost and sleet that first night.'

'The bloody English,' said Brendan bitterly. 'They'd wipe us out like vermin if they cou'd.'

'No, Brendan. Let's be accurate,' said Sam sharply. 'Adair was English, I grant you, but the men who pulled the houses down were Irish, and so were the police who stood by and watched. And as my mother often said, "We weren't the first, nor will we be the last." This isn't about nationality, Brendan: this is about power and privilege. It was the Sutherlands that evicted my mother's people in Scotland a century earlier. Read your history and don't go thinking that Irish people are the only ones to have suffered, or the English the only ones to have made them suffer. Name me the country and name me the century and I'll tell you a story as bitter and as sad,' he said, with a steadiness in his voice that surprised even himself.

Brendan looked sheepishly down at the door-stone, now swept clean.

'Where did youse go that night?' he asked, without meeting Sam's eyes.

'I'll show you,' Sam replied, standing up. 'Like them, we have a bite of food from home,' he said as he strode out into the rough grass and retraced his steps on the path he'd made. 'But unlike them it might not be the last bite we'll get.'

Brendan sat silently as Sam took the reins and urged the pony along the track, the heat of noonday now fierce where there were no bushes or trees to give shelter.

'There,' said Sam, pointing to a track running off to the right. 'That's where Casheltown would have been. They spent the night at the house of an old man called Daniel McGee. He was in his eighties and blind, but he was a great storyteller. He told his last story there. A week later, he died in the Workhouse,' he added, as he jumped down and tied the reins to a stone post that no longer supported a gate.

'We'll go over that way,' he went on, nodding to the other side of the track as he picked up the shopping bag Mary had filled for them. 'The cashel should give us a good view over the lough. After all, that's why it was built there in days long gone.'

They made their way through the tall, damp grass, skirting the brambles and the wet patches till they reached the great circle of rough unmortared stone. They climbed up cautiously and perched on its highest point, Mary's shopping bag between them.

The whole of Lough Gartan lay spread out before them, the calm water sparkling in the sunshine, the new green foliage at its freshest, small clouds of gnats rising and falling in the warm air.

Gratefully, they bit into Mary's bacon sandwiches

and shared the bottle of tea between them.

'I did hear some of them went to Australia,' Brendan offered, as he finished off the last of the sandwiches.

'Yes. Some say two hundred. The figures disagree,' Sam responded, still munching. 'But they were fortunate. Only a few died on the voyage and there were three babies born. Not many emigrant ships do that well, but the *Abysinnia* was properly run. They were luckier than most.'

'Did any of them come back?'

'Not that I've heard of, and I've asked around,' Sam replied. 'It's not only your mother that doesn't want to talk about it. I've been trying to put the bits together as best I could, but without Rose and my mother I wouldn't have got beyond thinking I was born in Kerry. I might not even have known that my father was Irish and my mother the daughter of a Scottish Covenanter.'

'What?'

Sam paused as he unwrapped a packet of fruitcake and looked at his nephew's face. He had seldom seen such a look of outrage and incomprehension.

'So, what difference does it make who our ancestors were?' he asked quietly. 'We're here now, in this place, with these problems. I do what I can or fail in the attempt. What more can a man do?'

'He can be ready to lay down his life,' replied Brendan firmly.

'He can. But he'd be well advised to consider whether it would achieve anything or not,' said Sam crisply.

To Sam's sober correction, Brendan did not reply. He simply looked away down the track towards the field with the freshly swept doorstone and blinked his eyes against the dazzling light.

Eleven

'Are we nearly there, Mama?'

Sarah opened her eyes. One glance around the railway carriage and then through the dusty window told her she was moving through unfamiliar countryside and that the pleasant dreams she'd been having bore no resemblance whatever to reality.

'Oh, Helen, I *am* sorry,' she said, collecting herself. 'I didn't mean to fall asleep. Yes, we *must* be nearly there,' she said, glancing at her watch.

She scanned the sunlit landscape that streamed past the open window, but she could recognise no familiar feature in the rich Gloucestershire countryside. Not surprising, as it was some four years since she and Hugh had last made this journey.

'Were you bored?' she asked, smiling, as Helen left her window seat and came to sit close beside her.

Helen nodded towards the opposite corner of the empty carriage. Her brother was totally absorbed in a book about the development of flying machines. She sighed wearily and shrugged her shoulders.

'Poor Helen,' Sarah said as they exchanged knowing glances.

Hugh was miles away, just as indifferent to the unfamiliar countryside slipping past as he would have been to the green fields and little hills on the familiar journey between Lisburn and Banbridge.

'Do you think Uncle Teddy will come to meet us?' Helen asked, a hint of anxiety in her voice.

'Well, perhaps not,' said Sarah honestly as she tucked an arm round her and drew her close. 'It depends on whether he has to be up in London, but Auntie Hannah will be there, and your cousins. Perhaps not Frances and John,' she corrected herself quickly. 'I'm not sure when their term ends. English schools go on later than ours.'

'Why's that?'

'I don't think I know why,' she said thoughtfully. 'We'll have to ask Auntie Hannah when we get there.'

Sarah became suddenly aware of the warmth of the small body leaning against her. At almost eight, Helen was an intelligent and imaginative child, her head full of the stories she was either reading or planning to write, but Helen was often anxious. Sarah had long since learnt to watch for the danger signs, which began with fatigue, moved through questions and irritability and could quickly result in tears and exhaustion.

Her father had always insisted it was the price she paid for being sensitive to the world around her. He felt it was not something they should try to cure, for the sensitivity was, in itself, a gift, but it was important she learn how to cope with her feelings and not to allow them to overwhelm her.

After Helen had to be put to bed on a lovely summer afternoon, Hugh once asked if she remembered an evening in her own childhood when she herself had to be carried off to bed, because she'd got so upset when he'd spoken of young children working in the mills.

'It was unthinking of me,' he explained, 'but you'd been sitting so quietly all evening, I'd forgotten you always listened to everything, even if you looked totally absorbed in your own concerns.'

'I don't ever remember anything like that, Hugh,' she said, shaking her head. 'What happened?'

'Well, I had been talking to Elizabeth and your father and mother about the upsurge in orders caused by the American Civil War and the shortage of cotton and I'm sure I said there was so much work in the linen mills that children as young as nine and ten were being taken on, because there were families so poor they'd let them go. And you, my love,' he added, 'immediately looked up at Sam and Hannah and demanded to know if your family was poor.'

'Did I?'

'Yes, and you were just as upset as Helen. Your dear mother had quite a job reassuring you. I went down next morning to apologise,' he ended ruefully.

Dear Hugh. Would ever a day pass without her thinking about him? Missing him. Thinking of things to tell him if only he were there.

It was four years now since they'd made the journey to Cleeve Court, judging that young Hugh and Helen, then six and four, would be old enough to cope with travelling and enjoy meeting their cousins. Hugh was able to stay only two weeks, but she and the children had had a whole month with Hannah and her little ones. It had been such a happy time for all of them.

The following year, Anne had been born and Hannah's visit to Ballydown had been postponed, but Sarah herself had gone over to celebrate Anne's first birthday. Before she set out for home, she and Hannah had made plans for the following year. A month later Hugh died.

Sarah hugged Helen and held her close, despite the warmth of the July afternoon.

'Do you remember the photographs of Elizabeth and Anne with their little pony that Uncle Teddy sent us at Christmas?' she said, making an effort to be lively.

Helen looked up at her and beamed.

'Do you think they'd let me ride the pony?' she asked quickly.

'I'm sure they would. You might even find there was another pony there for the holidays. Auntie Hannah knows you like to ride.'

'What will you do, Mama, while I'm riding?' Helen asked, her good spirits fading again. 'You won't have to go to the mills and you won't have all those papers in the dining room.'

'But I shall have Auntie Hannah to talk to when you and your cousins are having all sorts of games and expeditions with Mademoiselle Challon,' said Sarah reassuringly, picking up the thin edge in Helen's tone. 'And we'll be going to see Grandma Anne and Grandpa Harrington over at Ashleigh Court. Just wait until you see the flowers in

Grandma's gardens. You'll love them. And you'll have all the watercolours you need if you want to paint, because Auntie Hannah will lend you hers.'

'Do you think Mademoiselle Challon will make us speak French all the time?' Helen asked, her brow wrinkling ominously.

'No, of course not,' replied Sarah, laughing. 'It's the holidays. She'll be finding you games to play and taking you out for drives in the governess cart or one of the traps. She's a *holiday* governess, not a schoolroom governess. I'm sure she'll be very nice.'

It was clear from the look on Helen's face that she had no such confidence.

'Nearly there,' said Hugh firmly.

Surprised at the sudden sound of his voice, they both turned to look at him. They saw him put his father's watch carefully back in his pocket, shut his book and stand up. Sarah was about to enquire how he could possibly know they were nearly there, as he hadn't been to Cleeve Hall since he was six, when the train slowed visibly and Helen hopped up to look out of the window.

'We're here. We're here!' she cried excitedly. 'And I can see Auntie Hannah and Uncle Teddy and Elizabeth and Anne, but not Frances and John, just like you said,' she added, with a note of relief.

Suddenly, without the slightest warning, Sarah felt sure that after all that had happened since they'd said goodbye two years ago, the very sight of her dear sister was going to be too much for her. What on earth would she do if she greeted Hannah with a sudden outburst of tears?

Cleeve Court
Gloucestershire
July 1913

Dearest Ma,

You were right, of course. And you may say
'I told you so' if you wish, because you never
say it unkindly.

Yes, I do feel better, so much better I
can hardly believe how dreadful I was feeling at the end of June. It is just so lovely to
be here with Hannah and Teddy. I'd almost
forgotten what a charming house Cleeve is
and Hannah has made us so welcome. She
and I have had some lovely walks together
and Teddy has taken us to visit some of the
nearby villages where he has been photographing the splendid parish churches.

The children are having a marvellous
time. Mademoiselle Challon is the most
remarkable young woman I have ever met.
She is full of such a boundless energy that
just watching her makes me feel tired, but
the children adore her. She speaks French to
them nearly all the time as if she'd just
forgotten they don't speak it themselves. The
other day when Elizabeth tripped and fell,
little Anne promptly helped her up and said,
'Ah, *ma pauvre petite*.' I think Elizabeth's governess is going to get quite a surprise when
Anne joins her for lessons in September.

Grandma Anne has been over twice to
see us and she asked about you most carefully.

I know she's sad you couldn't come this year, but she does understand that we cannot both leave Da when things are so difficult at the mills. I can hardly bear to think of them at the moment, but perhaps I will come back full of enthusiasm and new ideas.

I have to confess that when Anne spoke of Hugh's death I did cry, though I had managed not to with Hannah. I think I've decided that it is not grief for Hugh that makes me cry, for I have become accustomed to that, but the tenderness of people like Anne. Hannah is my dear sister, but she has always had a cool steadiness that Anne certainly does not have. I think it was Anne who cried first and couldn't find her handkerchief, but then we hugged each other and talked about you and the children and some of the very happy times we've all had at Ashleigh.

We are all going over there for the last week of our holiday. Sadly, Teddy may have to go back up to London later in the week, even if Parliament is not recalled. We talk sometimes over dinner about the political situation, here and in Ireland. Hannah says it helps Teddy to have another perspective and another listener as he gets very depressed about what is going on in Europe and our own government's failure to see the seriousness of what is happening.

Do you remember a young man called Simon Hadleigh at Hannah and Teddy's wedding? It seems he is to join us for our week at Ashleigh. To my chagrin, I cannot remember him at all. He was one of Teddy's two close friends from Cambridge and according to Hannah, he carried around the tripod and lenses for that huge camera Teddy lent me to take the wedding pictures. He's an ambassador of some sort and I've been warned I'm not to ask him about his work. It all seems so strange. Do you think I might become a spy?

I'm being frivolous, which Hannah says is a good thing. We agreed the other evening that, however bad situations are in the big world out there, we have to cherish our homes and families and laugh as often as we can, if only at our own solemnities.

It is almost lunchtime and I haven't laid eyes on the children all morning. What an idle mother I am. I promise you they are well and send their love to you and Da and Alex, as do we all at Cleeve and Ashleigh.

Your loving daughter,
Sarah

The day planned for the journey to Ashleigh was the only really wet day in what had been a fine and settled summer. Sarah drew back her heavy bedroom curtains and looked in amazement at the rain which poured down steadily and silently, creating shallow lakes on the gravelled area in front of the house.

'Just like Hannah's wedding day,' she said, smiling to herself as she began to wash and dress. She wondered why it was that some memories returned so frequently while others disappeared so completely. She always thought of Hannah's wedding day when the rain poured down like this. Her mind moved back beyond that day itself to the previous summer, the summer when Lady Anne had invited Rose to stay after her dreadful illness earlier in the year.

'How long ago was that?'

She counted on her fingers. Hannah was married in 1897, the year after she'd met Teddy, so the visit to Ashleigh was '96. Seventeen years ago, more than half her lifetime. Then, she'd been a girl of thirteen: now, she was a woman of thirty, a mother herself, and a widow.

Weather, objects, places, colours. Since Hugh died she'd become so aware of the strange and varied things that had the power to release a stream of memories. Trivial things, like a pile of disordered papers, the sound of a motor on the hill, or swans flying in to land on the lake at Millbrook. After he died, she hadn't known whether to let the memories come or to try to protect herself from them. She thought about putting away his pens and paperweights so she wouldn't think of him every time she began work, but in the end she decided to leave them exactly where they were. Hugh was not to be hidden away. He'd been part of her life since she was six years old. She could never imagine a time when he would not be there in her mind.

Unlike Hannah's wedding day, when the old

gardener had correctly predicted it would clear before noon, the rain continued all morning. It was still drizzling when the family coach arrived from Ashleigh to add its capacity to the vehicles at Cleeve and it persisted all through the drive, strengthening to a heavy downpour as they arrived at Ashleigh itself.

'Oh my poor little ones, what a day. Run. Run quickly up the steps. Grandpa is there waiting for you and Mrs Partridge has a lovely tea for you.'

Sarah followed the children to the door of the coach as they greeted Grandma Anne, their voices high with excitement. They splashed down into the puddles and ran cheerfully through them towards the house. A warm, dry hand steadied her as she herself stepped down to the sodden gravel and embraced Anne, who was wearing what looked like a coachman's cape and a large pair of Wellington boots.

'Sarah dear, I'm *so* glad to see you here again. Do go on up with Simon while I go and say hello to Hannah and Teddy.'

It was only then Sarah discovered that the large umbrella moving overhead, attempting to shelter both Lady Anne and herself from the worst of the rain, was being held by a tall, dark-haired figure who peered down at them both with a slight, diffident smile.

As Anne shot away through the puddles, he nodded to her, offered his arm and marched her smartly through the confusion of grooms and house staff, who were collecting luggage all around them.

He said not a word till they reached the shelter of the portico at the top of the steps.

'Rather poor weather for photography, I fear,' he said soberly.

Sarah laughed heartily.

'I *do* remember you now,' she said happily. 'They've teased me unmercifully, because I thought I couldn't. But I don't remember you being taller than I was,' she added, looking up at him, a puzzled look on her face.

'That is quite simple to explain,' he said, pausing to shake the umbrella thoroughly before stepping into the carpeted entrance hall with her. 'I spent a great deal of time at your feet. I assure you, you looked through your lens much more often than you looked down at the humble servant who was steadying the tripod,' he said, his dark eyes now shining with merriment as he made her a deep bow.

'Oh dear, was I so dreadfully rude?' she asked easily, amused and delighted by his manner.

'Good heavens, no,' he retorted vigorously. 'Simply devoted to the matter in hand, with commendable application. As I should be at this moment,' he added hastily, excusing himself and hurrying back outside into the rain.

'Sarah, my dear.'

At the sound of a familiar voice, Sarah turned and found herself looking at Harrington. Her smile faded and she felt her heart sink as she observed a man much changed from the one who had greeted her four years ago. His face deeply lined, his shoulders drooped, his gait a little unsteady, nevertheless he embraced her warmly and led her through to the downstairs sitting room where she'd once photographed her mother and Lady Anne sitting side by side on the window seat.

'I think you've brought some real Irish weather with you,' he said cheerfully, as he reached for the bell rope by the side of the blazing log fire. 'This reminds me of Sligo,' he announced, as his wife reappeared, trickles of rain dripping from her cape, arm in arm with Teddy and Hannah.

'Yes, but in Sligo it could go on for days,' Lady Anne threw back at him, laughing. 'I'll only be a few minutes,' she said, nodding to the housekeeper and housemaids, who had just appeared bearing wide silver trays laden with china, scones and cake. 'Please *do* pour, Mrs Partridge, but even I cannot have tea in Wellington boots,' she said, blowing a kiss to her guests as she hurried out.

Sarah watched her stride across the pretty sitting room, bowls of summer flowers glowing on the well-polished furniture, a small, incongruous shape enveloped in a sodden cape who moved so quickly she nearly collided with a dark figure coming into the room.

'Sorry, Simon, didn't see you,' she said breathlessly. 'Thank you for rescuing Mademoiselle. Now do go and have tea. And get Teddy to introduce you properly to Sarah. It appears he neglected his duty most dreadfully when last you met. But then we must forgive him, mustn't we? Bridegrooms are *so* unreliable.'

Smiling broadly, Sarah turned to look at Teddy who had caught his mother's departing remark. To her surprise, she found he was watching her carefully. Immediately he caught her glance he grinned, came over and took her by the hand.

'Sarah, my dear,' he began with a bow, 'I should like to introduce to you my closest and oldest friend, Simon Hadleigh,' he said firmly, as if determined there should be no failure of manners this time. 'Simon, I apologise for my former neglect,' he went on in the same sober tone. 'This is my dear sister-in-law, Sarah Sinton.'

For the second time that afternoon, Sarah felt her cold hand gripped firmly, but gently, in a warm, dry one.

'How do you do. I've heard so much about you.'

They both spoke at the same time, their voices so perfectly in harmony that Harrington and Teddy laughed heartily.

'Well, I hope I've done it properly this time,' Teddy said, looking across at Hannah. 'You've no idea how I've been scolded, Sarah, for my perceived neglect.'

'My poor Teddy,' Sarah said, her tone heavy with irony. 'We all know what a difficult time you have with my sister, but it's all my fault really,' she added cheerfully. 'If Simon will forgive *me*, I think I can manage to forgive *you* and then we can all have tea,' she added, laughing happily, as Lady Anne came back into the room, still looking somewhat dishevelled, but wearing a most elegant tea gown.

Twelve

'Yes, he *is* delightful company and I do like him very much,' Sarah replied in answer to her sister's question. 'But there's something I want to ask *you*.'

'Yes, I thought you might,' Hannah said, smiling, as she sat back in the window seat of Sarah's small upstairs sitting room three days after their arrival at Ashleigh Park. 'I'll answer what I can,' she replied, nodding, 'but there are things about Simon I have always found puzzling,' she admitted, her face muscles tensing slightly.

'Well, that makes two of us, sister dear,' Sarah began lightly. 'Last week, when you heard that Simon was going to join us at Ashleigh, you warned me not to ask him about his work,' she said matter-of-factly. 'You also said he was *very* reticent, so reticent that occasionally he might seem quite rude, but *I* haven't noticed any reticence. Just the reverse, in fact. He told us those wonderful stories about being a very junior secretary in Paris and having no idea about the liaisons going on around him. And then he told us about the move to Petersburg and the problems he had with the Countess Fedyanova,' she ended, raising her eyebrows and bursting out laughing.

Hannah nodded and laughed too.

'Yes, I see your point, Sarah,' she said, still smiling.

Simon's account of his attempts to divert the advances of an elderly Russian lady had kept them entertained the previous evening over a very pleasant dinner. And although he had made them laugh, he had also made no secret of the seriousness of the situation, for the Count was an important person with whom Simon had just managed to develop a promising professional relationship.

'You do *always* notice things, don't you?' Hannah declared, with a little half smile. 'Anyone else would have been so enjoying themselves, they'd have forgotten what I said, or thought I was just misunderstanding the man or being silly about him. That bit of you hasn't changed,' she ended thoughtfully as she glanced out at the gardens where the flowers in the formal beds had recovered from their drenching and now raised hundreds of bright faces to the morning sun.

Sarah waited patiently as her sister stood up, leaned out of the window and waved to the small troupe of children dispersing across the sunlit lawns. Judging by the pieces of paper they were clutching, it looked as if they might be engaged in another of Mademoiselle's totally absorbing treasure hunts.

'Simon's given Teddy and me a bit of a surprise these last few days,' Hannah went on, turning back towards the room, the sunlight catching her still fair hair. 'I'll have to go back a bit to explain properly.'

'Right,' said Sarah, nodding vigorously as she settled herself to listen.

'Well, you probably know that Teddy's actually a year older than Simon, even though they were contemporaries at Cambridge,' she began. 'Simon's very bright, so he went up early, but he *was* dreadfully shy. Even worse than Teddy was, if you can imagine that,' she added ruefully. 'But he and Teddy took to each other immediately, just like you and Lady Anne when you first met. Having the same problem brought them very close. Then Teddy met me.'

Sarah nodded encouragingly.

'Soon after we were married, Simon came to stay. It was a very happy visit. He seemed perfectly at ease with me as long as Teddy wasn't too far away,' she went on. 'But I did notice that when Marianne came to join us, he couldn't cope at all.'

Hannah opened her hands in a despairing gesture. Teddy's sister was a dear friend to them both and it would be hard to imagine a young woman less threatening to a shy man, for Marianne had all of her mother's good nature and just as little regard for formality. Besides, she was full of fun and quite incapable of being unkind to anyone who didn't deserve it.

'Just before Simon was due to leave,' Hannah said, looking very directly at Sarah, 'he had a letter from the Foreign Office offering him a post in Vienna. Teddy was absolutely delighted. He knew Simon's languages were good, but he still thought it was a remarkable offer for one so young. He urged Simon to take it.'

'And did he?'

'Yes, he did. And he made a great beginning.'

Hannah paused, a strange bleakness coming into her expression.

'Oh dear, what went wrong?'

'Nothing at all, professionally. That's what makes it so sad. Almost as soon as he arrived in Vienna, he met a young woman and fell madly in love with her. They were married within weeks. About six months later, Simon was sent on an assignment to Berlin. He had to be away for several weeks. When he got back, he found his wife had died in childbirth. She'd already been buried in the English cemetery with her baby.'

'Oh Hannah, how awful!' Sarah gasped, her hand flying to her mouth. 'What a dreadful thing to happen. Poor man,' she said, tears springing to her eyes.

Hannah bit her lip and took a deep breath.

'There was worse to come, Sarah,' she warned, her voice darkening. 'The Ambassador had tried to keep it quiet, but it appeared the child was not Simon's. His wife was from a well-known Viennese family, but she'd had an affair just before he arrived. It was quite widely known that Simon had made a convenient father,' she said flatly. 'There was no hope of keeping it quiet.'

Sarah said nothing, perfectly aware of what such a scandal would mean in the small British community of a European capital.

'Another man might have coped better than Simon, but it drove him to the edge of breakdown,' Hannah went on. 'His ambassador sent him to Berlin, to get him away from the gossip, but he didn't let us know what had happened or where he was. When he didn't come home on leave, poor Teddy couldn't imagine what was wrong. We actually began to think he didn't want to see us again. Eventually, after two years, we had a letter from Paris. He did apologise for not writing and when he came to stay, he told us something of what had happened. The sad thing was, he was no longer the Simon we had known.'

'Oh, Hannah, how awful for you,' said Sarah quickly. 'And I expect Teddy managed to feel responsible for encouraging him to take the job in the first place,' she went on more thoughtfully, as Hannah sat silent, her eyes downcast, as if she couldn't bear to say any more.

'Of all the problems I've had with my dear Teddy, that one was the worst,' Hannah went on, collecting herself. 'He blamed himself for encouraging Simon to go to Vienna when he was so awkward with people he didn't know. If Simon had stayed in London, Teddy would have been able to keep in touch. What really upset him, though, was that he didn't even know where Simon was, just when he needed a friend most.'

'But surely Simon *could* have contacted him if he'd wanted to,' Sarah replied. 'There was no breach between them, was there? Teddy *would* have helped him.'

'Of course he would,' said Hannah, nodding. 'As I pointed out many times,' she went on wearily, 'for those two years, Simon needed to do whatever he did by himself. His confidence had been shattered. He had to put himself together again.'

'He seems to have done a good job of it,' Sarah said quietly.

'Yes, indeed. He does seem to have,' Hannah

responded, smiling broadly, 'but I can promise you he wasn't like this when he came last year. I can honestly say I've never seen Simon as happy as he's been these last few days.'

'Yes, he tells a good story,' Sarah replied, glancing away from her. 'But there's more to him than an amusing man with charming manners. He listens very carefully and his eyes never stop moving . . .' She broke off, puzzled by the expression on her sister's face.

'It's *so* lovely to have you here, Sarah,' said Hannah unexpectedly. 'I do love Teddy so dearly, and the children are a joy, but sometimes I so wish you and I could have tea together and solve all our problems like we used to do.'

'With damson jam?'

Hannah nodded and said nothing.

'What made you think of that just now, Hannah?'

'I was thinking of what Teddy confessed last night. He says he's never seen Simon so relaxed or so forthcoming in all the time he's known him.'

She paused and looked out the window.

'He thinks it's because of you.'

'*Me?*'

'Yes, you, my sister dear,' she said more firmly. 'And I have to say that Simon has brought my sister back to me as well. You're a different person from the good, brave woman who arrived at Cleeve Station three and a half weeks ago.'

'Am I?' demanded Sarah, startled.

'Yes. You've remembered how to laugh and you make everyone else laugh too. I haven't felt as happy in months.'

'Oh, Hannah, how are we going to manage without the damson jam?'

'I think we must try to see each other more often,' Hannah replied promptly. 'Perhaps with the children a little older, it will be easier. Teddy never minds me going over to see you, though he says he does mind me going to see anyone else,' she added, laughing.

Sarah nodded thoughtfully. The prospect of seeing Hannah more often was a great comfort, but what Hannah said next both startled and confused her.

'If you came to me in London, it would mean you could see Simon too. I think that would be a good idea, don't you?'

After the memorable rain storm that greeted their arrival at Ashleigh Park, the week that followed was in marked contrast. Soft, dew-laden dawns gave way to fresh mornings and warm afternoons, the build-up of heat from a cloudless sky tempered by the lightest of breezes. Dusk fell slowly, full of the perfume of flowers that bloomed all the more generously after their unexpected soaking. The late evening was especially lovely, the sky velvet-dark, pricked with myriads of bright stars, until the moon rose and dimmed them with the radiance of its silvery light.

Sitting late at night by her open window, the moonlight flooding down on the gardens beyond, Sarah thought again about what Hannah had said that morning. Much had remained unspoken between them, but some things were clear: that

Hannah missed her, as much as she missed Hannah, and that she thought Sarah should continue her friendship with Simon.

For a time, Sarah cast her mind back to her life at Rathdrum, her parents and Alex and the work that bound them all to the four Sinton mills. She saw the large figure of her brother Sam, standing in the doorway of Ballydown, Martha and Uncle Joe in the kitchen of Liskeyborough, the shouts of barefoot children playing in the orchard. She looked out at the moonlit garden and pushed her sad and troubled thoughts firmly from her mind.

'So few days left,' she said to herself as she recalled the pleasures that had followed her quiet morning with Hannah.

'And what exactly do you do at the mills, Sarah?'

She could hear Simon's voice as they walked in the rose garden after lunch with Teddy and Hannah.

'Hannah's told me how hard you work,' he went on, 'but I've failed to get her to explain exactly what you do.'

'Sometimes I wonder myself,' she replied, her tone flatter than she'd intended.

To her surprise, Simon laughed.

'That's something else we appear to have in common,' he said easily. 'The harder I work, the less outcome there appears to be. Perhaps you suffer that as well?'

'I've been told I mustn't ask about your work,' she replied, smiling.

'Who told you that?'

'Hannah and Teddy, of course. Who else?'

'Well I expect they mean to be kind,' he said thoughtfully. 'So much of what I do is so boring.'

Sarah laughed heartily.

'Goodness, I thought it was because it was a matter of national security. Or that you'd think I was a spy.'

'A spy,' he repeated, delightedly. 'Most of the spies I know are fat old gentlemen with gout. Now one like you might be a *real* threat. I'd be tempted to tell her all about my elegant, luxurious and terribly tedious life.'

'Do you know many spies?' she asked, wondering if he was teasing her again.

'Oh yes, occupational hazard of the job,' he said, peering cautiously behind a rosebush.

'Oh, Simon, I don't know when I last laughed so much,' she said, as he straightened up again. 'Are you always so funny, or is it the sunshine after a good lunch and it being the holidays?'

'Mmmm . . . interesting question. I must give it my proper consideration. Meantime, would you mind if we sat down in the shade? I cannot possibly go back to Petersburg with a peeling nose.'

He led the way to a small terrace where a wooden bench sat in the dense shade of a thickly thatched roof, supported by four sturdy tree trunks. They sat down together and watched Hannah and Teddy pause to inspect the intertwining clematis on a new pergola before moving on, quite unaware of their absence.

'Phew, that's better,' he said, mopping his brow with a large handkerchief. 'There's no breeze yet.

How do you manage to look so cool?' he demanded, looking her up and down.

'Would you like a short briefing on the properties of Irish linen?' she asked wickedly.

'If you do, I shall reply with the figures for the proportion of Russian flax now being imported into these isles,' he came back at her.

They fell silent as they watched the fluttering movement of butterflies on the rich purple blooms of a nearby buddleia and the shimmer of dragonflies over a small pool bordering the path.

'This reminds me of a seat in the garden at the Peterhof,' he began, looking up at the rim of thatch. 'The Czar has a youthful sense of humour. He likes practical jokes. Sitting here with you reminded me.'

'But why is that?'

'Well, you see, the court is full of beautiful young women and courtiers, who are often as bored as I am. A certain amount of . . . shall we say . . . dalliance . . . goes on,' he continued, his eyes sparkling. 'So, imagine the scene. Our two lovers are seated, as we are, their escorts having disappeared, or, more likely, having been given the slip. Can you guess what happens next?'

Sarah shook her head, unwilling to spoil his story.

'The roof of the shelter turns into a fountain. Water pours down from the edge of the thatch completely obscuring our lovers from view,' he said, waving his arms up and down.

'Good news for lovers, perhaps? she asked, raising an eyebrow.

'Sadly, not so,' he replied. 'Because if they attempt to leave they'll get wet. And if they stay, they'll be late for tea. Either ways, they'll be discovered. I think it's a rotten trick myself, but then it's my job to try to understand how people's minds work and the Czar's little tricks tell me quite a lot about him.'

'But how does the fountain work?' she demanded. 'Is the seat counterbalanced?'

'No, nothing so advanced,' he replied laughing. 'A couple of ancient retainers hiding behind the bushes. The machinery is simple. Just pedals they move with their feet. So easy, they can keep it up for hours.'

Sarah shook her head.

'It seems so strange to hear you talk about Petersburg as I might talk about Banbridge or Rathfriland. Is it very beautiful?' she asked, a hint of longing in her voice.

'I find it so,' he said, without a trace of lightness. 'There's something unusual about the quality of light from the northern sky. Have you been to Versailles?' he asked suddenly.

'No, but I've seen Teddy's photographs,' she said, surprised at the quiet intensity of his voice.

'The formal fountains and canals at the Summer Palace are copied from those at Versailles, but they look entirely different in Petersburg. They're much more dramatic, an extravagance of gold statues and cascades and long prospects. Yet somehow it's the light you're aware of, not the manmade things. With the Gulf of Bothnia beyond, there's just so much water and sky. I find it strangely moving,' he ended softly, turning to look at her.

'That's what my father said when he went to Kerry,' Sarah said, smiling. 'He'd never been far from

Armagh and he just couldn't get used to vast prospects of lake and sea. He could never understand how my mother could bear to leave it.'

'And how *did* she bear it?'

'My mother is a wise lady. She says life is about choices. You can't have everything, but you must make sure to appreciate what you *do* have. She'd *had* Kerry and all the good things it brought her, but in Kerry she didn't have my father, any of us children, her house, or her garden. I know she's right. Life changes. You have to accept that things you once loved move away.'

'And other things come in their place, if you are willing to be open to them?' he asked.

She nodded slowly.

'I always thought Ireland was my place and Ballydown my corner, but I'm not so sure about that now,' she said slowly, looking away down the long grass paths bordered by tall, flowering perennials. 'I sometimes feel such a longing to travel and see the things I've only read about or heard other people describe. I sometimes wonder how I could have changed so much.'

'Sometimes we surprise ourselves,' he replied gently. 'There was a time when I thought I would never trust a woman with any thought or any feeling I held dear. I decided that my best course was to teach myself to work in the world of men. In company, to play the jester when required.'

He looked at her directly and she met his gaze just as directly.

'You do it very nicely. It's such a pleasure to laugh

again. But I'd still like to hear about what you do.'

'Then you shall,' he said firmly. 'Providing only that you also laugh for me. I'll need your laughter when I'm back in Petersburg.'

Simon was as good as his word. Whenever there was the least opportunity, on watch as the children boated on the lake, sitting together guarding the prize for the latest treasure hunt, during their walks after lunch and in the evening, Simon told her how he spent his time in the handsome building overlooking the Neva.

She listened, fascinated to hear of the strange and varied ways in which information was conveyed from one European country to another and how the very exchange itself could affect so intimately what might happen as a result.

'Hannah and Teddy are right,' he said, one afternoon when Mademoiselle had requested their presence in a remote corner of the garden. 'I can't tell you what's going on at the moment, Sarah, but I can give you examples of previous situations that will let you see what has to happen if we are to maintain the peace. And I *can* say without giving any secrets away, that Europe is like a kettle on the boil. While the steam pours out it's noisy and uncomfortable, but there's still hope. But if someone, something, turns up the heat, the whole shoot will boil over. Does that make sense?'

'Yes, perfect sense. I think I can apply that image somewhat nearer home,' she said, shaking her head sadly. 'There's no secret about the Ulster Volunteers arming and the Irish Volunteers doing the same. Three quarters of the population want Home Rule and one quarter are so opposed to it they say they'll fight if it goes on the statute book. And what does that achieve? Does waving flags around feed starving families? Does it stop the exploitation of workers?'

She stopped abruptly, aware of the sharpness in her voice and the intentness with which he was looking at her.

'Sometimes one feels so helpless against the enormity of need,' she said more quietly. 'I get angry I can do so little. And I have to admit I get discouraged.'

'But how do you know what you achieve, Sarah? Can any of us judge properly? We only see part of what we do. You can always see failure if your hopes are high, but what's the point of aiming low?'

'Yes, that's true,' she admitted freely. 'But don't you ever get discouraged?'

'Oh yes. That's the hardest part of the job. Day after day nothing happens, then, when it does, it's bad.'

'So what do you do then?'

'Clear up the mess as best one can. Then look for something to set over against it. I go to the ballet. I read Dickens and Chekov or practise my Russian on my housekeeper. And I write letters,' he added, looking at her as if he might say more.

'Here you are. Here you are. I've got them all.'

Two sharp, excited voices broke the stillness of the afternoon as Helen and John arrived, breathless, and put down at their feet the six flowers and six fragments of foliage, named and located on the maps they were both clutching.

'Well done,' said Simon, giving them his total attention. 'Now, Helen first,' he commanded, as he held out his hand for her crumpled piece of paper.

The items laid before them would have to be checked most carefully. Only if they were the right ones and only if they were all there, could either Helen or John lay claim to the treasure.

Sarah was not at all surprised to see Helen's eyes close before she was halfway through the promised story. She glanced up at the top bunk where Hugh had settled himself and was amazed to find he was already fast asleep. To be on the safe side, she read on. It would not be the first time she'd stopped, only to meet a protest from one or other.

Tonight, there was no such protest. She stood up, slipped the book back in her travel bag and glanced through the porthole at the low evening sunlight, which still lay in bright patches on the adjoining deck. She was tired, but too restless to join the children in their bunks at this early hour. She opened the cabin door quietly and came face to face with the stewardess, an older woman she'd got to know on earlier journeys.

Without a single word spoken between them they agreed that Sarah would be on deck just a short walk away. If either child should wake, the stewardess would know exactly where to find her.

After the heat of the day, the slight breeze from the water was refreshing. She walked up and down the deck, grateful to be free of the confinement of the cabin and the airlessness ships always developed just before they sailed. As the last hawsers were cast off, she leaned on the rail and looked down into the churning water.

So slow to begin, this departure business. Inches at first, then feet, opening between them and the dock wall. An infinity of time to accomplish such a tiny distance. She listened to the slow throb of the engines as the ship freed itself from the city where it had spent the day caged, tended by engineers and stewards, waiting for this moment. Now, only now, with the sun low on the far horizon, did it come to life, surging out into the empty spaces of the Irish Sea. And once having freed itself from the confining concrete walls of the dock, there was no delay. The throb of the engines increased and the ripples ran back silently from the sharp bow as the ship turned towards the sunset, cleaving a path through the smooth, shining water.

'I wonder when I'll make this crossing again,' she said to herself, looking round the almost empty deck.

Hannah hoped she might come for Christmas if the weather weren't too hostile. Certainly she thought Sarah should come again next summer when Simon would have leave from Petersburg or might even have returned to London permanently to take up a place at the Foreign Office.

Sarah sighed. One didn't have to be a mind reader to see what Hannah was thinking, but she'd said nothing directly about the affection that had flowered between her and Simon, wise sister that she was, and

Sarah was grateful for that. It was too soon. Still too hard not to think of Hugh. Too easy to feel a kind of conflict between such a long, dear love, and the prospect of what might possibly be.

It had been such a pleasure to have a companion, someone at her side to whom she could talk and express her thoughts. Equally, it had been a relief to reach outwards and share Simon's concerns and in doing so, reach beyond the small and troubled island to which she was returning.

Simon had said nothing either. He didn't need to. All he'd come to feel was there in his eyes. In the way he walked beside her.

'Would you like me to come with you to Liverpool, Sarah?' he asked, as they stepped out after dinner into the gathering dusk. 'I could make myself useful with porters and entertaining the children.'

'That's very kind of you—'

'No, it's not,' he interrupted. 'It's an entirely selfish ploy to avoid parting with you tomorrow morning.'

'It is still a kind offer, Simon,' she said gently. 'But I would find it even harder to say goodbye in Liverpool.'

'Ships and seas always seem to separate more than marshes and steppe, don't you think?' he responded quietly.

He had looked at her directly then, his simple words seemed to imply so much more than they said.

'I don't know,' she replied honestly. 'I've lived my life in such a small compass. I cannot imagine the journey from Harwich to Berlin, or from Berlin to

Moscow, or Moscow to Petersburg. It is such a very long way compared to my brief night journey.'

He fell silent as they walked on through the rose garden to sit where he had once told her about the trick fountains in the Peterhof gardens.

'I shall adopt this fountain as my sitting place when I arrive back,' he said unexpectedly.

'And risk a wetting?' she said, laughing.

'There is no danger at all to a solitary male,' he said soberly, 'only to those who are accompanied.'

Suddenly she heard a tone in his voice she'd never heard before. It seemed as if a cloak of loneliness had wrapped itself around him. He sounded so sad, she wondered if there was anything whatever she could say to comfort him.

'I shall think of you going to the ballet and reading Dickens and Chekov, and practising Russian on your housekeeper, and writing letters,' she said gently.

'Will you really?'

'Yes, I will.'

'And if I were to write and tell you of my unexciting life . . .?' He broke off, uneasy.

'Then I could tell you of my infinitely more unexciting life,' she replied immediately, smiling up at him.

The look of relief and joy that passed over his face erased completely the sadness that had grown upon him. It was only later, sitting by her open window, thinking over the events of the day, that she realised how sad she herself would have been if no link had been made between them to span the time and distance which would separate them from any further meeting.

Thirteen

Bathed in chill sunlight, the little grey Molyneux church was full to overflowing for the funeral of Thomas Scott. He had been poorly since late summer, struggled through the autumn, but still tramped down to the forge on the brightest of the winter mornings. Even if he could no longer hammer a piece of metal, there were small tasks he could still do – the fire to light, old friends to greet – while his son Robert carried on the work.

On a short February day, overcast but not cold, they stopped work with the failing light, raked out the fire on the hearth and pulled closed the door behind them. As he sat smoking by the fire an hour later, Thomas's pipe slid from his fingers. With Selina there to support him before he fell from his chair, his youngest daughter, Isobel, ran to fetch Robert. It was as peaceful a departure as one might hope for. But it left a family and a community bereft.

Rose and Sarah sat close beside each other in the pew behind Selina. Her daughters, Annie and Isobel, sat on each side of her, then came her daughter-in-law, Ellen, sitting beside Selina's youngest son, Ned. The eldest of Thomas's grandchildren filled the remainder of the long pew. Beside Rose and Sarah,

Sam and Alex sat shoulder to shoulder, their pale, immobile faces as unfamiliar as their seldom-worn dark suits.

As they all watched, the coffin was lifted from the trestles in front of the altar and placed on the shoulders of the bearers. At the leading edge, John Hamilton, once Thomas's apprentice, and Robert, his remaining son from his first marriage, clasped each other's shoulders under the heavy oak casket. Behind them, James George, Annie's husband, and William Robinson, the eldest son of George Robinson, Thomas's neighbour for more than fifty years, steadied themselves and then moved slowly over the uneven stone floor leading to the west door.

Sarah glanced at her mother cautiously. She'd sat with her that whole afternoon after the news came, seen her weep inconsolably at first, then listened as she'd spoken of Thomas, moving backwards and forwards over her life in Salter's Grange, telling stories Sarah had heard many times before, laughing and weeping by turns. But now, Rose seemed quite steady as Selina stepped out into the aisle to follow the coffin, concerned to do what was needed at this solemn time and unwilling to allow her own feelings to break through.

Together they walked behind Selina's immediate family, those they knew from the front pew, and two older men who might be brothers, and a woman, most certainly her sister, who'd been seated across the narrow aisle. They passed between the packed rows of the congregation, standing unnaturally still, their dark suits and best dresses brought from the wardrobe on an ordinary working day.

The children from the slate-roofed schoolroom in the corner of the churchyard were lined up with their teacher in the pews at the very back, wide-eyed and silent. There was not one child among them who hadn't stood in the doorway of the forge and looked into the dark, absorbed and fascinated by the two men who laboured there. They'd watched the sparks fly, the water seethe and steam when hot metal was plunged into its oily surface and the horses that twitched and trembled till they felt the comfort of a familiar soot-streaked hand, a known body smell of sweat and smoke. Through every day of their short lives, the ring of hammer on anvil had been as much a part of life as the song of birds, or the movement of sunshine and cloud, or the walk up and down the hill between the schoolroom and their homes.

The low sunlight dazzled everyone as they emerged from the dimness and followed the coffin to the Scott burial plot, the newly dug grave like a narrow trench in the frosted, tangled grass. They waited till all those who wished to see Thomas laid in his last resting place had found somewhere to stand. Some of the younger mourners made their way perilously through the uneven ground between neighbouring graves. Others congregated on the path that ran beside the vault where the Molyneuxs themselves rested in the shelter of the church they'd built on the highest point in the townland, some four generations earlier.

'This,' thought Sarah to herself, as she looked about her, 'is why I cannot turn my back on this island. It is these people, their kindness and generosity, their willingness to help a neighbour.'

But even as the thought formed, she had to admit she had felt no such kindly feeling towards her countrymen for some time now. It was certainly not how she felt when she went to the mills and Tom, or one of the other managers, had to report yet another fight between the men kicking a ball around in the lunch hour. There was the name-calling, the waving of flags, the singing of party songs.

She was sick of it all, but especially of the endless marching columns. Ulster Volunteers and Irish Volunteers, with their belts and bandoliers, backpacks and wooden rifles, tramping across green fields or setting up targets for practise with real rifles.

Thomas would have none of it. Nor would her father. Long ago, they had said no to those who tried to intimidate them and they had both paid for it. Their partnership in the forge had to be ended when the master of the local Lodge gave the word they were to be boycotted and their work fell away. Her father had been forced to take a job in Drumcairn Mill, while Thomas struggled on, on his own, making barely enough to keep going until, once again, a Home Rule bill failed. Then, confident the world would always remain the way they wanted it, the drilling faded away. No, she thought bitterly, no one would ever change in the slightest minds that were so firmly made up.

Sarah looked across at Selina as she stood by the graveside, a tall, thin woman, her face lined. Sad, but not bitter. She had said often enough to Rose that what she and Thomas had shared all these years was an unexpected gift. She had not hoped for happiness again after her first husband died. Married to Mary-Anne, Thomas had given up all prospect of joy. But life had been kind. They had found each other.

Like everyone they knew, they'd suffered loss. Little Sophie, bitten by a rabid dog. Thomas's elder son gone to Canada, a few brief letters, then silence. Selina's beloved younger sister. But they had found such joy in each other and in their other two children, Isobel and Ned, in Annie's family and more recently in Robert and Ellen's.

Sarah felt her shoulders tighten as the chill of the fading afternoon began to eat into her. Aware of a small movement at her side, she glanced up at Alex and saw a strange, pained look on his face. As the rector began the committal, she saw him stand even straighter, as rigidly to attention as if he were on parade.

She'd been surprised when he'd asked for time off to come to the funeral and even more surprised when he asked if he might drive her motor and go via Liskeyborough to collect Sam.

'I didn't know you'd even met Thomas,' she said when he appeared in her dining room the morning after the news had come.

'Only once,' he said, his eyes sparkling with sudden moisture.

She waited, her pen still poised over the papers she'd been working on when she'd heard his gentle tap at the door.

'When I first arrived in Annacramp, Ned Wylie took me up to Thomas to see if he could give me a job,' he began. 'He couldn't give me a job, but he did what you did,' he blurted out unexpectedly. 'He accepted me. He looked at me and would've taken me in, even if I'd had no name at all,' he went on, his voice unsteady. 'As it was, he sent me to your Da. I wish there were more like Thomas and your Da,' he said, his eyes now glittering with tears.

She stood up and put a hand on his arm.

'Have you time for a cup of tea, or is Da expecting you back down at Ballievy?' she asked quietly.

'No, we'd finished there,' he said, collecting himself. 'He said to come up and see what you'd like to do on Friday. Go with them and let me collect Sam or come with me to pick him up. Whatever *you* want.'

They'd gone into the sitting room, where the morning fire was just beginning to blaze up. She sat down opposite him, studying the familiar face, the unknown young man who had walked into their lives and now was so much a part of the family and her own trusted friend. How long was it now since they'd made their pact?

'Alex, have you ever regretted leaving Canada?'

'No, not for one moment,' he replied firmly.

'But aren't there things you miss? People you were fond of or places you liked?'

'Yes, of course,' he said cheerfully, as Mrs Beatty elbowed the half-open door and put a tray of tea on a low table between them.

He waited till Sarah thanked the older woman and she'd closed the door firmly behind her.

'The things I miss most are all things that gave me heart,' he began, 'like the great countryside and the colours in autumn and walking out on a summer evening. There were working people like myself I used to talk to and we put the world to rights, as the saying is here, but nothing in Canada ever seemed to be my own. I was only a worker, a piece of human machinery. I'd been imported like a bale of linen. I was useful, but of no relevance to anyone,' he said calmly, without a hint of bitterness.

'But if you'd stayed, Alex,' she began, 'if you'd married and raised a family . . .' She broke off, suddenly wondering why Alex hadn't found a girlfriend among the spinners and doffers or the various young relatives of the Jackson's and their niece, Emily.

Alex laughed, so easily reading her thoughts.

'I have my eye on someone, Sarah,' he said slowly, 'but I'm in no hurry. I'll wait till you say yes to *your* man.'

'And what if I don't?' she came back at him, without considering very closely what she was revealing.

'You'd be a fool if you didn't,' he said promptly. 'You were a different woman when you came back from Ashleigh Park. Before you'd even come down the gangplank, I looked up at you and thought *that's it, that's why that letter to Rose was so different. She's met someone.*'

Sarah smiled ruefully. She'd said very little about Simon Hadleigh to anyone, even her mother, but she had not made it a secret either. Besides, the regular arrival of his letters with their exotic stamps, so prized by her son, was not something she could easily conceal, even if she'd wanted to.

She suspected that Alex had guessed months ago, when she'd made a plan to go and visit Hannah at Christmas, but this was the first time he'd spoken about it directly. Yet once again, Alex had sensed what she was thinking before she'd even recognised it for herself.

A handful of small stones fell into the open grave, rattling on the shiny surface of the lowered coffin. She came back abruptly to the present, bowing her head as the rector prayed, the light breeze now flapping the wide sleeves of his vestments.

The mound of earth piled neatly beside the long, raw trench diminished rapidly as two men with gleaming spades refilled the grave, their sleeves rolled up as if it were a summer day. Flowers were spread across the disturbed earth and the tramped grass as the rector walked away and one by one the watchers moved forward to shake Selina by the hand and say the familiar words of comfort.

'I'm sorry for your trouble.'

Sarah heard the phrase a dozen times before she was blinded by tears, the memory of her own loss suddenly as fresh as it had been that warm August day in the small Quaker burial ground at Moyallen.

She was grateful for the warmth of the house by the forge. In the big kitchen the doors of the stove stood wide open. In the sitting room beyond, tall flames rose from a log fire and reflected in the small panes of a corner cupboard where Selina kept her best china and in the heavily framed portraits of

American relatives. In both rooms, extra chairs were set against the walls and a laden table in the kitchen carried refreshments for those, like the Hamiltons, who had come a distance.

'Ach, d'ye mind the time . . .'

'George, how are ye? Shure I haven't laid eyes on you in years. What way are ye, man?'

'Ach, she's rightly considerin'. She always said she'd niver want to see m'father sittin' in a chair.'

Sarah listened to the voices around her, touched her warm teacup to her ice-cold cheeks and then drank slowly, grateful for the conversations that meant she didn't have to make an effort herself. Her mother was talking to Selina, their heads close together. Sam was shaking hands with Robert's wife, Ellen, an awkward-looking girl whose eyes never settled on the person she was speaking to. She said, 'Pleased to meet you,' then went on to complain about the cold and how long the rector had kept them standing at the graveside.

'Have a drop of this, Sarah, it'll warm you up. You're lookin' desperit pale.'

Sarah smiled up at her father. She'd never much liked whiskey but she wouldn't say no when he was doing his best to do his part, weaving his way through the crowded rooms, a bottle of Bushmills in his hand.

'Your Ma just told me you used to live opposite the forge,' Alex said, squeezing past Sam and Ellen Scott to come and stand beside her.

'Didn't you know that?'

'No,' he said, shaking his head.

Sarah looked at him in surprise. He seemed both agitated and anxious, as if this piece of information was of the greatest importance.

'Come and I'll show you,' she said suddenly, finishing her whiskey. 'It'll only take a moment.'

She turned to Sam, spoke a word to him and slipped out of the crowded kitchen into the fading afternoon, Alex close behind her.

'This way,' she said, as he paused at the front door, looking down the path to the forge and the lane running on down to the main road.

With the shadows gathering, the long-abandoned house over to their left looked like an overgrown wall, weighed down with ivy and screened by flourishing bushes. As she walked towards it, Sarah saw the thatch had finally fallen in at the far end. The roof of the main room sagged perilously but had not yet given way. She picked up her skirts, strode up to the door, turned the handle and stepped inside.

After the warmth and bright lamplight in the house, the air struck chill, but the smell of damp was offset by the fragrance of a stack of fresh logs piled against the door to the bedroom. She made her way across a pile of iron bars and between a few pieces of old furniture until she stood in front of the empty hearth.

'Da made this crane,' she said shortly, leaning forward and drawing the metal arm out from its place. The chain dangling, it swung over the blackened hearth with a muted creak.

Alex's face was in shadow. He nodded and said nothing, but she could see he was watching her closely.

As she stood there, all she could think of was the summer's day when she and Sam had ridden over from Richhill Station to visit Thomas. Brilliant light glanced from the rich foliage of high summer and the air was heavy with heat. They'd stood in the sunshine talking to him, and then she'd taken pictures of him and Robert together, working at the bench at the back of the forge where the dim light from the two dusty windows was just enough for an exposure.

Afterwards, they'd come to look at their old home. Sam had cut a spray of roses for her from a bush grown wild in the garden and she'd found the calendar for 1889 still hanging in the washhouse, the last days of their life there, some ten years previously, stroked off one by one in pencil. July 1889. The year of the disaster in which they had *not* perished.

'Has Ma told you about the Rail Disaster?' she asked suddenly

'Yes.'

'And the time Thomas nearly died?'

'Oh, yes,' he replied, as if it were the most obvious thing that Rose should tell him all the family history.

'But we were living here then. Didn't she say?'

Sarah couldn't imagine how either tale could have been told without mentioning the two-roomed house they'd had to move to when their landlord found the means to serve notice and give their house at Annacramp to his son.

'Maybe she did, Sarah, but I didn't make the connection. I thought you'd always lived at Annacramp, in that house Ned Wylie showed me.'

'But why does it matter, Alex?' she asked gently.

'Because it's part of *your* life, Sarah,' he answered firmly. 'We made a promise to help each other two years ago. Don't you remember? If I don't know about your past, I won't be able to understand why you're the person you are. I'll not be able to help you the way I want to.'

'Yes, of course, I remember. But I'm not sure I've done very much to help you,' she said sadly.

'Oh yes, you have,' he came back immediately. 'You took my word. You've shared your family with me. You've kept my secret.'

Sarah shivered and pushed the crane back into its place. It seemed such a strange thing that it had remained here, exactly where it had always been for the last fifteen years. The whole world had changed for her and for everyone else and yet the crane on which her mother had cooked over the open fire was just as Sam had left it when he pushed it back into its place that glorious summer day.

'We ought to go back, Alex. Back to the present,' she said ruefully, knowing now quite clearly that there was something in her present she could not bear.

'You've been good to me over my past, Sarah. I'll do my best to be good to you over your future,' he said firmly. 'I think I can see it clearer now after today.'

He held open the door for her and she walked past him out into the dusk. There were times when she couldn't understand Alex at all, but she had never had any cause to doubt his kindness, his goodwill, or his strange wisdom. He most certainly had kept his side of their pact.

'Are you foundered with cold?' John asked, as he and Rose pushed open the door and stepped into their dark, chilly kitchen.

'No, I'm not *that* cold, love. You had me well wrapped up in those rugs,' she replied, dropping her hat on to the nearest chair. 'But I'm cold at heart and so are you,' she said, looking up at him in the patch of pale moonlight that filtered through the front window. 'We'll light the lamps and make up a good fire,' she went on, putting a match to a single candle sitting ready on the windowsill.

She waited for the flame to steady, then carried it over to the stove so she could see to light the gas lamps.

'Are you hungry?'

'No. I can't say I am,' he replied honestly. 'Ach, shure I've no heart for food. But a mug of tea would go down well.'

'Come on then,' she said, encouragingly. 'You light the paraffin stove and I'll get the fire going. I've plenty of good kindling all ready here in the box and a bit of turf to hurry it up. We'll have a blaze in no time,' she went on, rubbing her cold hands together. 'Keep your coat on for a while till we get some heat. I think we'll have another frost tonight.'

'Aye. The sky was very clear coming back,' he said wearily, making an effort to sound less dispirited than he felt. 'But there's a good stretch on the evenings now.'

Rose knelt in front of the stove, piled in two large handfuls of bone-dry twigs and arranged slivers of turf around them before choosing small pieces of coal to go on top. The moment she set a match to the twigs they crackled into flame, the small, familiar noise bringing comfort. Moments later the turf smoked and glowed, filling the room with a perfume that lifted her heart. In all the worst moments of her life, she had tended the fire on the hearth for the sake of John and the children coming in from work, from school, from rain and cold.

She drew in the pungent aroma that took her back to her earliest years and remembered her mother bent over the hearth in the thatched house up in the Derryveagh Mountains. The flames flickered more vigorously. She added larger pieces of turf and more coal. Satisfied it was well alight, she got awkwardly to her feet, her back sore from standing, her body stiff with the cold and the tensions of the day.

'Away and change your clothes, John,' she said quietly, as he came back into the kitchen carrying a can of paraffin in case the oil stove might need refilling later. 'Maybe you'd bring me down that nice wool shawl you gave me at Christmas. It's in my top drawer.'

She saw the bleak look on his face soften slightly as he turned towards the stairs. It was even colder in the dairy as she filled the kettle to boil it on the gas, so she put the whistle on its spout and shut the door quickly behind her.

'That's more like it,' she said a little later, when John reappeared, his black suit replaced by corduroys, a Fair Isle pullover she'd knitted for him years ago and an old tweed jacket.

She slipped off her best cape, wrapped the shawl round her and poured from the waiting teapot.

'Ye were right about the fire,' he said, looking into the dancing flames as he sat down. 'It would put heart in ye.'

'Are you very upset about Thomas?' she began cautiously, as she sipped her tea, the warmth of the fire already thawing out her feet.

'Ach, I am in one way, but not in another,' he said slowly. 'Sure we all come to it. He was a good age and didn't suffer much. I'm more upset about Sarah,' he said abruptly.

'Sarah?' she repeated, completely taken aback.

'Aye. Shure, the wee pale face of her by that graveside. You maybe diden see her, for you were standin' beside her, but I was across from ye's after we put the coffin down. I could see her plain. Ach, I'm sure she was sorry about Thomas, but it was beyond that. She looked as if all belongin' to her was dead, as the sayin' is.'

Rose shook her head and thought back through the afternoon.

'You're right about me not seeing her,' she admitted. 'I thought she was steady enough and I had my eye on Selina.'

'Rightly too,' he said, nodding. 'But even when we got back to the house, her face was like one o' those marble sculptures in the church. I gave her a drop o' whiskey an' she took it, for all she doesn't like it,' he said sharply.

'It's only two and a half years since Hugh,' Rose reminded him. 'I thought she was much better after her holiday last year,' she added thoughtfully. 'She talked about going over to London at Christmas and seemed very keen, but then there was nothing more said about it.'

'D'ye think there's anythin' between her an' Alex?'

'Alex?' Rose repeated, amazed that John should even have thought of such a possibility.

'Aye. He was watching her all the time,' he said, nodding his head emphatically. 'Every time I looked over at her, I saw him looking too. And then they went outside together. An' she seemed more like herself when they came back.'

Rose smiled and refilled their mugs.

'Alex *is* fond of Sarah, you're quite right. And she's fond of him too, I know. But it's no more than that,' she said gently. 'If there is a man in question, I think it would be that friend of Teddy's that carried her camera at their wedding. The one she couldn't even remember. Simon Hadleigh. I told you he was there at Ashleigh in the summer and Hannah and Anne have said how well they got on together.'

'Would that be it, then?' John came back at her. 'Is she not settled in her mind what she should do? Sure Hugh would only want to see her happy, if this man was right for her. What do Hannah and Lady Anne think of him?'

'It's hardly as simply as that, love. I think they'd be very happy to see Sarah and Simon together, but Sarah's maybe thinking of the children. And maybe, indeed, of us. Simon Hadleigh is a diplomat. Anne says he's a very able man and will go far, but he's in Russia at the moment. He told her he was due to come back to London soon, but with the way things are going in Europe he may not get back.'

'What d'ye mean?' asked John, alarmed.

'Well, with all this talk of war, he might be needed where he is. I don't think you can choose where you go unless you're *very* senior,' she said soberly. 'Or perhaps very junior,' she added as an afterthought.

'Aye, well,' he said, finishing his tea and stretching out his legs in front of the roaring fire. 'It's hard to know what to do for the best. I'd be a happy man if she found someone even half as good as Hugh, God rest him,' he said with a great sigh.

'Even if she went to live in England like Hannah, or had to live somewhere far off in Europe?' she asked, a note of caution in her voice.

'Even so,' he said, nodding firmly. 'She's a grown woman, Rose, an' you and I are gettin' on now. You're sixty and I'm sixty-two. I hope we've a few more years yet, but we'll not always be here. I'd like to see Sarah look powerful different to the way she looked today.'

Fourteen

As in the rhyme Granny Sarah had taught all her grandchildren, the March of 1914 came in like a lion and went out like a lamb. After the cold of February and the rattle and bang of the wind, day after day, all through the early weeks of March, the change came with a suddenness that took everyone by surprise. A morning dawned in perfect stillness, the sun poured down from a clear sky and both plants and creatures responded to the real warmth in its rays.

Late in the morning, Rose finished the letters she'd had in mind for a week or more and came to the door to stand bathed in the sunlight. She cast her eyes along the garden path and smiled to herself. The daffodils, which only yesterday had pointed thickened spikes up at the stormy sky, now bent their heads and were beginning to unfurl even as she watched. All around her the birds were active. Sweet songs poured down from the trees and bushes, swooping flights descended upon the last of the crumbs put out at breakfast time, while others scuffled in the dried grass against the far wall of the garden as they struggled to pull out building material for their nests.

'Between one day and the next,' she said to herself.

She was amazed how easy it was to forget that change isn't always slow. Today, everything was different, but then, she reflected, some changes are long prepared. However wild and stormy the last weeks, they had not been particularly cold. The daffodils had continued to grow quietly and unobtrusively but it needed the warmth for them to bloom.

She tramped down the path to inspect the fat pink buds of her camellia. No sign at all of frost damage. She was so absorbed in her search for new growth she didn't hear the light step on the hill. Only when the garden gate clicked behind her did she turn to find her brother grinning at her, the sunlight glinting from his hair, thinning now, but still perceptibly red.

'Sam!' she cried, in delight. 'I wasn't expecting you for two days.'

'Hallo, Sissy,' he said, hugging her. 'I got my dates wrong. I said I'd be in Dublin for Lily's birthday. Then I thought you might *not* be pleased if I only stayed two nights.'

'You are *quite* right,' she said, trying to look severe. 'Where's your suitcase?'

'Left it at the station,' he said easily. 'Thought I'd ask Sarah to run me down later to collect it. I want to warn her about the vagaries of Dawson Street, among other things.'

'Tell me more about this visit,' she said, as they went indoors and settled themselves comfortably. 'I *was* surprised when Lily invited her *and* the children for Easter, but Sarah seems very pleased and Helen and Hugh are full of it. Apparently Lily mentioned the zoo *and* the seaside *and* Fairyhouse Races in her letter. D'you think she really means it?'

Sam laughed and shook his head as Rose offered to draw the kettle forward and make him tea.

'Oh yes, she means it all right,' he said, nodding vigorously. 'She doesn't have the best of health, but when she's well there's no stopping her. She loves being out and about. Just put a sketchbook and a sandwich in a bag and she's happy. I've never met such an extraordinary woman. Can talk to *anyone*. Not just people of her own class.'

'I'm still wondering why she never married, Sam,' said Rose thoughtfully, her mind moving back to the days at Currane Lodge when the lovely young Lady Lily had been surrounded by admirers. 'Do you think she was secretly in love with *you* all along?' she asked, teasing him.

'No, I'm afraid it was something much sadder,' he replied, his smile disappearing. 'Almost the first time we met in Dublin she told me quite openly that her mother was the reason she'd never married. From the time Lily could wear a dress, her mother talked to her about one thing only. Marriage and children. *Always* marriage and children. Who she should marry, where she should live, how many children she'd have. Poor Lily couldn't bear it. By the time she was fourteen she'd vowed she'd never marry at all. Isn't that a dreadful thing to happen to any girl?'

'Yes, it is,' she agreed promptly. 'It's a hard thing if a woman chooses badly, but even that might've been better than all those years looking after her father. She must have been lonely then,' Rose went on, suddenly thinking of the large, silent rooms and the echoing corridors she'd known at Currane when all the family were away.

'Oh yes,' he said, nodding matter-of-factly.

'But not now?'

'No. Lily being lonely was resolved long before I turned up. When I first asked her to dine at the Shelbourne, I'm afraid it was only from sheer selfish curiosity,' he said, smiling wryly. 'But she didn't seem to notice. She was so pleased to see me and wanted to know all about what I was doing. Unlike me, she has the gift of accepting people just as they are,' he said, looking his sister full in the face.

As the morning sun moved across the sky Sam went on to tell Rose how Lily's life had been transformed when she came to Dublin, how she'd kept open house and made many friends, in particular young men who were struggling as artists, or poets, or actors.

Rose listened, fascinated. Sam had never before spoken so freely or with such affection for this woman she herself had met only twice since she'd left Currane Lodge.

'Did you know that Lily went to the Slade?' he asked unexpectedly.

'Goodness no, I didn't,' Rose replied hastily.

She'd been listening to all he said, but a part of her mind kept moving away, back to the young Lady Anne. She thought of her violent tantrums and rages and the way she'd say, 'We don't need men, do we,

Rose? We'll go off to London and the continent and let my sisters have the babies.' She heard again the edge of anxiety in the words and saw the look of determination on her face.

So it was Lady Caroline, the delicate invalid, who had pushed Anne, as well as Lily, to the edge of despair. She could hardly bear to think what might have happened to her dear friend if she'd had no one to help her correct her violent reaction to her mother's continual pressure.

'When would that have been, Sam?' she asked, making an effort to reconnect with what he was telling her.

'Some time after I joined the Land League and you'd moved north. I'd no contact with Currane for years then. Not till Ma died and Sir Capel sent for me. She says when she went with her portfolio, they didn't think much of it and advised her against coming, but she'd had a legacy from her godmother, so she could pay the fees. Now, of course, she's rather good,' he said, in a satisfied tone that suggested justice had been done. 'I've tried to persuade her to sell some of her pictures,' he went on, 'but she won't hear of it. She still gives them away.'

'Yes, I know,' replied Rose quickly. 'And I'm the richer for that. Is she short of money, Sam? Was that why she moved to Dawson Street when Sir Capel died?'

He nodded briefly.

'Oh, I am sorry,' Rose said sadly. 'It must be even harder if you've come from a family that once had plenty. Not like us, Sam,' she said smiling ruefully.

'Don't worry about Lily,' he said awkwardly. 'She doesn't let it bother her. To tell you the truth, Patrick's sold another couple of old houses for me and I'm almost embarrassed to tell you how much that land is now worth,' he added, glancing away. 'I'm trying to find some way of helping her that she won't notice. I've tipped one of her girls to keep the bills for me,' he said with a grin. 'Would you believe, she just puts them in a drawer, and then she wonders why the coalman doesn't come!'

Rose smiled too. She was so happy that Sam should have such pleasure from this unexpected friendship, but what really delighted her was the thought that Lily's well-being was now being cared for by a rich man who'd once been her father's stable-boy.

'Speaking of your Patrick, tell me about the rest of my nephews and nieces,' she said, glancing up at the clock. 'Yours first and then Mary's. Any news about any of them since you last wrote to me?'

Having started on the news from two large families, they were still talking when Rose heard John's step on the path.

'Oh my goodness, is that the time?' she said, laughing, as she jumped to her feet. 'John dear, you've caught us gossiping and not a bite of lunch for you,' she went on as he paused in the doorway and beamed at them.

'How are ye, Sam? How's that shoulder of yours?' he asked, as he strode across to greet his brother-in-law.

'Just grand, John. Not a bit of trouble with it, provided I do nothing. Neither spade, nor slane, nor pen,' he retorted, laughing.

'Aye, well,' John said, hanging his cap by the door, 'we're gettin' on, aren't we?'

Rose glanced at him over her shoulder as she pulled out a drawer in the dresser. Beyond his pleasure and warm greeting, she could see he was weary, tired from some effort he'd had to make during the morning, but he'd not be pleased if she mentioned it in front of Sam.

'Sam was just telling me about Brendan,' she said, as she spread a clean cloth and began to lay the table for lunch.

'How's he doin' in Dublin now? Did he get another job after his friend's shop had to shut?' John asked, sitting down gratefully by the fire.

'Nothing great so far,' said Sam honestly, 'but I hear he's something of a celebrity at Liberty Hall on a Sunday night.'

'Doing what?' asked Rose, as she brought the morning's baking in from the dairy and put it on the bread board.

'It seems Michael Mallin plays the flute. He's got up an orchestra if you please. Four of them. And Brendan sings.'

'He does have a lovely voice, Sam,' said Rose quickly, pausing on her way back to the larder for cheese and cold meat. 'D'you think he might take up singing for a living?'

'Never thought of that, Rose, but there's enough pubs might be glad to employ him if they thought it was good for business.'

'How are ye managin' without him?' John asked abruptly, as Rose waved them over to the table and started cutting thick slices of new bread.

'I miss him, John, but I couldn't stand in his way. He worked hard for me, indeed he did, but he's no real interest in the land,' he said matter-of-factly. 'It's partly my own fault I've lost him. I've probably talked so much about the state of the workers in the cities, he thinks he should be doing something about it. I can hardly complain, can I? I was just the same at his age,' he added with a wry smile.

'Aye. It was a bad business that lock-out. All those poor people starvin' for months till the relief ships came from the unions in Britain. Sure it was just as bad as a famine, though it were in the city. D'ye think anythin' good will come out of it?' he asked, his face sombre, as he buttered a slice of wheaten bread.

'Well, it might,' Sam replied. 'Your good Belfast man, James Connolly, has moved to Dublin and he'll get things organised at Liberty Hall if anyone can. It seems his boss, Larkin, has gone to America. I don't know what to make of that. He might have given up trying, like I did, or he might be raising money. I sometimes think we don't know the half of what's going on, however much we read the newspapers and the manifestos. There's a lot of rumour printed as if it were God's truth.'

'You're right there, Sam,' John replied, nodding vigorously. 'I sometimes don't know what to think the way the world's goin' these days. All this talk of war and men drillin'. Hugh useta keep me right. Whatever I would put to him, he'd have another view to set alongside it. He was always that sensible. For all he might be annoyed, he'd never let himself get worked up,' he said, his tone full of admiration and longing.

In the silence that followed, Sam and Rose glanced at each other. Despite John's effort at conversation they knew he was not himself.

'How's young Alex making out?' Sam asked as the silence grew longer. With an eye to the clock, Rose got up to make a pot of tea.

'The best at all,' John replied, a touch more life in his voice. 'He's kinda quiet at times, an' I wonder what's goin' on at all in his head. An' then he'll give a big smile an' he looks a differen' man. An' he's sharp all right. Tell him a thing wonst an' ye'll not have to tell him again,' he added, as he waved Sam to his own armchair and pulled a kitchen chair over to the fire to sit beside him.

'Where are you for this afternoon, love? Back to Seapatrick?' Rose asked, as John drained his mug and cast his eyes towards the clock.

'Aye, but I hafta go to the hospital first.'

He paused as if there was no need to say anything else, but one look at Rose's face and he knew he'd have to confess what was troubling him.

'Ach, there was a wee lassie at Lenaderg fainted this mornin',' he began, looking at the floor. 'One of the weeman said it was that time o' the month. She fell forward an' the guard had been left off the loom by the maintenance men. She'll likely lose the arm,' he ended abruptly as he stood up. 'I'm away over to see her an' sign the forms for the report.'

An hour later, as the sun began to filter into the shadowy dining room, Sarah put down her pen, picked up Simon's long letter and read the final paragraphs yet again.

> I am delighted to hear that you are going to Dublin for Easter. I shall think of you on the banks of the Liffey as I stroll by the Neva. I hope by then the ice will have melted and the river will no longer provide a shortcut from one bank to another. Spring is so slow this year that I think longingly of the gardens at Ashleigh and try to imagine walking there with you. It is not only the warmth of the sun that I long for, but your laughter.

> My dear Sarah, I do so hope that the alarms of this turbulent year will not prevent our meeting in August as it did in December. Meantime, I comfort myself with music and books, imagining the conversations we might have, though in truth I would agree to a pledge of silence if I could just be with you again.

From somewhere outside she heard the sound of footsteps. She sighed, pushed the sheets quickly back into their envelope and dropped it into her drawer. A messenger, a request from a mill, she thought wearily. Mrs Beatty would open the door, but whoever it was would have to be seen.

She picked up her pen again, tried to collect her straying thoughts, but failed. When there was a tap at the door and Mrs Beatty appeared, she admitted to herself she was grateful for the interruption. There was something in Simon's letter that was unsettling. Not unwelcome, indeed, but most certainly unsettling.

'It's yer uncle, ma'am, but he says he doesn't want to disturb you,' the housekeeper began. 'He says he could come up later, or tomorrow.'

'No, Mrs Beatty,' she said, smiling, pleased that it was not another problem to be dealt with. 'Tell him I'll be out in a moment.'

She tidied up her papers, put some of them away, anchored others with a variety of paperweights. Then she locked the drawer in which Simon's letters lay in neat piles and dropped the key into a small, floral vase on the mantelpiece.

'Sarah, how are you?' Sam greeted her, as she came into the sun-filled sitting room.

'Happy to be interrupted,' she said as he kissed her. 'It's the fault of the sunshine. That's when I get really tired of papers.'

'Good. Then you won't mind if I ask you to drive me into Banbridge for my suitcase?'

'Glad of the excuse,' she said honestly. 'Actually, I've documents ready for Millbrook. Would you mind if we dropped those off first?'

'Not a bit. I love being driven round in your comfortable motor. It doesn't make me feel sick like some of these Donegal sidecars, though I can't blame the vehicles. It's the awful roads round Swillybrinnan and Creeslough are the problem. They're *much* better here in the affluent east,' he said, teasing her.

'They have to be, Uncle dear. No use having the means of production if you can't get the goods to market,' she said dryly.

Hearing the familiar phrase she'd used, Sam laughed. She'd written to him in Pennsylvania to ask him what exactly he *was* doing for the workers there. Her mother's explanation, she wrote, had not been very detailed. She'd been all of fourteen then.

Ever since then, either by letter or face to face, they'd talked and argued about the labour movement in Ireland and the local circumstances that made it so poorly developed compared with their sister island or other European countries. Even now, when he saw her regularly, she still sent him newspaper cuttings or reports of speeches he might not have seen.

Naturally, they didn't always agree. Sam would argue that strike action, properly organised and co-ordinated, was the only way to bring about the changes in working conditions that were so badly needed. Sarah said no, she had yet to read of a strike in Ireland that hadn't endangered lives. No one knew how many poor souls had died in Dublin in the recent labour disputes. The unions in Britain *had* sent ships full of food, but by the time they arrived it was too late for many. For her part, she was in favour of direct government legislation. She regularly quoted the work of Eva Gore-Booth and Esther Roper, who not only organized women but at the same time made their situation known in government circles.

As they walked out of the house and into the sunshine, Sam sensed a burden slip from her shoulders.

He'd been just about to tell her about the injured young weaver, but he decided to leave it for the moment. In the bright light, he became aware of the fine lines round her eyes. Sarah was thirty now. Still an attractive woman, he thought, as she moved lightly across to the motor house, the sun glinting on her dark hair, but not a happy one.

'So what's all this talk of war doing to the order books?' he asked, as they turned right at the foot of Rathdrum Hill.

'Filling them up, as far as I can see,' she said bluntly. 'It appears that linen is the fighting fabric. Everything from tents to kitbags. We've been warned that if war does come we'll be expected to quadruple production,' she added sharply. 'And the powers that be think we can do it by stopping hemstitching and making more cloth instead.'

'And can't you?' he asked innocently.

She looked at him crossly and saw he was grinning at her.

'Oh yes, of course we can,' she said sarcastically. 'One mill is the same as any other mill. There's no difference at all between spinning frames and weaving looms, is there?'

'No, of course not,' he said cheerfully. 'Not if you've never laid eyes on either one or the other, nor bothered to find out the difference.

'I don't think we'll have a declaration before Easter, do you?' he asked, as they wove their way through the traffic in Banbridge.

'Do you *really* think there's going to be a war, Sam?'

''Fraid so.'

'Why?'

'I think there's a kind of negative momentum building up,' he said soberly. 'Something's got to give way, but a European war would take the pressure off us here in Ireland. If Britain doesn't go to war against Germany, then it's more than likely you'll have the Ulster Volunteers and the Irish Volunteers at each other's throats.'

'Hardly a pleasing alternative,' she said wryly as they came out into open countryside again.

'What does your friend think? He'd be closer to the truth than we might be.'

'Simon?' she said, surprised how glad she was to mention his name. 'Poor man, he can say nothing in his letters unless they come to London in the diplomatic bag. That doesn't often happen. But he did say last summer that Europe was like a kettle on the boil. While it kept blowing out steam all was well, but it might boil over at any time.'

'Sounds like a fair description to me. Pity he can't say much,' he added sympathetically.

'Yes, it is. He writes good letters and I love getting them, but I'm aware of what he'd like to share but mustn't. Mostly, we stick to books and music. He's fond of ballet, which I've never seen, but he's interested in everything I do, which is nice. Don't you find, Sam, that explaining something to someone else really helps to clear your mind?'

'Absolutely,' he agreed. 'I've been guilty in the past of addressing my desk if there was no one else available.'

'Oh, I am glad,' she said suddenly. 'I got quite worried when I started talking to Helen's kitten.'

'Perhaps that's why I'm so keen for you to come to Dublin and forget all about work for a few days,' he said quietly. 'Lily's so looking forward to seeing you and the children.'

'She wrote me such a lovely letter after Hugh died, inviting me then,' Sarah replied, glancing towards him on the now empty road. 'I couldn't face going anywhere, not for ages. But she kept on writing.'

'Doesn't surprise me,' he said shortly. 'She's heard a lot about you from Anne and Hannah. You'll enjoy yourself, I'm sure, but for goodness' sake bring your warm clothes, Sarah. Lily's is the draughtiest house I've ever been in. I've been warmer in a sheepfold on a winter night.'

Fifteen

It was not often Sam Hamilton failed to fall asleep the moment his head touched the pillow, for his days were full, his work heavy and exhausting. When he wasn't making the longest of the delivery runs from the jam factory near Richhill, where he now worked, driving to Belfast, or Larne, Newry or Drogheda, or even Dublin itself, he was servicing the firm's road vehicles and maintaining the steam engines that provided the factory's power supply. Nor did his work end when he cycled home. He was well known for the quality of his workmanship, so there were always repairs waiting in his workshop.

Tonight, however, to his great surprise, he found himself lying awake. Wide-eyed, he stared at the pale outline of the window panes behind the flimsy bedroom curtains, his mind active and his body tense.

He was puzzled that sleep now deserted him when he had yawned his head off earlier, sitting by the fire, while Martha made the last tea of the day and handed him his mug in silence.

She was fast asleep now. She'd turned away from him the moment he went to give her a goodnight kiss and was now breathing heavily.

'*Never let the sun go down upon your anger,*' his

mother had always said when they were children. She always knew when there was some upset between them. Before they went to bed she would find out the whole story. Forgive and forget, she'd said. Don't we all upset each other without meaning to, no matter how much we might try?

He sighed. There was no forgiving or forgetting with Martha. When she stopped speaking to him, as often as not he didn't even know what he'd done, or not done, though this time he *did* know, for she'd made it absolutely plain. There was no use him thinking about it any more, for he'd made up his mind, made it up years ago, when yer man Thompson at the Tullyconnaught Haulage Company had given him his cards, not because he'd broken his leg, but because he wouldn't join the Lodge.

Suddenly he raised his head, sure he'd heard a movement in the yard.

'Probably that fox again,' he said to himself.

He dropped his head to the pillow again, relieved, for he'd shut up the hens himself just before dark, glad of the fresh air and the fine April evening after the smell of the acetylene burner in the workshop.

He thought about the welding a farmer up towards the main road had asked him to do. A funny kind of a man he was, always coming down to see how he was getting on with it and standing there looking round him, even when he'd explained it would take a bit of time, given he was only working in the evenings.

Perhaps he just wanted the chat, or an excuse to get out of the house. There was more than one man he knew glad of a chance to get away from a woman tired out with farm work and housework and the burden of her children. Like Martha.

He closed his eyes and pushed the thought out of mind. What was done was done and there was no mending it. He had a fine family to rear. Five boys and three girls, the two youngest children, Molly and Johnny, asleep in their cradles on Martha's side of the bed.

The night was still, not a rustle from the newly leafed trees, nor even the cry of an owl. He always thought of Sarah when he heard an owl screech. When she was a little girl, she couldn't bear to hear an owl call. If one woke her from sleep she'd cry until their mother came to comfort her. She said it sounded hurt and no amount of explaining would persuade her that it was just the noise an owl made.

It was James who solved Sarah's problem in the end. He'd mimicked the two sorts of owls who called from the trees and barns around Robinson's farm and taught her how to make the cries herself. After that, when she woke in the night, she knew which owl was calling and was comforted, for she knew no one had hurt them.

Sam often thought back to his own childhood these days. For him it had been a happy time. He'd never understood how James could turn his back on all the love there'd been in the three different homes their mother had made for them. In the end, he'd decided it had to be his ambition.

He remembered Hugh Sinton once saying, 'Ambition is a very limiting thing.' He'd been puzzled at the time, but the more he thought about James, the more it seemed to fit what he'd done. It taught him a simple truth. If you pursue ambition for ambition's sake, even if you achieve your goal, you can be sure you'll miss much of what life has to offer you.

He still felt sad whenever he thought of Hugh. And even sadder when he thought of Sarah. To his surprise, his eyes filled with tears as he remembered her with her camera one hot, summer day when they climbed Cannon Hill so she could try 'land-scape', as she called it. They'd gone to see Thomas and Robert in the forge and that was the day they'd walked round their old home, two rooms and a washhouse with a well in the orchard and Da's crane over the open fire.

He'd seen Sarah coming out of the old house with Alex on the afternoon of Thomas's funeral. He wondered then if there was anything between them and he hoped maybe there was. Though Alex was much younger and not educated like she was, he was a good, kind man. Sure, would any of that matter if they were fond of each other? Wasn't it all about love and comfort?

He strained his ear in the silence and caught the sound of a motor half a mile away on the main road. Late for anyone to be moving. It must be nearly mid-night. He lay still, concentrating on the unfamiliar sound, not able to identify the vehicle as belonging to anyone he knew.

Sarah had seemed better the last time he saw her, catching her by chance with his mother when he'd called on his way back from one of his runs to Newry. She'd just been in Dublin with the wee ones, staying with Lady Anne's sister, the one who'd painted Ma's picture. They'd had a great time, she said. Helen and Hugh had never been to a zoo before and couldn't stop talking about it. She herself loved walking by the sea on Dublin Bay. Uncle Sam Donegal was there with them. He'd taken them to the races at Fairyhouse on Easter Monday and won all his bets, though he'd only put a few bob on each race, for fun.

The motor was coming closer. He still couldn't place it, but one thing was sure, the engine was running rough. Either the driver wasn't very skilled or the vehicle was carrying too much weight. To his great surprise, the vehicle drove past the farm and stopped a little beyond it, just where the lane widened out near the entrance to the station. The engine must be overheating, for he could hear it vibrating even after the ignition had been turned off. The only cure for that was to let it cool, so there was no use getting up and going to offer a hand. Martha would not be best pleased if he disturbed her.

A few moments later, he heard footsteps in the yard. He waited, expecting a knock on the door, but when no knock came, he slipped out of bed, tiptoed into the big kitchen and squinted though its uncurtained window. Two silent figures were opening the door of the barn.

Hastily, he went back into the bedroom, pulled on his trousers and jacket and pushed his feet into his boots. He was grateful Martha didn't stir. In the kitchen, he picked up a powerful torch and slipped outside without switching it on.

The night had clouded over and fine spots of rain were blowing in the freshening wind. He stood with his back against his own front door, so that his outline wouldn't show up against the whitewashed walls of the house. Through the open door of his workshop he could now see a light but there was no sign of either of the two men.

He waited anxiously, wondering what precious piece of his equipment they might have their eye on. Perhaps he *was* foolish not to have a lock on the door, but who, saving neighbours, knew what he had in there? What did it say for trust in your fellow men to be locking and barring doors?

Footsteps were approaching slowly now from the road. He began to wonder anxiously how many of them there were. Peering into the darkness, he saw the gleam of two faces. As his eyes grew accustomed to the darkness and he heard, rather than saw, their slow movement towards the barn, a thought began to shape in his mind.

As the two bare-headed young men reached the barn door and appeared silhouetted in the faint gleam of light, Sam saw one of the men already in the barn move forward to meet them. A big, heavily-built man, his hair receding from a shiny forehead, he reached out his arms for the heavy, sacking-wrapped bundle one of the younger men was carrying.

'Good evening, gentlemen,' said Sam loudly, shining the torch full upon them. 'You've had a fine evening for the work.'

'Shush . . . Shush, man, keep yer voice down and put out that torch,' he hissed, as Sam walked across to stand beside them. 'Ye don't know who might be about, spyin' on us. Here, give us a hand,' he went on, as the pale, freckle-faced lad pushed the heavy burden into his arms.

'No. I'll not take any hand in this work,' Sam replied firmly, moving the torch around so that he could see all their faces.

The second of the older men looked familiar. He'd seen him often enough in Richhill. His name was Hutchinson, but he didn't know his first name or much about him. The bald one was a stranger, as were the two young men, bent over with the weight of what they were carrying.

'I'll give you a can of water for your radiator,' Sam said calmly, 'and you can be on your way.'

'What?' exclaimed the first man, pushing the burden back on the young man, who reeled slightly under the weight. 'What are ye talkin' about?'

Nodding to the heavy burdens the young men were still clutching uncomfortably, he turned to Sam. 'These are to go up in the loft over this barn,' he said. 'It's all arranged. Now give us a hand or get outa the way. We've work to do before dawn an' if you're any sort of a man ye'll be helpin' us.'

The younger of the two lads lowered his burden to the ground abruptly. A moment later the other lad followed suit. The metallic clank told Sam all he needed to know.

'So ye've got the guns,' he said mildly.

'Boys, we have,' said Hutchinson, his face lighting

up. 'There were *five hundred* motors at Larne, their headlamps on, waiting for the *Clyde Valley*, an' not one to hold up a hand against us. Twenty thousand rifles an' a million rounds of ammunition. They'll do more talkin' than all the speechifyin' we've been havin'. Now, c'mon, man dear, we haven' time to stan' here. There's others waitin' for their consignments,' he ended hastily, as he signed to the two boys to pick up the bundles of rifles again.

'I think you may not have heard what I said,' said Sam slowly. 'I said I'd have no hand in this work. There'll be no rifles going up into my loft. Now take those away outa this.'

'Is this Liskeyborough?' the older man demanded angrily.

'Yes, this is Liskeyborough.'

'Ach, there's no mistake, Charley,' broke in his companion, impatiently. He took a piece of paper out of his pocket. 'Sure we have the directions and the instructions exactly where to put them. We haven't come all this way to be held back by some traitor to the cause.'

'An' what cause wou'd that be?' Sam asked, his voice still calm and steady, almost relaxed.

'The cause of *freedom*,' Charley replied, his voice low and intense, hissing out the words. 'Freedom from these Papishes that wou'd take us over and have us under the heel of Rome. We'll defend our good Protestant traditions an' our right to worship our God in our way.'

'An' what about keepin' God's commandments?' Sam asked, not troubling to lower his voice.

'What d'ye mean?' came the furious retort from the bald man.

'I had in mind "Love your neighbour" and "Thou shalt not kill",' Sam replied quietly.

'Is the wee fella givin' ye some trouble?'

Sam turned quickly to see the unshaven face of Uncle Joe, his trousers pulled on over his nightshirt.

'I'm Joe Loney an' I'm right glad to see you gentlemen,' he said, his face wreathed in smiles as he greeted the older men. 'I'm sorry about this one,' he said, nodding unpleasantly towards Sam, 'but we'll not let him annoy us. Did all go well?'

'Aye, powerful well,' said Charley, relief spreading over his face. 'Does this man here work for you?' he went on quickly. 'Will ye tell him to give us a hand an' stop givin' us cheek and keepin' us back?'

'Ah will, aye,' said Joe quickly. 'Away back t' yer bed, wee fella,' he began, looking Sam up and down, 'an' let these good men get this stuff inta my barn.'

'*Whose* barn?' asked Sam, as the two young men bent to pick up the rifles.

'My barn,' said Joe irritably.

'No, Joe, it isn't *your* barn,' Sam retorted. 'Your name's on the paper the bank has for the farm all right, but *I* pay the rent of this barn an' without that money you'd not have a penny to pay the mortgage. An' you'd hardly have a bite to eat either but for what I give my wife every week to feed you and the children. Now, tell your friends to go an' take their guns with them.'

There was a moment's stunned silence.

'I cou'd put you an' your family out on the street in the mornin',' rasped Joe, hopping with fury.

'You cou'd, you cou'd indeed,' replied Sam shortly. 'But you'd have to give me a week's notice in writing for the barn.'

Before Joe had digested this latest comment, Sam moved quickly past the two uneasy-looking young men and pushed between the older men who had come out of the barn doorway to speak to Joe. He caught hold of the door handle, pulled it firmly shut behind him and leaned against it, his torch beaming down on the parcels of guns lying on the ground. Through the coarsely woven sacking covers, the metal barrels glinted in the strong light.

'Maybe ye'd like to get one loaded up and start killing for your cause right here,' he said, looking at the two older men, his face immobile, his eyes steady upon them 'That's the only way ye'll be gettin' past me inta this barn.'

'C'mon, Charley, we're wastin' time here wi' this fool of a man. We've work to do and plenty glad to help us,' Hutchinson said, signalling peremptorily to the two boys to lift the guns and get them back to the motor.

Charley stared at Sam and then looked round at Joe, whose face had crumpled into a bitter grimace.

'I'm sorry for you, sir, with this man to deal with,' he said, nodding towards Sam. 'But we'll not forget him,' he said nastily, as he followed Hutchinson and the two lads out of the yard without a backward glance.

Martha was standing in the doorway in her bare feet, a cardigan pulled on over her shift. Joe pushed his way past her without a word, his face like thunder as he made straight for his bedroom on the left-hand side of the kitchen. The door banged loudly and from the bedroom on the right-hand side one of the babies sent up a wail of fear and anxiety.

'Ye may see to that,' said Sam coolly. 'I'll make us a drop of tea.'

He lit a lamp, raked up the fire and pulled the smaller kettle forward over the flames, put the teapot and caddy ready on the edge of the table and sat down to wait. The kettle boiled before the child's howls had subsided, so he made the tea, and fetched milk and sugar and two mugs from the dresser. He sat waiting for Martha, his head in his hands.

'You're a nice one,' she declared, glaring at him, as she closed the bedroom door quietly and stamped back into the room. 'Ye ought to be ashamed of yourself, lettin' us down like that,' she began, her hands on her hips. 'Who do you think you are? What right have you to give orders roun' here? This is Joe's place an' it'll be mine one day.'

'I'm your husband, Martha,' he said steadily. 'I'm the father of your children and the one who sees that you're all well cared for, though from the way you treat me you'd never think it,' he said, standing up. 'But I've come to a decision tonight,' he continued, not once raising his voice as he poured tea into the two mugs. 'Unless you and Joe stop talkin' behind my back, callin' me names and makin' little of me, I'm leavin' this place. I'll see you an' the children don't go without, but Joe can shift for himself. I'll sell my stuff in the barn till I can find somewhere to begin again, some place where I'm not ashamed of the company I keep.'

'An' are you sayin' that you're ashamed of me, Sam Hamilton?' she demanded furiously.

'I'd be ashamed of any woman that did what you and Joe did behind my back.'

'Sure it was for your own good,' she said shortly. 'Ye haven't a bit of wit. The neighbours laugh at you with your queer ideas. An' you're not one bit loyal.'

'Loyal, Martha? What does that mean to you? Does it mean standin' by me, encouragin' me, or does it mean cuddlin' up to me when ye want what ye want and ignorin' me round the house, except when ye need me to mind the children?'

'I mean loyal to your country,' she retorted, ignoring what he'd said. 'What kind of a Protestant d'you think you are, turnin' them men away after all the trouble they had to get them guns? I suppose you'll just let the Fenians walk all over you, the way you walk over me an' Joe.'

Sam looked at her closely, a small, angry woman in a flimsy shift, her breasts drooping, her belly protruding under the thin fabric, her bare legs paper-white, her feet dirty from the yard.

There was no use talking to her. From long experience, he knew she could keep at it all night, throwing things up at him, complaining at what he did, or didn't do.

'Martha, I'm not goin' to argue with you,' he said suddenly. 'You don't love me, an' I sometimes wonder if you ever did, but we have eight children to rear an' I'll not have them neglected. You do your work an'

I'll do mine, but keep a civil tongue in your head or we'll have to come to some other arrangement,' he said, drinking the remains of his tea at one long swallow.

She stared at him and looked, for a moment or two, as if she would simply begin to berate him as if he hadn't spoken. Instead, she turned on her heel and went back into the bedroom.

He sat for a while, staring into the tiny blaze. For too long now, there'd been no pleasing her – outside of the bedroom, he thought wryly – and he'd no heart for any more of that now. Suddenly he stood up, raked down the flames and covered them with ash, ready for the morning. Picking up his torch, he unhooked his heavy winter coat from its place by the door and went out into the damp, windy night.

He crossed to the barn, picked up the lantern his visitors had lit and climbed the wooden stair to the loft above. He looked around to see if he had some old sacks somewhere, but if he did he couldn't find them. He blew out the lantern carefully, wrapped himself in his greatcoat, lay down on the dusty floorboards and fell fast asleep.

Sixteen

Despite the growing tension that followed the very successful gun-running in Ulster and the continuous disturbing news from Europe, springtime in County Down proceeded, quite indifferent to the affairs of men and women. The hawthorns dipped their branches, so richly showered with creamy blossom they could have been laden with snow. The gorse bushes flamed an unbelievably brilliant yellow, the meadows glistened with new growth and cow parsley danced along the hedgerows, a lacy white curtain in the warm breezes.

When Rose and John drove to Armagh on the second Saturday in June for the Annual Celebration Day with the Sintons, Hugh's older brother and his wife, the sky was a perfect blue. From the tall windows of James and Mary's handsome Georgian house, the assembled company surveyed the familiar summer scene. Beyond the shady tree-lined walk that encircled the Mall, the white figures of the cricketers moved through the heat haze shimmering above the pitch. White-haired, but still robust, James pointed out to his guests that drought had already worn bare the short grass of the outfield. The pitch itself was as hard as nails.

Everyone was in good spirits. Elizabeth and Richard had been an addition to the original family parties for many years, but Sam Hamilton had not appeared in Armagh since his marriage, though he'd always been such a favourite with Mary Sinton. Both James and Mary were clearly delighted to welcome Alex for the first time. He'd been invited the previous year, but he hadn't felt he could quite manage such an important family occasion so soon. It helped Alex make up his mind when his good friend Sam announced he was free to come.

'I don't approve of speeches,' said James, standing at the head of the lunch table, 'so this won't take long, but I can't let today pass without a word.'

There was a murmur of warm encouragement from the assembled company.

'You may not have done the calculation, but it is twenty-five years ago this week since Rose and Sarah celebrated their joint birthday on the Armagh Methodist's excursion to Warrenpoint. We all know what happened that day,' he went on, a little more soberly. 'Without our dear Rose, some of us would certainly not be sitting here today.'

Rose blushed as she always did whenever James spoke of her part in persuading his family to jump out of the runaway train. Even after all this time, she still could hardly believe what had happened.

'We have met now for twenty-five years, each year a different mix of Hamiltons and Sintons. We have suffered our losses,' he continued crisply, not wanting to cast a shadow on such a happy occasion, 'but we have had our gains. And today we welcome Alex.'

He beamed broadly at the young man.

'Friends,' he said, 'let us give thanks as we do each year, for love and life and friendship.'

'For love and life and friendship,' they repeated, as they stood and raised their glasses.

After a long, leisurely lunch spent catching up on news of all the absent family members, they strolled across the road, heading for the dappled shade on the Mall. As they followed Sam and Mary Sinton down the shallow steps leading to the White Walk, Sarah found Alex at her side. Rose had warned Sarah that Mary was having trouble with her hips, but Mary made light of it, though Sarah could see how glad she was of Sam's strong arm to help her down the steps.

'Sam's in good spirits today, isn't he?' Alex said quietly, after they'd paused for a moment to let Sarah point out the Courthouse, the cathedrals, the two Presbyterian churches and the library.

'Yes, he is,' said Sarah, beaming at him. 'Did *you* persuade him to come?'

'No, ma'am,' he said, grinning at her. 'Much as I'd like to take the credit for it. It was *he* persuaded me.'

'Well, I *am* delighted. I haven't seen Sam look so happy for a long time.'

Alex fell silent.

'There's something you're not telling me.'

'Correct.'

'And why is that?' she said, a hint of anxiety creeping into her voice.

'Can't think how to put it,' he confessed wryly.

'Just say it, Alex. When have I ever been annoyed with you for telling me something I needed to know?'

'Right.'

Sarah waited patiently. He was normally so direct with her; she couldn't imagine what was giving him such difficulty now.

'You know when I've a day's holiday and I borrow your motor, I go over and work with Sam,' he began easily enough. 'Well, two weeks back I had all Saturday as well as Sunday, because there's been a lot of overtime.'

'Yes, I remember,' she said quickly. 'You said you might stay over if I didn't need the car.'

'Sam offered me a bed.'

'Good Heavens!' she exclaimed. 'Where on earth *did* he put you? Ma says the four little ones are top and tail in one big bed, Charley and Billy are in with Uncle Joe on mattresses, and there are two cradles in Martha and Sam's room.'

'Up in the loft, Sarah,' he replied, looking at her cautiously. 'He has his bed up there now and two proper beds for Charley and Billy. I had both the mattresses, one on top of the other. Very comfortable they were too.'

'And how was Martha?' Sarah asked cautiously.

'Better than usual. She was actually quite civil for a change.'

'And Uncle Joe?' she went on, wondering what could possibly have happened to make Martha behave decently.

'No great change there. A face that would sour milk, as I think the expression is in these parts, but he didn't say very much about anything, certainly not in front of me.'

'And the children, Alex,' she continued, puzzled by the picture that was emerging. 'What about them?'

'Wearing shoes and boots,' he replied, raising an eyebrow.

'Oh, Alex, what wonderful news,' she said, beaming at him. 'Ma will be *so* pleased. She really did worry about them in the bad weather. But why were you so uneasy about telling me all this?' she asked suddenly.

'Well, I thought you'd be upset about the bed in the loft.'

'Yes, I can see that,' she said, nodding. 'But I'm not sure what joy there ever was for Sam in that other bed,' she added, her lips tightening. 'At least this way he seems to have taken back his self-respect.'

Alex nodded vigorously.

'You won't go doing what Sam did, will you, Alex?' she said after a pause. 'I don't think I could bear it.'

'Don't worry about that, Sarah,' he replied, his face lighting up with that sudden beaming smile which made him look almost handsome. 'In Canada, farm servants like me were invisible because they didn't matter. If there was one thing I had plenty of opportunity to observe, it was the misery a man and a woman can inflict on each other if they have no love and no respect, each for the other.'

Sarah's good spirits rose even further when she and Alex drove Sam back to Liskeyborough. When they arrived, Martha was nowhere to be seen, but an older woman introduced herself as *Aunt* Charlotte. She said she looked after the children on Saturdays while their mother went visiting.

A pleasant person, whom the little ones obviously liked, she scooped up the sweets and chocolates Sarah and Alex had bought for them in Armagh and distributed a modest ration.

'Oh Alex, it has been such a good day,' Sarah said, as they turned into the drive at Rathdrum. 'I'm just so delighted that things are better for Sam. Will you stay and have a bite to eat with me, or have you a lady friend awaiting you?' she asked, her eyes shining with pleasure.

'I'll stay,' he said, grinning. 'I'm still a free man. I'll not tie the knot till I see you settled,' he said, laughing, as he gave her a hand down from the motor before he put it away.

The letter was sitting on the kitchen table where Mrs Beatty knew Sarah couldn't miss it. It was thin, almost certainly only a single sheet, and postmarked Berlin. She was still staring at it anxiously when Alex came back into the kitchen.

'Sarah, what's wrong?'

'I don't know yet. But something is,' she said, her hands shaking as she tore open the envelope.

'Here, sit down and read it properly,' he said, pushing a kitchen chair up behind her.

'It's from Simon,' she said distractedly.

Alex had to smile to himself. Who else was likely to be in Berlin? He ran the tap to get fresh water and set the glass on the table beside her.

'Can I help or is it private?' he asked quietly.

By way of reply, she handed him the brief note written from Petersburg but posted in Berlin.

My dearest Sarah,

I fear our well-laid plans have gone awry. My leave in July has been cancelled, but I shall shortly be leaving for Berlin with messages from Sir George to our ambassador. I shall be there for some days. I am then required to attend Lord Grey in the week beginning Monday 23rd of June.

How long I shall be at the Foreign Office I do not know, but at least I will be in England. I have requested some days to visit Cleeve and I am about to write to Hannah and Teddy asking if I may come to them after my engagements in London.

I shall be glad to see them, but it is you, my dearest, I long to see. Is there any possibility whatever that you might be able to come to Cleeve in the last week of June?

Alex carefully averted his gaze from the loving good wishes and the scrawled signature.

'What's the problem, Sarah? You can go over next weekend, can't you? You want to see Hannah anyway.'

'But what about the children and their holiday? And work?' she asked distractedly. 'I can't just go off like that. It would mean sailing next Saturday night.'

'I'm free next Saturday afternoon. I'll take you to

the boat,' he said, amused, yet sympathetic, when he saw how agitated she was.

'But the children, what about them?' she asked, her eyes wide and staring.

'Well, they're at school till the twenty-seventh, aren't they? I can ask for time off and take Rose over to pick them up. They can stay with Rose, or Rose and John can move in here till you come back,' he said practically. 'You'll just have to take them to Portrush or Ballycastle instead of Cleeve and Ashleigh.'

'But I can't take *more* time off,' she said shortly.

'Sarah, you're a director, not a weaver,' he said gently. 'Of course you can. Besides, you know perfectly well Elizabeth, or Richard, or both, would stand in for you if you want to give the children a holiday later on.'

'It's so sudden,' she said, staring at the thin sheet of paper.

He followed her gaze and noticed the date. 'It *has* taken a long time to come,' he said soothingly.

'No, it hasn't,' she said, shaking her head. 'That's the date in Russia. There's twelve days difference between the Gregorian calendar and ours. He was in such a hurry, he forgot to correct it. Sometimes he puts both.'

'That must make life difficult when you're doing business with other countries,' Alex reflected.

'Yes, it does,' she said, putting the letter down and picking up the note Mrs Beatty had left, staring at it as uncomprehendingly as she had at Simon's missive.

'You *must* go, Sarah,' he said quietly.

'Why?' she replied baldly.

'Because you love him,' he said simply. '"Love, life and friendship," as James said. That's what it's all about. You can't turn your back on that. It would be like not getting out of the train when you've been told why you should.'

She nodded slowly.

'Perhaps, you're right,' she said, sounding quite exhausted. 'Mrs Beatty has left us a shepherd's pie. Is that all right?'

He smiled and nodded. 'Lunch was lovely, but it seems like a long time ago now,' he said enthusiastically. 'Perhaps a bite to eat would help settle you. Would you like me to heat it up?' he asked, still smiling, as he went and found the matches and lit the stove.

'I can hardly believe I'm here, Hannah,' Sarah said with a sigh, as she looked round the familiar sitting room at Cleeve Hall the following Sunday afternoon. 'Only a week ago, I was in Armagh talking to Mary and James about you and Teddy and the children. I never dreamt I'd be sitting having tea with you so soon.'

'I'm so delighted to see you, Sarah,' Hannah replied warmly. 'I *know* it's a big disappointment about Simon's leave, but *I* have you here *now*, all to myself for at least a couple of days. I'm going to enjoy every minute of it,' she said smiling, as she sat herself down in the window seat. 'Now where shall we start?'

They both laughed, for there seemed so much to share it was difficult indeed to know where to begin.

Hannah was as pleased as Sarah about the changes Sam had made in his life and delighted at Helen and Hugh's progress at school. Then she asked about the labour difficulties troubling the four mills and how both their parents were responding to it.

In turn, Sarah wanted to know exactly how the current state of affairs in the country and in Europe was affecting Teddy. His seat in Parliament was considered a safe one, but Teddy himself was increasingly critical of the cabinet and their failure to address the problems the outbreak of war might produce.

As they talked, Sarah grew increasingly aware that Hannah's life was far from easy, her responsibilities growing all the time. Teddy was working long hours and wasn't always free to come home at weekends, but if Hannah wanted to spend time with him in London, it meant leaving eight-year-old Elizabeth and six-year-old Anne with the housekeeper and their governess. She was constantly having to divide herself between two homes, both of which needed her active presence.

'There'll not be a problem next year when they both go to school,' she said practically, as she explained how she could be so busy that she scarcely had time to write letters, 'but it's *now* that matters, isn't it?'

Sarah was surprised to find her sister's tone so firm, her look so sombre.

'Somehow I feel one is being pressed more and more to make decisions about now. *Just* now,' Hannah said, after a pause. 'It used to be one thought about the future and talked about all sorts of plans and possibilities. At least Teddy and I always did. But suddenly, the future seems so uncertain, so difficult to predict, that all one can do is think about *now.*'

She paused and turned towards her sister, her eyes anxious and troubled. 'What do *you* think?'

'Well, yes. Now that you ask me, I think I have to agree,' Sarah replied quickly. 'I'm not sure I'd actually come to that conclusion, but if I look back over the last months, that's really what I've been doing, just making decisions from day to day and week to week.'

Sarah broke off. Hannah had always seemed so calm, so unperturbed. Something of the sense of stillness was still there, yes, but Hannah was no longer so composed. Why this should be so, she couldn't yet tell, but what Hannah said next made it rather clearer.

'Sarah dear, you've been so good and so brave since Hugh died. You never complain about the work at the mills and all these disputes and strike threats, but I'm not blind. I can read between the lines,' she said, smiling wanly. 'It's not the life you planned for yourself and it's never going to be. Not now. Not the way things have changed.'

'Oh, it's not so bad, Hannah,' Sarah said abruptly. 'The children are such good company. We had a wonderful time when we went to visit Lily. And Ma is always understanding when I get fed up . . .' She broke off, saddened and distressed by the look on Hannah's face. 'I'm sorry, Hannah dear. You're right, I'm not being honest with you,' she said apologetically. 'Perhaps I'm not being honest with myself,' she added wryly. 'I do my best, but apart from writing to

Simon and working in the garden, there's not much joy in it. And not much prospect of it getting any better.'

'I wouldn't say that, Sarah. I wouldn't say that at all,' replied Hannah vigorously. 'And if you really believed that was the case I don't think you'd have come, would you?'

To Sarah's surprise and chagrin she found herself blushing. She laughed and stood up, walked the length of the pretty sitting room, stretched her arms and shoulders and came back to stand looking down at her sister.

'I have the feeling, sister dear, you have it in mind to give me some good advice,' she said soberly, though her eyes were sparkling. 'I've never been much good at taking advice, but seeing it's you, I promise I shall listen carefully. In fact, since I'm being so honest, I've no idea *what* to do next. I've almost begun to dread seeing Simon again, because I'm so agitated about so many things.'

'Well, in that case,' began Hannah, smiling, 'I think it's rather fortunate that Lord Grey requires his services for a day or two, till we see what all these things might be. Now how about a little walk in the garden before the children have their supper?'

It was not until Thursday afternoon that a telephone call from Teddy in London announced that Simon was at last free to travel down to Cleeve Hall that evening. Teddy was proposing to come with him, albeit accompanied by a large briefcase full of work to be done at the weekend.

Hannah was beaming when she came to find Sarah, who was reading to Elizabeth and Anne in the nursery on their governess's afternoon off.

'Are you still feeling anxious?' Hannah asked, as the two little girls went off to play in the garden.

'Yes,' she said honestly. 'Just as anxious, but in much better spirits. It really is a treat being here with you. Perhaps it's because I do have Ma and Alex to talk to that I hadn't realised how lonely I was.'

'I know how you feel,' Hannah replied. 'I miss Teddy so badly when he's up in town all week. And I hate it if he has to stay for the weekend as well. You and I make quite a pair, don't we?'

They laughed together and hugged each other, grateful for the time they'd had to spend together, glad too the waiting was over and whatever was to happen next would soon emerge.

Sarah was alone in the sitting room when she heard the sound of wheels on the gravel. Not only had the train been on time, but the single cab at the station had been available. Within moments, Simon had come upstairs and was crossing the room towards her.

'Sarah, Sarah, my dear, I thought the days would never pass,' he said as he took her hand.

For a moment, she thought he might kiss her, but she checked herself. Simon was not a man to presume. Whatever his feelings, he would not do anything that might distress her. However loving their letters might have become, nothing had yet been said between them to move them beyond warm friendship.

'Simon, it's so good to see you. I began to think Lord Grey would never part with you,' she said, laughing. 'Are you exhausted?'

'I was,' he said, looking at her tenderly. 'Teddy had to read his newspaper for entertainment all the way down, but I seem to be recovering remarkably rapidly.'

'Poor Simon,' she said sympathetically, as they moved towards the window seat and sat down together. 'Hannah did explain about Lord Grey. Is it true he had you come all the way from Petersburg because he doesn't trust telegrams or memoranda?' she asked lightly.

There was a tension about Simon she had not experienced before, but she reminded herself that she'd never encountered him after he'd just spent four days in continuous contact with officials at the Foreign Office and with Lord Grey in particular.

'Lord Grey is a force to be reckoned with,' he said wryly, 'but I've got a more difficult assignment than him on my mind at the moment. Sarah, what time is dinner?'

Sarah laughed.

'Oh dear, are you starving? I'm afraid it's a bit late. Hannah said nine o'clock, so Teddy could spend some time with the children.'

'No, I'm not hungry at all,' he said, shaking his head emphatically and glancing at his watch, 'but I ought to change and there's something I must say to you. If I'm quick, could we go and walk in the garden? It's still warm and rather nice.'

'Yes, of course. I'll wait for you here.'

The garden was lovely, the air warm and still, the grass paths bone dry, the varied perfumes of roses and flowering shrubs lying on the air. For once, however, Simon seemed quite indifferent to his surroundings as he walked through them more quickly than usual till they were some way beyond the house.

Still puzzled by his behaviour, Sarah said nothing as they paused on a small terrace overlooking a lily pond. There was a conveniently placed seat where one could enjoy the reflections in the water and the pattern of ripples as the fish jumped, but Simon ignored it. He simply looked back towards the house, out of sight behind a small group of poplars and an enormous cedar with sweeping branches that almost touched the ground.

'Simon dear, what is it?' she said, unable to bear the tension for a moment longer.

He paused and took a deep breath.

'Sarah, the kettle's about to boil over,' he said quickly. 'Something is going to happen, if not tonight, then tomorrow. If not tomorrow then in a few days' time. And if it does, I shall have to go. Instantly.'

The look he turned towards her was so distraught it was all she could do not to put her arms round him and comfort him.

'That would be so sad,' she managed.

'It would be disastrous, for me, at least.'

'But why, Simon? Would you be in danger?' she asked, suddenly anxious, wondering what kind of assignment might put him at risk.

'Yes, indeed I would. You see, I'd be in danger of losing the love of my life. I'd hoped we'd have a fortnight together in July. Then I hoped we'd have a week here at Cleeve, but if the telephone were to ring right now, we'd have only the time it takes for Teddy to come and find us.'

'We could go and hide behind the bushes,' she said, trying to show a lightness she was so very far from feeling.

'Oh, Sarah, this isn't the way it ought to be,' he said with a bleak smile. 'But this is the only moment I've got.' He turned to face her once more. 'Sarah, I want you to be my wife. I know there are difficulties for both of us, but I love you as I've never loved anyone before. If you can say yes I'll be the happiest man alive. If it's too soon, I hope you'll forgive me and go on being my friend. I couldn't bear life if I hadn't you as my friend.' He paused. 'I'll wait as long as you want,' he added softly.

For one long moment, Sarah hesitated. She had no doubt in her mind she loved him, but there were so many other people she had to consider. Hannah had made her go through them all, reassuring her that she was not being selfish. That she had a right to happiness.

'Simon dear, it's not too soon to ask me if I love you,' she said gently. 'I *do* love you and I would dearly love to be your wife, but I think we may have to wait a little before we can be together, for both our sakes,' she said, looking up at him.

'Oh, Sarah, Sarah, dearest. How I wish I could run away with you!' he exclaimed, catching her up in his arms and swinging her round him. 'I am the happiest man alive.'

He put her gently back on her feet. 'No, don't repeat the warning. I will hear that *tomorrow*, but not tonight. Tonight the telephone hasn't rung, we are here, now, together and you love me. What more could I ever ask?' he said, drawing her into his arms.

It was the happiest of weekends. Hannah and Teddy were overjoyed by Simon's ecstatic announcement. The weather was ideal, warm and sunny, so they could spend most of their time walking, talking about the life they could make when, as they put it, *the kettle boils dry*. However much they had to speak of the realities of work and family commitments, they did not allow them to break in upon the suddenness of their joy.

If they only had until Monday morning, then so it must be. Every hour was to be cherished. Whatever happened, they now had a hope and a possibility and the outline of a future that would give them strength for whatever would be asked of them in the months to come.

On Sunday they all went to the little village church nearby where the vicar prayed for peace and shook hands with them all as they departed. He recognised Sarah and Simon as visitors and hoped he would see them again soon.

The telephone rang as they were finishing lunch. None of them heard it over the laughter and the rattle of dessert plates.

'Telephone, sir,' the housekeeper said, as she came quickly back into the dining room only moments after she'd brought the apple pie.

Teddy stood up at once. For a moment no one realised that Mrs Greenaway was shaking her head.

'Please, sir, it's for Mr Hadleigh.'

'Come on now, finish your nice apple pie and you can go outside if you want,' said Hannah firmly, as Elizabeth and Anne watched Simon go.

They had just left the room when he returned.

'That's it, my friends,' he said slowly. 'The kettle's boiled over. Franz-Joseph and the Countess Sophie have been assassinated in Sarajevo.'

Seventeen

On Sunday afternoon, following Simon and Teddy's hasty departure for London, Sarah and Hannah drove over to Ashleigh Court and spent a few days with Lady Anne. The three women enjoyed the short time they could spend together and took much pleasure in sharing Sarah's good news, but the days themselves were overhung by the growing tension in the country and by Anne's anxiety about Harrington, who was now having some difficulty in walking.

When they parted on Wednesday, a sultry afternoon in that first week of July, they knew life was about to change for all of them. There were no tears, but the embraces at the foot of the great stone staircase at Ashleigh and at the small local station near to Cleeve Hall, a day later, were more heartfelt than usual.

As each day of that long month passed, the sense of unease grew. Nothing in the newspapers gave the remotest sign of hope that the die had not been cast in a remote city in Bosnia that no one in Ulster had ever heard of before. On the fifth of August, when the news reached Banbridge that war had been declared after a meeting of the Privy Council late the previous evening, there was a palpable sense of relief. Now that the worst had happened, at least everyone would soon know what might be demanded of them.

After hearing Sarah's account of Harrington's deterioration, Rose wanted to go and see her old friend, but from the moment the news of war had come, she could see the burden that had descended upon John. With the problems at the mills multiplying by the hour, she just couldn't leave him to cope on his own, never mind worry about her safety, now that German submarines were reported in the Irish Sea.

'Hallo, love, I wasn't expecting you,' Rose said, when Sarah appeared in the doorway one crisp, pleasant morning in September. She put down her sewing, took off her spectacles and got to her feet. 'I hope you've got some good news. I've had nothing but bad this morning.'

'Oh dear,' Sarah replied sympathetically. 'Tell me your bad news first and then I'll think if I can find anything good.'

'Dan Willis, our postman,' Rose said abruptly. 'He applied to join up and they had to wait for a medical report, but it's come through and he's going. I'm not sure if it's the Inniskillings or the Irish Rifles,' she said abstractedly. 'He mentioned both. He finishes on Friday. He'd nothing for us this morning but he came up anyway to ask me if I'd write to him in France. He says the few friends he has have already joined up and they're in other regiments. He has no one at all to write to him. Isn't that sad, Sarah?'

Sarah nodded and dropped down in her father's chair as Rose pulled the kettle forward on the stove.

'Cup of tea?'

'Yes, I'd love one. I'm on the way to Lenaderg and I'm dreading it,' she said honestly.

'Oh, Sarah, what now?'

Rose looked carefully at her daughter. She was quite composed on the surface, but couldn't hide the anger beneath from so experienced an eye as her mother's.

'Nothing new really,' Sarah replied with a sigh. 'That recruiting drive we had in Banbridge last week was a great success. Lenaderg has lost a quarter of its workforce and the orders are piled high. No one asks how we weave cloth when the most experienced engine men and weavers go off to join up. There are even those who suggest our fall in production is *disloyal*, Ma. Disloyal! Can you believe it?' she said furiously. 'They just don't understand that you can't run machines or human beings twenty-four hours a day, non-stop.'

'What about the new half-time women?'

'Oh, that will help,' Sarah agreed promptly. 'Any pair of hands that can be trained will help, but it takes time. It's at least two months before one of these new women can do the work of a young man that's gone.'

'More headaches for you and your father, Sarah,' Rose said gently, as she brought out the cake tin and offered Sarah a slice.

'Which reminds me,' Sarah said, watching her cut

the cake. 'Did you hear that Peter Jackson's going? Did Emily tell you?'

'Oh dear.' Rose sighed. 'I haven't seen Emily yet this week,' she said with a weak smile, as she thought of her lively young neighbour. 'She came up last Saturday afternoon. She says the studio is terribly busy with all these young men being photographed in their uniforms before they go off to camp or join their regiments. She's late home most evenings.'

'Doesn't it seem funny to think of Emily working in the studio where I had my first job, Ma?' Sarah said suddenly. 'When you took the cake tin out, I suddenly thought of my last day at school. Do you remember?'

'Yes, I do,' Rose said, laughing. 'I'd planned to have tea all ready for you coming home, best china and cake,' she continued, waving her hands towards an imaginary tray with an embroidered tray cloth, 'and then Mrs Jackson arrived and kept me talking. Poor woman, I must go down and see her. She can't walk the hill now and she's bound to be upset over Peter going and him with a wife and three little ones.'

'Good thing she still has Emily at home,' Sarah said quietly. 'And Alex, of course. I know he's only their lodger, but he seems so much part of the family. I know he helps Michael with the cattle and Emily told me that whenever he's not studying, he always helps with jobs in the house.'

Rose smiled. Alex was one of the good things in life and Emily was another. Though she didn't see much of her these days, her visits to deliver eggs and milk and butter were always a pleasure. Emily standing smiling in the doorway reminded her of the days when Sarah came in from work, full of what she'd learnt in the darkroom, who'd had their picture taken and what she had to do the next day. A time that now seemed so long ago, it almost felt like a different life.

'Any news from Petersburg?' Rose asked shyly.

'None at all,' Sarah replied, laughing. 'Petersburg no longer exists.'

'What *do* you mean?' Rose demanded, her alarm somewhat offset by Sarah's amusement.

'The powers that be have decided St Petersburg is too Germanic a name for a Russian city,' she began solemnly. 'I must now address my missives to *Petrograd*. But, having said that, Simon *is* well. I just don't know how he manages to write such lively letters when most of what he does he can't mention, but we do have long discussions about books. I've read everything by the Russian authors in Banbridge Library and Hannah, bless her, has promised to find me some more recent ones when she's got time to go to a bookshop in London.'

Sarah put down her empty mug and stood up, brushing crumbs from her skirt.

'I must love you and leave you, Ma, as the saying is,' she said, grinning. 'But I do have *one* piece of good news. Your grandson, Hugh, has just been awarded his first big prize – the Pearson Memorial Cup for a sustained project,' she said proudly, as she saw her mother's face light up. 'I had a letter from him yesterday.'

'Was that what he was working on last term? The

development of aeroplanes?'

Sarah nodded. 'The projects were judged over the summer, but it seems the headmaster had to find an engineer to read it for him. He was pretty sure it was good, but he couldn't claim knowledge of the subject himself. Apparently, the engineer was very impressed. Dear Hugh is so delighted.'

'And so am I, love,' said Rose, her face lighting up. 'I think this calls for a little extra pocket money. Is that all right with you?'

'Perfectly all right, Ma,' she said beaming. 'I don't have to worry about what he does with it. He *never* spends any on sweets. Books, books and more books. Though he did mention a slide rule,' she added quickly. 'Either ways, I've no worries about his teeth.'

'I'll write him a wee note after lunch,' Rose said, standing up and walking to the door with her.

'Isn't it a lovely morning?' Sarah said, as they parted at the garden gate. 'Sometimes you can almost forget what's happening in France.'

Rose nodded. Sometimes when the mountains looked their loveliest, when there were flowers to pick and birds to feed, and ordinary everyday things to talk about, one could indeed banish the images of the burnt-out shells of French towns and the lines of trenches marching across the pleasant, well-cultivated landscape of Flanders. Sometimes, but not often – and certainly not for very long.

Swillybrinnan
20th September, 1914

My dearest Rose,

Thank you for your ever-welcome letter.
The news of young Hugh's success is something to set against all the bad news that
overwhelms us daily. I shall certainly arrange
to be with you for his twelfth birthday at
Halloween. How fortunate that half term
falls so happily this year.

The only comparable news I can share
with you is my own very minor achievement:
the publication in a farming journal of a piece
of work Brendan and I did when I first came
home. 'Alternative cultivation techniques for
saturated soils' will hardly be widely read or
implemented, but one has to do what one can.

Mary sends you her love, but I have to
say she is in very poor spirits. She did not
appreciate that her two older sons were still
on the reserve list after serving with the
Royal Irish Fusiliers. As you know, they
were called up immediately and are now in
France. She has had one very cheerful letter
from Patrick, but it was written from
Shorncliffe in the south of England and it
was devoted to a full account of their
send-off from Armagh. It seems Armagh did
them proud, the streets lined with cheering
people. He says the 300 reservists were
escorted to the station by the band of the
3rd Battalion, the mounted troop of the

Ulster Volunteers and the local UVF company singing patriotic songs.

For some reason, the Nationalist Volunteers with St Malachy's band were not permitted to join the procession, but they were there at the station and played and cheered the soldiers on their way. As the train steamed out for Greenore, the station-master and his men let off fog signals.

I'm afraid I cannot find it in my heart to cheer with the crowds, for I fear many of these men will not return. The only cause for pleasure is that the common enemy has achieved the impossible, Irishmen of all persuasions marching side by side and cheering each other on. Would that they were not marching to a battlefield.

Of my own eldest son, Patrick, the news is even more distressing. He has left for Germany, ostensibly to visit Eva's family. I cannot possibly believe it is as simple as this, though he has talked about going for a long time. Possibly he is being used as a messenger by one of the Irish nationalist groups active in New York, but he is certainly not admitting that to me or any of his family. I feel particularly sorry for his wife, who cannot possible be happy about the plan. For myself, I try to remember my own days in the Land League and how passionately I felt the wrongs of the world. It seems passion of all kinds diminishes with age.

You asked most kindly about my shoulder. It is certainly better when I use the rub Richard recommended, but I still forget that pushing a pen vigorously is as hard on the muscles as digging turf or drainage channels. So, my dear, I must stop. It will not be long before I see you, but please don't let that prevent you writing to me whenever you have an opportunity.

My fondest love to you and my good friend John,

Your loving brother,

Sam

As the warm, pleasant autumn moved on, so the focus of daily life changed and adapted to the new world of war. In August, the newspapers had reported Lord Grey's comment that it would be 'business as usual', but it was soon very clear this was not to be so. The hundred thousand men of the British Expeditionary Force sent to France and the might of the Royal Navy would not be able to fight the war for the country while life continued unmodified at home.

As each month passed and Rose read the daily and weekly newspapers, she began to feel she was having to learn a new language. Like all those years ago, when they first came to Ballydown and she'd had to ask what a stenter was, why beetling hammers jammed, what pouce was and why it was dangerous, she now had to master the language of war. Brigades and battalions, companies and platoons, fusiliers and lancers were all new to her, and the formal titles of

regiments, their battalion numbers and their nick-
names, she found completely confusing.

It was during the retreat from Mons, always
referred to as the 'retirement', that she began to
grasp the importance of every hump and hollow in
the landscape, why a hill could be an important
objective, and why trenches gave such protection.
She struggled to understand, as if by doing so she
was supporting the men who crawled across stubble
fields under shell fire and rifle fire, snatched rest
wherever night found them, and lived on apples and
damson from unharvested orchards when rations
could no longer reach them.

There were no more marching columns in
Ballydown now. The men who trained with wooden
rifles in Edward Carson's Ulster Volunteer Force he
had encouraged to join the British Army. John
Redmond had encouraged the Irish Volunteers to
do the same, each man assuming that a grateful
British government would give them what they
wanted when the war was over.

Thousands of men were now in training. Some
from nearby Clandeboye came home to Banbridge
on leave at weekends, full of enthusiasm for their new
life. They couldn't wait to get to France. Their greatest fear, it seemed, was that the war would be over
before they were called upon, but the war showed
not the slightest signs of being over by Christmas, as
had been so widely predicted, and the newspaper
reports of local men lost grew ever larger.

'Is there anyone we know?' Rose would asked
anxiously each week as John scanned the pages of

the *Banbridge Chronicle* while she prepared to serve supper.

There were always names they knew. Sometimes a family name, known because the family had sent generations of spinners and weavers to the mills. At other times the loss came closer: brothers, fathers and husbands of women who now worked at the mills. The retirement from Mons had claimed the sons of a number of local farmers. In November, two young men from Seapatrick were killed, one from the Irish Guards, one from the Royal Irish Rifles.

'An' they said it would be over by Christmas,' John said bitterly, after he'd read out their names one foggy evening as Rose sat knitting socks for the local soldier's support group.

'The papers did, John, but you remember what Sarah told us,' Rose replied quietly.

'Aye, I'd forgot. Her man Simon said it might start small, but it would grow to be a big thing. I think what he was sayin' was that we diden know the half of it, though those wou'den be his words, wou'd they?' he asked with a hint of a smile.

Rose smiled too. If there was one thing that did give her pleasure it was the way John always referred to Simon as 'her man, Simon'. Even before Sarah's visit to Cleeve, John had referred to him as *her* man.

She remembered how he'd done the same thing with Alex some years back. He'd spent a few hours in his company, asked a few questions, and by the end of the evening he simply referred to him as 'our cousin, Alex'. That was John's way of summing up a situation he'd figured out to his own satisfaction. She didn't know how he did it so quickly, but he was seldom wrong. He'd known from Sarah's response that Simon Hadleigh was right for her, and that was that as far as he was concerned.

'What about Alex?' Rose asked, her mind following its own logic.

'How d'ye mean?'

'Do ye think he'll go?'

'No, I don't,' he said firmly. 'I've put it plain to him. I'll not be able to keep things goin' if he does,' he said, shaking his head. 'What's the use of one more soldier at the front if we can't keep up the War Office orders for the gear to keep them fighting?'

'But is it not hard on him, John?'

'Aye, there's more than likely been the odd jibe from boys too young to go,' he said coolly. 'An' maybe he's had a white feather. I wou'den know, but Alex is very like our Sam in some ways. If they make up their minds what's right, they'll not shift. An' Alex knows I just can't do without him.'

In the months that followed there was no good news for anyone. The winter, wet and cold in Ballydown, was even more severe in Flanders, where men spent days on end in flooded trenches under continuous artillery fire. In March 1915, Patrick Doherty and his brother Sean were killed in the battle for St Julien. Their wives, Eileen and Bridget, received identical letters on the same day telling them their husbands were missing, presumed dead. Sam wrote to Rose asking her to come and visit Mary, who was so distraught the doctor had to be called.

Rose went to Donegal and did her best, but Mary was not to be comforted. She was so locked in her own grief she seemed quite indifferent to their plight. Nor was Sam any more successful in his efforts to rouse her. He at least had the comfort of knowing he could ensure none of his eleven great-nephews and nieces would starve on the pittance of a war widow's pension.

Rose came back home and struggled for weeks with a chest infection picked up from one of the children. Sarah had to postpone the visit to Dublin she and the children had been looking forward to in the Easter holiday, so she could look after her. Rose had just managed to get to her feet again when John started coughing. It was the beginning of May before they were both well again.

Rathdrum House
20th June, 1915

My dearest Simon,

Of course I'm disappointed. Yes, I admit, I did shed tears in the privacy of my bedroom. The thought of seeing you has kept my spirits up through all these long months, but having confessed to my weakness and my sadness, I'm now trying to look at the other side. You are far away, but you are not in the trenches. However threatening and difficult the work you are doing, you are not actually being physically bombarded all the time. Unlike my poor cousins' wives, I will not receive a letter telling me you are missing.

My love, we must be thankful for that, at least. Our hope still lives. The plans and promises we made in the gardens at Cleeve last year are still there to support us. While we are both alive and well, the only thing that separates us is time, and time will eventually shrink the distance between us and allow us to make the life together we so desire.

Don't let go of that hope, my dearest, however sad you may be that you will not be allowed to travel to England this summer.

We cannot know how soon things might change. When my mother became ill, I had to comfort the children who'd so looked forward to visiting their Auntie Lily in Dublin. Perhaps we will be able to go in the summer. But, if not, then there is next year. Our invitation stands. They know that what was promised will come about, even if they have to be patient. Like the children, we must find comfort and put our trust in patience. Our promise to each other stands.

I assume you will be given leave, even if you can't come home. You must begin to plan where you can go and what you can do. Will you be allowed to leave Petrograd to visit the surrounding countryside, or will you have to stay in the city in case you are needed urgently?

The children are most sympathetic about your leave and they recommend Lake

Ladoga. I had to smile when I found them studying the atlas and discussing your problem. I did not point out that Lake Ladoga may not be as beautiful as it sounds, for I remember you telling me once how badly bitten you were by mosquitoes on the Volga. A very romantic location, so Helen says.

Summer has come, my love, and the tedium of work is off-set by driving to the mills under blue skies, the birds singing all around me. I neglected my geraniums completely while I was packing my share of the food parcels for the 8th Battalion, but they have distinguished themselves. Without my care, they have done much better than usual and are a mass of bloom, just when I was beginning to think I had inherited a little of my mother's skill as a gardener.

She is quite well again, I am glad to say, and always asks for you most kindly. As do the children, when they are here. Hugh asks me to thank you especially for varying the stamps you use each time you write. He says he now has a full set, but the others are very useful for 'swaps'. Like everything else he does, Hugh collects stamps with a meticulousness I find quite intimidating. His efficiency quite puts Helen and me to shame.

It is time I was taking my morning's work to Millbrook, so I must stop. I can post this letter on the way, hoping it will get to you soon. I am so grateful that I'm permitted

to use your Foreign Office address; so much
shipping is being delayed, damaged, or lost,
that I fear our surviving letters would be
very infrequent. Perhaps when the war is
over, I shall thank Lord Grey in person.

Meantime, my dearest, be of good
cheer. My loving thoughts are always with
you,

Sarah

'What'll you do, Sam, if it *does* come in?'

Sitting on an empty five-gallon can of lubricant,
Alex Hamilton looked across at his friend one late
October afternoon, the light in the workshop
already dim, though it was not long after four
o'clock.

Sam drank deeply from his mug of tea, arranged
his small daughter, Rose, more comfortably on his
knee and considered for a moment.

'Well, being a Quaker there was never any question of going to fight,' he said slowly. 'I was clear in
my mind about that from last August, but I did think
maybe I ought to apply for the Ambulance Corps,' he
said slowly. 'Then the boss asked me to consider what
would happen if I went. I suppose he said much the
same to me as Da said to you. Sure, you can't keep an
army in the field if there isn't the supplies.'

Alex nodded encouragingly.

'Mind you,' Sam went on, a slight smile creasing
his oil-streaked forehead, 'you could argue we could
do without jam in time of war, but I've heard it said
that poor people who live on bread and tea would

be in a bad way if it weren't for the wee bit of sugar and jam they have to give them energy. An' we have our quota for the troops as well.'

'So you wouldn't go?'

Sam looked down at the dark head tucked into his free arm. The child sat quite still, content and slightly sleepy. But Sam wouldn't answer Alex's question in front of her. He knew there was little that Rose missed.

'Good girl,' he said, sliding her gently to her feet. 'Take Da's mug over to the house. Ma'll be wondering where you've gone.'

She took the mug, gave him a great beaming smile and shot her hand out towards Alex.

'Yours too,' she said sharply.

Alex laughed, finished his tea in a long swallow and handed it to her.

'Thank you,' said Sam as she took it silently.

'Thank you,' she repeated obediently as she turned away and ran off through the open door.

'I wouldn't want to go,' said Sam. 'I've thought long and hard an' I've decided my job is to stay here, but surely with conscription I'd have no choice but to go,' he said doubtfully. 'I know in England they let Quakers go into the Ambulance Corps, but they still make them go. If it came in here, surely they'd do the same, wouldn't they?'

'I honestly don't know, Sam. One paper says one thing and the next one something different. But one thing's for sure, I'm likely to get called up before you do, unless I take a trip down the aisle.'

Sam looked puzzled until Alex gave him a big smile.

'Did ye not read that in England there's an awful lot of proposing going on?' asked Alex, laughing. 'Single men are to be called up before married men.'

Sam managed a smile.

'Have you someone in mind, Alex?' he said slyly.

'If I had, I wouldn't insult her like that,' Alex came back at him.

'There's not much we can do till we see if it goes through,' said Sam slowly. 'There seems to be a lot of opposition to it in this country. Maybe, if the worst comes to the worst, we could go together. Would you be willing to consider ambulance work?'

'More than willing, Sam,' he said vigorously. 'My problem is I'm not a Quaker, nor of any religious persuasion, but I cannot bear the thought of killing a man. Maybe I'm a coward,' he said uneasily.

'How would that make you a coward, man? Sam retorted vigorously. 'Sure, what's brave about killin' a fellow creature?'

'I see your point, Sam,' he said, standing up, 'but I'm not convinced that I'd be much good if I was faced with the muzzle of a gun, or found myself under fire.'

'Sure, how do any of us know what we've in us, till it's put to the test?' Sam said, as he walked back over to the workbench. 'I'd say m'self ye'd be right reliable in a tight corner, but for both our sakes I'm hopin' we'll not be put to the test.'

Eighteen

The fourth Monday in April 1916 was a bank holiday throughout Ireland, but while bank officials might be looking forward to enjoying the blue skies and warm sunshine that had settled in over the preceding weekend, it was not a holiday for shops, offices or factories. If the spindles were silent at Millbrook, it was only because of the major maintenance work begun on Saturday, which would take until Monday evening to complete.

At Liskeyborough, Sam Hamilton woke at five, bright light already streaming through the skylight of his barn making bright patches on the narrow beds of his two eldest sons and the spare one now installed for Alex when he stayed overnight at a weekend.

He carried his clothes downstairs, washed and dressed in the room adjoining his workshop. It had once been a stable and he'd set it up with cupboards and washstands and a water tap supplied from a tank on the roof. Still wearing some comfortable old shoes, he tramped over to the house to make his breakfast.

All was silent, the sunlight pouring through the back windows as the sun rose higher. Moving round quietly, he blew up the fire, put the kettle on and cut slices of bread from a baker's loaf, which he buttered liberally. Only when he had eaten and drunk two mugs of tea did he take off his shoes, reach into the cupboard for his boots, and pull them on.

For a moment, he stood in the centre of the room, looking around him as if there was something in his mind he'd forgotten. He shook his head. Whatever it was, it wouldn't come back to him. He'd told Martha he'd be away early and back very late and reminded her to wake the boys. He had the key to the gate of the works in his pocket, his watch in his waistcoat, some money in his wallet and a handkerchief in his trouser pocket. All he had to do was lift his coat from the peg and put on his cap.

Running his eyes round the empty kitchen once more, his breakfast things neatly gathered up on the table, his eye caught the small shelf where he kept his books – not the manuals and specifications; they had their place in the barn – but his Bible and a few volumes of prayers and reflections. He had little enough time ever to read them, but they were there, a source of inspiration and a comfort, when the world seemed full of badness.

'*Lord, you are there at my going out and my coming in,*' he said to himself, wondering where the phrase came from. Was it something he'd read recently or something he'd memorised a long time ago?

Or perhaps, he decided as he pulled the door quietly closed behind him, it was a gift of the spirit to hearten him for the day.

By a quarter to eight, he and Mickey Doyle had loaded the lorry, checked her out and were ready for the road. As they left the yard, the women workers hurrying up the hill pulled out their white head-covers from their pockets and waved at them. Mickey waved back, but Sam returned their greeting with a big smile as he manoeuvred carefully down the narrow access.

The lorry was running sweetly and Sam was well pleased with her. He relaxed at the wheel and settled himself for the long drive. Mickey was no trouble to anyone. A small, wiry man, much stronger than his height and breadth would suggest, he sometimes talked away about the passing scene, or his family, but he never minded if he got no reply.

'Isn't it a powerful day, Sam?' Mickey began, as they headed south. 'Won't the wee ones have a great time trundlin' their eggs? Where do your ones go?'

'Up to the obelisk,' Sam replied, his eye on an approaching vehicle.

'Where's that?'

'On across the railway from our house and up the top of the next hill,' Sam replied, glancing at him now the road was clear. 'Sure ye can see it for miles around. Have ye never noticed it?'

'Ach, aye, I know where ye mean now,' Mickey said, light dawning upon him. 'The stone finger on Cannon Hill. I diden know ye called it an obelisk.'

Sam smiled to himself. Mickey was no great scholar. He'd left school at the first possible moment and he had some difficulty writing. Fortunately, he had a good memory. He'd learnt the bills of lading off by heart, so he could check those out himself without any difficulty, but anything new was a trouble. More than once he'd had to help him out on the quiet.

The journey went well, down through Dromore and on to Newry, the Mourne Mountains to their left a sharp outline against the clear sky. Sam thought of his mother standing by her door looking out at them, as she so often did. Suddenly and unexpectedly, a pleasant, windy day on Church Hill came back into his mind, a day he'd trundled his egg with James and Hannah and Sarah.

For many quiet miles thereafter, his mind moved so far away into that world of childhood he almost forgot about Mickey, so they were already halfway over the bridge at Drogheda when he realised that Mickey had made his usual joke.

'Aye, an insignificant wee river to have caused such a lot of bad feelin',' he agreed, smiling, as they crossed the Boyne and turned off the road to an eating-house where they knew they'd be well looked after.

It was not yet noon, but they were hungry and grateful for the generous meal of meat and vegetables, well covered in a rich gravy. Sam was always amazed at the quantity of food Mickey could put away. He was so thin, he looked as if a proper meal would be too much for him.

They'd made good time so far, but they didn't linger over their meal, for Sam reckoned the next part of the journey would be slower. He always let Mickey drive the lorry from Drogheda to the outskirts of Dublin to give himself a break before the difficult manoeuvres in the crowded streets, but, being less experienced, Mickey found it hard to keep up speed.

The traffic built up quickly after Sam took over again on the outskirts of the city. There were family parties in sidecars going out for the afternoon, the occasional motor with young men in blazers and women in motoring hats, the ends of their veils streaming out behind them as they spun merrily northwards. Twice, they had to slow down until the road was wide enough to overtake columns of marching men out on manoeuvres.

'Boys, they're doing a good speed,' Mickey declared when a party of cyclists wearing bandoliers and armbands whizzed past them as they turned into Dorset Street.

But Sam needed all his attention for the road ahead, for they were into the heart of the city with trams coming and going as well as all the carts and delivery vehicles. He thought the streets seemed busier than usual, but perhaps it was just the number of people strolling around in the sunshine.

As always, Mickey was memorising the route against the day when he hoped to be driving it himself with his own helper, but Sam paid little attention to his recital of street names as he came down Capel Street and turned right along the Liffey. Watched by the holiday makers and followed by small boys swinging their arms and not looking where they were going, were yet more parties of green-clad figures. Sam had to reduce speed and creep along behind them until he was able to make a detour to avoid them. The side streets round St Patrick's Cathedral were quieter, if narrower. Shortly after crossing the river, he saw the familiar twin towers of the biscuit factory.

Weary now, but grateful the last half hour was behind him, he swung wide in the roadway so as to place his vehicle neatly between the entrance pillars. As he drove through he heard an ear-splitting burst of gunfire. A bullet whistled past his cheek leaving his shattered windscreen to collapse in tinkling fragments as a crowd of shouting green figures swarmed round them.

'Jesus, Mary and Joseph,' said Mickey in a whisper, crossing himself.

'Out, at the double, hands up,' a voice roared. 'Higher, higher. Hands above your head. Round here to the front of the vehicle,' the figure continued furiously, waving its rifle up and down as if to emphasise the point.

With his legs still stiff and vibrating from the effort of the last hour's driving, Sam climbed awkwardly down from the cab, his hands above his head.

As the soldiers pushed him towards the front of his lorry, a bayonet poked him in the back. He could feel the heat of the engine on his shoulders as the soldiers closed in around them. Somewhere to his right, he heard another fusillade of shots.

'What *is* going on here?'

The voice was quiet, educated and angry. The green-clad figures parted to allow an officer to come through their ranks and stand looking at them. The officer said something, but although Sam saw his lips move, another burst of gunfire close by made it impossible to hear what he was saying.

'Go and tell those fools to hold their fire,' he said furiously to the man who had roared at them to put their hands up. 'They are *not* to shoot anyone or anything, unless we are attacked from the castle or by the British Army. Is that clear? And see that gate is shut and guarded,' he went on, whirling round to address another armed man. 'And get back to work,' he said more quietly to the remaining watchers.

'I think I can possibly handle two unarmed prisoners without your help,' he said sarcastically as the rest of the volunteers melted away.

'Now who are you and what is your business here?' he said sharply. 'Don't you know that Dublin is now in the hands of the Provisional Government and this factory is a military strongpoint? We are entitled to shoot at sight anyone threatening our security. What is this vehicle carrying?'

'Jam, sir,' said Sam, whose arms were beginning to ache.

'Raspberry and strawberry and a small quantity of marmalade,' added Mickey helpfully.

'Well, we'll see about that,' he said curtly. 'Right, you two, over here, against the wall,' he went on, taking a pistol from his belt and waving at them. 'You, McDairmid, have that lorry searched. Take six men and open those containers. Send two more men to cover this pair while I question them.'

Sam was grateful for the patch of shadow that lay against the wall to which they were now directed, but one look at the two young men who had pointed their rifles at them told him they were in more danger from them than from the officer's pistol. He had never in his life handled a rifle but he'd watched many a man handle equipment in the workshop. You could always tell when a man knew what he was doing. This pair didn't have much idea.

'Where are you from?' he began curtly.

'Richhill, County Armagh, sir,' replied Sam coolly.

'A good Orangeman, I suppose, from that part of the world?' he said, looking pleased with himself.

'No, sir.'

'What? What's your name?' he said, looking at him curiously.

'Sam Hamilton, sir.'

'That's a good Protestant name,' he said firmly. 'And you're not an Orangeman?' he said, disbelieving.

'I'm a Quaker, sir.'

'Are you now?' he said, his tone softening slightly. 'All right. Put your hands down.'

Sam lowered his arms gratefully. He'd done many an awkward job up over his head, but he'd no idea how painful it was to keep your arms in the one place for so long.

'Name?' he said, swinging round towards Mickey.

'Mickey Doyle, sir.'

'And are *you* an Orangeman then?' the officer snapped.

'No, I am *not*,' he replied promptly. 'I'm an Irish Volunteer, the same as you are yourself, sir,' he said proudly.

'In the name of goodness, if you're a Volunteer, what are you doing here?' he asked furiously. 'Why aren't you out with your company in Richhill?'

'Because the manoeuvres was cancelled for yesterday,' Mickey said crossly. 'It was in all the newspapers. But a man came up from Dublin and told us forby. He said the whole thing was off.'

The officer looked back over his shoulder to where his men were unloading drums from the lorry. Sam thought he caught a curse and a comment about traitors, but the noise of rolling barrels and a further outbreak of rifle fire drowned out the rest of his comment.

'Put your hands down, Doyle,' he said, looking at him impatiently. 'I don't propose to take prisoners, you'd only be a nuisance when we're attacked,' he announced, looking from Mickey to Sam and back again.

'What is it, Kearney?' he asked, more agreeably, as a dark-eyed young man approached him, his rifle held somewhat more confidently than the two who still eyed Mickey and Sam uneasily.

'Jam, Commandant. As they said. Raspberry and strawberry. Rather good actually, sir.'

Somewhat to Sam's surprise, the commandant smiled warmly at the young man, then swung round to address him again, a slight hint of amusement still touching his lips.

'Sam Hamilton,' he began wearily, 'can you explain to me why you should be bringing jam to a biscuit factory?'

'Yes, sir. If you open a tin of the fancy ones they're mostly squares and rectangles,' he explained, trying not to look at the young fellow with the rifle pointing at him, 'but in between you'll see two or three wee oval shapes. There's a bit of a dint in the middle of them and that has the jam in. They're very nice,' he added matter-of-factly.

'We've unloaded the lorry, Commandant. Was that correct?' asked the young man.

'Quite correct, Kearney. Might come in useful,' he said with a pleasant smile. 'See it's stowed in the kitchens and tell the Cumann na mBan women.'

'Right, you two. We're likely to be attacked at any moment. You, Doyle, will you vouch for your Quaker friend here if I let the pair of you go? Straight out and back up to Ulster. I'll give you a pass to get through our men. They'll have closed the roads by now.'

'Yes, sir,' said Mickey Doyle enthusiastically.

The commandant searched all his pockets before he found a piece of paper. He scrawled something on it and handed it to Sam, who thanked him and tucked it carefully away in his waistcoat.

'Your people did good work in Cloughjordan, so I've heard, Sam Hamilton. It wouldn't be my way, but then we can't all be the same, I suppose. Now, on your way. Get out of here as quick as you can.'

Pausing only to remove the shattered glass from the metal bodywork covering the engine, they turned the lorry in the yard of Jacob's, waited for the gate to be opened for them and drove straight out, up the road past Dublin Castle and back across the Liffey.

The first time Sam and Mickey had to stop on their way out of the city was when they encountered a half-constructed barricade surrounded by small boys, who appeared to be enjoying themselves thoroughly. The moment they stopped, they climbed up the wheels and into the empty back.

'Will you lot go home *now*?' the irate officer

shouted to them as he reached up to Sam's window for the piece of paper he held out to him.

The boys paid no attention to him whatever, but Sam was pleased to see the cheering effect of Commandant McDonagh's piece of paper on the harassed officer. He smiled at them, asked if they'd been delivering supplies, if the position at Jacob's had been secured, and what other activity they'd seen on their way out of the city.

Sam let Mickey describe the arrangements at the biscuit factory. Despite his close encounter with two rifles and a pistol, he'd managed to observe both the deployment of snipers in the two towers which dominated the route north from Portobello Barracks to Dublin Castle and the setting up of a first-aid post and a kitchen by one of the women's groups.

When the officer handed Sam back his authorisation and waved him on, the small boys refused to get down from the lorry. Mickey waved his arms furiously at them, shouted abuse and got nowhere.

Sam turned off the engine, walked slowly round to the back of the lorry, stood looking at them and said nothing. He went on standing there till first one, then another, climbed down. A small group of older boys remained firm, unwilling to lose face in front of the younger boys already on the ground.

'Have you boys ever been to Drogheda?' Sam asked in a conversational tone.

Heads were shaken.

'Well, ye're in the right place for goin',' he said, smiling agreeably. 'Drogheda's my next stop. Mind you, it's a fair step back. You'd hardly foot it before dark.'

The boys took the hint and a few minutes later, they were on their way.

There were no more barricades, but the road was blocked by a lorry unloading a group of men carrying rifles and pickaxes as they ran close by the railway line going north. Waiting patiently for the lorry to move out of the way, they saw the first of the men make their way across to the railway line. Some began digging up the lines, others began excavating shallow trenches.

'Heavy work that,' said Sam, as they set off again, managing to pick up speed as the traffic became lighter and the delays fewer.

Despite the brilliant sunshine and the warmth of the afternoon, the draught through the missing windscreen rapidly froze them both. Halfway to Drogheda, Sam drew into the side of the road to let them warm through and put on their jackets.

'Boys a dear, there's some heat in that sun,' said Mickey, shivering with cold.

'Aye, it's great. Ye can feel it doin' ye good,' Sam agreed, as he turned his back to get his shoulders warm. 'Maybe we should warm our coats before we put them on. The heat might last longer,' he said suddenly. 'My Ma use to do that when we were wee. She'd warm ours in front of the fire before we went to school,' he went on, as he spread theirs on the rough grass by the roadside.

'What's happened your sleeve, Sam?' Mickey asked, as he looked down at the garments on the sun-warmed grass.

Sam bent down, puzzled by a burn mark that hadn't been there when he put it on.

'Hold on a minute, Mickey,' he said, climbing back up into the cab. 'I think I know what did that.' He took out his penknife and levered a bullet from the wooden panel behind their heads. 'There you are,' he said, dropping it into Mickey's hand. 'D'you want it as a souvenir? It might just as well have been in your head or mine.'

'Aye, an' what wou'd our childer do without us, Sam? Your eight and my five,' he said, shaking his head in distress.

Sam began to pull on his coat, for there was a long journey still ahead and he was sure they'd have to stop again to get warm.

'I'll tell you what, Sam. I'll say nothin' to my missus, if you'll say nothin' to yours,' Mickey said suddenly.

Sam nodded agreeably. It had never occurred to him to tell Martha.

'What'll we do with that?' Sam asked, puzzled that Mickey was still staring at the bullet so intently.

'I'll tell you what, Sam,' said Mickey quietly. 'While you're drivin' over the bridge at Drogheda, I'll throw it in the Boyne an' we'll never say another word about it. No one will be a bit the wiser.'

The journey back to Richhill took longer than either of them had reckoned, the cold eating into them savagely as the sun went down and the sky paled into dusk. A meal in Newry warmed them, but it was no more than a brief respite, for they'd barely thawed out by the time they had to be on the road again. By the time they got back, unlocked the factory gates, put the lorry away and locked up again, it was a clear, star-filled night, the temperature dropping like a stone.

The two men parted at the foot of the access road, bidding each other goodnight in few words, silent with fatigue and cold, as they mounted their bicycles to cycle home. Sam put his bicycle away in the barn, picked up his torch to light him across the yard and pushed open the door into the silent kitchen. He switched off the torch and sat down by the stove to take off his boots. There was still a little warmth from the stove and a smell of cooked food lingered on the air, but he hadn't the energy to stir the fire and make tea. For a few minutes he just sat, listening to the tick of the clock and the distant rumble of Joe snores.

Lord you are there at my going out and my coming in.

The words came again and echoed in his head. From somewhere nearby he heard a barn owl call. Immediately, he thought of Sarah and her old, childish fear that the owls cried because someone had hurt them.

He got to his feet, put his boots in the cupboard and pushed his feet awkwardly into his old shoes. As he put his hand on the door latch, holding it carefully so that it wouldn't make a noise and wake the children, he remembered what he'd not been able to remember in the early morning. Sarah was in Dublin at this very moment, with wee Helen and Hugh, on an Easter visit to their Aunt Lily.

Nineteen

Sarah opened her eyes in the darkness. A narrow shaft of sunshine, bright as the beam from a torch on a moonless night, spilled through a tiny gap in the heavy velvet curtains and cast a shimmering patch of light on the faded wallpaper at the far side of the large, high-ceilinged room.

'Another lovely day,' she thought, smiling to herself as she turned on her side. 'How lucky we've been so far.'

She lay, warm and comfortable, as the shapes of Lily's furniture began to emerge, the tiny spill of light now reflecting from the frame of a handsome watercolour of Currane Lodge. She liked this house, its well-loved contents, its worn but still beautiful carpets, the velvet curtains with their tasselled ropes, the small pieces of delicate china that Lily liked to spread around on every available surface.

The pretty cups and saucers collected over the years used to worry her when the children were younger, but not now. At eleven, Helen was more careful with them than ever Lily was herself. As for Hugh, nearly two years older, he simply removed the delicate objects to a safe place when he needed somewhere to spread out his books.

She lay listening to the unfamiliar sounds of Dawson Street. It was so strange to hear traffic go past the door. Even when her father or Alex turned the motor outside the gates of Rathdrum, the sound was so far away that it was absorbed by the lime trees in the avenue, overlaid by birdsong in the garden, or by familiar noises from the kitchen.

This morning the traffic was already busy, although the house itself was still silent. She could hear footsteps and the jingle of harness and the creak of delivery carts. Any moment now, there would be a perfunctory knock at the door and Lily's girls would appear. Maureen, the elder, would fling back the curtains, tell her what a grand morning it was, then show her sister Bridget where to put the tray with her morning tea. A beautiful dark-haired girl with the sweetest of tempers, Bridget had been placing her tea tray on the same bedside table every morning since they came, but she never showed the slightest sign of being bothered by her sister's bossiness.

She stretched out a hand and picked up the bedside clock. Although her eyes had adjusted to the dimness of the room, she couldn't see the figures, but something about the movement of that bright beam of sunshine made her wonder if it was later than usual. At that moment, there was a discreet knock at her door.

'Come in.'

She sat up in bed and reached quickly for her dressing gown. The draughts which had plagued the house when first they'd visited were much reduced, but there was no heating upstairs and the room was very cold, despite the brightness of the late April morning. To her great surprise, it was her uncle who came in.

'Morning, Sarah. Sorry to trouble you,' Sam said, pulling back an edge of curtain so they could see each other. 'We have one or two problems about going to Fairyhouse today. Lily has a migraine and is still in bed, and we seem to be without Maureen and Bridget.'

'You mean they're not in the house?' Sarah asked, aware now that it *had* all seemed unusually quiet.

'No, no sign of them. Breakfast is laid, but they did that last night as they always do. But that's all.'

'They went to a dance last night,' Sarah said helpfully. 'I know that, because they told me it was at Liberty Hall and I wondered if Brendan might be singing, but I'm sure they came back as I was going to sleep.'

'Yes, they did,' he agreed, nodding. 'I was reading in the sitting room but I heard their voices on the stairs. I've been up to their room. Beds made, all tidy. No note.'

'How strange,' Sarah said, perplexed. 'Oh, but poor Lily, Sam. Is her head a bad one?'

'Mostly eye strain, I would think,' he said reassuringly. 'She sat sketching in the full sun yesterday with the light off the sea. You know how bright it was. She says she just needs to sleep it off. It was when I went down to fetch her a cup of tea that I found the birds had flown.'

'Well, we can make our own breakfast,' Sarah said easily, 'but it's very strange.'

'What about Fairyhouse?'

'Oh, we can't possibly go and leave poor Lily, Sam,' she protested.

'She says she doesn't mind a bit; she'll be asleep. She doesn't want the children to be disappointed.'

'No, Sam. We've had a lovely time and been out so much, we'll just have a quiet day here,' she reassured him. 'Helen is sure to want to go and feed the ducks. I can take them both for a walk this afternoon.'

'Well, whatever you think. I admit I could do with some breakfast.'

Sarah laughed. Sam had the look of a man who'd been up and about for some time and more than ready for something to eat.

'Right. If you wake Helen and Hugh I'll be down very shortly and we'll see what we can do.'

Breakfast was rather more difficult than Sarah had expected. There was neither bacon nor eggs, very little butter and only two rather tired-looking ends of baker's loaf. The smaller one was distinctly mouldy, but the larger one could probably be saved. With careful cutting and trimming she reckoned she could produce six slices for toast.

There was half a jug of milk in the larder and the coronation tea caddy was half full, but when she tried to light the stove, she discovered there was no gas. The sitting-room fire was still smoking, but Hugh rearranged it to accommodate the kettle and used the elderly brass bellows to good effect. While the tea brewed Helen and Hugh made toast on the now red fire.

There was no marmalade either, but there was a new jar of damson jam which Rose had sent with a Simnel cake as a present to Lily.

'The baker usually delivers on a Monday morning,' said Sam, as they cleared away breakfast. 'The milkman should have been here. He brings the butter and eggs as well. I think I'll just go out and buy a paper, and I've letters to post. Have you any?' he asked, raising an eyebrow.

Sarah smiled back and blushed slightly. She'd spent most of the previous evening writing to Simon. 'Yes, I'll fetch it for you,' she said, smiling. 'Are you sure Lily is all right?'

Reassured that she really did want to be left to sleep, Sarah found a paper bag for the mouldy bread and asked Hugh whether he would like to come with them to feed the ducks. To her surprise, he said he would. Remembering you needed a key to come in by the front door, she collected one from the drawer in the hall table before they all stepped out into the loveliest of spring mornings.

'Ma, this is even nicer than going to the races,' said Helen happily. 'I didn't think trees in a city could look so beautiful,' she went on as the three of them walked briskly up Dawson Street and crossed the road into St Stephen's Green.

'They're digging trenches,' said Hugh in amazement, as they came through the northern gate and headed for the pond. 'You can't do that in a park,' he protested, 'even if you *are* on manoeuvres.'

Sarah looked around at the uniformed figures moving purposively backwards and forwards. They were all armed and wearing ammunition belts. An officer was giving orders and a number of trenches were under way between the shrubbery and the railings.

'Look, Mama,' Helen gasped, 'a lady with guns.'

Sarah followed her gaze. She was quite right. Standing under the memorial archway at the far side of the park, a tall woman wearing a dark-green uniform with trousers surveyed the scene. From time to time, she waved her arm imperiously at a number of young girls who were carrying bags and bundles towards a small summerhouse where some older girls were unpacking them. Stuck into her belt were two pistols.

'Look, there's Mr Kearney, Mama. He looks very annoyed,' said Helen urgently, dragging her eyes away from the woman with the pistols.

'Well so would you be if someone started digging up your park,' said Hugh sharply. 'He's responsible for damage to the place. He's not just here to look after the ducks.'

Mr Kearney, by now an old friend, was working his way towards them. He stopped to speak to a young man in uniform sitting on a summer seat, his arm round a pretty girl, watching the trenches being dug. Already some of the ones just behind the railings were large enough to accommodate three men. More men were arriving all the time.

'Oh, let's ignore them,' said Helen firmly, pulling her bag of bread from her pocket as she strode forward to where the ducks stood by the water's edge, preening themselves or floating lazily on the sparkling water.

As she put her hand into her bag, a shot rang out. The ducks at her feet rose in a flurry of noise and flapping wings, startling her. She stepped backwards so quickly that she nearly fell over, the bread dropping at her feet. Sarah was just about to suggest they should leave when Mr Kearney appeared at their side.

'I'm sorry, ma'am. I must ask you to go,' he said, shaking his head angrily. 'Ye might get hurt when the military gets down from the castle to clear this lot out. They should be shot,' he said furiously. 'An' me with five sons fightin' in France. I'm ashamed of them. Ashamed.'

'Mr Kearney, will they shoot your ducks?' Helen asked desperately, her voice cracking slightly as she tried to stop herself from crying.

'They'll have to shoot me first, miss,' he said firmly. 'Now don't worry. They'll be all right. A day or two and we'll be fine again,' he said encouragingly, as he hurried away to speak to other people walking in the sunshine, watching what they thought was yet one more manoeuvre.

It was now just after noon, the trees spreading pools of deep shadow at their feet. They retraced their steps across the park, crossed over the road and made their way back down Dawson Street. As Sarah put the key in the door, a series of explosions echoed on the still air. The loud detonations were followed by some erratic gunfire. They went inside quickly and she went straight upstairs to make sure Lily was all right. The heavy shutters on her bedroom closed firmly against the light, she was fast asleep and didn't stir as she quietly opened and closed the door again.

Back down in the sitting room, Hugh was mending the fire, and Sarah had just taken her jacket off when she heard a cab draw up at the door. Looking out through the sitting-room window, to her amazement, she saw Sam get out carrying a newspaper.

'Sarah, the fools have risen,' he said, as he strode across the pavement to meet her at the open door. 'Go upstairs and pack as quick as you can. Get Helen and Hugh to help you. The sooner I get you on a train going north the better. The cab's waiting for us.'

Seeing how distressed he was, Sarah asked no questions, but simply ran upstairs and packed up her possessions with all the speed she could manage. Helen packed her own things in record time and helped Hugh to do the same.

Downstairs again, her arm aching from manoeuvring the heaviest suitcase, Sarah could see the cab driver was having trouble with his horse. Fidgety and difficult, it was reacting to the sudden bursts of firing from St Stephen's Green and somewhere nearer at hand. Sam and Hugh were trying to load the small suitcases into the oscillating cab, Hugh hampered by his short stature, Sam by his bad shoulder.

'I'll say your goodbyes to Lily when I get back,' Sam called to Sarah as he saw her pause at the front door. 'There's not a moment to be lost,' he added, as he came back, lifted the heavy suitcase and half carried, half dragged it to the waiting cab. Sarah ran to help him, then went back and closed the front door as Helen and Hugh got into the cab ahead of her.

'What's happening, Uncle Sam?' asked Hugh coolly as the cab lurched forward, the horse now trotting enthusiastically away from the kerbside. 'Is it a rebellion?'

'Yes, you could say that, Hugh,' said Sam, equally coolly.

Sarah looked out of the cab window. It was fifteen minutes since they'd heard the explosions, but the streets were still full of people going about their business as usual. With the midday sun pouring down, cabbies passing in the other direction had taken off their jackets and were driving with their shirt sleeves rolled up.

It felt so normal a spring day, and yet she felt sure Sam had the measure of the situation. She looked at him hopefully as they bowled along. He was pale and very tense, but covering his anxiety for the most part. She was aware he mightn't wish to say much in front of Helen and Hugh.

'I posted your letter, Sarah,' he began suddenly. 'But I'm not sure when Simon will get it,' he said, keeping his tone conversational. 'As I came out of the GPO, it was taken over by the Irish Volunteers. I couldn't quite believe what was happening, so I stayed to watch. Padraic Pearse came out and read a proclamation,' he said, taking a folded sheet from his pocket and offering it to Hugh, who began to study it carefully.

'He and James Connolly shook hands and Connolly said he was happy to have lived to see the day,' he continued. 'The volunteers then knocked out all the windows and have barricaded themselves in. There's a splendid green flag flying, a fair amount of random firing going on, and I now know where

Maureen and Bridget are,' he said, peering out of his window again to see what progress they were making.

'Oh, Sam, no. Surely not,' Sarah said, horrified at the thought of the quiet, gentle Bridget shut up behind the barricaded windows.

'Yes, I saw them going in. A detachment of the women's group, Cumann na mBan,' he said flatly. 'You ought to approve, Sarah. Don't you always advocate women playing their part? No discrimination and all that?'

'Of course, I do, Sam,' she said firmly, irritated by his tone. 'But I don't approve of *anyone* taking up arms and killing other people. I may not be a Quaker myself, but I agree with them that killing is not the best way of solving problems. But I can't bear the thought of poor Bridget in there,' she ended anxiously.

'Will they get killed?' said Helen, a dangerous waver in her voice.

'What about Maureen?' said Hugh, speaking at the same moment.

But neither Helen nor Hugh got an answer to their questions. They heard a high-pitched neigh from the horse as the cab stopped with a jolt and began to rock backwards and forwards as the horse jittered uneasily on the cobbles.

'Sorry, sir, ma'am,' a young man said, glancing from Sam to Sarah as he flung open the door. 'I shall have to ask you to get out.'

He ran his eye over Hugh and Helen and to Sarah's amazement offered his hand to Helen, holding it till she was safely on the ground.

One glance through her window told Sarah why they'd been stopped. A half-completed barricade stretched across the road. Men in full uniform and others wearing only armbands and bandoliers were piling up furniture and mattresses and weaving wire between the heaviest items. They were working quickly, shouting to each other and calling for more material to complete the blocking of the road.

'I suggest you get indoors as soon as you can, sir,' the officer said courteously. 'We're expecting an attack at any moment,' he added, as Sam jumped down and turned back to help Sarah.

'You, sir,' the officer shouted up at the cabby. 'I must ask you to get down. Take your horse out of the shafts and lead him away. I'm requisitioning this vehicle in the name of the Provisional Government. They will compensate you for any loss you may incur,' he added quickly when he saw the look of bewilderment cross the cabby's face.

'You will, be damned,' said the cabby furiously, pulling on the reins to turn the cab away from the barricade, just as Sarah was getting down.

As the cab rocked violently, she held on to Sam's hand and jumped. Landing awkwardly, she tipped forward and just managed to avoid falling headlong as a loud report rang out just beside her. She felt something whiz past her like an angry insect and a moment later there was a scream of agony as the horse pitched forward on its knees, blood pouring from its wounded leg.

Clinging desperately to the roof of the cab, the driver managed to slither to the ground just before the poor animal fell sideways, pulling the cab over with it. It lay there, its eyes rolling, emitting heart-rending groans.

'You bloody fool,' the officer shouted, spinning round and glaring at a pale-faced lad who stood horror-stricken, his rifle still pointed towards them. 'Put the safety catch on, *now*, this minute. And get back to work,' he shouted angrily, as he unslung his own rifle, sighted carefully on the struggling animal and shot it neatly through the head.

'Sorry about that,' he said gently, looking down at Helen and Hugh. 'I love horses, but there was nothing else I could do for the poor creature.'

He signalled to his men to add the body of the horse to the barricade and use the cab to complete the blocking of the street.

The suitcases now lay on the road beside them. Sarah shook her head as Sam went to lift the largest one. 'Leave it, Sam,' she said quickly. 'We've a long walk back. We can probably manage the two small ones. You take the lighter one and Hugh and I'll share this one.'

She put her arms round Helen, whose face streamed with silent tears.

'He didn't suffer, darling,' she said, dropping to her knees.

As Helen buried her face in her shoulder and sobbed, she saw Sam take out his wallet and give some notes to the cabby. Over the noise of men dragging furniture and hammering nails to anchor the strengthening wire, she caught only the odd word, but she saw the cabby nod and look less furious as he pocketed the notes.

'I'll see ye next week then, sur,' he said, tipping his hat to him as he turned away. 'God bless ye, sur.'

He walked with such a very bad limp, Sarah wondered if he'd been wounded in the Boer War.

'Now, darling, dry your eyes,' she said, stroking Helen's long hair back from her damp face. 'We must go home and see how Auntie Lily is. She's all by herself and she won't know what's happened.'

Helen sniffed, accepted Sarah's hanky and collected herself.

'I don't think she'll be frightened,' she said thoughtfully, as Sarah took her hand and led her to the pavement where Sam and Hugh stood waiting. 'But she *might* be lonely. And she'll wonder where we've all gone.'

They walked in silence, two by two, trying to keep in what shadow there was as the afternoon grew hotter and hotter and dazzling light reflected back at them from streets and buildings. The noise of gun-fire was sporadic and mostly distant, but several times they saw a shop, or a house, being occupied as they passed busy road intersections.

An officer, usually a young man, like the one in charge of the barricade, would knock on the door and explain that the building was needed for the security of the new government. The inhabitants were given the option of leaving or retreating to the back rooms or the cellar.

At one handsome three-storey house, there was no one at home but a very young maid. She stood at the open door, trembling, a small figure in black

with a white cap and a minute white apron, staring
at the heavily laden figures who confronted her.

'Away and get your coat and go home to your
Ma,' said one of them kindly. 'When they come back
from the races, we'll say we chased you out. They'll
not blame you,' he said reassuringly, as she hovered
in the doorway, close to tears.

Sarah had no idea how far it was back to Dawson
Street. The cab had got up a good speed and they
were certainly well on their way to the station when
they'd been stopped. She didn't know the city all
that well, but what was certain was that Helen was
not a good walker. At the best of times she tired
easily and, after her experience at the barricade, this
was not the best of times. By now, she was walking
so slowly that Sam and Hugh were having to stop
regularly to let them catch up.

'Let me carry the case now for a bit, Hugh,' Sarah
said, smiling encouragingly.

'No, Mama, I'm fine,' he said firmly, as he swung
the case to his other side and prepared to set off
again.

'Ma, I'm so thirsty,' Helen whispered, stopping
again only a few minutes later.

Sarah was longing for a drink herself. It was
hardly surprising they were all thirsty and hungry.
They'd shared the toast at breakfast, a slice and a half
each from a modest loaf. They'd only had one cup of
tea, all the kettle on the fire could produce if they
were not to wait indefinitely, and that was a long
time ago now.

'How far is it now, Sam?' she asked cautiously.

'A bit yet,' he said coolly, 'but there's a shop that might be open not too far away. A fruit shop. Grapes and oranges and big juicy pears,' he added, rolling his eyes, so that Helen managed a small smile and Hugh brightened visibly.

It must have been at least another half mile to the shop. The awning was still out to cast a shadow on the window, which was full of beautiful fruit. Lined up in rows, resting on pink, white, or silver paper, or displayed in baskets with paper shavings, they saw mouth-watering grapes and melons, pears and oranges. But the door of the shop was firmly shut and barred.

'Never mind,' said Sam, looking at their downcast faces. 'It's not far now. We can take a short cut down the alley behind the hotel and come in the back way. The kitchen door is never locked. There might be some lemonade in the larder,' he said hopefully, as they turned off Grafton Street into the narrow alley-way that ran behind the Royal Hibernian Hotel.

There was no lemonade in the larder, but there was plenty of water in the tap. They all stood and drank large glasses full before Sam went to look for Lily and Helen and Hugh ran upstairs to the lavatory.

It was only as they hurried out of the room that Sarah noticed a loaf on the kitchen table. Freshly baked, with some of its new-bread smell still lingering and partly wrapped in a piece of paper, it had a set of grubby fingerprints on one soft, white side, and a dint in its dark upper crust. She picked up the loaf to examine it more closely and saw lying on the table the same lines of print she'd glanced at quickly in the cab when Hugh passed over the piece of paper Sam had brought back from his visit to the Post Office.

She sat down abruptly and began to read:

POBLACHT NA H EIREANN
THE PROVISIONAL GOVERNMENT
OF THE IRISH REPUBLIC
TO THE PEOPLE OF IRELAND
Irishmen and Irishwomen: in the name of
God and of the dead generations . . .

She broke off as Helen reappeared. Still very pale, but smiling now, she came and put an arm round her mother.

'Ma, I'm so hungry,' she began. 'But Auntie Lily is up and dressed and she says there's sure to be something to eat in the larder. Maureen and Bridget only took one day's rations so there should be plenty left.'

Lily was a very optimistic person, but her optimism was not always well founded. By way of lunch, all Sarah could produce was bread, thinly spread with butter and plenty of damson jam, followed by generous slices of her mother's Simnel cake. There was tea as well, once the kettle boiled on the hot fire, but there was no more milk.

'My goodness, what a long walk you've had,' said Lily as she finished off her cake. 'Why didn't you take a cab?' she asked, looking from Sarah to Sam and back again.

'There weren't any to take, Lily,' Sam said quietly. 'It seems we are in the middle of a rebellion.'

'Oh dear,' she said. 'I was afraid something un-pleasant was going to happen. Poor Willie told me last week he might not be able to come to our Thursday painting session,' she said sadly, 'and now I suppose he's in the Post Office with his brother and you say it's all barricaded up.'

'Who's Willie, Auntie Lily?' asked Helen promptly, her delicate colouring and good spirits restored by her unusual lunch. 'Is he one of your young men?'

Lily laughed merrily. 'Yes, he is, Helen,' she said, smiling. 'One of the painters. Willie Pearse. Not a very good painter, but a dear boy. I just wish he wouldn't follow his brother everywhere he goes. He won't like it one bit in the GPO if it's all barricaded up and there are guns going off.'

'Sam, dear, did you say you'd seen Maureen and Bridget going in as well?' Lily asked suddenly.

'Yes, I did. There was a whole group of Cumann na mBan, loaded down with stuff. I think they were carrying first-aid kits.'

'Oh, you don't think anyone will get hurt, do you?' she said, with a look of startled amazement.

Sarah busied herself with the empty teacups and left it to Sam to reply. Lily's vagueness and unrelat-edness could sometimes be endearing, but the look on Sam's face suggested he was having difficulty keeping his impatience in check.

'Well, provided the British Government doesn't take it amiss that they're being attacked in time of war and don't bring in troops and artillery to clear them out, they ought to be all right,' he said steadily. 'Did Maureen and Bridget leave you a note then?' he went on quickly, hoping to turn the conversation before either Helen or Hugh joined in.

'Oh yes, dear girls,' she said, smiling. 'They left it under my paint box,' she explained, waving her hand towards a table with a half-finished watercolour. 'They said they'd been mobilised, whatever that means, and they'd each taken a day's rations. They said they'd pay me out of their wages for their rations and they hoped I'd be all right until they came back in a few days' time.'

Sam sighed and bent forward to make up the fire. It might be hot outside, but the sitting room was now in shadow and getting uncomfortably cold. As he placed lumps of coal on the fire, a burst of gun-fire broke the silence in the room. It went on for some time, during which no one said anything.

'Well, how about some Scrabble, Helen?' said Lily easily. 'Perhaps, Hugh, you'd like to play too. I can finish my painting later.'

She stood up and moved her drawing board aside to make a bigger space between her collection of Chinese porcelain bowls.

'Good idea,' said Sam. 'Sarah and I will just do the washing-up and see what we're going to have for supper.'

He picked up the tray she'd just loaded and headed for the kitchen, leaving her to follow with the other half of the Simnel cake.

'What are we going to do, Sarah? he said anxiously, as she shut the kitchen door behind her. 'We can't survive long on that cake, and things can only get worse.'

'In what way, Sam?'

'Well, it might only be a matter of hours, a day or two at the most, till the fighting starts,' he said matter-of-factly. 'The British will send in the troops to clear out the rebels. A lot of people will be caught in the crossfire.'

He dropped his eyes sadly and caught sight of the proclamation which she'd smoothed out and begun to read at the kitchen table.

'There's something I couldn't tell you, Sarah, on our way to the station.'

He paused awkwardly and studied the crumbs on the bread board where Sarah had carefully cut a thin slice from the loaf to remove the dirty fingermarks.

'I think I know where the loaf came from,' he said, nodding at the crumbs. 'On the way to the GPO I saw a group of uniformed men stopping a bread cart. I thought they were just buying loaves for their own use, but I think now they probably requisitioned the lot, like the cab and the furniture.'

He paused and Sarah felt herself grow unbearably tense. To her surprise, he dropped down in one of the kitchen chairs, his eyes glistening with tears as he buried his head in his hands.

'Sarah, I saw Brendan there in St Stephen's Green with Michael Mallin. I'm sure that's who sent the loaf.'

Twenty

When Rose drew back the curtains on Easter Monday a beautiful spring morning greeted her. Immediately she thought of all the jobs that would be so much easier to do on such a bright and fresh day. With John at Millbrook until early evening she'd have a clear run right through the day.

'What a lovely day for the races,' she thought, as she put out crumbs for the birds.

It would be so good for them all to have a real treat. She sighed. Perhaps in Dublin, with Lily and her friends, there wouldn't be so much talk about what was happening in France.

Sometimes she felt all people ever talked about these days was the war, especially since the Ulster Division had left for the front and rumours circulated that a big offensive was being planned for the summer.

However hard she tried, the steady flow of men from the four mills lost in action depressed her spirits, and now there seemed no prospect of an end to it. At the beginning of the war everyone had clung to the hope that a man reported missing might reappear, but now they all knew that except in very rare cases, it meant they'd been killed. The worse the battle, the less chance of burying the dead, and there would be no comrade to remove the identification papers.

'But should you not put it out of mind?' Rose asked herself, as she came downstairs with the first pair of curtains for the wash.

If you thought about it all the time, it was much harder to laugh. And that seemed wrong. Losing your capacity to laugh was only going to add to the weight of the burden, not help you to support it. But if you didn't keep in mind what was happening at all, what did that say about *you*?

That was the sort of question she always put to her dear friend Elizabeth as they packed parcels or knitted socks for the local Red Cross to send to the front. The sort of question she could never resolve to her own satisfaction.

She smiled to herself as she lifted the first kettle of water from the stove, carried it through to the deep Belfast sink in the dairy and shivered as she felt the chill of the dairy envelope her. She turned on the tap, stood back as the powerful stream of icy-cold water splashed droplets on her apron, then turned it off quickly. An inch or two was all she needed.

John had been talking about building at the back of the house, enlarging the dairy and putting in a boiler that would give hot water and feed two radiators. He said he noticed the cold more now he did less physical work himself, but she'd always felt the cold, so it must be worse for her. Back in the summer she'd made light of it, but after another winter, she had to agree with him.

Suddenly and unexpectedly, she thought of their very first meeting. By the side of Currane Lake, he'd climbed up a hillside to ask for her help, the coach he was attending halted in the hot sun, one of the horses having lost a shoe. She'd been so reluctant to come down and talk to a young man wearing a coat at least two sizes too small for his broad shoulders.

Standing in for one of Sir Capel's regular grooms, he'd laughed when she pointed it out. 'Shure a blacksmith niver needs a coat.'

She drained away the dirty water, well satisfied with its dark colour, and began rinsing the pretty patterned curtains till the water ran clear, letting her thoughts run on over all the long years of their time together. They'd shared such happiness and such sadness. She'd known too many couples who'd grown out of love as time went by, others who'd replaced love with resentment. She gave thanks that John still loved her, even to thinking about her red hands on cold mornings when she rinsed clothes in an unheated dairy.

By the middle of the morning, all the curtains were blowing on the clothes line. She dried her damp hands on her apron, chose a small teapot from the dresser, made tea, and sat down gratefully by the fire, wrapping her red hands round her mug to warm them.

'It's desperate quiet without Sarah.'

Only the previous evening John had put his newspaper down and spoken those words. She'd almost laughed, the image of the turbulent young girl who blew into the house like an east wind conjured up before her, but the look on John's face was no laughing matter. Bereft almost, as if Sarah's absence opened up a silence he could hardly bear.

'Yes, you'd miss her popping in, or hearing the motor on the hill,' she replied gently.

'Ach, I know it's only a couple of days this time, but I was thinkin' of when she goes for good, as surely she will. An' harder on you, love, than me, with you here at home all the time.'

'Yes, I'll miss her,' Rose agreed calmly. 'And the young ones too, though it's only in the holidays they're in and out every day.'

'I was thinkin' that maybe when she goes, we might move to Dromore,' he said abruptly. 'There's some nice houses there, not far from Elizabeth and Richard. Ye'd have more company and less hard work keepin' the place right. We're not gettin' any younger, ye know.'

'Well, that's true enough, love,' she agreed, hiding her surprise that he should have been thinking ahead in this way. 'I suppose it would all depend on who we got in Rathdrum. I don't think Sarah would want to keep it lying empty for most of the year, and she did say Simon was very likely to be posted abroad.'

John nodded silently.

'Like enough she'll sell it,' he said sharply. 'There's nothing worse than property left empty, even though we'd keep an eye on it. Is there any word of Simon gettin' his call back home? She says he'd applied for it before the war started. That'll be two years in August.'

'I think the war changed everything, John. In the ordinary way, he'd have applied and been moved in a couple of months perhaps, but if there was no one else to do his job in Petersburg, he'd have had to stay. Not every man at the Foreign Office speaks Russian and German and French.'

John's face softened briefly, but the desolation soon returned.

'An' you think she'll marry him?' he asked shortly.

'Oh, yes. She will. It's just a matter of time,' she said reassuringly.

'Would ye think of a move then?' he asked shyly.

'I'd miss the mountains,' she said after a long pause. 'And the garden. And the Jacksons, especially young Emily, but you're right. It's all going to be so different when Sarah goes, and I'd be happy to be near Elizabeth and Richard. I promise I'll think about it, love, I really will.'

'Aye. You do that. And mind, you don't have to sell this place. It's yours. An' if you weren't happy in the town, we could come back. Aren't we lucky as has the choice?'

'We're fortunate, John, but we're not *lucky*,' she went on. 'We made our luck, or you did, mostly, by working so hard and doing so well. That's why we can think of a move if that's what we want.'

John nodded and looked pleased, but when he continued, his tone was almost solemn. 'I'd never have got anywhere without you, Rose. My mother always said that an' she was right.'

She laughed and suddenly saw herself back at Annacramp, a bride of some two weeks, being welcomed by Granny Sarah. The old woman had embraced her, then turned to her son, an irreverent grin on her face. She'd laughed up at him as he bent to kiss her.

'Aren't you the lucky one? Didn't I always say you were the one that would land on yer feet whether you were rich or poor.'

Sam Hamilton was tired out after his long drive to and from Dublin, but he lay awake that night for a long time. Sarah and the children were due home on Tuesday, but there was no chance of that happening with the city full of barricades and the railway lines dug up. He wished he knew the layout of the city better. He'd like to feel she was somewhere out of the way of the trouble, but from all he'd heard Lily Molyneux's house was not that far from Sackville Street and Grafton Street and they were central streets where the men in green were sure to be active.

He thought of his mother waiting to welcome her home and found his mind drifting off to times long gone, when he'd come in from work, tired and cold. There was always a welcome and a kind word and maybe a wee joke. He sighed. He'd had to learn to live without warmth and kindness. It was not in Martha to welcome anyone, even the children, though he knew she cared for them in her own way. The only one to welcome him these days was little Rose.

Dark-haired and bright-eyed like his own mother, she would hold up her arms whenever she saw him, expecting him to bend down and gather her up. Such a wee scrap of a child she was, though nearly seven. He'd worried about her until his mother herself told him how small she'd been at the same age, but at least she was safe, not like Sarah and her wee ones somewhere in the heart of Dublin.

Eventually he fell asleep and woke at his usual time, his mind clear it was up to him to find a way of getting her back. The only person he could think of that could help him was Alex and he was in Banbridge. There was little chance he could get time off today, but he'd ask for a half day on Wednesday and that would give him time enough to go and see his mother as well.

Tuesday passed slowly. Mickey Doyle didn't appear for work and there were routine problems from the previous day as well as the damaged windscreen to be repaired. The boss had gone up to Belfast on business and wasn't due back till late afternoon. While he worked and waited, Sam did his best not to worry. Thinking things through was one thing, but worry quite another, for it undermined the strength of spirit you would surely need.

'And your sister is in the city, Sam?' old man Piele asked, after he'd given a full account of the previous day's delivery to Dublin.

'I'm afraid she is, sir. Our Uncle Sam is with her, which is a good thing, but she has the wee girl and boy.'

'Dear a dear. We live in hard times,' he exclaimed, shaking his head sadly. 'Well, the first thing we'll do is telephone the Friends in Dublin. They'll tell us all they know. And you can certainly go over to Banbridge tomorrow. There's a small order for Brookmount. Do that first and we'll not count it as time off. I'll go and make some calls and come back and tell you what I've found out.'

Sam returned to his work, pleased he'd not lose a half-day's pay but anxious about the news from Dublin. He hadn't long to wait before his employer came out of the office looking grim.

'Sorry, Sam, I've no news. It looks like they've cut the lines. I tried six different people I know. There's nothing but silence,' he explained, shaking his head. 'We'll have to put them in God's hands till we see our way, but go to Banbridge tomorrow and tell your mother before she maybe sees something in the papers. There's nothing about it this morning, but there might be by tomorrow.'

As Sam drove up the main street of Banbridge the next morning, he suddenly realised who else might help him. He parked his lorry and went into the Post Office.

'Good mornin',' he said pleasantly to the girl behind the counter. 'I'd like to see William Auld,' he continued, remembering that his former flagman, 'Wee Billy', had made his way up in the world.

'*Mister* Auld is very busy,' she replied sharply. 'He's in his office and not to be disturbed.'

'Then perhaps you could tell him Sam Hamilton would like to see him and will wait here till he's free.'

She turned her back on him without another word and disappeared through a door marked Postmaster and Telegraph. Moments later she returned, made a feeble attempt at a smile and directed him round the counter to the door behind her.

'Ach, Sam, how are ye?' Billy Auld said, meeting him at the door and grasping his old friend by the hand. 'It's great t' see ye. It's been a while now.'

'Aye, it has. I don't get over that often. Plenty o' work to do for the sake o' the wee ones,' he explained, returning the handshake warmly. He came to the point directly. 'Billy, our Sarah's in Dublin, an' I know there's trouble there, for I was down on Monday an' was lucky to get back. That's why I've come. Can ye help me at all?'

'Sam dear, that *is* bad news. Whereabouts in Dublin is she?'

'A place called Dawson Street. I've niver been there, but it's near Grafton Street and St Stephen's Green and not that far from Sackville Street.'

Billy shook his head and looked anxious. 'I'll tell you what I know,' he began, his voice lowered, 'for your Sarah's a real lady an' has always been kind to me. Aye, an' your mother too. But what I tell you is highly confidential. If it got out I'd lose m'job.'

'I'll not say a word, Billy. I'm just tryin' to think of some way of gettin' her and the wee ones home safe.'

'Has she wee Helen and Hugh with her?' he asked, his eyes opening wide.

Sam just nodded and waited for him to go on.

'Well, ye know there's been a rising. The rebels has taken over a whole lot of places in the centre, the City Hall and the Four Courts and the railway stations, and the GPO is their headquarters. They've cut the telephone lines, but they didn't get the exchange, so we can still get messages in and out. The army's been sent for from England and there's a thousand troops gone down from the North, a field gun from Athlone and a gunboat's sailed up the Liffey. They're well outnumbered, so it can't last long, but there's been heavy fighting in some places. There was reports this morning of buildings on fire. There's twenty girls of our staff still working to keep the military in touch with the castle and with London.'

'But there'd be no way of contacting Sarah, would there?'

Billy shook his head. 'Normal telephones, telegrams and post are all out of action. If it weren't for the exchange and a few lines the engineers managed to lead into private connections, we'd be completely in the dark. We're having to relay messages, which is why I know as much as I do,' he explained as he watched Sam's face grow very thoughtful.

'But you'd know if things quieted down, wouldn't you?'

'Oh yes, we'd know, right enough.'

'Billy, if I was to send my cousin Alex in t' see you every day, cou'd you tell him when we might be able to get through in a motor?'

'Well, I'll know when there's a surrender,' he said thoughtfully. 'But that might not be the end of it.'

'No, it might not, but the roads would likely be open. We'd have to take a chance on that.'

'How would I know your cousin Alex?' he asked abruptly.

Sam laughed, the strong lines of his face softening. 'He looks a bit like my father an' he has a Canadian accent, but ask him who gave me my cards when I wouldn't join the Lodge. He'll tell you all right. I'm hopin' he'll come with me. If my Uncle Sam wants to come back as well, that's four and luggage. Far too much for one motor.'

'Aye, an' ye might find a shortage of petrol too,' Billy warned him. 'Ye'd be advised to take a few cans with you for the way back.'

Sam nodded and stood up.

'You're a busy man, *Mister* Auld, so yer woman out there tells me,' he said grinning. 'D'ye mind the day ye went for my Ma to see me drivin' the new Fowler for the first time?'

'Ah do indeed, Sam,' he said, smiling, as he looked around his office and then got up and walked with him to the door. 'We've both come on a bit since then, haven't we? Tell Alex I'll be expectin' him,' he said, dropping his voice as they came out of the general office. 'An' good luck, Sam.'

'Thanks, Billy. You're a good friend. I'll let you know how it goes.'

He strode out through the main door, climbed up into the parked vehicle and headed out on the road to Ballydown.

Rose finished turning the heel of her sock and took a deep breath. However often she turned a heel, she felt sure it wouldn't go right if she didn't give it her full attention. This morning she'd felt so preoccupied that she'd been thoroughly irritated by having to concentrate so hard. Now the critical bit was over she could relax.

She sighed and glanced at the clock. No use whatever thinking Sarah might arrive as early as this. Even if she'd got an early train from Dublin, it was nearly three hours to Portadown and then at least another hour to get the local train and drive out in a cab from the station. Mid-afternoon was a more likely time. But she was sure to be back sometime today and it would be so good to see her.

She knew she was going to miss her so much, but then she'd always had a feeling Sarah would go. Indeed, she felt she'd have gone long ago, if she hadn't married Hugh. But that was as it should be. A woman must make her way. If she clings to her mother and her life as a girl, she'll never become the full woman she should be. That was what her own mother had said to her, sitting in their tiny room at Currane Lodge, drinking tea by the fire, when Rose confessed she'd said 'yes' to John.

She got up suddenly and went to the dresser. Among the delph and china they used every day there was one cup and saucer more delicate than the rest which had its place but was never used. Rose picked it up and smiled to herself as she found it was full of dust. By right it should be in the china cabinet in the new parlour, but she'd always kept it on this shelf where she could see it, for it was her only tangible link with her own past.

Her mother had given her the pretty cup and saucer the last time she'd seen her, the night before she was married. She'd told her that her own mother had given it to her the night before *her* wedding. As she turned it in her hand, her mother's words came back to her.

'*I want you to take it with you. And maybe, sometimes, if things go a bit hard with you, you'll sit down by yourself and drink from the cup, even if it were only spring water you had.*'

Rose took the cup and saucer out into the dairy to rinse them under the tap. She dried the fragile pieces carefully on a clean tea towel and carried them back to their place.

Yes, she'd drunk from the cup herself, more than once, but for the most part life had been good to her. She had her family, her home and a man she loved. Now what she most wanted was for Sarah to marry the man she loved and move into a world which would give her scope for all her qualities to blossom.

She had just set the cup and saucer carefully back on the shelf when she heard the scrape of boots on the doorstep.

'John and Alex, what a surprise! I was just going to make tea in the wee pot,' she said, beaming delightedly as they came in and kissed her.

'Ach, we thought you might feel lonesome,' said John casually.

'And we knew we'd get cake if we came,' added Alex, knowing it would make her laugh.

It was not completely unknown for John and Alex to walk down from Rathdrum for a cup of tea if Sarah were away, but it didn't happen often, and today Rose was grateful for their company.

'Did you enjoy the Easter Monday dance, Alex?' she asked, as they settled by the fire.

'Well,' he replied cautiously, 'I haven't really got the hang of it yet. Emily says I've got two left feet.'

'Never worry, Alex,' said John vigorously. 'Shure, isn't dancing only an excuse to get your arms round a girl?'

'John!' Rose expostulated. 'Do you think Alex would need an excuse if he found the right girl? He's more up to date than you were, you know.'

Alex blushed slightly but John laughed heartily.

'Aye, I diden have much idea in those days, but I caught on quick once I got a bit of encouragement.'

'God bless all here.'

'Ach, son, we diden hear you coming,' said John, getting to his feet, a broad smile on his face as Sam walked across the threshold. 'Are you delivering in the town?'

'Aye, Brookmount,' he said, bending down to kiss his mother.

'That's a fair bit out,' she said thoughtfully.

'Aye, it is, but Piele's given me the half day to come and see you,' he replied quietly, as Rose fetched another a mug from the dresser and cut more cake.

She stopped in the middle of pouring tea and looked at him steadily.

'Sam, something's wrong. You've bad news to tell us?'

'No, Ma. Not *bad* news as far as I know,' he responded, with an effort at a smile. 'But I came before you might see somethin' in the *Banbridge*

Chronicle tonight that'd upset you. I know you were expecting Sarah yesterday,' he went on, 'but she'll not be home today either. There's trouble in Dublin, bad trouble. In fact, she may not get home till I go for her.'

'What sort of trouble, son?' asked John shortly, his face grim and drawn.

'It seems there's been a rebellion,' Sam replied bluntly. 'There's volunteers in green all round the place. They were there at Jacob's on Monday when Mickey and I went to deliver an' we were lucky to get away before the roads was barricaded. On the way back, I saw a party goin' to pull up railway lines to keep the troops from comin' in.'

'But why is there no news of this in the papers, Sam?' asked Rose, her face suddenly pale.

'All the ordinary telephone lines are cut, but I went to a friend of ours and found there's some still working and he's heard the army's been sent for, so there'll be fighting before it's over. He told me the rebels have set up their headquarters in the GPO. Where would that be, Ma, from where our Sarah is?'

'Not far enough, Sam,' she said calmly. 'A nice wee walk up past Trinity College and over O'Connell Bridge into Sackville Street if you've a letter to post.'

'There's no post either,' Sam added.

'Oh dear,' said Rose with a sigh, 'and I forwarded her a letter from Simon that came the morning they left.'

'So when are we going down, Sam?' said Alex, who'd already worked out that Sam would need help.

'Now ye can't talk about goin' yet,' John broke in. 'If there's trouble, it'll get worse before it gets better. Sarah is sensible and they have Uncle Sam with them and he knows the ins and outs of Dublin from when he lived there. If there's dangerous places, he'll know. Who's this friend ye mentioned, son?'

Sam smiled. 'An important gentleman who sends you his regards, Ma. The postmaster in Banbridge, no less. Wee Billy Auld.'

'An' ye mean to say wee Billy knows what's goin' on an' none of the rest of us do?' John came back at him.

'Indeed I do. He said it's highly confidential, so we keep it to ourselves. If it got out, he'd lose his job, but if Alex calls in each day he'll give us the word when things improve enough for us to chance it.'

'Well that's good of him, indeed it is. We've known wee Billy since he was Sam's flagman, ach, twenty years ago, an' he's always been good-hearted,' John explained to Alex. 'But this is very decent of him. Very decent indeed.'

'And you think you ought to go down and fetch Sarah?' Rose asked.

'Aye, I do. It might be a while before the trains is runnin'.'

'And you'd go with him, Alex?' Rose continued calmly.

'Yes, ma'am,' said Alex promptly. 'I'll be glad to go. She's told me I can use her motor any time she doesn't need it.'

'Even with the British Army and the rebels sniping at each other?' Rose went on, a warning tone in her voice.

'We'll know from Billy when the worst is over, Ma,' Sam said reassuringly. 'It'll be safe enough by the time we go.'

But Rose knew perfectly well that however careful they might be the situation was bound to be a dangerous one. She felt herself shiver despite the warmth of the stove. In the days ahead, just like all the women around her, she would have to live with the knowledge that her dear ones were at risk.

Twenty-One

Sarah's eyes opened with a jerk as her fountain pen fell from her hand and dropped to the floor with a small thud on the very worn carpet. She was amazed she'd fallen asleep despite the firing, which had started up again from St Stephen's Green and from Grafton Street.

She picked up her pen and looked anxiously across the dim room. Helen was still fast asleep. Even the crack of machine-gun fire hadn't wakened her. Fatigue, or perhaps familiarity, she thought. In the feeble light of the single candle reflected from the white ceiling, she could just make out her long, dark lashes, so sharp a contrast with her pale, shadowed face.

Sarah looked down at her letter and smiled. At the point where she'd fallen asleep a word was half finished and a small trail of ink marked the pen's departure.

One of the few comforts she'd found in these long, weary days was writing to Simon after Helen was asleep. It didn't matter that he might not receive what she wrote for a long time; simply writing to him brought him close to her and gave her the steadiness she needed to face the night. It would be a long night and there might be little possibility of sleep before the end of it.

Suddenly her mother's words came back to her. She'd spoken of her long letters to Uncle Sam, when he was in Pennsylvania.

'When I write to him, I have to shape my own thoughts, to make up my mind what I think and be prepared to argue with him if he doesn't agree.'

Those words made such sense now. Focusing on someone a long way away, and doing your best to share what is happening to you, is a very powerful tool for coming to terms with them yourself.

Not that Simon was likely to *disagree* with what she was writing. She was simply telling him what was happening. Could he read the half-written letter at her hand, the only thing that would matter to him was her safety. The rights and wrongs of what was going on outside the shuttered windows would not have been uppermost in his mind.

She picked up the letter and re-read the previous paragraphs, trying to reconnect with her train of thought before she had nodded off.

> We have been shut up indoors now since Monday afternoon, when the first troops began to engage the rebel positions nearby. Our only outing is a somewhat perilous but mercifully brief journey to the Royal Hibernian Hotel, further up Dawson Street, where Lily and Sam are well known. The manager has taken pity on us. They give us a very good lunch each day and fill a small

basket with bread, a little cold meat and some milk to keep us going overnight. Today, there were two oranges for the children, which were most appreciated.

Lily has a great friend staying at the hotel, a Mrs Norway, whom my dear Helen has twice called Mrs Sweden! The poor woman lost her elder son in France some months ago. He was only nineteen. She and her husband moved into the hotel because she couldn't bear their house in Blackrock after the news came of his death, for he and his younger brother, Nevil, had so loved it. Her husband is the head of the Post Office in Ireland and has had a very dangerous time trying to get to and from Dublin Castle and Phoenix Park, to take counsel with his superiors. Fortunately he was not in the GPO when it was taken by the rebels, as he would most likely have been shot.

Yesterday we were formally advised by proclamation to stay indoors and indeed it is good advice. Several people were shot dead in the Shelbourne Hotel, a short distance away, while simply looking out of the window. We sit with the front shutters closed and have heard the odd bullet ricochet from our brickwork. It is remarkable how one adapts to the situation, finding it for the most part boring rather than frightening. Though that may co—

Sarah straightened the wick of the candle with the unburnt end of a matchstick, for the flame was in danger of drowning in a pool of wax. She tilted it carefully and allowed the wax to flow down into the candle holder. Immediately, the flame rose up again. There had been a whole box of candles in the pantry on Monday when she and Sam had surveyed their resources, but now, even with undressing in the dark or the meagre light from the unshuttered back windows, the box was more than half empty.

She picked up her pen, completed the word 'come' and prepared to continue.

These three days have seemed incredibly long, though the children have been so good and complained very little about their imprisonment. Hugh, of course, wants to go out with Uncle Sam and see what is happening. Sam has persuaded me he himself is perfectly safe as he knows exactly where the rebel positions are and how to avoid them, but he properly refuses to allow Hugh to go with him. He says the streets are full of sightseers, as well as the looters, who are having the time of their lives.

He brings back the most extraordinary rumours, which, as he says, 'proliferate in this loquacious city', and equally extraordinary stories, which help to amuse us. The story I liked best was about an old woman who had made up a great bundle of shoes of all kinds and then another of clothes. She couldn't carry both, so while she was carrying away the clothes, she'd had to leave the shoes waiting on the pavement. When she came back and found they'd gone, she complained bitterly that there was no justice in the place and not a soul to look after a poor old woman's belongings!

Lily encourages Helen with her water-colours. I wish she'd been able to teach, for she has a real gift, and Helen has responded so enthusiastically. Hugh reads continuously but he did have a stroke of real good fortune. Mrs Norway's son, Nevil, who is seventeen and on holiday from Shrewsbury School, is keen on aeronautics. He has lent Hugh his entire collection of books because he has offered his services to the Red Cross as a stretcher-bearer, for they have been overwhelmed by the number of casualties, military and civilian.

I have never taken much pride in my competence as a seamstress, though my mother taught me most carefully, but yesterday I found some real pleasure in deploying my skills. Lily and I spent the day making a flag for the Red Cross. Sadly, the white flag is no longer respected. Both military and rebels have been fired on when bringing out wounded. I think we may have to make another tomorrow, but while we have plenty of white sheets, I know Mrs Norway is anxious lest we are unable to find enough bright red material for the cross.

Dearest Simon, how extraordinary it seems to write to you about sewing at such a time. No, it is not an evasion. There is danger and I am aware of it. A large part of the city is on fire, which is why I am sitting up till two o'clock, when Uncle Sam will take over my duties. It depends on the wind whether we will have to leave the house and find shelter somewhere else.

We've been told the fire began with looters letting off fireworks in a toy shop, but the rebels prevented the Fire Brigade from dealing with it, so it has spread, gaining ground all day. From the attic we can see the whole sky alight with a red glow, flames rising hundreds of feet with great swathes of sparks almost like a firework display. It is a most dramatic and awesome sight. Beautiful, almost. I go up to the attic every hour to see if there is any sign of the flames leaping towards us. And here I must pause, my dear, for an hour has passed since I sat down to share my thoughts with you. It is only ten o'clock, so I have plenty of time to continue, if all is well.

Sarah slipped out onto the landing, her hand carefully shielding the candle flame from the effects of her movement. She left the bedroom door ajar because the loud click it made when it closed might well waken Helen.

The house itself was silent and dark, but the roar

of artillery hammered on her eardrums so furiously as she moved along the landing and up the narrow flight of stairs towards the roof, she felt she just wanted to turn and run away. She could hardly believe that this all-enveloping sound was what the soldiers at the front had to endure, day after day, as well as the actual danger of the shells that fell on them. Only the shelter of solid walls and the knowledge that it would stop soon had kept her going since the army had first deployed its field guns and a patrol boat had begun firing from the Liffey.

Despite the noise outside, she still tried to move quietly. Lily had gone to her room early to save her eyes from candlelight. Sam had lain down, fully dressed, at the same time as Hugh, his clock set for two in the morning. Adjusted to the continuing noise outside, an unexpected sound from within the house might waken any of them.

The stairs to the attic were narrow and uncarpeted. The bare boards creaked underfoot as she made her way up through the enveloping darkness. Pushing open the small door into the attic room and bending under its low lintel, she gasped for breath. Beneath the low ceiling, the whole room was lit by the red glow of the fires and the air around her vibrated with the gunfire, the sound now filtered only by the roof slates and not by the stout walls of the old house. From near at hand, almost as if it were in the next room, came the sudden crack of rifle fire.

She paused, her heart racing, the shock of sound and light making her hand shake. The candle flickered and went out, but it made little difference. The light pouring through the one small window and the skylight in the roof was more than enough to reveal the passage to the window she'd cleared earlier in the day, through the trunks and boxes untouched since Lily came to the house.

She put the candlestick down on the edge of a large chest and was about to make her way towards the window when she heard footsteps and a scrabbling sound overhead. The red glow disappeared from the skylight above her. A few flakes of ceiling plaster floated down as it was thrown open and a dark figure prepared to lower itself into the attic.

She stood rooted to the spot as a pair of legs swung back and forth, and watched in amazement as she saw one hand reach up to lower the skylight window till it rested gently on the hand that still clutched the wooden frame, bearing the entire weight of the young man's body.

A moment later, the skylight fell back into place and the figure dropped the short distance to the floor, knocked over an old umbrella stand and fell headlong on to a pile of discarded curtains.

'Shhhh . . . you'll wake the children,' she said, the noise of his landing temporarily blocking out the boom of artillery.

There was a long moment while he rolled over, unslung his rifle and sat up. Bright eyes peered at her from a blackened face.

'What are ye doin' up here?' he asked. His voice was calm, though puzzled, his accent certainly not a Dublin one. It seemed somehow familiar, but she couldn't place it.

'I'm checking on the fires to see if we've to get out,' she replied, returning his gaze as he studied her closely in the strong flickering light.

'Ye'll be all right,' he said shortly, as he leaned back wearily against a chest of drawers and made himself more comfortable. 'The wind's gone round and there's spits of rain on it. There's a real good view from behind your chimney stack.'

'Have you been up there all day?' she asked, remembering the lunchtime talk at the hotel about a sniper who'd survived all attempts to remove him.

'Yes. Two days in fact, but last night was fairly quiet. I got a good soaking, but I'm none the worse. Lad with me had to go to hospital this morning. I think he's got pneumonia.'

'How on earth did you get him to hospital?' Sarah asked in amazement.

'Half carried him to the College of Surgeons by the back alleys. There's two or three houses where we can come in the back and go out the front and a few has tunnels to the next one,' he explained when he saw the look on her face. 'I took him to one of Madam's girls and she went for the Red Cross.'

'Madam?'

'Aye. The Countess Markievicz. Some calls her Madam, some Connie. She's quite a character. Wants us all to fight for "Ahland",' he said, mimicking the lady's aristocratic accent. 'Quite willing to have a go herself.'

For a moment, Sarah couldn't think why the Countess should want them to fight for 'Ahland'. Then it dawned on her. Of course, it had to be

Ireland. Lily said she was a mad rebel fighting for 'Ahland'.

That had been on Monday afternoon, after they'd finished what passed for lunch. Helen gave Lily an account of the day's adventures and described 'a lady dressed like a man' with guns in her belt whom they'd seen in the park.

'Oh, that'll be Connie,' Lily interrupted, laughing. 'The Countess Markievicz. Connie married a Polish count, Casimir. Lovely man. But he went back to Poland. They're still friends, as far as I know, but I can't imagine anyone being able to live with Connie. I knew her when I was at the Slade.'

Lily always enjoying talking about the enormous numbers of people she appeared to know in Dublin.

'Mad keen Republican. Her father was a Gore-Booth,' she added helpfully, as if Sam and Sarah were sure to know who he was. 'They have huge estates in Sligo. Poor, dear man, both his daughters were rebels. Eva, the younger one, lives in Manchester and campaigns for women's rights. I think she might even be a suffragette.'

A soft voice brought her sharply back to the present.

'I don't think you remember me, Sarah.'

Startled at the use of her name, she looked more closely at the reclining figure, who seemed almost at ease on his pile of curtains. She supposed he'd blackened his face to be a less visible target, but even thus disguised there *was* something familiar about him, particularly the bright eyes, the leisurely way of speaking, and the soft accent.

'It's many a long day since we played football in the back field at Creeslough,' he said, his eyes twinkling.

'Brendan!'

'The very one. I hope I didn't frighten you,' he said, looking at her with a grin. 'But you're not easy frightened. Never were.'

'I am if it's the children,' she said honestly.

'Sure, so you should be. Are they both all right?'

She nodded, touched by his concern.

'We're sleeping at the back; Helen's with me and Hugh has moved in with Uncle Sam. Lily refuses to move anywhere – she won't even close her shutters – but so far we're all right. What about you?' she asked.

'We've held out for three days,' he said proudly. 'We'll try for a few more. Against a couple of battalions of well-trained troops, we stand no chance. Never did really, but it had to be done.'

'Why, Brendan, why?' she said, tears springing to her eyes. 'All those lives, volunteers and soldiers and ordinary people who had no part, neither one side nor the other. Maybe *your* life as well if you go back and fight on,' she said, aware that tears were streaming silently down her face.

'Don't cry, Sarah,' he said kindly. 'I knew what I was doing when I joined Michael Mallin at Liberty Hall. Even if McNeill hadn't cancelled the manoeuvres and messed up the whole thing, we'd still not have had much chance. But we can't let the English walk over us, treating us like natives, like they did with the Boers. Even if we fail, we've reminded Ireland she's a nation, not a colony.'

'But wouldn't that have come with Home Rule? Wasn't it worth giving it a try?' she said quickly, wiping her tears brusquely with her sleeve.

'Live old horse an' you'll get grass,' he said bitterly. 'All Ireland has ever had from England is promises an' poverty for the workers. Your family has gone up in the world, Sarah, an' you've done your bit for those at the bottom o' the pile, an' so has Uncle Sam, here an' in America. But it's not enough. Individuals can only ameliorate. Change has to come where the power is an' that means force of arms.'

Ameliorate. The word set up an echo in Sarah's mind. A strange word in the mouth of a country boy from Creeslough, who'd left Massinass School at the first possible moment. But then, he'd progressed to a more powerful school in Liberty Hall, studying with Michael Mallin and Jim Larkin, just as Uncle Sam had studied with Michael Davitt and the Land Leaguers.

'And the innocent victims?' she prompted.

'The cost of freedom is always high,' he said calmly.

Sarah was about to retort when there was a sudden dip in the light level and a sound overhead.

Brendan was alert instantly. With a single gesture, he signalled to her that her face and pale wool cardigan might catch an eye. At the same time, he moved silently back into the deep shadow cast by an old wardrobe. Sarah dropped to her knees beside the pile of curtains he'd just abandoned, pulled one of them up and over her head and lay looking at the bare floor, the smell of dust and rotting fabric all around her.

As she drew her legs up under the heavy curtain and eased herself further into shadow, she wondered if she could have retreated the necessary few steps to the narrow stairway and pulled the door behind her. But there had been so little warning. The echo of her feet on the stair or the creak of the attic door closing might be as audible out on the roof as the sounds from overhead were in the crowded attic.

Even as she questioned whether she'd done the right thing, she heard voices above them. She couldn't make out what was being said, but the speakers were certainly English. It sounded like a soldier from somewhere in the Midlands, which it might well be, for Mrs Norway had told her the Sherwood Foresters were among the recently arrived battalions.

The footsteps moved back and forth across the slates, the men calling to each other, sometimes closer, sometimes further away. Sarah got a crick in her neck holding her head up from the dirty floor. She lowered it gingerly without a sound. If one of the soldiers above were to drop down as Brendan had, he would land right on top of her. They could lift up the skylight from outside and get in as easily as Brendan had.

The floor was hard and the smell of the old curtains became more and more oppressive. All Sarah could see from under her heavy covering was the few inches of floor just beyond her nose. She watched the red glow from the burning buildings flicker on the bare boards, her ears straining for any sound. Mercifully, for the moment, the artillery fire had almost faded away.

Minutes passed slowly. The hard floor and the confined space became even harder to bear. Twice she painfully suppressed a sneeze. Still the feet tramped overhead. Once, she thought someone kicked the edge of the skylight, but the curse that followed suggested he'd merely tripped over its raised edge.

She had no idea how long she'd lain absolutely still. If a soldier did decide to investigate a possible hideout for a sniper, could she get to her feet in time to insist that she'd just come up to observe the fire? And what would Brendan do? Would he stay out of sight? How could she bear it if he shot a man in front of her? Or if a soldier shot him?

The thought of bullets flying in the tiny space was terrifying. Were it to happen she reckoned her chances of getting back to the children unharmed were fairly small.

From overhead came a shout, a third voice, calling to the others, louder than them. Before there was any reply, there began a violent drumming on the roof, a crescendo of sound like a roll of drums she couldn't identify. She felt herself tighten with an unbearable tension until she realised a squall of rain had moved in quickly and was now pounding the roof. Even as she realised what it was the fierce battering eased to a steady downpour.

The floorboards beneath her vibrated and she felt rather than heard Brendan move. Cautiously, she turned back her covering and scrambled painfully to her knees, her back sore and her legs stiff. One foot had gone to sleep. Brendan pointed to the door.

Together they made their way silently downstairs by the faint reflected glow of the fires spilling through the back windows. Only when they reached the sitting-room door did Sarah speak.

'Stay here till I light the candle,' she whispered. 'It's pitch black with the shutters closed.'

She did not point out that he was almost certain to knock over one the tables laden with Lily's precious china if he attempted to follow her.

She crossed the room cautiously, felt for the cold marble edge of the mantelpiece and ran her hand back and along behind the clock. The matches were in their usual place. The moment the flame flared in her hand, he came silently after her, weaving his way deftly between the obstacles.

As she lit a candle, it suddenly occurred to her that Brendan's flexibility of body and speed of response had probably saved his life more than once already.

'I must get back, Sarah,' he said quickly. 'Would there be any chance of a bite to eat? And I need some water,' he added, unhooking a water bottle from his belt.

'I'll see what I can find,' she said, taking the empty water bottle from his hand.

She lit a second candle and hurried out to the kitchen as quickly as its flickering light would permit, wondering what there was left to give him.

'Not much choice,' she said to herself, taking half a small loaf from the bin.

She cut off a slice for Lily and one for each of the children for breakfast, wrapped them in a cloth, put them back in the bin and used the last of her mother's damson to make jam sandwiches from the rest.

There was half a pint of milk in the bottle standing on the marble slab in the larder. She poured about an eggcupful into a jug for Lily's morning tea and drained the rest of the bottle into a glass. She gazed around hopefully, as if there might be something she'd forgotten, but she knew the only thing in the larder was some soup she'd made the previous day. Sam had come home clutching three cauliflowers he'd bought from a man who'd braved the bullets and was doing a roaring trade from his horse and cart on the south side of St Stephen's Green.

She put the candlestick on a tray with the milk, sandwiches and the refilled water bottle, made her way up the steps that led from the kitchen and moved along the corridor running towards the front of the house. Before she'd gone very far she was startled to hear low voices coming from the sitting room.

'Sam,' she said quietly, as she pushed the door shut with her shoulder. 'Did we wake you?'

'No, I didn't hear a thing,' he said, smiling up at her. 'I woke up and couldn't get back to sleep when the firing stopped, so I came for my book. Maybe a good thing, maybe not,' he said, looking at Brendan, who seemed not at all troubled by his uncle's sudden appearance.

Brendan eyed the tray as Sarah set it down. She moved the candlestick to join its match on the table. A pair of beautiful Georgian silver candlesticks to light the table and only jam sandwiches to eat, she thought ruefully.

'Sorry, this is all there is,' she said, handing over the plate and the glass of milk. 'Not even butter, but it's Ma's damson jam,' she added wryly. 'No gas either, so I couldn't make you tea.'

'This is great,' he said, taking a huge bite from one of the generously cut triangles.

She watched as he munched vigorously. It was perfectly clear he hadn't eaten for some time.

'Brendan, there's a bedroom in the attic where Maureen and Bridget sleep,' Sam began quietly. 'We can find you some clothes and hide the rifle safely.'

His mouth full, Brendan simply raised his eyebrows.

'What's to be gained going out there to be killed? It's only a matter of time,' Sam went on, a growing urgency in his voice. 'They've got a ring round the centre and they're closing in. They've got as far as Abbey Street and taken one of the bridges,' he continued, his agitation visible even in the softness of candlelight. 'It might be tomorrow, it might be Friday, but sooner or later they'll tighten the noose, pound the GPO to bits and come and clear out what's left of your lot. What's the point, Brendan, throwing your life away?'

Sarah looked from one to the other, then dropped down in one of the dining chairs from where she could see both faces, pale in the dim light, Sam full of an edgy tension, Brendan drinking his milk as easily and enthusiastically as if he were lowering a Guinness in a pub with a friend.

'I made a promise, Sam,' he said quietly after he'd thrown his head back to drain the very last drop.

'After the lock-out and all those people starving till the relief came, I saw things I never want to see again. The Citizen Army has to stick to its promise.'

'But, Brendan, this rising isn't what you made your promise for,' he said, his voice hissing slightly as he tried to make his point in a whisper. 'That's why McNeill called it off. He knows something we don't know, but I can make a guess at what it is. Padraic Pearse is no Sinn Feiner. I think the Brotherhood is behind this, and they've made use of McNeill and the volunteers for their own purposes. It's the wrong thing at the wrong time, Brendan. Look at who's suffering. The very people the Citizen Army was formed to defend, thrown out of their houses, burnt out of their jobs. Over five hundred civilians have been killed or injured so far . . .'

His voice trailed off as Sarah watched Brendan shake his head.

'Thanks, Sarah,' he said very quietly. 'Tell Auntie Rose she makes great jam. I'll come an' see her one of these days if my luck holds,' he added, standing up.

Sam stood up too and looked at his nephew, a lightly built young man no taller than Sarah, his bright eyes flicking from one to the other as he hitched his gun more firmly on his shoulder.

'If Pearse surrenders,' Sam began again, a touch of desperation in his voice, 'don't for any sakes be heroic. When the battle's lost, live to fight another day.'

Sarah watched the two men shake hands. As Brendan was about to turn away, he changed his mind. He turned and embraced his uncle and the two of them clung together for a long moment.

'I owe you a kiss, Sarah, when I've a clean face,' Brendan said lightly, turning towards her.

'Good luck, Brendan,' she said quietly as he walked to the door.

She was almost sure she could see tears glittering in his eyes.

'Back, front or roof?' she asked coolly, as she picked up a candlestick to light his way.

'Back,' he replied, following her into the corridor without so much as a glance behind him.

A few moments later, he disappeared into the dark shadows of the strip of garden that ran towards South Frederick Street and Sarah returned to the sitting room where Sam sat, his head in his hands.

She came and sat down near him. She was about to speak when a furious barrage of artillery opened up. The vibrations made the candles flicker.

'They're getting closer,' he said, having to speak loudly to make himself heard. 'He doesn't stand a chance.'

There was no comfort to be offered, nothing she could possibly say that would touch the look of desolation she saw spreading across Sam's face. She wanted to tell him that at least he had tried, but the noise was now so great they couldn't hear each other speak. Sam indicated that he was going to try to read, Sarah that she was going back upstairs to make sure the children were all right.

As she passed through the hall, a gleam of light from the fanlight over the front door fell on the face of the grandfather clock at the foot of the stairs. The night would indeed be long. It was still only midnight.

Twenty-Two

When Alex Hamilton was shown into the post-master's room in Banbridge Post Office on Saturday 29th April, 1916, he knew there was good news, before a single word was spoken.

Two days earlier he'd gone into the town to make himself known and discover the present state of affairs in Dublin. Billy Auld had jumped to his feet and waved his visitor to a chair.

'Any friend of Sam's is a friend of mine,' he declared.

Alex had been ready to answer any number of questions to establish his identity, but Billy asked only one.

'How's Sam's mother?'

'As good as she can be. She's worried about Sarah and the wee ones, but she tries not to let it show. You know how she always does her best to keep up spirits.'

'Aye, I know that fine well,' replied Billy, smiling. 'An' I knew you for a Hamilton as you walked through the door.'

'Well,' said Alex, looking enormously pleased.

He'd called in the next day as well, and there'd been no change, but today Billy's broad smile and bright eyes suggested something more hopeful.

'There's been a surrender,' Billy began, 'but don't get too excited. Pearse was burnt out of the Post Office and moved to Moore Street. He had no way out from there without bad losses, so he decided to ask for terms. The military said unconditional surrender or nothing. Pearse agreed and wrote out the order, but some of the other commandants don't believe it, so they're fighting on. I know that Jacob's is holding out for one and so is some chap called Dolores, or something like that, a foreign name, at Boland's Mills. I'm sure there's others too. Apparently, there's a wee nurse being used as a go-between and some of the commandants are being taken to see Pearse for themselves, so it'll take a while.'

'But we *could* go tomorrow?' Alex said levelly, doing his best not too sound too excited.

'Well . . .' he began cautiously.

Alex grinned at him. 'If it was your sister or your good friend?' he said, still smiling.

'Aye,' Billy admitted, nodding his head. 'I'd do it m'self, but I hafta tell ye, there's still a lot of fighting going on. There's roads blocked and snipers who maybe won't hear word of the surrender for a while. There's a mobile unit north of Dublin near a place called Ashbourne has killed a dozen or more police-men. I don't know exactly where these places are, but ye might find Volunteers trying to ambush army patrols if ye go by the main road.'

Alex nodded. 'I'll tell my boss,' he said, smiling. 'Sam was down on Monday. That'll maybe help him think out the best way into the city. Is there anything else I should tell him?'

'Aye, maybe ye should warn him of the destruction. I spoke to one of our wee girls at the telephone exchange. She says they've been trapped there since Monday, sleeping in a cellar in turns. She got a look out this morning and she says she couldn't believe it, you'd think you were on the Western Front. Half of Sackville Street is destroyed, all the big shops and hotels, and there's only the walls of the GPO left. It's still smoking, though a lot of the other fires is burnt out. And there's no food shops open so people can get nothin' to eat.'

'We'll go well prepared,' Alex said, nodding. 'And we'll certainly take petrol, like you said to Sam on Wednesday.'

Alex stood up, held out his hand and said his thank you.

'If I hear anythin' to the bad, I'll walk up to Ballydown this evenin',' Billy promised as he got to his feet. 'Are you for Liskeyborough ?'

'I am. As soon as I've told Rose and John the news, I'll take Sarah's motor and go over for Sam. We'll need a few hours before dark to make sure both vehicles are in top form. Say one for us in the mornin'.'

'Indeed, it'll be more than one if I see the inside of the church at all,' said Billy warmly. 'Give Sarah my best wishes when you see her, and her Ma too,' he added, as he walked with him out of the room and across the floor to the main door.

Sam was to stay overnight at Ballydown, sleeping in the room he had once shared with his brother. His mother was glad to have both Sam and Alex for supper and even more grateful they'd keep John company through the long afternoon. She guessed the two well-cared-for vehicles would need little in the way of maintenance, but seeing they were as good as they could be was a way of passing the time.

Parked outside the large, empty barn John rented from the Jacksons at the foot of the hill, the three men worked together. Points were greased, cables tested, oil applied.

No hand with vehicles himself, Michael Jackson came to keep them company, offering bits of news gleaned from the *Banbridge Chronicle* or the *Belfast Evening Telegraph*.

'Sure the rumours is somethin' chronic,' he said, leaning against the barn wall as they worked. 'Apparently there was supposed to be a German invasion of England while the rebels were creatin' a diversion in Ireland, but all it came to was a few shells on some wee place in Norfolk, a couple o' people killed and the British Navy after them in no time. An' there was to be fifty thousand coming from Galway and yer man Larkin back from America to command the Citizen Army.'

'It all helps to sell newspapers,' said John tartly, as Emily came out of the house with four mugs of tea on a tray and a slice each of well-buttered currant bread.

'Half day today, Emily?' asked John, as he put down his spanner and helped himself.

She smiled at him, her dark eyes sparkling. 'Yes, thank goodness. I get so fed up being polite to people,' she said so promptly that they all laughed.

'She makes up for it when she gets home,' Alex said quietly, as she offered the tray to him.

Sam straightened up just in time to catch the look that passed between them. So that was the way the wind was blowing. He smiled warmly at Emily as he took his tea, heartened by what he saw.

'What is it they say about home, Emily?' Sam asked, as he picked up his slice of currant bread. 'Ma has it embroidered on one of those sampler things she made when she was a wee girl. "*Home, the place where we grumble the most and are treated the best.*"'

'That's right, Sam. There's a whole lot of those sayings that wee girls had to embroider,' his father replied. 'They came out of a copybook. Yer Ma and I think we had the same one, tho' we were at the far ends of Ireland from other.'

'*The coneys are a feeble folk, but they build their houses in the rocks,*' said Alex unexpectedly.

'Where did ye hear that one, Alex?' Emily demanded, her tone light and teasing. 'Is that a Canadian one?'

'I don't know,' he said honestly.

'Now *my* mother had that one up on the bedroom wall,' said John quickly, a sudden image coming back to him from long ago. 'I mind I asked her once what a coney was and she said "a rabbit", but then I told her rabbits don't build in rock.'

Alex looked towards him, grateful that no one had noticed his own confusion and puzzlement at the sharpness of a memory that had just come to him.

'What did she say to that, Mr Hamilton?' Emily asked politely.

'I think she told me I was a wee question mark,' he said, laughing, as he finished his tea, so grateful for this easy talk with friends when he found it hard to think about anything else but Sarah.

Rose spent the long afternoon baking bread and cake to send to Lily along with the tins and packets she'd already packed in cardboard boxes. There was room for Lily and Sam to come back with Sarah and the children if they wanted to, but she had a feeling Lily wouldn't want to leave Dublin and abandon a house where so many people felt welcome, just when they might need its comfort most.

She hoped Sam might come up for a day or two, just to give her all the news, and then go back when the trains were running again, but she wouldn't rely on it given how concerned he'd be about Lily.

She sighed as she took a fruitcake from the oven. It had been a truly dreadful week. Since the moment Sam had warned them of what was happening in Dublin, there'd been nothing but bad news. Bad news from Dublin itself as the casualties rose, then a letter from Ashleigh Court, and finally, only yesterday, one from France.

Lady Anne had written, telling her that her beloved Harrington was now so weak he had to be fed. For weeks he'd been struggling to walk, and now he was confined to bed. His speech had deteriorated so much they had to play guessing games like children when he wanted anything. The doctors who'd come down from London had just shaken their heads and said it was only a matter of time.

Two days after she'd replied to Anne, the postman brought one of the familiar envelopes that everyone dreaded. For a moment, Rose had been puzzled. No one in her immediate family had joined up except her sister's two sons, and they'd been killed in action already. She'd ripped open the envelope and seen the name of her former postman, who'd asked if he could write to her because he had no one else to write to.

Dan Willis had left her everything he possessed. Her name and address was on his will, found in his pocketbook by the comrades who'd buried him. She was informed that she would shortly receive by post two medals, a New Testament, a wallet containing a ten-shilling note and a text which said 'Be strong and of good courage'.

If she let herself think of Dan, she wept. If she let herself think of Anne, watching over Harrington through the long days, tears poured down her cheeks. And all the time, Sarah and Helen and Hugh were shut up in a house in Dublin with a bitter conflict going on all around them.

When Sarah opened her eyes on Saturday morning she couldn't quite believe her ears. Last night, Helen and Hugh had returned to their own rooms, the danger from the fires now passed. She had donned one of Lily's nightdresses and slept the whole night through. Now, there was a bird singing in the narrow strip of garden at the back of the house. Although she could still hear artillery, the sound was muted and distant, and there was no rifle fire.

'Good mornin', ma'am, it's a fine mornin'.'

She sat up abruptly and stared in amazement at the neatly dressed young woman who was putting a tray of morning tea on her bedside table.

'Bridget!' she exclaimed. 'Are you all right?'

'Yes, thank you, ma'am,' the girl replied with a polite smile.

Sarah took a deep breath and rubbed the sleep from her eyes.

'You won't give us away, ma'am, will you?' Bridget asked calmly. 'If the military find we were out, we'll be put in jail or sent to England.'

'But how did you get here?' Sarah asked, now fully awake. 'I thought you were in the GPO. Where's Maureen? Is she all right too?'

'Maureen has a few burns, ma'am, but not bad. We had a doctor was captured early on. An Englishman, but very nice,' she admitted, her tone giving away her surprise. 'He dressed them for her and he says she'll heal well. It was a bomb she was carrying went off, but it was one of the dud ones an' it didn't get her face, just her stomach,' she explained, drawing a hand across her own waist. 'Drink your tea, ma'am, it's gettin' cold,' she said briskly, as Sarah pulled a dressing gown round her shoulders.

'So where's Maureen now? In hospital?'

'Not at all,' replied Bridget, smiling. 'She's taking Lady Lily her tea and then she's going to cook the breakfast while I do the fires.'

'Cook? But there's no gas. And we've only half a

loaf,' Sarah protested.

'The gas is on now,' Bridget said easily. 'I made the tea on it and we brought bacon and eggs back with us,' she continued. 'Mr Pearse told us yesterday he would like us to go for our own safety. He said we'd done our bit an' he was proud of us. So we went home and got cleaned up. There was a few women stayed, two of the nurses and Miss Carney,' she added thoughtfully. 'Of course, she wouldn't leave James Connolly when he's in such a bad way.'

'What happened him?'

'Shot in the foot, but the doctor thinks it's gangrene,' Bridget said coolly. 'He needed to get to hospital. Poor man, he's in agony all the time,' she went on as she again motioned to Sarah to drink up. 'Ye won't tell on us, will ye, ma'am?' Bridget repeated as Sarah put down her empty cup and she took up the tray again.

'No, I won't tell on you,' she said, nodding, as she got out of bed to wash in cold water and put on the same clothes she'd been wearing since Monday.

Now that there was no need for her to struggle with brewing tea on an open fire or make sure the children didn't burn their only piece of toast, she didn't hurry. She tried to collect her thoughts and fit together what Bridget had told her and the rumours of a surrender that had reached the Royal Hibernian Hotel before they left after lunch.

Bridget was quite transformed. The quiet girl her sister was so ready to boss had emerged from the week much stronger in herself. She wondered if she should be glad that the rebels had allowed women to take their part as equals in the struggle, facing the same dangers as the men, or sorry that the women had not stood up and suggested that there was some other way. But then, the men wouldn't have listened anyway.

The deaths of so many weighed upon her. Bad enough to think of the deaths of so many Volunteers, or the Citizen Army, who'd known what they were choosing, or the soldiers who'd been trained for the job. Much worse were the civilians – the men, women and children caught in crossfire, shot in their own homes or fleeing from the fires, left without food or shelter, their livelihood destroyed. What of them? What choice had they been given?

Sarah made the bed and tidied the room, quite forgetting that Maureen and Bridget would expect to do it after they'd served breakfast and cleared up afterwards. She paused by the window, the curtains now drawn back, the sunlight beaming down on the narrow strip of garden.

An elderly magnolia had come into bloom in the course of the week. The waxy white spires had begun to open on the south-facing side of the tree as if nothing whatever had disturbed their yearly routine. The pink-tinted cups held up their petals to the morning sun.

'Come in.'

Sarah turned quickly when she heard the knock at the door. Maureen came across the room towards her and dropped down into a chair in front of her.

'Ma'am, I'm sorry,' she said, her face pale and

anxious. 'I went up with tea for Mr McGinley a wee while ago. He's not in his room an' his bed's not been slept in,' she went on, close to tears. 'I've searched the house before I wou'd come up to ye, but he's not here.'

Twenty-Three

Rose woke long before the early alarm on Sunday morning and lay still, not wanting to deprive John of the last of his short night's sleep. The previous evening they'd sat on by the fire with Sam after Alex had left to walk down the hill to his own bed, not saying very much, but reluctant to make a move. She turned gently on her side and comforted herself as she eyed the light filtering through the freshly washed curtains. At least the morning was fine. Even before the sun was up, she was sure the sky was clear. It was going to be a fine day.

After breakfast, John walked down the hill with Sam and waited to see the pair of them off, leaving Rose to stand by the gate, the shadows long in the rising sun, sparkling beads of dew hanging from every blade of grass. Fingers of light pierced the hawthorn hedge across the road. The birds were already active among its spiky twigs and their own blackbird sang from the chimney pot.

She took a deep breath as she heard the engines burst into life, the sound vibrating on the still air in the quiet of a Sunday morning. Moments later, first Sam and then Alex drove out of Jackson's yard and turned onto the main road. Tears poured down her face unbidden. She spoke sharply to herself, wiped them quickly with the back of her hand and composed herself as she saw John come out of the farmyard, take one last look at the departing vehicles and walk slowly back up the hill towards her.

It would be a long day and no one could be sure of its ending.

For several hours the journey went well. It was a familiar road to Sam, but quite new to Alex, a delight he had not expected, his first drive beyond the mountains that had bounded his horizon since his homecoming. For all his thoughts of what might await them, he drove along with a joy he'd rarely felt before, his mind totally enthralled by the changing perspectives of mountain and lowland, the sudden shock of delight as he saw the sea, incredibly blue, calm and glittering in the morning sun as they moved steadily southwards.

They stopped every hour to check the radiators, have a word or a mouthful of tea from Rose's flasks and a walk behind a nearby hedge. After Drogheda, they made a longer break to eat some sandwiches. Sitting on a stone wall by the roadside, the sun warm on their shoulders, the sound of bees visiting the bright faces of dandelions all about them, they agreed it was very hard to imagine what had been happening in Dublin.

Beyond those few words they said little. Alex was well used to Sam's silence and today his own mind was so full of the extraordinary beauty of the countryside he was happy to be silent himself.

It was another hour beyond Drogheda before they were brought to a halt. Near the brow of a long, slow incline, a military vehicle was stopped in the middle of the road. Even if they'd not been waved down by a soldier, there was no possibility of getting past.

'Where are you from? What's your destination?' a young soldier demanded as he marched up to them.

Sam climbed down from his father's motor. The soldier's tone was hostile, but his posture led Sam to think he was less sure of himself than his manner suggested.

'We're from Banbridge, going to collect my sister and her children from Dublin,' said Sam equably. 'Are you having trouble with your vehicle? We might be able to give you a hand,' he added quietly as he watched the lad try to decide what he was supposed to do with the answer he'd been given.

'I'll speak to my officer,' he replied, clearly relieved at not having to deal with a situation for which he'd not been briefed.

Some minutes later the officer approached, ran a sharp eye over the two gleaming motors parked carefully by the roadside, and addressed Sam, who was eyeing the lads who stared uneasily at the open engine of their vehicle. Clearly, they hadn't the slightest idea what to do about it.

'You have some mechanical knowledge,' he said shortly.

'Yes, sir, we do. Would you like us to take a look?'

'Thank you,' the officer said abruptly, as he turned to the soldier who had waved them down. 'Stop any traffic there might be a hundred yards away and keep an eye on these vehicles. I'll send someone to help you.'

Sam and Alex walked over to the War Department lorry and nodded to the group of young men, one of whom was applying oil generously, if indiscriminately, to the moving parts. He looked from one uneasy face to another.

'Who was driving her?'

'Me . . . sir.'

Alex smiled to himself. The pale-faced lad was so young he clearly wasn't sure how to address a man in his thirties.

'Tell me now just what happened,' said Sam encouragingly, as he ran his eye over the engine.

Alex saw his friend wrinkle his nostrils slightly and guessed what was coming next.

'I was driving up the hill, sir, an' I saw a sheep, so I slowed down. An' then there was a whole crowd of them goin' across in front of me an' I had to put the brakes on. An' when the road was clear, she wouden start. I tried and tried. An' then my mate tried, but she wouden shift.'

'Right. Now, my friend an' I'll show ye what to do if this happens again, but it's better avoided in the first place,' began Sam quietly. 'You let your revs drop on the hill, so she probably stalled before you even touched the brakes. Then ye flooded her. D'ye smell that smell? That's the petrol evaporatin'. Wait an hour or so an' she might clear, but there's a quick way. Watch what we do an' ye'll know for again,' he said helpfully as he climbed up into the cab and nodded to Alex as he applied himself to the starting handle.

A few minutes later, the vehicle was ticking over nicely and the soldiers sitting by the roadside began to climb up into the back. The officer who'd been keeping an eye on the road south came over to them.

'I'm afraid these lads have little training and no experience,' he explained. 'The battalion is well below strength since Ypres,' he added shortly. 'Are you aware what conditions are like in Dublin?'

'We have some idea, sir.'

'And you're still set on going?'

'We are,' replied Sam quietly.

'Well, I've no powers to detain you, and I owe you my thanks,' he said with a sharp nod, his eye moving to the lorry now loaded with men and ready to move. 'I've probably not got much more information than you, but my last orders were to report to barracks, avoiding St Stephen's Green and the Royal College of Surgeons, if you know where those places are. It seems the rebels are still holding out there. At least they were last night.'

Sam nodded slowly. 'Thank you very much, sir. I appreciate that,' he said as the officer walked away and climbed up beside the driver in the vibrating vehicle.

Alex smiled to himself. It didn't surprise him that Sam hadn't told the officer that the area he mentioned was precisely where they were going.

There were three more stops on the way. At the first, an officious young officer from the Irish Rifles questioned them separately, ordered his men to search both vehicles and interrogated them about the boxes of food and cans of petrol they were carrying. Eventually, he waved them on when another vehicle came in sight.

In the city itself, they had to stop at a barricade. An officer from an English regiment apologised for the delay. As they waited, his men finished dismantling a collection of furniture, carts and tangled wire. Some snipers had occupied the nearby houses the previous day, the officer explained. They'd only recently been cleared out so that work could begin.

'Unpleasant job,' said Alex sympathetically, as he watched two men dragging a dead horse to the side of the road.

In the heat of the day, the smell was unpleasant, but the trail of blood was an even sharper reminder of what had happened in the last week.

Beyond that point, the smell of burning lay on the warm air. There were houses with smashed windows, some still barricaded, others where maids in neat white aprons were sweeping up the broken glass.

As they approached the river, burnt-out buildings became more frequent, but there were plenty of people about in the streets, and although the sound of artillery reached them from the other side of the city, the only rifle fire they heard was from much further west.

Alex followed close behind Sam, which was easy enough as there were few other vehicles around. Occasionally he glimpsed a name he'd heard mentioned as Sam and John pored over a street map of Dublin the previous evening. They drove past an imposing building, which he was sure must be Trinity College.

Soon after, they swung across a major thorough-fare and into a smaller street leading south. Coming towards them was a procession that took up the whole road. They pulled over and stopped just as the first figures came level with them, only a soldier's width away.

Led by a small dapper man with thick, dark hair and a long moustache and a haughty-looking woman wearing trousers, a band of men in uniform, their heads held high, marched past them, escorted closely on both sides by soldiers, row upon row, and disappeared in the direction of the quays.

Studying the faces of the young men and boys and the handful of women, one of them carrying a Red Cross flag, as they passed so close to him, Alex realised what he was seeing. These were the defeated rebels from one of the more tenaciously held strong-points. Disarmed, they were now being escorted by the army to await sentence.

As Alex followed Sam up Grafton Street and they turned left into Duke Street, he didn't know that their long journey from Ballydown was almost at an end. What neither he nor Sam knew was that just behind Michael Mallin and the Countess Markievicz, they had both seen Sam's cousin, Brendan Doherty, marching proudly with the remainder of the Citizen Army from their post at the College of Surgeons.

*   *   *

By Sunday morning, a whole day since Maureen had brought her the news of Uncle Sam's absence, Sarah felt the hours had been even longer than any of the previous days they'd endured. She'd gone up to his room immediately and searched for a note or any possible explanation as to where he might have gone. She found nothing except the tangled heap of clothes on the surface of his undisturbed bed.

Maureen followed her up. 'Look, ma'am,' she began anxiously. 'All his good stuff is in the wardrobe. This is what he wears every day,' she added, pointing to the familiar items, 'but the things he kept here for when he did bits of jobs roun' the house, that's all gone.'

Sarah had to admit she was right. Earlier in the week, when Sam raked the fire and took out the ash, he'd worn an old pair of trousers and a brightly checked shirt her mother had once said made him look like a lumberjack. Both shirt and trousers were gone. So was his oldest tweed jacket.

'He must have taken clothes to someone,' Maureen insisted, as Sarah stood staring down at the bed, wondering if there was a perfectly reasonable explanation that had not yet occurred to her. 'Ma'am, two of our brothers got out the night o' the surrender when me Ma brought them clothes hidden under her shawl. They'd hid their guns an' got through holes from one house to another and were back safe home in no time,' she said, tears forming in her eyes.

'Mister McGinley has been awful good to Lady Lily and to the both of us,' she said, now weeping loudly. 'Sure she'd 'ave been put out o' this house if it wasn't for him payin' all the bills. But he'd niver stay out at night. Something's wrong, I know it is. How am I goin' to tell her, ma'am?' she ended, subsiding on the bed in floods of tears.

'He might have been arrested by the military, Maureen,' Sarah said steadily, anxious to check Maureen's noisy sobs before they reached Helen or Hugh in their nearby rooms. 'There *is* a curfew, so he was breaking the law being out at all.'

Maureen sniffed and looked unconvinced, her tear-stained face the picture of misery.

Just at that moment, Bridget opened the door.

'Breakfast is ready, ma'am,' she said briskly, as the welcome smell of bacon and toast wafted into the bedroom. 'I've told Lady Lily that Mister McGinley must have gone out for the paper. There's no point upsettin' her till she's had her breakfast,' she said briskly.

After the limited nature of breakfast for the last week, the meal should have been memorable. Not only was it tasty and plentiful but it was served in the usual way on a spotless linen cloth, with pretty china and silver chafing dishes on the sideboard.

Sarah forced herself to eat normally, but she would willingly have exchanged her well-filled plate for a single slice of smoky toast and Sam's familiar presence. She did her best to sustain Bridget's fiction till everyone had eaten well and he still had not reappeared.

In the end, she told them all as simply as she could that Uncle Sam had gone out last night and had not yet arrived back. She admitted it was worrying, but he might have had to take shelter if firing had broken out. As she spoke, there was still rifle fire from the direction of St Stephen's Green and the heavy thump of field guns vibrated on the morning air, though that was to the south of the city.

Lily seemed quite unperturbed by the news. When Bridget came to clear the table, she seemed more concerned that Helen would now be able to paint a magnolia bud from the garden. If Lily was happy, then Helen was happy, for the two of them had become great friends. They went out to the garden together to choose a bloom for their morning's work.

Sarah could see that Hugh was more upset than Helen, but he said nothing. Several times during the week, he'd asked to be allowed to go and help Nevil Norway carry stretchers for the Red Cross. Sarah hadn't the heart to say he was too lightly built for the job. Instead, she'd insisted she might need his help if they had to evacuate the Dawson Street house. She'd observed how Hugh listened to all that was said in the sitting room of the Royal Hibernian and always talked to Nevil on his rare appearances at lunch. Back at home, he pored over Lily's elderly street plan of Dublin. She suspected that Hugh was probably as aware of the danger to his great-uncle as she was herself.

They went for lunch as usual on Saturday, telling their friend Mary Norway what had happened. Sarah considered going to visit the nearby hospitals in case Sam had been injured, but several residents of the hotel convinced her it was still too dangerous, with crossfire likely to occur almost anywhere as the army continued to move against entrenched snipers.

After a sleepless night, Sarah felt sure Sam had been injured, perhaps seriously, but to her amazement Lily remained quite unperturbed at breakfast. Even when Helen and Hugh asked if any message had come about Uncle Sam Donegal, she didn't react, just continued with her toast, though her habit of looking slightly preoccupied was distinctly more marked than usual.

They did not go out for lunch. It was a question of waiting and hoping that a message would come to tell them where Sam was. The telephone was working again and Mrs Norway phoned to ask if they had news, but they had not. Neither had she, though she'd made what enquiries she could.

As Bridget and Maureen were anxious to perform their usual duties, Sarah had no work to do and found the passage of the hours even more intolerable. She felt too agitated to read and was reluctant to write to Simon, so great was the weight of anxiety hanging over her.

Sometime after lunch, firing stopped completely. Shortly afterwards Bridget came in and folded back the shutters, which they'd kept partly closed since the day before when they'd been unbarred for the first time. The light fell on Helen's magnolia bud, now slightly open, and the daffodils Lily had brought in from the garden. But for Sam's absence, the room looked almost as it had done a week earlier before they'd set off on their outing to walk on the beach at Blackrock.

'Mama, Mama. Look! It's Uncle Sam outside,' Helen shouted, jumping up from the window seat where she'd been reading.

For one wonderful moment, Sarah's heart leapt with joy and relief as she hurried to the window.

'It's Uncle Sam Liskeyborough,' added Hugh quietly.

To Sarah's amazement, she saw the familiar figure of her own dear brother. Never before had the sight of his smiling face been such a disappointment.

She stood, stunned, as she watched not only Sam, but also Alex, park the familiar motors in front of the house and lift out baskets and boxes before moving towards the front door.

Helen got there first, with Hugh close behind her, long before either of the two men had freed a hand to ring the bell.

'It's my brother Sam and our cousin Alex,' Sarah said quietly to Lily, who'd dozed off after lunch.

'How nice,' she said, smiling sweetly as she roused herself. 'Though I shall be sorry to part with you. I expect the children really should be back at school,' she added, standing up to welcome the new arrivals as Helen and Hugh brought them into the room.

Sarah watched as Lily greeted Alex and Sam, rang for tea, and enquired politely about their journey as if it were an ordinary Sunday afternoon. She wondered what on earth she was going to do about her uncle. All she longed for was to be free to go home, but how could she leave the city without ensuring that he was safe?

The children were delighted to see Sam and Alex, and Lily was her liveliest self. She loved visitors and Sarah listened patiently as she explained to her guests that she'd been sadly deprived this week, for all her 'young men' seemed to have other things on their mind and none of her women friends had even phoned.

So lively was the conversation that it was Bridget who went to the door when the bell rang some time later. Sarah caught the mention of her own name, so she slipped out into the hall and found Nevil standing there.

'I think I may have bad news,' he said quickly, drawing an envelope from his pocket. 'I once heard you mention Ballydown.'

The envelope was bloodstained. Someone had tried to clean it and the paper was still damp. It was addressed to Mrs John Hamilton, Ballydown, near Banbridge, County Down. The handwriting was unmistakable.

'Where did you get this, Nevil? Is Uncle Sam injured?' she asked, her hands shaking as she took it from him.

'I found it at a temporary shelter,' he said reluctantly. 'We took someone else there and I saw . . . someone . . . I thought I recognised.'

Sarah stared at him, feeling for his difficulty and struggling with her own. Nevil's job was to collect the fallen. Some were taken to a hospital, others to a temporary shelter, a euphemism for a makeshift mortuary.

'There were no papers and no wallet in his jacket.

They'd probably been stolen. Just this,' he said, nodding bleakly at the crumpled envelope.

'So he's been badly injured, Nevil,' she said slowly.

'No, not very badly injured,' he said, shaking his head sadly. 'But I'm afraid we didn't find him in time, so he's dead.'

Twenty-Four

It was no hardship whatever for Rose and John to walk to church on such a beautiful spring morning, but once home, the midday meal eaten and cleared away, the long afternoon stretched interminably before them, with an equally interminable evening to follow.

John fell asleep in his chair after lunch, his face slack, the wrinkles more pronounced in the absence of his usual animation. At sixty-five he was still a fit and active man, she thought, but he tired more easily, was grateful for Alex's unbounded energy and sometimes now took the motor into Banbridge when once he would have enjoyed the walk. Still, she sighed, he was here, alive and well, when others younger than him had gone. She could only give thanks.

For herself, the idea of sleep never entered her mind, for she felt a tension that could only be sustained by waiting and watching patiently for what was to come. Her part was to hold her family in mind for as long as this journey took. Others might call it prayer, she thought to herself, and perhaps it was, as she imagined the two motors moving ever southwards to the violated city where once she'd come as a bride and marvelled at its beauty.

When John woke, he buried his nose in the Sunday papers, but she wasn't surprised when he said suddenly that he wanted a word with Michael Jackson. When he came back, she suggested they walk up to Rathdrum House to see Mrs Beatty, who'd gone to visit her sister earlier in the week, but had now returned and been on her own since Saturday morning.

Slowly, so slowly, the hours passed. Rose was grateful for a visit from Emily, bringing a gift of eggs from her aunt. 'Rose might have a houseful for a very late supper,' she'd said. 'They might come in handy.'

She stayed a while and made them laugh, telling them about the people who came to the studio in Banbridge to have their pictures taken. It reminded them both of the days when Sarah came home and told them just such stories before she made her move to Belfast.

As the day faded to a pale, golden sunset, bands of cloud appeared in the west. Blue-grey against the setting sun, they lay like islands in the sky. As dusk deepened, a fine rain began to fall and John stood at the open door eyeing the gathering clouds uneasily.

'They'll have to stop and put the top up,' he said, as he closed the door against the sudden chill of the evening and came back to the fire, picking up the paper he'd already read from corner to corner.

'What's the shortest time they could make *if* there were no delays?' Rose asked, just to break the silence.

He considered carefully. 'I'd say about five hours each way. They'll keep up the best speed they can and they're both good drivers, but it'll be slower now it's dark, even with the new headlights. Sam knows the road like the back of his hand, but it's all new to Alex.'

It was now after nine. Some fourteen hours had passed since their early departure, so something *had* come to delay them.

'What about a drop of tea?' she asked when another hour passed with no sight or sound of a vehicle.

'Aye, that would do well,' John replied wearily, putting down the service manual for a new delivery vehicle at Ballievy.

As she stood up to draw the kettle forward on the fire, she caught a sound, but John was already out of his chair, the door open, striding out into the teeming rain that glinted grey in the flare of headlights.

'Alex, good man. Are y'all right? Where's Sarah?'

'She's fine. She's behind with Sam,' he said, lifting Helen out of the back seat and handing her to John, still asleep, while Hugh scrambled down from the passenger seat and ran along the streaming path to his grandmother, who held out her arms.

'Are you tired out, sweetheart?' she asked, gathering him in a hug.

'Yes, I am,' he said directly. 'Mama said we could stay the night with you if it wouldn't be too much trouble,' he added politely, while trying to stifle a huge yawn.

Helen was reluctant to wake. She clutched John round the neck and would have gone on sleeping on his shoulder if Rose hadn't asked him to carry her upstairs to the room Sarah and Hannah had once shared. Hugh followed his grandparents silently and was sitting on the bed in Sam and James's room taking his shoes off when Alex appeared with their two small suitcases. He opened both, searched through them and found Hugh's pyjamas and Helen's nightdress.

'So yer all safe,' John said, as he and Alex came downstairs, quickly followed by Rose, after tucking both children into bed.

Rose glanced at him as he was about to speak. She knew immediately something was wrong. She waited patiently, watching him.

'There may be bad news, Rose,' he began cautiously. 'We think your brother Sam has been wounded. Sarah's gone to the hospital.'

Rose felt a great silence well up inside her, a strange feeling that someone had already told her this news, but she hadn't been listening properly.

'To the hospital, Alex?' she repeated, looking him full in the face.

Alex glanced at the stove where John had stopped in the middle of making tea, the kettle in his hand.

'He's dead, Alex, isn't he?' she said, waiting for him to turn back towards her, her voice as normal as if she were enquiring for the well-being of a friend or acquaintance.

There was never a problem with Alex. He could never lie. The answer would be there in his eyes.

'We're not absolutely sure, Rose,' he said firmly, 'but I wouldn't want to raise your hopes. Sam should be here in another hour or two. He'll know for sure.'

'What about Sarah?' said John sharply, his voice rough with emotion.

'Sarah's grand,' Alex replied, nodding vigorously to reassure him. 'But she wasn't sure she could leave Lily if the news was bad,' he went on, his face now pale and strained. 'She told me you'd understand,' he said softly, looking across at Rose, who stood immobile by the table.

'Of course I do. Do you think she'll be safe if she stays?'

'Yes,' he said honestly. 'We met a whole column of rebels who'd just surrendered. All the barricades have been cleared and she told us herself it had been quiet there most of the day.'

'Here, love,' said John suddenly, drawing his eyes from Alex's face and looking round at her. 'Come an' sit by the fire.'

He drew her over to his chair and let Alex finish making the tea.

'Your hands is stone cold,' he said, rubbing them in his own large, warm ones, desperately trying to comfort her. 'Maybe your Sam'll be all right.'

'We'll have to wait and see, John,' she replied in the same calm tone. 'Do we know what happened, Alex?'

She paused as he fetched milk from the dairy and then curled her cold hands gratefully round the warm mug he handed her.

'We think he may have taken clothes to Brendan to help him get away before they surrendered. No one knew he'd gone till one of Lily's girls found he hadn't slept in his bed and his old clothes were missing.'

Rose dropped her eyes and drank carefully. 'I can imagine that,' she said slowly. 'He once admitted to me he felt closer to Brendan than to any of his own sons, but then Brendan was more like him than any of his sons were. He always wanted to change the world and so did Brendan. They didn't agree about the means, but they did agree about what needed doing.'

They sat in silence for some minutes until the American clock on the wall by the dairy door gathered itself and struck eleven, its strange, muted note echoing in the silence of the gas-lit room.

'Alex, do the Jacksons know you're safely back?' Rose asked.

He nodded but said nothing more, wondering if she had guessed Emily was sitting up, waiting for the sound of the motor and for the brief note on the horn which he'd promised.

'Then I think, John dear, you should go to bed. You're tired out and you have to go to work in the morning,' she said firmly. 'Alex will keep me company till Sam gets here, and maybe Sarah too, if all's well,' she added, with a lightness that amazed her. 'If that's all right with you, Alex?'

Alex nodded gratefully. After all his years of loss and loneliness, there wasn't much he wouldn't do for this woman who'd made him feel he had at last a place in the world.

It was after midnight when Sam stopped briefly outside the Post Office in Newry to allow Sarah to drop three fat envelopes into the box. A squall of wind and rain followed her back into the car and she shivered as she drew the travelling rug back round her.

'Are ye right?' Sam asked, as she settled herself.

'As right as I can be,' she said wryly. 'What about you?'

'I'm *very* sorry about Uncle Sam, but it's Ma I could weep for,' he said slowly. 'How're we goin' to tell her?' he asked, without taking his eyes from the wet road.

'She'll know as soon as we cross the threshold,' she replied simply.

'D'you think she'll still be up?' he asked, surprised. 'It must be after midnight.'

'She'll be up. She'll not go to bed till she knows we're safe.'

They drove on in silence, Sarah grateful it was Sam at the wheel, for the wind had risen and small twigs were blowing into the windscreen. The moon was now completely obscured and the headlights cut a broad swathe through the deep, rain-sodden darkness, the road a glistening strip that looked as if it might end abruptly at any moment.

To prepare herself, Sarah went through the events of the afternoon yet again. Together, she and Sam had gone to the old warehouse where bodies were laid out in numbered rows. It was her uncle all right. Even as they approached between the rows, they recognized the thinning red hair and the handwoven tweed jacket he'd bought in Donegal when he first came home.

There was a stain on the jacket where the bullet had caught his bad shoulder, but his face was unmarked, so pale that the freckles of his creamy skin had faded to nothing. They stood together looking down at him until a young man brought a form to fill in, asked his questions, then handed it to them to sign. He'd brought a luggage label which he also filled in and attached to Sam's foot. It said simply *Samuel McGinley, Swillybrinnan, Donegal, c/o Lady Lily Molyneux, Dawson Street.*

'If we park on the hill, we wouldn't wake the Jacksons,' Sarah said abruptly as they turned on to the Ballydown road.

'Aye, I'd thought of that. I can chock the wheels if Alex is still there,' he replied, almost as though parking the motor on the steep slope was the only thing he'd been thinking off in the last silent hour.

When they finally heard the motor, Alex let Rose go to the door ahead of him. She met Sarah halfway down the sodden garden path, the rain still gusting round them, fallen petals of camellia strewn across the path.

'I'm sorry, Ma, so sorry,' she said as they hugged each other.

'He's gone, hasn't he?'

'Yes, he has,' she said simply, as her mother drew her indoors and brought her over to the fire.

John didn't even stir when Rose finally slipped into bed after Sarah and Sam had gone to their own old rooms where Helen and Hugh had been fast asleep for hours. She didn't move towards him, for her body was so icy cold from tiredness she was afraid she might startle him from sleep.

As she lay, wide-eyed, listening to the wind, his warmth began to enfold her and her mind began to move back, far, far back.

She was in a turf cart, creaking slowly along a rutted cart track, a red-headed baby in her arms, sleet blowing in her face, its icy points sharp as pins. The only warm bit of her was where she cradled the baby in her arms, her mother's shawl draped over them both. Babies were always warm, she thought, as they made slow progress, her father leading the donkey, her mother and Mary carrying bundles, their heads bent, her brothers leading the cow, who didn't want to go.

'Don't look back,' her mother said. 'Don't look back.'

She didn't know why, but if her mother said she was not to look back, then it was for the best.

Rose dreamt the short night through. She woke to the alarm and the knowledge of what had happened with a calmness that amazed her. It was her dear John who showed such great distress when she had to tell him the news, comforting him as best she could before a day's work that he couldn't set aside.

At breakfast, Sam seemed to be his unperturbable self, Sarah composed, the children silent and sad, but not shocked or surprised. They'd waited the two long days for news of Uncle Sam Donegal and neither their mother nor Maureen and Bridget concealed the truth from them.

The storm had blown itself out and brilliant shafts of sunlight came and went between the ragged clouds as Sarah drove the children up to Rathdrum, spoke to Mrs Beatty and then walked back down the hill to spend the morning with her mother.

As she stepped into the kitchen, a single glance told her the morning jobs had been done, the floor swept and the fire made up. On the table, two camellia blooms, broken off by the wind but still undamaged, sat in a saucer of water. Her mother sat by the fire knitting another sock for the Red Cross parcel.

'How are you, Ma?' she asked gently, sitting down opposite her.

Rose smiled. 'I'm perfectly well, but I've not lived in this new world for very long yet. I've loved Sam for even more years than I've loved your father, or any of you children. I'll have to wait a bit longer to find out what it's like.'

'There's something I didn't tell you last night, Ma,' Sarah began uneasily. 'Maybe I forgot or maybe I just couldn't manage to tell you. I hope you won't be annoyed with me. Sam wrote you a letter. It was in his pocket when the stretcher party found him.'

She took the stained envelope from her pocket, handed it over, and watched as her mother opened it carefully and took out the two closely written sheets inside.

How often she'd seen her mother open Uncle Sam's letters, scanning them quickly to make sure all was well, then sitting down to read them carefully, or putting them in her pocket to enjoy when the house was quiet, with everyone at work or school. She waited patiently for what seemed a very long time.

'How like him,' Rose said, smiling, as she handed over the pages to her. 'Read it for yourself.'

Sarah took the sheets from her mother's hand, fumbling so awkwardly she nearly dropped them.

Friday evening
28th April, 1916

My dearest Rose,

I don't know whether it is army regulations or simply a habit that has become institutionalised in time of war, but it seems these days that when 'going over the top' one is required to write to one's dearest and to make one's will. My will has been long made, but perhaps, in order not to tempt Providence, or whatever the fate that shapes our ends, I should write you a few lines of farewell in the fond hope that you will not actually receive them.

The week has been an extraordinary one and no doubt future historians will produce as many versions of it as there were eye-witnesses. For my own part, I fear many young and not so young men will lose their lives to no great purpose. Already thousands of the most needy in the city have been deprived of even what shelter they had and what food they had the means to buy.

I have thought out how best to infiltrate the College of Surgeons, where Brendan and the Citizen Army retreated from the indefensible positions in St Stephen's Green. I tried to persuade him of the hopelessness of the position on Wednesday evening and failed, but now that Pearse has actually surrendered I hope I shall have more success. All he needs to make good his escape are civilian clothes and his own intimate knowledge of the city.

Should I be prevented from giving you an account of this adventure myself, I should like to leave the following thought on record.

Call no man happy until he is dead.

Well, I should be sorry to leave, but thanks to my dear Eva and to you, my dearest·sister, I have been happy and have managed better in this naughty world than one might have expected given my prospects at birth. I set out to do one thing, but actually did something quite different. I failed to improve the lot of the poor, or make any great improvement to agricultural practice, but I have been able to provide for Lily and all my extended family, and for the education of many young men and women from the trust fund of which you and Sarah are to be the executors. I could have done much worse.

I shall not ask you not to grieve for me. Where there is no grief there can have been no love. And I have been loved. But I would remind you that death has been at my elbow many times, the first time, perhaps, when we left Ardtur and were rescued by those elderly Presbyterians in Ramelton. Countless times in my work with the Land League, and later in Pennsylvania with the Trade Unions, I was at risk. I am exceedingly glad that death did not finally catch up with me in a state-room aboard the Titanic. That would have been against my principles.

It is almost time for me to go. One last message for you to deliver for me, my dear Rose, should need be. Tell Sarah that she too must go. I hope Simon will return to claim her and that she will find happiness again. But, if that should not happen, nevertheless, she must still go. Perhaps for the same reasons that I had to go. She is cabined and confined. She will do best what she has it in her to do in another place.

I am, as always,
Your loving brother,
Sam

Twenty-Five

The weeks that followed Sarah's return from Dublin were some of the unhappiest and most exhausting she had ever spent. She started off bravely enough as she took Helen and Hugh back to school where she visited the headmaster and explained to him exactly what they had experienced in the last two weeks.

Confident they were in safe hands, she applied herself to the accumulated papers on the dining-room table. Some piles were so high they were in danger of overbalancing and sliding to the floor. The enormous activity at the mills as a result of War Department orders was generating even more paperwork, and while Elizabeth and Richard had willingly taken on her social work while she was away, neither of them had the experience to handle the documents ordering materials, confirming production schedules, or enabling shipments to be despatched.

Although Sarah saw no signs of her mother losing the steadiness with which she had borne her brother's death, her father's state of mind was a different matter. He seemed to be permanently anxious about one mill or another. At the same time, the continuous round of meetings necessary before the company finally became public both taxed and wearied him. Alex came to see her almost every evening and freely admitted he was as concerned about her father as she was.

As if all this were not burden enough, both Sarah and Rose began to receive distraught letters from Lily. When Sarah and Sam had brought her the news of their Uncle Sam's death she had been coolness itself. She'd insisted that Bridget and Maureen would help her arrange for Sam to be buried in the Molyneux family grave and not in the hastily organised burial ground for the bodies of unclaimed victims. Sarah's place was with the children, Lily insisted; she must go home at once to her dear Helen and Hugh.

As the first news came of the shootings of the rebel leaders, however, Lily was inconsolable. She wrote passionately about 'poor Willie', whose only crime, she said, was to be his brother's shadow. He was a man who had probably never even held a gun, but he had been there with his brother, Patrick, in the GPO, and so he'd been shot.

Rose and Sarah read each other's letters and asked themselves whether one of them should go down and see her, now that the trains were running again. Rose admitted she couldn't leave John at the moment and Sarah confessed that even a short visit would undo all the hard work she'd put in catching up on the mills' administration.

The news from Dublin city itself was utterly distressing. Thousands of people were in need of relief.

As details of Easter week began to emerge, the news came through that three innocent people, one a well-known pacifist, had been shot without trial by a British officer, who was thought to be unbalanced.

It came as no surprise to anyone that the signatories of the rebel Proclamation were executed, but some days later they read that Brendan's friend, Michael Mallin, had also been shot along with two comrades. Thomas McDonagh, the officer who'd ensured Sam's safe return from Jacob's biscuit factory, was another victim. Through the first weeks of May, the shootings continued. When James Connolly, a Belfastman and a socialist, was shot on the twelfth of May, sitting in a chair because he was too badly wounded to stand, Sarah broke down and wept, overwhelmed by the unreasoning retaliation of the military in charge at Dublin Castle and her certain knowledge that what was being done now would only plant the seeds of future bitterness.

Brendan Doherty was safe and well, though imprisoned in Wales, and that was a real comfort to Rose and Sarah, but it had little effect on his mother, Mary. She'd responded to her brother's death just as she had to the death of her two sons, with an inconsolable grief that made her incapable of the slightest compassion for anyone else.

Sarah was surprised when she returned home and found no letter from Simon awaiting her. She'd reassured her mother about the loss of the letter which she'd forwarded to Dublin, telling her that there'd be another one very soon to make up for it. But no letter came.

Day after day, the post brought only receipts and invoices. Letters from Lily and notes from Helen and Hugh. Even some from Sam, who was not much given to writing, but took up his pen to ask how they all were between his usual visits. Yet there was still nothing from Simon.

Sarah found herself counting on her fingers. Could he have sent a letter to Dublin to reach her for Easter? Even if he had, he wouldn't have sent anything after Easter Monday, knowing she was due home the next day. As the first week of May passed and the second one began with no sign of the familiar envelope and his large, generous hand, she became more and more anxious, however much she tried to reason with herself.

Normally, he wrote a little every day, posting his missives every three or four days, as she herself did. Even allowing for the mail, which had remained remarkably consistent despite the war, she could no longer manage any simple explanation to account for this absence.

On a beautiful May morning almost halfway through the month, the trees fully clothed, the cow parsley a froth of white in the hedgerows, Sarah walked down the hill to see her mother without noticing either the warm sunshine or the bright faces of the buttercups.

'Any news?' Rose asked.

She shook her head dejectedly as she sat down.

'Sarah dear, there's no point waiting if there's anything you can do to ease your mind,' she said, looking down at Sarah's pale, shadowed face. 'Why don't you telephone Teddy and ask him to contact the Foreign Office? He's almost certainly got a friend there who can help him.'

Sarah smiled wryly. 'Ma dear, why didn't I think of that?'

'Because, my love, you are tired out and you have too much on your mind already.'

'And what about you?' she protested. 'Da's not himself, Lily writes to you every two days and Aunt Mary sends messages demanding you go and see her . . .' She was about to say, 'and you've had no letters from Uncle Sam,' but she stopped herself in time. He was the one subject she couldn't bear to talk about, not because of her own sadness, but because of the message he'd left for her in his last letter. *Tell Sarah she must go.*

The words had echoed and re-echoed in her mind for days now. He'd said he hoped Simon would come and claim her and that she would then find happiness again. That was not what disturbed her, for he'd said as much to her himself many times, but his letter insisted she must go, *even if there were no Simon.*

Did he have some intuition that Simon would not survive the war? The thought appalled her. She could face leaving her home and the place she loved, however bitter and angry it often made her, to follow the man she'd committed herself to, but where could she ever find the strength of spirit to leave if she lost him? Besides, could she now find happiness in a world that had no Simon?

Her mother was quite right. She simply had to find out why there had been no letters. She went straight back up to Rathdrum, took out the car, and drove over to Millbrook to telephone Hannah. Tom's office was private and welcoming and a few minutes after she arrived she found herself talking to her sister.

'Oh, Hannah dear, how lovely to hear you. I wish I could pop in for tea,' she said, amazed that the line was so clear her sister's voice sounded as if it were in the same room with her.

'Sarah, I wish you could,' Hannah responded vigorously. 'Ma's told me what an awful time you're both having, though you were so good about Dublin in your last letter. I'm sorry I haven't replied. Perhaps we should use the telephone more often.'

'Yes, we should. Even a few minutes would help.'

'But tell me quickly why you've rung in case we get cut off. It happens here quite often.'

Sarah told Hannah about her anxiety over the lack of letters from Simon and registered Hannah's crisp tone as she promised to contact Teddy immediately. Then there was a significant pause.

'Sarah, I would've been writing tonight or tomorrow, but there's something I need to tell you,' she began, catching her breath.

'Go on, Hannah dear.'

'Harrington had a heart attack yesterday. He's still with us, but the doctors say there will probably be another one.' She paused again. 'If you saw him, Sarah, you'd hope it would come soon.'

'Poor Harrington,' she replied sadly, thinking of

the failing but welcoming figure she'd last seen nearly two years ago. 'How is Anne?'

'Brave. But she'll be heartbroken.'

A whirring noise on the line warned them they *were* about to be cut off. 'I'll ring or telegraph the moment I have news for you. Bye, Sarah,' she added hastily, just before the phone went dead.

Sarah placed the large black receiver back on to its stand, sat down at Tom's well-ordered desk, dropped her face in her hands and wept.

The telegram that arrived next day brought absolutely no peace of mind for Sarah, but it did provide some information.

> *Simon recalled end April. No further details yet.*
> *Keep chin up. Love Teddy.*

A second telegram appeared the next day. Sarah tore it open before the delivery boy had even got back on his bicycle.

> *Harrington dead. Please tell Ma.*
> *Fondest love Hannah.*

Sarah immediately abandoned her papers, spoke a word to Mrs Beatty, and followed the telegraph boy back down the hill to break the news to her mother.

'It may have been a blessed release for Harrington, but it's heartbreak for Anne,' she said, wiping a tear briskly from the corner of one eye. 'She always loved him so.'

'Do you want to go over and see her?' Sarah asked. 'I'd look after Da. Or I'd try to,' she corrected herself, knowing that clean shirts and food wouldn't go far to comforting her father.

'No, this isn't the time,' Rose replied, shaking her head. 'She'll be busy and she has Hannah to help her. It's later she'll need me. And your father's still in a bad way, what with Uncle Sam *and* the launching of the company. You know how he hates meetings and all the effort of selecting these bright young men for the new accounts department. He'll not be right till it's all over and he becomes an employee of Bann Valley Mills.'

'It's taken so long, Ma. I thought it would be months, but it's been nearer a year. I began to think it would never happen.'

'Waiting is hard work,' said Rose, smiling. 'You know that yourself.'

'Yes, I do,' Sarah agreed. 'But I forget,' she added, smiling herself. 'I thought those days in Dublin would never pass, shut up in the back room because the sitting room was too dark with the shutters closed. Cold, because we had to ration what fuel we had, and hungry, except in the afternoons after our dash to the Royal Hibernian.'

'*All things pass, both good and bad,*' said Rose thoughtfully.

'Is that another one from the copybook?'

'I was wondering about that myself. Sometimes it's the copybook, sometimes it's the voice of my own mother, other times I've no idea where the thoughts come from, but they come. And sometimes they do help out when one is perplexed, troubled and dispirited.'

The next day, at long last, a letter arrived from Simon. It was loving and full of joy, telling her with delight the news of his recall to London, but it had been posted in Stockholm all of twelve days earlier.

Harrington was buried in the graveyard adjoining the little church where Hannah and Teddy had been married some eighteen years earlier, the church full of friends and former colleagues from Westminster and the entire staff of his estates. Hannah wrote a full account of the funeral for her mother and Sarah, and confessed to them her apprehension for the future now that she and Teddy had become the Earl and Countess of Bridgehampton, titles which Harrington and Lady Anne used only on state occasions.

As for Simon's whereabouts, there was still no news, though Teddy rang a colleague in the Foreign Office every morning.

Helen and Hugh came home from school for a weekend and Sarah did her best to be enthusiastic about all their news. Hugh was most concerned when he inspected his seven oak trees on Saturday morning. They'd grown so vigorously in the warm weather, they would definitely need transplanting in the autumn. Helen was disappointed that more of her flowers were not in bloom. She'd wanted to make a bouquet for Grandma, but Grandma's flowers were nicer than her own, she declared.

It was Alex who solved the problem of Hugh's oak trees. He said they were just what was needed to strengthen the hedgerows around Ballydown. Together, they spent a long afternoon marking out the positions with bits of wood from the workshop. Come the autumn, Alex promised, they'd lift the young trees and take them to the places they'd chosen.

'I've had another letter from Auntie Lily, Mama,' announced Helen over breakfast on Sunday morning.

'Have you?' Sarah asked cautiously, suddenly anxious that Lily might have written to her about 'poor Willie'.

'Yes,' she went on enthusiastically. 'I was worried about the ducks, so she went to see Mr Kearney and asked about them. He said they were all fine. When the army and rebels were shooting at each other, they had a cease-fire twice a day, so he could go out and feed them. He says there are some ducklings now as well.'

Another telegram arrived on Monday afternoon.

> Swedish packet hit mine off Dogger. Simon on board.
>   All passengers rescued. Repeat all rescued. No arrivals yet confirmed.
>   Teddy.

Sarah was torn between sheer relief to hear something of Simon and renewed anxiety. Ships that hit mines usually sank, but they sank slowly and Dogger was on the edge of busy shipping lanes. On the other hand, it was near enough to the German Bight to be a bad area for submarines. And she could never forget the first reports from the *Titanic* that declared so optimistically that all passengers had been rescued.

'Well, any news?' asked Alex, as he came to find her in the garden.

She took the crumpled telegram from her pocket and handed it to him, watching the expression on his face as he read and reread it. Why was it, she wondered, that the fewer the words, the more often one seemed to need to read them.

Alex smiled at her.

'He'll be all right,' he said firmly, sitting down beside her.

'What makes you think that?' she demanded.

'Can't say. Just a feeling.'

She sat silent on the old wooden bench that Hugh used as an aeroplane. Yes, perhaps she too felt it was going to be all right, but there was a tight knot in her stomach telling her that it wasn't.

'Even if he is, I'm not sure I can go, Alex.'

'Not go? But you love the man.'

'Yes, I do, but I'm so much needed here. Ma's been so good, but she's had nothing but bad news lately, first Uncle Sam, now Harrington. Even her postman was killed on active service. And Da's beside himself between the loss of Uncle Sam and the changeover. You know that yourself.'

'Sarah, you forget. No one is indispensable. If you'd stopped a bullet in Dublin, we'd all have had to cope.'

To Alex's amazement, Sarah laughed.

'I almost did,' she said easily. 'If I hadn't slipped and nearly fallen it might have got me. It came close enough to tear my skirt.'

'Did Sam confess to you about his jacket?'

'What jacket?'

'His fairly new, everyday one,' he said lightly. 'Your mother spotted a hole when he came over to see her and he told her it looked like a burn. She mended it one night while I was there, so I knew perfectly well what it was. When I tackled him about it, he finally admitted he got it when he took the jam down to Jacob's factory.'

'You're quite right, you know. No one *is* indispensable,' she said, after a long pause. 'But that's not the point, is it? I *have* survived – and so has our Sam, thank God – but how can I leave them now, Alex? They've never needed me more,' she said, tears springing unbidden to her eyes.

'What would Rose say if you told her that?' he asked quietly.

She wiped her eye with the back of her hand. 'She'd repeat what her own mother said to her,' she began steadily. 'I can't remember the words, but it's to the effect that no woman should ever hold on to her daughter and no daughter should ever stay when she meets the man that's right for her.'

'Well then?'

She sat silent, weary as after a long effort.

'I have something in mind that might make the going easier,' he said.

'You have?' she repeated.

'Yes,' he continued briskly. 'John has been talking about moving house to make life easier for Rose. If you were to go, they could move up to Rathdrum. I would then ask her if I could rent Ballydown for my wife and myself.'

'Alex!'

'I have an understanding with a young woman, but I shall not marry till you do,' he said firmly. 'I made up my mind about that when we agreed you needed a brother.'

Sarah had just opened her mouth to reply when she heard a cry from the direction of the back door. She screwed up her eyes against the sunlight and peered down the garden. Mrs Beatty was waving a tea cloth, her usual way of announcing a visitor.

'Shall I go?' Alex volunteered.

'Thank you,' she said gratefully.

He returned a few minutes later. To her great surprise, he was followed by Billy Auld. Alex, who had been looking so happy some minutes earlier, had grown tense and anxious.

Looking from one face to another, Sarah wondered what more unhappiness was about to descend.

'Sarah, this must have come in as we were shutting down. I hope it's not bad news,' said Billy as he handed over the sealed official envelope.

It seemed an age before she was able to pull out the telegram itself.

> Hope to be in London tomorrow. Await your call.
>
> Simon.

She had to read it three times before it registered that Simon was safe.

'It's good news,' she said, tripping over the words. 'My fiancé is back in England. His ship hit a mine and I was told he'd been rescued . . . but . . .'

She handed the telegram to Billy, who was looking enormously relieved. 'Actually, Sarah, your man's in Scotland,' he said, beaming at her. 'He must have come home on a destroyer,' he added, pointing out the stamp of the Post Office where the telegram had been despatched.

'War Department base near there,' he said. 'That's why you'd no word sooner. Destroyers can't use radio for fear of submarines.'

'I told you he was all right,' said Alex, grinning at her.

'But you *didn't* tell me you were going to get married,' she came back at him, a sudden joyous sense of relief sweeping over her.

'Billy, Alex and I are getting married,' she said, laughing at the ambiguity of her remark. 'I'm marrying Simon, but *he* hasn't told me yet who he's going to marry. What kind of a cousin is that, Billy?'

'Ach, I can't get over it,' said John for at least the third time as Rose brewed up the final tea of the day. 'Sure we've had nothing but bad news for weeks and now this. The poor man must have been in an awful way not bein' able to let her know he was all right and having to go away up to Scotland before he was put ashore.'

'As bad as Sarah, cooped up in Dublin and not knowing if she'd get home safe,' replied Rose promptly.

'Aye, they've both had their hardship. An' so have we, one way an another.'

She smiled at him as she poured their tea and then sat back in her chair, relieved that he'd laughed for the first time in weeks.

'What d'ye think of this idea of us movin' up to Rathdrum when Sarah goes?' he asked casually.

'I'd rather go there than Dromore,' she said honestly. 'I'd miss the mountains. An' you'd have your workshop for when you retire.'

'Well, if you were happy an' had less work to do, I'd be for it.'

Rose smiled to herself. She'd always loved what she still sometimes thought of as 'Elizabeth's house'. She knew the garden as well as her own and if they moved there they'd have plenty of room for visitors, and young Helen and Hugh would always have their first home to come back to.

'What about this house, John?'

'Well, that's up to you,' he said promptly. 'It's your house, but if you want to rent it to Alex and Emily, I'd be all for it. We'd have good neighbours there,' he said warmly. 'Aye, an' there'd still be Hamiltons at Ballydown.'